PORTRAITS OF DECAY

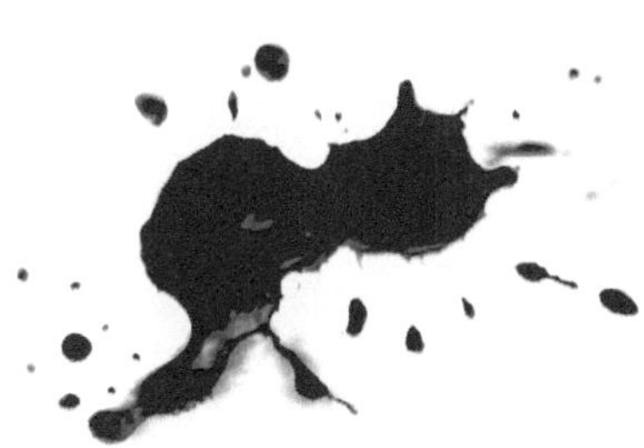

BOSTON, MA

To my parents, Thomas and Suzanne.
Thank you for encouraging me to use my imagination.

I am the scorn of all of my adversaries, a
horror to my neighbors, an object of dread
to my acquaintances, those who see me in
the street flee from me

I have passed out of mind like one who is
dead; I have become like a broken vessel.

Yea, I hear the whispering of many—
"Terror on every side!"
As they scheme together against me;
as they plot to take my life.

—Psalm 31: 11-13

FOREWORD

What if you couldn't do your art?

That question began a conversation between author, J.R. Blanes and a musician friend. Their conversation led to a short story. And that short story expanded into the novel before you.

As a visual artist, a painter, I've often wondered this myself. I was once asked by a stranger why I create. I told him creating is like breathing. If I can't create, I'll die.

For an artist, creativity is who you are. Beyond your identity *(I am an artist)*, it is your essence. Your soul. What happens when you lose your creativity? Or worse: What happens when your creativity is taken from you?

This is the core of *Portraits of Decay*.

When I first graduated from art school, I spent a good amount of time in New Orleans visiting a friend who had moved there-an artist and fellow graduate from the art school I attended. Before art school in New England, I grew up seeped in southern culture while living in Below-the-Mason Dixon Line, Bible Belt cities: Birmingham, Nashville, Jacksonville,

Atlanta. New Orleans is a place all to itself, unlike any other southeastern city, unlike anywhere else in the United States. Really, unlike anywhere else on earth. Its blend of cultures and customs provide a backdrop teeming with color, sounds and smells. Perfect for pursuing inspiration. The barriers between various ethnicities, traditions and beliefs are blurred in ways not readily experienced elsewhere. The veil is of a gauzy material sheer and easily crossed. That especially pertains to the supernatural. Its pervasive presence is palpable, most times an amused and amusing companion escorting you through the streets, alleys and cemeteries, hot on your heels. Other times, it brushes past you like the ample Spanish Moss draping in the trees, gentle yet heavy laden with a mystical history. And at unwanted, unwelcome moments it encircles you, as inescapable as the humidity.

In New Orleans, the paranormal is as commonplace as air. I remember my friend mundanely mentioning over coffee that her new boyfriend had visited a voodoo priestess-one he met with regularly-to procure a spell so that my friend would fall madly in love with him.

J.R. was struck by the uniqueness and vibrancy of New Orleans from the moment he first arrived. His job required him to spend four days a week there, allowing him over the next few years to dive deeply into the different facets of NOLA life. Head over heels in love with this city, his desire was to capture every aspect as authentically as possible. Miles of streets were trod, with a lot of time particularly dedicated to exploring the arts district. Hours were invested in interacting with the locals; hearing stories from every creed and color, learning their voices. J.R.'s devotion to the flavor of the area and its people is what drew me in when I began reading *Portraits of Decay*. I could *see* and *smell* and *taste* New Orleans. I was again that young artist, exploring the bayou while swatting at bugs so big they shouldn't exist. Trying, and failing, to hold messy powdered sugar at bay while eating beignets. Dancing the night away to zydeco music while immersed in a swath of sweating happy bodies of every skin tone.

Oh, the life of the young artist, wanting to take it all in and toss it back out to the world. To find a way, your way, to leave a mark. To still be new, and therefore impulsive, at making choices, art, love. As I read I was hurled back in time to those fresh hopes and fresh hurts. I saw a bit of myself in Jefferson; a lot of myself in Nevaeh. More than I want to admit, I saw a lot of myself in Gemma too.

What if you couldn't do your art?

Portraits of Decay is about twenty-somethings in the New Orleans art scene. It is about being youthful and passionate and ambitious. It is about trying to figure life out in a place where Baron Samedi comfortably strolls the streets, cigar in hand. It is about a love triangle that goes horribly and horrifically wrong—far beyond the ways all love triangles do. It is about dreams and identity, and the lengths one may go, the methods one may resort to when these treasures are threatened.

I am so very honored to have had the chance to join J.R. on this journey. You can't walk together without learning a lot about each other. Countless virtual sessions, emails, phone calls, and texts equal the meeting of two creative minds. I appreciate J.R.'s earnest mission to represent New Orleans well, and his ability to breathe life into these characters who have a wonderful story to tell. I am grateful for the unexpected opportunity to relive the struggle of a young artist when it feels like the deck is stacked against you. Longing for life to go well in work and romance, while every moment is amplified by the raw verve of youth. I am grateful J.R. trusted me as an "expert" in all things art and artist: what attending art school is like, methods and materials visual artists use, studio setup, how galleries work, etc.

What if you couldn't do your art?

This is a book I truly love. I hope you find it as captivating and entertaining as I do.

Yours,
Anna Koon

PROLOGUE

At the dining table, Angelique trembled, steaming hot coffee spilling over the lip of her mug onto her hand, the skin red and puckered. Despite the blistering pain, she refused to let go of the handle. The handle was the only thing keeping her from doing what the voice demanded.

Kellan lay in the crib, no more than ten feet away, where Angelique had put him down for a nap only fifteen minutes ago. She looked at the bedroom through the crack in the doorway. At the sun-shaped light switch and the sky-blue wallpaper teeming with puffy white clouds. When she decorated the room, her pardner Lyle Allen said it was sissy. As in, *you're going to make my boy a sissy*. But Kellan was only a baby. Shouldn't his innocent soul know the joys of the world before life stripped it away?

The chimes of Pachelbel's Canon rung like a death knell beneath Kellan's howling wails; each of his cries fracturing her brain. Softly, she begged her sweet baby boy, *please quiet, child, please.*

The voice urged her to silence the fucking brat.

Silence him for good.

But Angelique wouldn't do it. *Let the voice be damned.* She'd fight him with every last drop of willpower in her body. No matter how much he tempted her. No matter how often he whispered in her ear. No matter how loud and long Kellan screamed.

She would not hurt her baby boy.

Once, not long ago, Angelique had thought of herself as a caring mother, one whose child blinked at her adoringly and smiled at her silly voices and snuggled against her for protection when he was sleepy.

After breakfast, weather permitting, she'd place Kellan in the stroller, closing the canopy to shade him from the sun. Together they'd stroll along the fronatown, often ending in the park down the road. Kellan seemed to enjoy these excursions, just as his mommy did, cooing to the chirping of birds and sniffing at the sweet fragrance of the hibiscus and stretching his chubby hands toward the sky as if he could clutch it in his tiny fingers. Angelique would tickle his chin and feet. His plump belly. He'd laugh in that squealy giggle she found adorable.

At night she'd swaddle Kellan in his favorite blanket, decorated in pictures of the farm animals for which he did not yet know the names, and sing "Hush, Little Baby," as he fed on her breast before falling asleep. Even when her arms went numb, she wouldn't move to shake away the tingles, afraid to wake her sweet baby boy. Sure, Kellan would fuss every now and then, but no more than any other infant. Her family was amazed at how lucky she was to have such a well-behaved child.

Count your blessings, they'd tell her.

Then one day, everything changed. Or maybe it was she who had changed? What had happened to her that her child no longer loved her?

Now Kellan glared at her in disgust, as if he couldn't believe this tired, baggy-eyed woman with tangled hair and sour stench and saggy body hidden beneath slobber-stained sweatshirts could've possibly birthed him. This woman ravaged by sleepless nights, who wandered from one narrow end of their shotgun house to the other, through one cluttered room to the next, muttering to herself that she wasn't losing her mind when she damn well knew she'd crossed that line some time ago. This woman who forgot to feed or change him, letting him spend hours in a shit-filled diaper—despite the horrid stench that turned her stomach—until Lyle Allen told her to. Just like he told her when to take off her clothes and pleasure him. Just like he told her when to speak and what to say.

This woman who now sat at the dining table, burning herself with hot coffee, and mumbling the same phrase over and over again: *Please quiet, child, please…*

Still, Kellan continued to cry. He was probably hungry. She should feed him. If only he wouldn't reject her offering, spitting and turning his head away when she slipped her nipple into his mouth, like Angelique's milk had curdled and turned rancid.

If that was the way Kellan was going to act, he deserved to starve. Wasn't that what Lyle always said? That they weren't going to raise no spoiled brat?

No! She refused to listen to the voice inside her head. She loved her child. *Didn't she?*

But wasn't it she who should be spilling tears? Lyle blamed Kellan for ruining her body. Said she'd been pretty until the baby came along. And she was pretty. A dark-haired beauty that could've had any man.

But she'd stupidly settled for Lyle Allen. Then a few months later, the son-of-a-bitch had impregnated her. The rest was downhill from there.

Outside the window, Angelique saw Lyle in the driveway working on his truck, dirty boots sticking out from beneath the undercarriage, jeans streaked with grease. She wanted to call him to come and quiet his child. Change Kellan's diaper. Give him a bottle. Rock him. Whatever the hell the boy needed. As long as she didn't have to be near their son. It was safer if she stayed away. She no longer knew what she was capable of.

Lyle always did call her a crazy, stupid bitch. But he didn't mean it. He said so himself. The words just slipped out when he got angry. But perhaps he was right. Perhaps she was crazy.

But she shouldn't bother Lyle. Kellan was her responsibility. Lyle told her so. Which was why she was in the house listening to their baby scream while her pardner fiddled around on his automobile.

Besides parenting, Lyle Allen expected Angelique to clean up after him and do laundry and cook meals. She was more of a housekeeper than a wife. But she performed her chores dutifully. Without question. Even when she wanted to throw a plate at his head or set his clothes on fire or tell him to go fuck himself. It was all *yes, honey* and *no, honey* and *whatever you want honey.*

An empty valise sat inside the closet. How often did she gaze out the window and think about leaving? Away from Lyle. Away from the voice in her head. Then why didn't she? Because she couldn't. That was why. She'd tried that once. Had everything for her and Kellan packed, ready to move in with her sister who had prepared the extra bedroom, even bought a crib and toys. But the moment Sofie arrived to whisk them away, Lyle answered the door and refused to let Sofie inside. Her sister tried to yell past Lyle's hulking frame to Angelique. Pleaded with Angelique to come with her. Said she didn't have to listen to Lyle Allen. But she *did* have to listen to Lyle. Speaking through Angelique's mouth, in her voice, Lyle told Sofie to go away.

Sometimes Angelique wondered whether Lyle had put some kind of spell on her. What was it he'd said to her when he'd found the texts between her and Sofie? "You can bet the devil, I'll raise the fires of hell before I let you leave."

Maybe that was exactly what he'd done. That was what her sister thought anyway. Sofie said she'd noticed something strange about Angelique right around the time she decided to stay. *It's like you no longer have your own thoughts or opinions,* her sister said. *Whatever he says, you do. No questions asked.* But Angelique didn't believe in superstitions. Black magic and voodoo and witches didn't exist. They were only spooky stories the New Orleanians told to scare tourists. And she still had a mind of her own. She was in love with Lyle. He knew what was best for her.

Angelique quit going over to her mamma'n'ems, as Lyle demanded. She ignored her sister's phone calls, and whenever Sofie came by the house, Angelique would act like nothing was wrong. *Busy, that's all*, she'd say. Just as Lyle had taught her.

Perhaps she was sick. Schizophrenia ran in her family. Both an uncle and cousin suffered from it. Neither one of them were around no more. Uncle drowned in Lake Pontchartrain, his body washing up in Mandeville days after he went missing. The cousin, well, police found her in a tent under the Green Bridge in a grassy area off of State Road 47. She'd been living on the streets damn near ten years by then. This was after she'd been in and out of every institution in Louisiana. Angelique was certain her dad had the disease too. He kept his doors locked and slept with a gun beneath his pillow. Said it was to keep the Rougarou from breaking in. Had the sickness now gotten her too?

Kellan continued to scream bloody murder until his voice went hoarse. The voice shouted at her to "shut that child up." The voice sounded just like Lyle.

The porcelain handle of Angelique's mug shattered in her hand. The cup dropped and spilt a river of brown on the wood surface of the table. Blood trickled down her wrist from a slice in her palm.

Please quiet, child, please.

But there was only one way to please the voice. She had to stop Kellan's screaming. Only then would the voice allow her peace.

Angelique scooted from the table, her chair legs raking the linoleum, crossed the kitchen, and slipped inside the bedroom. Baby toys squeaked beneath her feet as she approached the crib, the mobile spinning above it, miniature birds dangling from strings going round and round. Leaning over the rails, she watched as her sweet baby boy squirmed on his soft white mattress like a tick being burnt by a match, hands folded into tiny fists of rage, eyes squeezed tight, pushing tears down his hot red cheeks, legs kicking dead air, his toothless cavern of a mouth stretched wide, blaring like an alarm with no shut off button.

She stroked the fine hairs of his sweaty forehead. Wiped away the tears with her thumb.

She had to stop Kellan from crying before Lyle heard. After a hard day's work, all he wanted was some fucking peace and quiet. Was that too much to ask? It shouldn't be this difficult to quiet a goddamn baby. She was just a bad mom, that was all.

From the crib, Angelique lifted a pillow. It was cloud-shaped with pink cheeks and a smiley face. She squeezed its fluffy softness. Then lowered it onto Kellan's face and pressed down hard. A hush fell over the room. The quiet silenced the voice inside Angelique's head. She closed her eyes and hummed along to Pachelbel's Canon.

She didn't hear the front door open. Didn't hear Lyle

calling her name as he stomped through the house. Didn't hear that their son had stopped screaming. Stopped squirming. Not until Lyle stumbled into the bedroom and pushed her aside and ripped the pillow from their son's face, shouting at her to stop, stop, stop. Angelique collapsed against the closet, shuddering awake.

Lyle lifted Kellan. Stuck his finger under the baby's nose. Rested his ear against his chest. *What the hell did you do, you stupid bitch?* Holding Kellan against his shoulder, Lyle frantically patted the child's back. *Come on, Kellan, breathe, breathe!*

On shaky legs, Angelique slid up the wall to a standing position. She touched Lyle's arm, but he shook her off. Shouted at her to stay the fuck away. To not come near their child. He called emergency services and pleaded with them to hurry.

Angelique backed into the corner. Clamped a hand over her mouth as it dropped open. Gaped in her horror at Kellan's still body. At the boy who'd never again coo. At the boy who'd never crawl across the floor. At the boy who'd never call her mommy.

Then the voice began again. *Please, quiet child, please...*

PART ONE

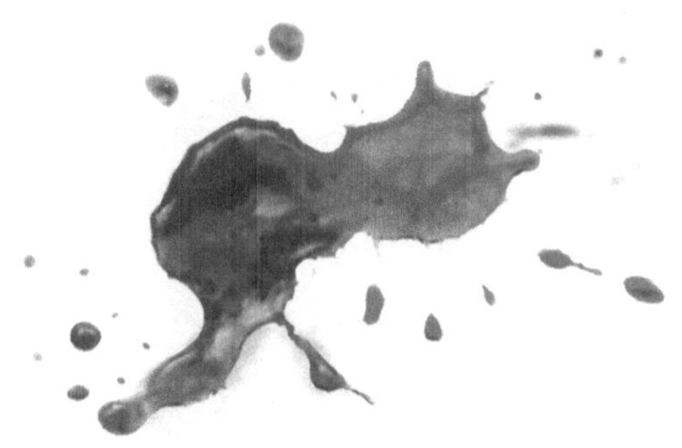

1. JEFFERSON

They'd only arrived at the Carondelet Street Gallery minutes ago when Gemma began bickering with Camile. Jefferson ducked through the doorway, carrying the first paintings of his collection from the van. He stood at the threshold, waiting to be told where to put them, completely invisible to the quarreling duo.

"If you put Jefferson's paintings in the back by the bar no one will notice them," Gemma argued, "The guests will be too busy filling their cups."

The gallery was a camelback row house, L-shaped in structure. The entrance opened into two front showrooms, separated by a thin wall with a narrow passage. Big island windows faced Carondelet Street and provided pedestrians a clear view of the artwork. Off the downtown showroom, a short hallway branched into an oddly cramped back room, where a miniature bar hooked along a staircase leading to an upstairs office. This was normally where guests mingled while wetting their whistles with beer and wine. This was also where Camile displayed first-time artists' work. Visible yet hidden as Jefferson was now.

"It's not like I'm stuffing his work in the attic," Camile said in her southern Brooklyn-esque accent.

"No, but it's the next rung above," Gemma said.

Camile paid Gemma little attention as she typed a text message into her phone, appearing as unwrinkled by the complaints as her charcoal suit. Jefferson highly doubted Camile ever broke into sweat, even on the muggiest of days, which was almost every day in New Orleans. He stepped out briefly to unload more art from the van. When he stepped back inside…

"Listen, we have less than three weeks to put this show together. Now's not the time to be arguing layout. His work will get just as much exposure as the other artists."

Gemma jabbed a finger in Camile's direction. "Then you should've mentioned this earlier instead of laying it on us at the last minute."

Camile's phone dinged. She pouted her lips, either annoyed by what was said in the message or by Gemma's small outburst. "So, Jefferson may have to hustle a little. All he has to do is put on a winning smile, chat about his art, and he'll do fine. As big as he is, it's not like you can miss him."

"I'm right here," Jefferson said, setting down a canvas.

"I know he'll do fine. He'll do amazing. You know there's renewed interest in his brand of veristic surrealism—"

"Which is why I decided to include him in the show."

"—and why I think it's a mistake hiding him in the back. There are plenty of galleries along Royal who'd love to put his work front and center. I can tell you."

Pausing her texting, Camile said, "Then why not go to them?"

Camile's response didn't please Gemma one bit. Then again, Jefferson didn't know if anything could please her. Why did she have to push so hard? Why couldn't anything ever be enough? In the eight months since they started dating, Jefferson had done everything he could to make her happy, but it never seemed to satisfy. He guessed that was what happened when you grew up wanting for nothing.

Jefferson opened his mouth to give his three cents, but Gemma beat him to the exchange.

"Because I think we can really help each other here." Gemma looked at Camile incredulously. "Jefferson's style fits perfectly with the theme of this exhibition." Gemma snatched one of the paintings leaning on the wall next to Jefferson—a painting of street cars racing around the Fairground horse track—and thrust it in front of Camile. Jefferson cringed, afraid she'd drop it as she attempted to make her point. He motioned for her to give it back, but she either didn't notice or didn't care. "And you're the perfect gallery to showcase his style of work. But not if his work is stuck where no one will see it."

"What are your thoughts, Jefferson?" Camile asked as he was about to step back out. The two women turned in his direction.

Caught between their collective stares, Jefferson's massive frame felt wedged into a corner. In truth, he didn't care where his paintings hung. He was thrilled to have finally gotten his feet in the door of the Carondelet Street Gallery. There were artists who'd gladly push him under a streetcar for such an opportunity, which was why he wanted to stay on Camile's good side. She had connections that could make things happen for him professionally. Get him noticed. On the other hand, if Jefferson went against Gemma, he'd never hear the end of it. It was because of her that he was here. She'd convinced Camile to take a chance on his work.

Fuck! Why'd they have to put him on the spot like this?

"I mean, it'd be nice to be in the front showrooms—" Gemma smirked; Camile sucked on her teeth—"but I'm fine either way, really."

"Then it's decided. He stays in the back room." Camile returned to her text as if there were nothing more to say.

As she handed back the painting, Gemma withered Jefferson with her steely gaze. He wasn't going to hear the end of it when they got home. Unable to stand Gemma's focused anger any longer, Jefferson admired one of Nevaeh's photographs, the Doullut Steamboat Houses reflected in a puddle of rainwater.

"Fine, fine. Have it your way. I just thought as someone who has invested a lot of money in your gallery and is sponsoring this show you might be open to my suggestions," Gemma said.

Jefferson couldn't believe Gemma had aimed so low, but he wasn't surprised either. Wasn't that how she'd haggled their way into several exhibits and a couple of magazine profiles?

Camile stopped texting; slid her phone in her pocket and folded her arms over her chest. "Okay Gemma. Let's say I entertain your opinion. Where would you suggest I hang Jefferson's paintings?"

Gemma waved her arm around the sunlit showroom. "How about in here?"

"But Nevaeh's photographs—"

Once again, Gemma shot Jefferson a look poisonous enough to wither the gaillardias in the window. Jefferson bit back his words. He'd dug a deep enough hole already. No reason to dig any further.

"He's right," Camile said. "I can't rightfully ask Nevaeh to switch rooms. I already promised her the space."

Gemma took a couple steps toward Camile, clicking her tongue against the roof of her mouth like a clock counting down to an explosion. "Then I guess the next time your gallery gets in a lurch you can ask *her* for a sizable donation."

"That's not how donations work, darling," Camile said, no longer disguising the irritation in her voice.

Jefferson couldn't stand listening anymore. He wasn't about to let Gemma push Nevaeh aside—or anyone else for that matter. "Gemma, I'm sure there's another solution—"

"Baby, please stop interrupting."

"Fine, I'll talk to her," Camile said between gritted polished teeth. It was obvious from her pained, glossy-lipped smile that she was annoyed at having been beaten. "But I'm not promising anything," she added, unwilling to fold entirely.

Gemma smiled sweetly. "That's all I'm asking."

Minutes later, after Jefferson had finished emptying the van, the heavy wood door creaked open behind him. Rays of sunlight framed a figure, enfolding them in a shimmer of white light. Nevaeh strolled in, singing slightly out-of-tune to a pop song playing over her earbuds. She stunned in a long sleeve summer dress she'd refashioned from a hideous pair of paisley jacquard pants she'd purchased last week from a thrift store on Magazine Street. Jefferson knew this because he had been out shopping with her, poking fun at the flowery trousers Nevaeh had now transformed into a fashion statement.

Jefferson would've complimented Nevaeh on her wardrobe, but it'd only draw Gemma's suspicion. Instead, he gave Nevaeh a cursory nod. Taking out her earbuds, she replied with a casual "hey."

Clapping her hands, Camile trotted up to Nevaeh and pulled her into a hug. "Darling, how are you? It's good to see you," she said, kissing Nevaeh's cheeks like they were close friends—which they weren't. Jefferson doubted Camile considered anyone a close friend.

Nevaeh blushed from the attention. "Awright, I guess."

While Camile and Nevaeh exchanged niceties, Gemma strolled across the room to join Jefferson. She latched onto his arm, dug her nails into his bicep, and pulled him down to her level. "What are you doing?" she hissed in his ear.

"What are you talking about?" Jefferson muttered out of the corner of his mouth.

"You know exactly what I'm talking about. Taking Camile's side over mine."

"I wasn't taking sides."

"No? 'Cause it sure sounded like it to me."

Camile held Nevaeh at arm's length to admire her. "Girl, you are snapping! This is the cutest outfit. Where did you get it from? You looking like you ready to pose for a vignette."

"I sewed it myself," Nevaeh said, somewhat awkwardly.

"You did?" Camile's eyes popped open in mock surprise. "Can I hire you as *my* tailor?"

Gemma chortled. "The poor thing. She probably stole the material from her dead granny's closet."

Jefferson shook free of Gemma's grasp. "Would it kill you to say something nice?"

"Jesus, it was a joke, Jefferson. But I'm glad to see you have *somebody's* back."

"What does that mean?"

"Nothing."

With an arm around Nevaeh's shoulder, Camile escorted her toward the rear of the gallery. "I was wondering if I could talk to you privately for a second, darling."

Nevaeh glanced back at Jefferson. He dropped his eyes toward his feet, afraid to meet her gaze. Gemma watched with a satisfied smirk as Camile led Nevaeh away. Jefferson wished he could think of something nasty to say to wipe the wicked grin from Gemma's face, but all that came to mind was: "Looks like you got your way."

Taken aback, Gemma pressed her palm against her breastbone, gasping like Jefferson had knocked the wind from her. "Excuse me? Wow! Here I was expecting a *thank you*, and instead, you throw the favor in my face like I did *you* wrong."

"You did *somebody* wrong."

"What do you care about that skeeta hawk?"

A lump wedged in Jefferson's throat. He'd pushed too hard. Why? Because it was Nevaeh losing out from this deal. She hustled twice as hard to land a spot in this exposition, hanging her photography anywhere that gave her a chance, until she'd finally caught Camile's attention. She deserved to be displayed in the front room.

But he couldn't tell Gemma that.

"I don't want to make waves," he said, unable to think of a better excuse. "I'm lucky Camile agreed to hang my work." *And probably wouldn't have if it weren't for Gemma.*

Standing on her tippy toes, Gemma wrapped her arms around Jefferson's neck, and pulled him down until their noses touched. "Why do you say things like that, my sweet giant?" she said, staring directly into his eyes. "You have real talent. And soon everybody in New Orleans is going to see it."

"You think so?"

"You know I wouldn't say it if I didn't." Gemma fingered a button on his shirt, unsnapped it, stroked the dip in his throat beneath his Adam's apple. "Now you relax and let me take care of everything." She bit his lower lip, sinking teeth into the pinkish flesh, before letting go. "And don't interfere again."

Jefferson touched his mouth and came away with two droplets of blood on his fingers.

"Not interrupting anything, am I?"

Jefferson and Gemma had not heard the front door open. Startled, they turned to find Marcel Romero watching them from behind a pair of bottle top sunglasses. He smiled a mouthful of silver, visibly amused by their row. Both Jefferson and Gemma were shocked to see him. Far as they knew, he was blacklisted from every gallery in town.

Marcel leapt forward, scooped Gemma off her feet, and spun her in circles. Arms held at her sides, Gemma demanded he put her down. Marcel did as she requested but rested his hand against her cheek. Gemma slapped it away.

"Gemma, you charmer, gorgeous as ever. Been a long time. See you still hanging with this boyo." Marcel offered Jefferson his hand.

Jefferson ignored the ringed appendage like Marcel planned to shock him with an electric buzzer. It wasn't just that Marcel was Gemma's ex. When Jefferson first started trying to get noticed in the art scene, Marcel did everything possible to shove him aside, treating their art like a competition he couldn't bear to lose.

"Not going to shake?"

"Rather not."

"You still sour over all that stuff?" When Jefferson didn't respond, Marcel sputtered his lips. "Gotta let it go, Jefferson my man. These are better days."

"What are you doing here, Marcel?" asked Gemma. "Shouldn't you be peddling down at Jackson Square?"

"Camile offered me a show."

This came as more of a shock than Marcel appearing unannounced. Just as Jefferson was about to inquire further, Camile glided back into the front room, trailed by Nevaeh, who, judging from her clenched jaw, had learned the news of her relegation. Jefferson tried to slyly grab her attention to apologize, but she wouldn't look his way.

"Well, if it isn't trouble walking through my door." Camile and Marcel embraced.

"Hey now, I'm from the Catholic District. Brother Martin Preparatory, class of 2010."

"Don't bullshit a bullshitter. You a nutria from the Lower Nine. And the better for it. Don't want no toots 'round here. Oh Marcel, have you met our other artist, Nevaeh Parker?" Camile ushered Nevaeh forward.

"Don't believe I have." Marcel offered his hand. "Pleasure."

"This here is some of her photography," Camile said, holding up a frame.

Pushing down his sunglasses, Marcel admired a photo Nevaeh had snapped of a group of men shooting craps in the middle of a flooded street during Hurricane Ida. "You got quite the eye." He studied Nevaeh up and down before sliding the glasses back up his nose.

"Thanks," Nevaeh said. "At least somebody thinks so."

The remark twisted like a knife inside Jefferson's gut, but he couldn't do anything except stand there in silence. He'd have to talk to Nevaeh later. Make sure she knew he had nothing to do with Camile's decision.

Gemma wedged herself between the trio. "What's he doing here?" she asked Camile, nodding her head at Marcel.

"Oh, I didn't tell you?" Camile said, feigning forgetfulness. "Sambola had to drop from the exhibition. Personal reasons. Marcel kindly took his place on short notice."

"How thoughtful of him," Jefferson said, sarcastically.

"Gotta problem, Big J?" Marcel cracked his knuckles.

"Boys, please, act like adults," Camile said.

Gemma cleared her throat harshly. "Do you really think this is a good idea? No offense, Marcel, but you're not exactly Mr. Popularity. Not after you talked trash about half the galleries in this town."

For once today, Jefferson agreed with Gemma.

"You're one to talk. What's this about you accusing Barbara Stone of ripping you off?" Marcel clapped back.

Shit! Jefferson had hoped this wouldn't come up. But what did he expect? Gossip spread through the art community like a can of spilled paint. Once it got rolling, it mixed into a glob of lies and half-truths. "There was a misunderstanding," he said.

"What is there to misunderstand?"

"Things got blown out of proportion. Barbara and I talked it out. Everything is fine now," Gemma assured Camile.

That was a blatant lie. It was Jefferson who'd smoothed things over after Gemma accused Barbara of withholding some of their money from the exhibit's sales.

Nevaeh stepped from the shadows. "Sounds to me y'all have rubbed a few thorn bushes. What I don't get is what this has to do with what we're doing here?"

Once again, Jefferson tried to catch her eye, but having said her piece, Nevaeh slipped back into the shadows. Taking a risk, he pulled his phone from his pocket and texted her a quick message. *Talk later?* Eyes on Gemma, who was focused on making Marcel's head explode with her mind, he slipped the phone into his pocket.

"Spoken like the true voice of reason," Camile said. "What's important is we put on the best exhibition this city has seen. Then no one will care who did or said what. Agreed?"

Everyone did, though somewhat reluctantly. But what choice did they have? It was either this or hope something better came along. Which was a laugh. They had to make it work. Everyone who was anyone in the art community had shown at the Carondelet.

Jefferson's text alert beeped in his pocket. He checked the message. It was a reply from Nevaeh. It read: *Yeah, ok.*

2. GEMMA

Later that evening, Camile led the krewe over to Bar Marilou for cocktails, a sort of pre-exhibit celebration she threw before every show to slither into the good graces of her artists.

Hidden on the side of the Maison de la Luz Hotel, inside a converted Law Library, Bar Marilou was a speakeasy that sold fancy cocktails with avant-garde names—Midnight Marriage, La Luz Espresso—to middle-aged jesters who dressed like street performers but lived in newly refurbished homes in Lakewood and Audubon. The whole place masked its pretentiousness behind bohemian New Orleans swagger. Everything from the tiger print carpet to the golden stools to the pink floral wallpaper and red mood lighting common of '70s French decor screamed, "Look at me! Look at me!" They'd even kept the shelves of books from the former library. The whole charade made Gemma want to burn the place down.

Camile ordered a round on her tab from the snazzily tuxedoed bartenders. She shook hands and kissed cheeks with the staff and introduced half the bar to her new collective like she had sculpted them into existence. No one else seemed to mind. Not even Jefferson. For once, Gemma's hatchling broke from his shell and chirped happily with some hippie folk musician about an obscure band she'd never heard of.

Maybe this was because Camile treated them like part of her circle and not like outsiders hovering around the edges. The few times Camile remembered to introduce Gemma, she'd called her a patron of the gallery, as if Gemma hadn't saved Camile's ass when she'd needed it. But Gemma made it known exactly the sizable portion she'd kindly donated. Her boasting garnered her a few raised brows and awkward silences. Gemma didn't care. She enjoyed watching Camile squirm.

At thirty-six, Camile Davies was grasping onto whatever straws remained in the jar. She had to feel they were getting shorter and shorter. This was evident by stringing herself to Marcel. They flirted openly, Marcel hugging Camile's shoulders while she giggled over something he said. She wondered what that sneaky bastard could've possibly offered Camile for her to risk a chance on him. Dirt on Gemma? Why else would the nasty little shit bring up the Barbara Stone incident? To embarrass her, that was why. Well, she could play that game too.

What Camile didn't know was Gemma had spoken with the landlord of 841 Carondelet. Ms. Davies had fallen months behind on the rent. Which was why they were at Bar Marilou. Everybody here owed Camile favors, but soon the favors would run out. That was when Camile would have to cut Gemma in on the gallery. That, or watch helplessly as Gemma swiped the gallery's brass key from around her neck.

Then there was what to do about Jefferson. His talent matched his size, but his confidence whittled him to nothing. He'd still be peddling hand-painted postcards in front of Jackson Square for a couple bucks a pop if she hadn't come along. But if he listened to her, and did what she said, then she'd make something of him yet. Together, they could own this town.

After they'd all gotten a drink, Camile corralled them around a plush sofa surrounding a dark wood table near the casement windows. The girls scooted to the middle while the boys flanked the ends. For a long moment, no one said anything, taking turns sharing polite smiles. Gemma couldn't take her eyes off the brass key resting against Camile's chest. She wondered how that precious metal would feel hanging around her neck.

"You an artist too?" Nevaeh asked Gemma, breaking the ice.

"Gemma attended classes at Parsons in New York when she was younger," Jefferson said, proudly.

Gemma choked on her iced tea. She really wished he hadn't brought that up.

"Really?" Camile sounded unconvinced.

"You never said nothing to me about it," Marcel acted as if he'd caught her in a lie.

Gemma plucked the cherry from Marcel's Chambery Stroll. "I never told you a lot of things." She bit into the bourbon drenched fruit and winced as the juices squirted down her throat. "But yes, I went there for a summer program when I was sixteen. Took part in a one-day workshop on expression in painting with Toby French—"

"Toby French?" asked Camile, flabbergasted. "The British Impressionist."

"Now I know she's fibbing," Marcel cut in, but Jefferson hushed him.

"The one and only."

Gemma remembered having to paint the face of a mannequin head that sat on a table in the center of the room. Toby French had instructed the class to imbue its blank expression with emotion. While other students somehow managed to make the mannequin cry with sadness or beam with joy or burn with anger, Gemma's rendition remained as blank as the mannequin's expression. As if she'd replicated its emptiness. As if she couldn't imagine a life behind those dull, vacant eyes. Just thinking about that mannequin's head staring at her coldly from the canvas brought a shiver up Gemma's spine.

Nevaeh continued to stir her drink. "What did Toby French say about your work?"

Humiliation warmed Gemma's neck. It was like she could still feel Toby French standing over her shoulder, draping her sixteen-year-old self in dark shadow, Toby's wheezy asthmatic breaths blowing in Gemma's ear as he sighed with disappointment. The kerosene chemical stench of Liquin on Toby's khakis as he pointed a paint crusted finger at the face on Gemma's canvas, the bile in the back of her throat as Toby said her painting had as much life as the inanimate object she'd composed. Gemma had run out of class and spent the rest of the afternoon in her dorm sobbing, swearing to never paint again.

"He complimented my technique. Said my lines had nice form and real depth." Which wasn't a complete lie.

"Bullshit," Marcel said, pushing away his half-full cocktail.

Finished with the conversation, Camile strolled over to the next table to chat with a man coated head to toe in silver.

"Why would she lie?" Jefferson said, Gemma's unsung hero coming to the rescue.

"Because that's what she does," Marcel said, stirring his cocktail.

"Why'd you stop painting?" Nevaeh asked.

Because her parents never approved of it. They pressured her to go into business, which in the long run maybe wasn't such a bad idea. She made a better representative than a painter.

Scooching closer to Jefferson, Gemma ran her fingers through his curly dark hair. "I found better use for my expertise."

Blushing, Jefferson smiled at Nevaeh to hide his embarrassment. Nevaeh shifted in her seat uncomfortably, avoiding eye contact.

"Managing Jefferson's career, of course. I think he's going to go far." Gemma glared right at Nevaeh. "Don't you?"

"Is that why you asked Camile to switch us?" Nevaeh challenged her.

Marcel whistled through his grill.

"I'm glad you understand."

As Nevaeh reached for her drink, her sleeve pushed up on her arm, displaying a crosshatch of scars on her wrist. She looked up, catching Gemma's eyes from across the table. Gemma pouted her lip in mock sympathy.

"Did them myself, if that's what you're wondering," Nevaeh said.

"I didn't say anything," Gemma said, looking at Jefferson like she didn't know what Nevaeh was talking about.

Tapping Maurice on the shoulder, Nevaeh asked him to let her out. "I'm going for a smoke."

Jefferson watched as Nevaeh weaved through the crowd toward the front door. "I think I'll join her," he said, voice cracking slightly. "If you don't mind, babe?"

Gemma did mind. She didn't like him being alone with that skeeta hawk. Sure, they'd been friends since college but ever since Nevaeh had come back into his life Jefferson had seemed somewhat distant. Not that he'd ever do anything. He'd have to grow some balls first.

But saying no would make her look desperate. "I'm not your mommy."

Jefferson kissed her on the cheek before hustling a bit too eagerly to catch up with Nevaeh.

"Where did everyone else go?" Camile nudged Marcel over as she returned to the table.

Marcel jabbed a thumb toward the entrance.

Outside the window, Jefferson joined Nevaeh where

she leaned against the gate, smoke drifting from her pierced nostrils, cigarette clutched between her fingers. She didn't seem happy to see Jefferson, nodding as he spoke, but lips clenched tight.

Excusing himself, Marcel slid from the booth, leaving his half-finished drink to water down. While letting him out, Camile noticed Jefferson and Nevaeh outside together.

"So, you and Jefferson, what's going on there?" she asked with a smirk.

"What do you mean?" Gemma played ignorant.

"How long you been a couple?"

Bending down, Jefferson lit his cigarette from Nevaeh's. "None of your business," Gemma said.

"Touché." Camile raised her sherry. "Still, I can see why you corralled him." The leather squeaked as Camile sunk into the cushion. "To represent him, I mean. He's definitely talented. Marketable, too." She glanced over her shoulder at Jefferson and Nevaeh. "But he lacks…poise. Nothing that can't be fixed." Camile turned around. "But you know this."

Gemma tied the cherry stem into a knot. "What's going on with you and Marcel?"

Camile snickered. "Now who's getting personal?"

Over at the bar, Marcel was chatting with a troupe of burlesque dancers. He leaned his head back, raised his hands above him, and gestured as if he was sticking a sword down his throat. He hopped around and waved at his tongue like he'd eaten a scorching hot pepper. The troupe laughed at his ridiculous charade.

"I just don't know why you'd take a risk putting him in the expo?"

"Marcel got a bad deal. He never did all those things people say he did. I think he deserves another chance…"

No longer listening, Gemma slowly rose from her seat as she watched Jefferson place his hand on the small of Nevaeh's back as he opened the door for her. Gemma stepped toward them and almost collided with the returning Marcel, causing him to spill his fresh drink on his shoe.

"Damn, girl. Watch where you're going. You made me scuff my shiny derby." Marcel pulled a handkerchief from his pocket and polished clean his black leather footwear.

"That took a while." Gemma flashed Jefferson her watch.

"We were having a smoke," Jefferson said. "You said it was okay."

"Do you always have to ask her permission?" Nevaeh jabbed.

"No, of course he doesn't have to ask permission." Gemma laughed off the accusation. "Right honey?" She touched Jefferson's wrist. "You do whatever you like." *As long as you stay away from that skeeta hawk.*

"I'm going to grab another drink," Jefferson announced. "Anybody need anything?" His eyes landed on Nevaeh. She shook her head.

Camile shook her empty glass. "Would you mind grabbing me another, darling, while I visit the lady's?"

Before Jefferson could answer, Camile rushed off down a dimly lit hall running past the bar.

Once again, Jefferson left Gemma holding court. She almost went chasing after him but didn't want to appear clingy. *Can't he go anywhere without you on his coattails?* Gemma could hear Nevaeh asking. So, she sat back down and tried to act cordial. At least if Camile was there, she'd have someone to spar with, but these two were as dull as the old ladies gabbing down at the Republican Women's Club her mother was always dragging her to.

"How did you meet Camile?" Nevaeh asked Marcel.

"Oooo-we! Now that there's a story. It was when she was still the registrar for the original Carondelet Street. When it was still owned by Margaret Carroll. Oh, I guess it was about eight or nine years ago. Now you have to understand I was a cocky young player barely old enough to drink then, but I had this scheme I was rolling where I'd scope out busy galleries with small numbers of employees and go up to customers like I worked there and bullshit them about art. Once I had their interest, I'd start telling them about a hot new artist hitting the market. Of course, that artist was yours truly…"

Gemma scoffed. "Isn't that what you always do? Charm your way into every gallery?"

"Better than buying my way," Marcel fired back. "Anyway, where was I? Oh yes, so I'm gabbing with customers at Carondelet Street…"

Gemma tuned Marcel out as soon as Camile came strolling from the bathroom and saddled next to Jefferson at the bar as he waited for their drinks. There was nothing propositioning about her posture. No accidental brushing of limbs. Nothing that suggested Camile was interested in Jefferson personally, which was what bothered Gemma most. If Camile wasn't flirting then she was talking business. And it appeared Jefferson was listening.

Gemma gripped the edge of the table. It was all she could do to keep herself from launching from the sofa and racing over to stand between them. *Just be patient,* she told herself. Soon enough Camile would dig her own hole. And this time, Gemma wouldn't be there to pull her out. No, this time she'd bury her.

"…Wait, so Camile pretended like she was a customer and let you try to sell her your art?" Nevaeh asked, astounded.

Marcel shrugged. "She was already interested in the product. She just wanted to hear my pitch."

Gemma read Jefferson's lips as he said, "Thank you, I appreciate it," to whatever Camile had offered. The sourness of the lemony iced tea stirred the acid in Gemma's stomach.

"And that's how you ended up working together?"

"Yeah, until…" Marcel aimed his gaze at Gemma. "Now I'm more into a mix of digital painting and video mapping."

"I've been thinking about moving more into the field of photo-painting," Nevaeh said.

Gemma slammed her empty glass on the table, startling the two. "Jesus, do you two ever stop squawking?"

Nevaeh and Marcel looked at each other, astonished. Before they could rebuke, Gemma stood to meet Jefferson and Camile as they approached the table. Placing her hand on his chest, Gemma stopped Jefferson from taking a seat, looking up at him, with what she hoped was a pained expression. "We need to go home."

Jefferson held up his brand new beer. "Right now?"

"Please Gemma, don't run off just yet. Grab another drink—a real one this time—and relax," Camile said.

It took all of Gemma's willpower not to wipe that sneaky grin off Camile's face. "I'm not feeling well."

"Is something wrong?" Jefferson asked, concerned.

"I'm just not feeling well, and I'd like to go home."

Jefferson placed his full beer on the table. "Sorry y'all, but we're gonna head out. I'm glad we got the chance to hang. Let's do this again." He glanced at Nevaeh.

She sipped her drink and acted like it was no big deal, but her nonchalance showed she was annoyed.

"Couldn't you stay? I feel we haven't had the chance to chat," Camile implored Jefferson. "We could call Gemma an Uber. You wouldn't mind, would you, darling?"

So you can sink your claws into him deeper. "I'd really prefer Jefferson take me home," Gemma said, hating herself for sounding weak.

"I better go," Jefferson said, unable to hide the disappointment in his tone.

"Have it your way," Camile said, obviously disappointed.

As they were about to leave, Nevaeh called after Jefferson. He turned around, far too eager to hear what she had to say. Nevaeh raised the glass. "Thanks for the beer."

Before they reached the door, Gemma overheard Nevaeh say to the others, "That was awkward."

Gemma knew they'd gossip about her as soon as she was gone. She could almost feel her ears beginning to burn as Jefferson hailed them a cab from the sidewalk. *Let them have their fun. Soon enough they wouldn't be laughing.*

As they cruised along in the cab down St. Charles, Jefferson watched out the window at the branched arch of oak trees growing over the sidewalk and the pedestrians moving in and out of the small local shops. Gemma rolled down her window to kill the stench of cigarette smoke on Jefferson's clothes.

"I really wish you'd give up that habit," she said. She sniffed her dress. "The smell is even on me now. It's like I stepped from a brushfire."

Jefferson mumbled a noncommittal reply. Gemma could tell he was steaming about being dragged away from the party. He hadn't said a word since leaving Bar Marilou. But Gemma didn't know what he should be so angry about. It wasn't like *she'd* flirted with anyone else or whispered behind *his* back.

"What did you and Camile talk about?" Gemma asked, no longer able to tolerate being left in the dark.

"When?" Jefferson said, not even looking at her.

"At the bar."

"We were just talking about the show. How we both thought it was going to be a big success. Though I still don't think you should have made a fuss about the curation. Nevaeh was quite upset that you convinced Camile to move her art from the front room."

"What do you care what that skeeta hawk thinks?"

"I don't," Jefferson replied much too fast. "I just don't think it was right. And will you please quit calling her skeeta hawk? She hasn't done anything to you."

When had he suddenly grown a pair? "You two were awfully chatty."

"Nevaeh and I have been friends for a long time. You know that. It isn't like you haven't met her before."

Gemma rolled her eyes.

"She's a nice person. I think you'd like her if you gave her a chance."

"Were you friends before or after she cut herself?"

Jefferson's jaw tensed. "Everyone has issues."

Gemma grabbed Jefferson's limp hand and placed it in her lap. "Yes, but a girl with those kinds of issues only causes trouble. She could ruin everything we've worked for. Now why don't you tell me what you and Camile were talking about."

"I already said. The show."

"Don't lie to me, Jefferson. I can always tell when you're lying. Your voice rises in pitch."

"She said I should drop you and let her represent me." Gemma dug her nails into Jefferson's flesh. He jerked his hand away. "But I told her I could never do that. I told her we were a team. That it was because of you I'd gotten this far."

"How did she react?"

"Disappointed." He touched her knee.

"Good." Gemma took Jefferson's hand again, guiding it up her thigh. "Because I don't know what I'd do if I lost you."

They rode the rest of the ride home in silence. Though she had some doubts about Jefferson, Gemma did love him. He was the only person who ever really listened to anything she had to say. Who didn't treat her like a spoiled rich girl. Who appreciated what she did for him.

Which was why if he ever broke her heart, she'd rip his out.

3. NEVAEH

"When are you going to tell Gemma?" Nevaeh asked, holding her position beneath the archway between her bedroom and front room.

"Can you lean forward a little bit more and spread your arms to your sides?" Jefferson responded, avoiding the question as usual. Nevaeh did as he asked. "Perfect."

Circling around to her left, Jefferson sketched in his notebook, concentrating on the work at hand, the scratch of his pencil tracing the lines of her slender body. Shading the bold lines of the cuts on her arms. Slashing the strands of her kinky hair and sharp cheekbones. Then gently rounding her breasts, eyes, and lips in softer, sweeping gestures. Drawing her into existence.

She knew this all without watching. The soothing sensation swept across her as he traced her every crevice, every charm and flaw. The tingle of his fingers sliding along her skin as he took in every detail and reproduced them on the paper. This was why she modeled for Jefferson. She loved seeing herself through his eyes. Somehow, he made her beautiful in ways nothing else, and no one else could.

Jefferson flipped the page. She arched her back and slipped one leg slightly back behind the other. "Relax a bit," he said.

For a half hour, Nevaeh had struck various poses while Jefferson focused on capturing the essence of her movements. The muscles in her limbs burned with a pleasant ache, vibrating beneath the sweat beaded skin. *Why did it have to be so fucking hot in New Orleans?* The air conditioner slobbered coolant onto her warped tile, and the rotating fan whipped the humidity into an oven roasted hurricane, siphoning the oxygen from the room.

Nevaeh concentrated on the painting on her wall Jefferson had done while hanging in City Park. It was her favorite. There was something melancholy about the blurry image of an older man seated on a bench near Langles Bridge, the thick layers of acrylic on the cotton fabric creating a sweeping motion, as if the figure was blending into the world around him, becoming part of the different pigments of nature. For a moment, she expected the old man to turn toward her and wave. Invite her to join him for a peaceful afternoon away from stress and worry. Some days, Nevaeh swore she heard raindrops splashing in the lagoon and wondered if she could step into the painting and become part of it just like the old man.

Nevaeh had asked Jefferson about the man once and he'd said he'd seen him in a dream.

Unlike the surrealism of his other work, the painting blurred the lines between the realistic and the abstract, with its striking contrasts of unblended colors and visible brushstrokes. To Nevaeh, this was the painting that reminded her of Jefferson, outwardly simple yet deceivingly complicated. He'd given it to her as a gift the night of the Nouveau Collective Exhibition. The night they first slept together after reconnecting.

Jefferson stepped around to her backside as she turned slightly at the waist to look at him in profile. He moved around her slowly, capturing her from different angles.

They'd known each other since they studied at the Academy of Fine Arts. As fate would have it, Nevaeh became friends with Jefferson by accident. He was running late to their first Art History class and the chair next to her was the only seat available. While putting down his things, he spilled café au lait over their table and drenched her backpack. Apologizing profusely, he tried cleaning the mess for her, but she told him to forget it. She'd wash it in the bathroom after class. She complimented him on the smell of the coffee, which he'd bought from one of her favorite roasters, Cherry Coffee. The very next class, Jefferson brought her a café au lait. It was the sweetest gesture.

The following week they started meeting at Cherry Coffee Roasters and walking to the Academy together. Sometimes they'd grab the streetcar, and go hang out at the New Orleans Museum of Art. They'd eat beignets in the sculpture garden before roaming the wondrous halls, bonding over a shared love for Expressionism. Other times they went to the Contemporary Arts Center for lectures and performances, or Jefferson would take her shopping at White Roach, a record shop inside a mint green building on Magazine Street. They'd go to his cramped studio apartment—long before he moved in with Gemma—where they'd lay on his bed and listen to obscure bands like 16 Horsepower, Budos Band, and Surprise Chief. Bands that were now part of her playlist.

As much as she wanted him to, Jefferson never made a move. She knew now that he was too shy. But back in 2018—when she was only 19—Nevaeh thought he wasn't attracted to her. The weird girl with the bulging forehead and flat nose and scrawny boyish body. Sometimes she'd leave Jefferson's place, wishing he'd fall in love with her and whisk her away from the brutal reality of her strict upbringing. An upbringing which she never confessed to anyone. Not even the therapists at Tree of Life.

Nevaeh raised her arms over her head, and spread her fingers apart, lifting up on her toes like an angel taking flight. Jefferson halted, captivated. "That's it. Hold it right there," he said, flipping the pad to the next sheet of paper.

Naked, with her wounds exposed, Nevaeh felt free of the restraints that had been placed on her most of her life. It was one of the reasons she modeled for Jefferson. Why she wanted to be with him. Her scars didn't repulse him, in fact, Jefferson said they made her all the more beautiful. He often traced them with his fingers as if his touch could heal her. Placed his lips on them as if he could kiss away the pain of those memories.

He'd asked her about her scars once, but she couldn't bring herself to tell him the truth. At least not the whole truth. She didn't want him to blame himself for what happened. Instead, she'd told him she could no longer live under her parent's authoritarian rules and thought death was her only escape—a decision she regretted but was not ashamed to admit. They were proof of the suffering she'd endured. Jefferson had accepted her explanation and never asked about it again. Now, she was no longer ashamed of her scars. They were a testament to her survival.

"I need to take a break, Jefferson."

"Almost done." He quickly finished his final drawing. "Man, babe, I got some fantastic sketches. There's real emotion."

Nevaeh came to have a look as Jefferson flipped through the images. She saw exactly what he meant. He'd somehow managed to capture the shades of love, anger, and sadness battling inside her. Could he read what was going through her mind? No, she didn't think so. Otherwise, he'd know that she was still upset about what happened at the Carondelet.

"My butt looks too big," she said.

"Looks right to me."

"Hey now, mister." With a quick pivot, Nevaeh wrapped her arms around Jefferson's neck. He dropped his sketchbook on the bed, lifted her by the waist off her feet, and kissed her softly on the lips. Damn it! Why'd he make it so hard to stay mad at him?

No, he wasn't getting off that easily. He still hadn't answered her question about talking to Gemma.

Tapping his shoulder to put her down, Nevaeh wormed

out of Jefferson's embrace and moseyed over to a chair in the corner of the room where she'd tossed her clothes. She slipped into black slacks and buttoned on a white shirt, snagged her cigarettes off the dresser, and strolled out to the gallery to smoke and watch the tourists ambling along Chartres.

Jefferson followed her out. "What's wrong?"

"You never answered my question."

He sighed heavily. "I'm fixing to talk to her—"

"You've been saying that for months."

"—after the show."

"The show your girlfriend is now running."

Jefferson leaned over the railing and hung his head. "You know I had nothing to do with that."

"But didn't put up much of a fight against it neither," Nevaeh said, blowing smoke from her nostrils.

"Let's not argue about this again. I said I was sorry."

Across the street, a nicely dressed couple exited an Uber, grabbing their bags and sharing a laugh before kissing and entering the red American Townhouse of the Le Richelieu Motor Hotel.

Nevaeh turned toward Jefferson. "And I accept your apology. I understand you're doing what's best for your career."

"That's not it at all. Listen, I know Gemma puts up a tough front, but she has feelings too. Part of the reason she's that way is because no one really cares about her—"

"Maybe if she learned to treat people with respect instead of stabbing them in the back—"

"What do you want from me, Nevaeh? I can't control what Gemma does."

"You do whatever you want." She took a final drag before stubbing her smoke out on the railing and marching back inside the apartment to get ready for work.

As she grabbed a pair of black socks from her dresser, Nevaeh heard Jefferson step in behind her. "I know this is hard for you. It's hard on me too. But I can't break up with Gemma before the show. I would've never got my foot in the Carondelet's door without her connections. I'd feel guilty cutting her out now."

"Seems to me you're stringing the poor girl along," Nevaeh said, unable to keep her annoyance from creeping into her tone as she sat on the bed. Or was he stringing *her* along?

Jefferson stepped into Nevaeh's line of sight. The light from the open shutter cast a shadow across his face. "I'm not stringing her along. She'll get a cut of whatever I sell. But this is my chance to finally get my name out there. It's not like I want to paint murals for the rest of my life. Having everyone tell me what to paint then complaining when it doesn't come out exactly how they want it."

Nevaeh hated it when Jefferson bellyached. "There's nothing wrong with painting murals. We all have to make a living." She shook her server apron at him.

"Don't you hope to make a living off your art?"

From atop her dresser, Nevaeh scooped enough change for the streetcar into her hand then shook her fist at Jefferson. "Sure, but I'm not willing to use other people to get there."

"I'm not using her. I'm *not*. I just haven't figured out how to let her down. I know it doesn't always seem like it, but Gemma cares about me. And though I'm not in love with her anymore, I don't want to see her get hurt. You understand that, don't you?"

Nevaeh did. She may have not liked Gemma—or how she treated Jefferson—but to find out the one you loved was no longer in love with you would have to be devastating. Which was what she found so frustrating about this situation. For her to be with Jefferson, he had to break Gemma's heart—and *she* was the cause.

She slipped on her shoes by the front door then began searching for her phone. Where the hell had she put it?

"Do you need me to call it?" Jefferson asked, reading her mind. He dialed her number. The phone buzzed in her pocket. She felt like a complete idiot. "Jesus, I'm so angry I can't even think straight."

"I guess that's on me too." Jefferson slipped on his canvas shoes by the door.

In some ways, yes it was. But she'd played a part too. "Jefferson, wait. I didn't mean it. Not like that anyway."

Jefferson paused with his hand on the doorknob. "It's okay. I deserve it. You're right. I need to tell Gemma. But Camile's putting in a lot of effort to market this show and she's promised big returns. For everybody. It could be good...*for both of our careers.*"

Did he mean for them or him and Gemma?

"Then after the show's finished, I'll break things off. I

promise. Now's just not the right time. Not with only a few weeks left."

This wasn't exactly what Nevaeh had hoped to hear, but she understood where he was coming from. "You want to walk with me?"

A smile stretched across Jefferson's face. "I'd love to."

They strolled along Chartres Street through the heart of the Vieux Carré, weaving through the throngs of tourists carrying go cups of Hurricanes and the horse-drawn carriages clacking along the brick roads, a cool evening breeze cutting the stifling humidity. Nevaeh wondered how much longer she could wait around for Jefferson. She liked him. A lot. But she wasn't nobody's side piece. He needed to decide soon. Either her or Gemma. She couldn't wait forever.

She'd wasted enough time allowing others to make decisions for her.

After she'd escaped, Nevaeh often considered moving back home. Her parents had done a number on her self-esteem, and she always doubted her decisions. Until she was on her own, they told her what to wear, when to speak, and how to think. Clothes laid out for her every morning. Allowed only to open her mouth to answer a question or say "Yes, sir" or "Yes, ma'am" when scolded for performing her chores wrong. And every idea that popped in her head—well, it was judged by God.

Then she met Jefferson and she saw what freedom could be like. Once she'd had a taste, she refused to be tethered to her parents again. And they punished her for it. So, she took her life into her own hands and got locked up for it. There the doctors and nurses made the decisions for her.

Once she was out on her own for good, and those decisions fell squarely on her shoulders, Nevaeh often felt lost. At least the horrors at home were familiar. For a while, even something as simple as choosing what to eat threw her into a spiral, but Nevaeh knew if she crawled back she'd never escape again. So she stuck it out. Things slowly improved. She'd got a job serving tables. Found her own place. Concentrated on her photography. Even started selling some on her Instagram account, which led to a few exhibits, first in places like libraries and cafes, then in small galleries. Sure, she fell on her face a few times along the way, but those scars taught her lessons she wouldn't forget.

Nevaeh wanted Jefferson to be with her because he wanted *her*. Because they shared something special. Because they connected on a deeper level. But for that to happen, he first needed to break things off with Gemma.

4. NEVAEH

Soon as the ugly, five story brick building came into view, the logo in bold white letters across the top, Nevaeh's heart clenched and she struggled to breathe. The Tree of Life Recovery Center. She'd promised herself she'd never come back to this place. Never walk through those sliding doors again. She swore she saw her younger self staring out the barred bedroom window on the third-floor corner, the room where she'd lived imprisoned for six months. If living was what you'd call it. Existing was more like it.

With a few deep breaths, Nevaeh clutched the bag with her camera equipment and approached the entrance. The moment she walked through the sliding glass doors she was hit with a gust of freezing air conditioning that raised goosebumps on her flesh. The empty lobby stank of mothballs and lemon disinfectant. From somewhere behind the locked steel doors, a woman shouted, "Get away from me, fuckers!" A nurse calmly asked the patient to settle down. The woman screamed back, "Help, these fuckers are hurting me!" Then as quickly as the commotion began, it ended. Blood rushed through Nevaeh's veins as she pictured a needle sliding into the woman's arm and her nodding off into oblivion.

At the reception desk, the orderlies appeared to recognize Nevaeh. She may have cut her natty hair into a curly pixie and gained weight to fill out her once gaunt face, but when they heard her name, all they saw was the unhinged girl who'd been dragged kicking and screaming into the facility, butchered arms stitched and wrapped in gauze, parents loudly praying over her, pleading with God to save her haunted soul. Her parents didn't know haunted. If they did, they never would've stuck her in this godforsaken place.

The receptionist greeted Nevaeh with a cold expression and shoved a guest sign-in sheet in her direction, appearing to judge her as crazy for entering these halls again willingly. And maybe Nevaeh was.

The receptionist took Nevaeh's phone and purse and made her remove her jewelry. She'd purposely worn flats without laces. They checked her temperature and asked about any flu-like symptoms. At least they didn't ask if she was experiencing anxiety or having suicidal thoughts. The receptionist handed her a visitor's name tag and told her to wait in the lobby.

Minutes later, a buzzer sounded, and the metal security door creaked open. Ms. Hebert strode into the lobby, heels clacking across the tile floor, carrying a clipboard of documents, the same youthful black woman Nevaeh remembered from her days inside. Soon as Nevaeh saw Ms. Hebert's infectious smile it brought a smile to her own face.

Ms. Hebert was the Activities Director at the facility. When she'd learned Nevaeh had an interest in photography, she'd encouraged her to pursue her creativity, even letting Nevaeh borrow an old Canon EOS she'd brought from home. For the last six weeks she was there, Nevaeh spent two hours every day with the camera strapped around her neck, snapping photographic memories of the worst year of her life. The orderlies and nurses weren't fond of her privilege—thought it bred resentment among the patients—but none of Nevaeh's close friends at the facility seemed to mind. They enjoyed the attention. And since the doctors approved, the staff couldn't do squat—though they constantly threatened to revoke Nevaeh's privilege if she broke the slightest rule, which was why she was careful to remain on her best behavior. She would've bashed her head against the wall if they had forced her to go back to staring at a television for 14 hours a day.

"Hey stranger," Ms. Hebert said, wrapping Nevaeh in her warm embrace, "You're looking good."

Nevaeh snuggled against Ms. Hebert's soft body. Buried her face against her shoulder to stifle the tears.

"Let me take a good peek at you." Ms. Hebert held her at arm's length. "Wow! What a difference a few years make. I almost don't recognize you. What are you up to these days?"

"Got a job serving tables at the Two Sisters. An apartment. Working on my photography." She raised her camera. "Even got into the Carondelet."

"Wow! You go girl!" They high fived. "Is that what this project is for?"

"Maybe. We'll see."

"How about a boyfriend?" Ms. Hebert gave her a slight hip bump.

Nevaeh couldn't help but blush. She told Ms. Hebert about reconnecting with Jefferson and how they'd been spending time with each other again. She left out the part about him dating Gemma.

They stood there in silence for a minute. Ms. Hebert stuck her hands in her pockets and rocked on her heels. Her smile never left her face. "You ready to see a couple of old friends? Not many around no more. Like you, most got out. Valentin and London are still here, of course. I told them you were coming for a visit and they're super excited. Oh, and Emery is back, I'm afraid. I'm sure she'd love to see you."

It hurt Nevaeh hearing this. The day of Emery's release, they'd made a pact never to return. Guess some promises couldn't be kept. "How long now?"

"Seven months. She keeps finding ways to stay. I'm beginning to think she likes it here. I thought maybe you could change her mind."

"Doubtful. She's as hard-headed as—"

"You were. Except you were always looking for a way out."

"Looks like Emery and I are both back."

"Just make sure you don't stay too long."

After a security screening, Nevaeh followed Ms. Hebert through the steel doors and down the checkered tile hallway. Classical music played over the speakers during the daylight hours to present a cheerful atmosphere. They passed rooms with views of the beautiful homes across the street; daily life unfolding obliviously outside these walls. Orderlies made beds, removed the dirty laundry and trash, wiped the shelves and toilets with sanitizer, and sprayed that goddamn lemony air freshener. Patients wore their clothes and had their own TVs and were allowed a few personal items. These rooms were for the patients who'd completed their programs and were now waiting for release.

They turned left down another similar long hallway, passing staff who waved and smiled, and patients who did the same, though it all felt feigned. Sadly, these were the saner of the bunch. The rest were kept locked and sedated on the upper floors.

"Now, I understand you know the rules, but I have to repeat them anyway," Ms. Hebert said, turning right down another hall. "It took a lot of ass-kissing with the board to pull this favor, so please don't break any of them on any condition. I can't stress this enough."

Nevaeh nodded.

"You're only allowed to take photos of the patients that signed the agreements. You know who they are. Any complaints and we're looking at pending lawsuits. Got it? Visitor Tag must be always worn in view. You will need to stay in the designated visiting areas—cafeteria, lounge, and garden—with staff supervision. If you need to use the bathroom or want to see other parts of the facility—"

"I'd like to take photos of my old room, if possible."

"I'll make arrangements to have a staff member accompany you. You're not allowed to hand out any gifts, including food or drink. Any disruptive behavior that puts patients' or staff's safety into question, the visit will be terminated, and security will escort you from the premises."

They stopped outside the doors of the cafeteria, and Ms. Hebert passed the clipboard of documents for Nevaeh to sign. After she finished adding her John Hancock to several papers, Ms. Hebert opened the doors.

The smell of reheated food substances made Nevaeh's stomach turn the second she stepped inside the cramped sterile lunchroom. Two rows of long tables surrounded by uncomfortable plastic chairs crowded the rectangular space. Thin rays of light fell through the slits in the barred windows. Orderlies in white uniforms served lumpy egg salad sandwiches on trays to those patients in their charge.

The routine was sickly familiar. As if Nevaeh were just here this morning for breakfast. Some days she couldn't tell what the slop was she put in her stomach. She'd dropped twenty-three pounds in this place; her biceps and calves thin enough to wrap a hand around.

Ms. Hebert led Nevaeh to Valentin and London's table. They hugged her and shared pleasantries. They both looked well compared to the last time she'd seen them. Valentin spoke rationally and London wasn't fidgeting as much.

"I'll let you three catch up," Ms. Hebert said. "Just have an orderly page me when you're finished," she told Nevaeh.

They spent the entire lunch talking. Valentin had stopped

seeing the ghosts, but the voices still murmured, telling her about the souls drowning in the black waters outside Holt Cemetery. London didn't scratch all the time, although she was still convinced bugs were laying eggs in her pores. Nevaeh was happy they were both doing better. "Better" being a relevant term.

But they were more interested in Nevaeh's stories about life on the outside. Her apartment in the Vieux Carré. The places where she'd shown her art. She even told them about Jefferson. They glanced through pictures she'd recently captured. Bourbon Street completely empty, the puddles reflecting the neon signs of the bars. A single light burning in an upstairs room at the Le Richelieu Hotel. A blue jay perched on the lace ironwork of her gallery, its square patterned wings spread as if about to take flight.

Nevaeh's friends were more than happy to pose for a few photos. She snapped some great shots of them playing cards—something they'd done all the time when she was here—and making aghast faces at the horrible food. She laughed so hard her ribs ached. She'd forgotten how much she'd missed these two. They'd made her time in this hellhole bearable.

After she left Valentin and London, an orderly escorted Nevaeh to the courtyard, a greenspace in the center of the building that didn't see much sun. Seated on the park bench, a menthol dangling from her lips, ash an inch long, Emery smoked in the shade of the singular cypress tree, monitored by a security guard with a balloon head strung to neckless torso. A rope burn scarred the skin around Emery's neck and gauze wrapped her arms in white wristbands. She watched Nevaeh approach but didn't lift her hand in greeting.

"What you doing here?" Emery asked her as soon as Nevaeh sat down.

"Could ask you the same thing," she said, ignoring the orderly staring a hole into her back.

"Couldn't hack it out there. I tried; I swear. Had a job shucking oysters and everything. Then the pandemic whipped through and threw my life into chaos." Emery ground her cigarette beneath her slipper. "How'd you survive it? The outside?"

Nevaeh raised her camera. "This was how. I took all those penned up emotions and filtered them through art." She snapped Emery flipping the bird.

"Wish something like that worked for me, but I figure I'm better off staying here where it's safer."

The guard snorted.

"Eventually, you'll have to check out of Motel Crazy," Nevaeh said.

"Fuck I do. They let your buddies Valentin and London stay."

"They're a different story and you know it."

"What about your ex-neighbor?"

"My ex-neighbor?"

Emery said a name Nevaeh hadn't thought about since she walked out of Tree of Life. Nevaeh pictured the orderlies wheeling that poor woman into her room across the hall, her muttering the entire time, *Please be quiet, child, please.*

The only words Nevaeh ever heard her utter. Her stomach twisted as she remembered the putrid stench of fruit gone rotten. Shook away the memory of the woman's anguished expression; the way her mouth hung wide open as if she were silently screaming.

Glancing at her watch, the guard mentioned it was time for Emery to return to the facilities.

"Angelique is still alive?"

"Her and the legion of flies. Though she doesn't get out too much. None at all, really. They keep her locked up in her room. Only the staff allowed in or out. Occasionally a doctor comes for a visit. And the woman's sister."

"Ms. Hebert?"

"That's enough, Ms. Doucet. Time to go," the guard said, squeezing Emery's bony arm in her hammer of a fist.

Emery shook free. The guard stepped forward. Wiggling her fingers, Emery invited her to do something. The guard huffed.

"I've seen her go in there, but she mostly avoids it. Don't blame her. There's something off about that woman. And this is coming from someone who has tried offing herself multiple times."

"Ms. Doucet!"

"What?"

The guard tapped her watch. "Break is over."

"The warden says I gotta go."

Nevaeh drew her friend into a hug and said she'd see her soon. Emery hoped she didn't. "Stay sane, babe," Emery said, before allowing the guard to drag her away.

After getting Ms. Hebert's permission, the elevator cranked Nevaeh and the guard to the fifth floor to visit her old room. Nevaeh was greeted by a deep chill and a windowless steel door the guard opened with a keycard. Here, the Tree of Life wasn't the four-star hotel it pretended to be on the lower level. Foggy windows blinded the outside world from the madness that went on beyond the locked doors. Video cameras watched their movements from the ceiling. They strolled the carpeted corridor past the barricaded nurses' station, a cluttered room of paper strewn desks and cabinets overflowing with medical supplies. Every morning and afternoon, patients lined up single file in front of the glass encased counter to receive their paper cup of meds: sedatives to help make you forget you were even alive.

On each side, a series of doors housed those considered a danger to themselves or others. Trailing the guard, Nevaeh glanced into the thin, rectangular windows where patients in matching tan scrubs mumbled incoherently, cried for loved ones, held conversations with imaginary friends, or screamed vile threats at anyone within the vicinity. Unknown stains splattered the mattresses, the orderlies attempting to hide them with wrinkle-free sheets and cozy blankets. Nevaeh still had a crook in her neck from the stone hard pillows she couldn't punch into soft submission. Any object a patient might harm themselves with had been removed from the rooms. This included televisions, curtains, or personal care products. They weren't allowed belts or shoes with laces or hoodies with strings. No jewelry. No accessories like hats or sunglasses.

How was it she'd once belonged here?

Nevaeh hardly remembered the girl with the bandaged arms, who on her first night, bashed her head against the steel door hard enough to knock herself unconscious. But the Tree of Life Recovery Center had never quite left her completely. It had branded itself on her deep enough to scar. Maybe that was what this project was about, putting her past to rest.

A buzzing sound droned as they approached Nevaeh's former residence hall. Bodies of dead flies speckled the light fixtures. One landed on Nevaeh's shirt. She shooed it away. Then another and another. With a shaky hand, the guard took the keycard from her pocket. It was obvious she was nervous too.

They finally reached Nevaeh's old wing, her former room at the far end. Shadows of flies swarmed in the square streak of sunlight from the window. Darkness stretched from the end of the corridor toward the rooms as if something demonic were reaching out, threatening to wrap around her ankle and pull her into oblivion. This lingering dread was accompanied by a frigid coldness she hadn't noticed in other parts of the facility. The kind of coldness that sunk its teeth into your flesh, all the way to the marrow. The kind of coldness that rattled your teeth and burned your lungs.

Taking in the scene, Nevaeh and the guard halted, not moving a muscle. Finally, with a resolved sigh, the guard started her journey down the hall. Still, Nevaeh couldn't bring herself to take that first step forward; feet firmly planted as if she'd grown roots into the carpet. The flies swarmed her head, their buzzing deafening any thoughts.

"Are you coming?" the guard asked, voice trembling. It was obvious she didn't want to stay in this hallway any longer than necessary.

Nevaeh swallowed her fear.

As she shuffled toward the guard, moaning and frantic mumbling from some of the rooms harmonized into a deranged soundtrack. It was as if Angelique's lunacy had spread like a contagion. Of course, Nevaeh was being ridiculous. This was a psych ward. They may have called it a recovery center, but a psych ward it was. The patients didn't catch the crazy, they brought it with them.

But there was something about Angelique that had always terrified Nevaeh. That anguished look on her face reflected the pain Nevaeh felt inside. The torment she'd suffered at the hands of her parents. And she wasn't the only patient who felt that way. Many of them thought Angelique was a malevolent spirit that had come to the facility to haunt them with the tragedies they'd suffered. Even the staff complained when they drew her name on their rounds. Some refused to go into her room to administer her bath or meds. Those that would enter said evil lurked in her presence.

The guard stopped in front of Nevaeh's former room, checked through the tiny glass window to ensure no patient was inside, then slid the keycard through the lock. A red light flicked to green. Hand shaking, she turned the handle.

Flies crawled on Angelique's door, bustled at the narrow opening beneath. Buzzing. Buzzing. Buzzing. Right as the guard swung the door open to allow Nevaeh inside, a voice whispered in a craggily voice, *please quiet, child, please.*

Nevaeh stopped. She took a step backwards as the persistent buzzing of the flies grew to a deafening pitch. Still, beneath the cacophony, Nevaeh heard Angelique's cryptic mantra, as if she were whispering it into Nevaeh's ear, as if her voice was inside Nevaeh's head. Annoyed, the guard asked if she was coming. They didn't have all day. But Nevaeh couldn't stay in the hallway another second. She apologized to the guard for wasting her time. The guard shook her head and slammed shut the door. Nevaeh hurriedly backed away.

When she reached the end of the hall, Nevaeh turned the corner sharply, running right into Ms. Hebert. "Whoa, child. Where you off to in such a hurry?"

Nevaeh tried composing herself, slow her racing heartbeat, come up with a viable excuse, but all she heard was Angelique speaking those words, *please quiet, child, please.*

"Nevaeh sweetheart, you okay?" Ms. Hebert looked down the hall leading to Angelique's room; concern deepening the creases in her face as she realized where they were. She looped her arm through Nevaeh's and pulled her toward the elevators. "Why don't we take you back to the first floor? There's nothing nice to photograph up here."

Nevaeh nodded in agreement.

As they waited for the elevator to take them down to the ground floor, a fly landed on Nevaeh's cheek.

5. JEFFERSON

Jefferson tried his best to remain still on the stool, despite dying to loosen the choking top button of his collared shirt. From behind the ceaseless clicking camera of the photographer from the *Pelican Bomb*, Gemma motioned for him to lift his chin slightly. He did as she asked. They both wanted things to go smoothly. This was a huge opportunity: his artwork and name in a major magazine.

But having the spotlight thrown on him wasn't something Jefferson was comfortable with. He preferred the solitude of working alone in his studio. Having this many people crammed inside his workspace, forcing him to move his stuff around to make room for the lighting rigs, felt like an invasion of his privacy. Gemma had spent the entire morning staging the place, hanging the paintings she thought best represented his style–something they'd never agreed on, especially since he'd begun straying from the kitschy commercial art that she insisted was his bread and butter. Art that lately had begun to suck the joy from his beloved passion.

From the smiles Gemma gave him, Jefferson assumed she

was happy with how things were going. At least she hadn't fought with anyone today. Not even after Camile had brushed her aside and taken control of the entire feature—a feature that was only happening because of Camile's connections.

Camile sat behind the desk he used as his supply table, engaged in an interview with the magazine's journalist—who recorded the exchange with his phone while scribbling notes on a pad—about the gallery surviving the pandemic and the future of the Carondelet. After catching Gemma's fiery gaze, Camile briefly mentioned her as a sponsor for the upcoming exhibit when the journalist inquired about the gallery's finances. The response drew another smile on Gemma's face. And why shouldn't it? Today she was getting exactly what she wanted.

"All finished," the photographer said. "Mind if I take some photos of your studio?"

Jefferson wiped the beads of sweat from his forehead and nodded. "Yeah, that's—"

"Of course, he doesn't mind," Gemma interrupted. "Now if you ask my opinion, these here…" She pointed to three paintings hung on the wall behind him, "…are his very best."

Jefferson would've disagreed, but he knew better than to open his mouth, especially in such *distinguished* company. Why spoil Gemma's good mood? Let her have this moment. She deserved it.

Gemma strolled over and whispered in his ear, "I'm so proud of you, babe," before kissing him on the cheek.

Still, Jefferson felt guilty about stepping over Nevaeh,

despite her assurance that she didn't hold it against him. It should've been her photo and words gracing the article. There was only one way for him to make it up to her and that was breaking things off with Gemma. But today was not the day. Soon enough.

"Jefferson, why aren't you selling this piece at the show?"

From his desk, Camile lifted a recent piece he'd painted on an old streetlamp head. He'd rewired the lamp to plug into an outlet and replaced the four panels of glass with thinly stretched canvas. Painted on the canvas, a figure strolled down Magazine through various neighborhoods of New Orleans. When you flipped the light switch it changed the scenery from day to night, shifting the emotion from content and relaxed to contemplative and moody—at least that was what Jefferson had strived for.

Before Jefferson could reply, Gemma jumped in. "Doesn't really match with the rest of his collection, don't you agree?"

"If you ask my opinion," Camile said, carefully turning the piece in her hand, "*this* is your best work. Don't get me wrong, your other paintings are good, but this…" She shook a finger at the lamp head. "*This* is unique."

Now it was Jefferson's time to smile. But his smile didn't last long.

"Nobody pays to decorate their homes with old junk," Gemma said. "What they *will* pay for is art that enriches a room. You know…that adds some class." She waved her hand at the paintings on the wall.

The rising tension in the studio squeezed Jefferson's hands into fists.

"How silly of me. You're right, Gemma. What do I know? I've only run a successful gallery for eight years." Camile cradled the lamp in her arms. "But since it's *my* show, I'm going to insist we include it. I even have a nice stand for it to sit on that will look perfect in the center of the room."

Gemma smirked. "Of course. It's *your* show."

"What's under here?" The photographer lifted the bottom corner of parchment paper covering Jefferson's most recent painting. A portrait he'd painted of Nevaeh. A portrait that, if Gemma ever saw it, the journalist's questions wouldn't be the only ones he'd have to answer.

"No!" Jefferson shouted, startling the photographer stiff. He dropped the corner of the parchment paper and backed away from the easel.

"Jefferson!" Gemma scolded, regarding him like a misbehaving child. "What's gotten into you?" She moved toward the parchment paper. Reached for it.

Beats of sweat sprouted from Jefferson's forehead once again. His muscles tightened.

Gemma began to peel the parchment paper back, revealing just a few inches of red-tipped darkness and smooth flesh tones.

Jefferson launched forward on autopilot. "Uhhh, yougonnahafta—" With startling imprecision, he snatched up the easel and ferried it to the corner, turning the portrait—parchment paper still intact—to face the wall. Clumsily, he turned to face the others in the room, all of whom stood gawking. "S—sorry," he stammered. "I never show anyone a work-in-progress."

Gemma crossed her arms over her chest. "If it's for the show, then I don't see why we can't—"

"Mind if I ask you a few questions for the article, Jefferson," the journalist butted in, stepping in front of Gemma.

Jefferson swore he heard Gemma grinding her teeth in anger. "Of course," he said. Anything to divert from Nevaeh's portrait.

They took seats across from each other on stools. From over the journalist's shoulder, Gemma scowled. Jefferson averted his gaze to the journalist, a hipster dude with a pompadour and a lumberjack's beard. The journalist hit record on his phone, placed it on his lap, and readied his notepad.

"I hear you're a muralist," the journalist started. Jefferson nodded. "This must be a big change. Going from painting in private homes to having your work shown at one of the most prestigious galleries in the city. Can you describe to me how that feels? Going from virtual unknown to a soon-to-be established artist overnight?"

"Established? I don't know about that." Jefferson laughed. "But I didn't get here on my own. I had a lot of support along the way. A special someone gave me the confidence to take the next steps. To move from the gates of Jackson Square to the Carondelet."

Gemma's expression softened and she dropped her arms to her sides. The beginnings of a smile twitched at the corner of her lips.

The journalist asked a series of questions, mostly about his creative process and techniques, his influences, and his favorite medium, which Jefferson answered amiably and without hesitation. It looked like he might survive this interview after all unscathed until…

"One last question before we finish up," the journalist said, tapping his pencil against his pad. "Where do you derive your inspiration?"

An image of Nevaeh as he last saw her floated to Jefferson's mind. They stood beneath the gallery in front of the Deurty Boys as the rain began to fall, the droplets glowing like crystals in the sunshine. Both of them took a quick glance around, afraid of getting caught, though Jefferson knew Gemma avoided the Vieux Carre at all costs. Refused to dirty her boots on the liquor drenched sidewalks and subject herself to such debauchery. He and Nevaeh had kissed, a quick smooch, then she was off, heading up Chartres. Glancing back only once with a quick wave.

"She is my muse." The words slipped out before he could stop him.

"Who?" the journalist asked, leaning forward.

Gemma's lips slowly dropped into a frown.

"The city, of course. New Orleans," Jefferson uttered. "She is my muse. My inspiration. If you haven't guessed by what you've seen." He motioned at his art.

The journalist clicked off the recorder. "Well, I think we have everything we need," he said, dropping his notebook into his bag. He turned toward Camile. "I'll be in touch when the feature is ready for your perusal."

Camile thanked him kindly.

Crushed beneath the overwhelming weight of guilt, Jefferson asked the journalist whether they would be interviewing Nevaeh—"And Marcel, of course," he blurted, attempting to cover his tracks.

Gemma cleared her throat, drawing his attention. Arched her brow, silently condemning his sudden display of camaraderie.

The journalist glanced at Camile, who smirked with pleasure at Gemma's discernible irritation. "Well, normally we only run a piece on the featured artist…"

"But I think that's a fine suggestion, Jefferson," Camile said, enjoying watching Gemma twist into knots. "It proves that the Carondelet supports artists as a *community*. Don't you agree, Gemma?"

"Wholeheartedly," Gemma replied, not taking her eyes off Jefferson.

Why did he have to open his stupid mouth? Because they'd stolen the spotlight. It should be Nevaeh's face in the *Pelican Bomb*. Not his.

But Gemma would never forgive him for this stumble—that was for damn certain. As the rest of the party filed out of the studio, the journalist and photographer politely thanked him for his time before following Camile out to their car. He almost begged them not to leave.

Once everyone else was out of earshot, there'd be nothing to keep him from being entirely at Gemma's mercy.

Seated across a small table at Compére Lapin, Jefferson hunched over his barely touched plate of snapper collar, pretending to pay attention to Gemma, her words drowned beneath the white noise of whirring espresso machines, clinking glasses, and the cacophony of conversation that, at the moment, was giving him a raging headache. How was he supposed to hear a goddamn thing with all the noise in this place? He couldn't even hear himself think. He pushed his plate to the side, no longer hungry for the deliciously fragrant food, and sneaked a sniff of his nicotine-stained fingers.

It'd been hours since his last cigarette and the fits were wreaking havoc. If he didn't get one soon, he'd grind his teeth to dust. But he knew Gemma would throw a fit about it. She thought it made him stink like a burning sawdust factory.

Besides, she'd guilted him enough for one day. Refused to drop the subject of his little slip about Nevaeh being interviewed. "Why would you want to share the spotlight?" she'd said in the car on the way over. "Sometimes I feel like you don't appreciate what I do for you."

It wasn't that he didn't appreciate it. He was just tired of her stepping over everyone else to get what she wanted then pretending she did it all for him.

Nodding along, Jefferson caught snippets of the conversation. Gemma was still miffed about Camile including everyone in the *Pelican Bomb* article. A mistake she'd thrown in his face at every opportunity. But it wasn't like Camile needed either of their approvals. It was her gallery, and she could promote whoever she wanted. As long as Nevaeh received her due then he'd gladly share the limelight with Marcel too.

Jefferson had begged Gemma to forget it, but once she had a grudge, she had a hard time letting go. For days now she'd prattled on about how she'd run things differently if she owned the gallery—something Jefferson didn't ever see happening.

While Gemma grumbled, Jefferson ordered a third sazerac from the server, hoping the bourbon might temper the pain in his head. He thought of what Camile had said about Gemma at Bar Marilou: *Better be careful. She finds out you're with Nevaeh and it's all over for you. Just look at what she did to Marcel.*

Jefferson had pretended he didn't know what Camile was talking about, but he was never a very good liar. *Every time you look at that girl I see your heart leaping in your chest. And don't think Gemma doesn't too. She may be a lot of things, but she isn't stupid. I don't mean to tell you what to do, but you might want to cool things down until after the show. I have a lot invested in this, and I'm not going to lose everything because your girlfriend freaks over you falling in love with one of* my *artists.*

It'd irked Jefferson that Camile had hung this particular noose around his neck. It wasn't his fault her gallery was having money troubles. He didn't tell Camile to accept Gemma's contribution and offer to sponsor the exhibit. She should've known darn well Gemma would expect to run the show.

Of course, he'd gotten something out of her contributions

too. What would Gemma ask in return when his time to pay came around?

That was a good question. One Jefferson stupidly hadn't considered.

How about we help each other? Camile had said as their drinks arrived that evening. *Cut the loose string. Then we can both have what we want. Because you know, sooner or later, when she's tired of you, Gemma's going to do the same.*

But Jefferson didn't believe that to be true.

For one thing, Gemma genuinely believed in his art. More so than anyone else. She'd taken him to every gallery in the area and introduced him to people in the community he wouldn't have met otherwise—people like Camile Davies—bragging to them about his artwork. Back then he'd found her confidence sexy and intimidating. Gemma had a salesperson's ability to talk anyone into giving her anything if she wanted something bad enough. She flirted with the men as if she'd known them intimately all her life. By the end of a conversation, she'd broker a deal. She gained women's trust by building camaraderie, connecting through their common experiences of exploitation and disadvantage. Which was why Gemma often did the speaking for Jefferson. She'd gloat about his work and share photos from his Instagram page. He glowed from the attention.

Even now, here in the restaurant, as she babbled on and on—about what? he couldn't say—he felt drawn in by her confidence. From his pocket, Jefferson grabbed a fine point pen. He pulled a cocktail napkin in front of him and began drawing her portrait. Sketched the diamond shape of her face. Traced the long, flowing hair that draped along her slender neck. Shaded in her tapered eyebrows. Outlined her hooded, gray eyes and duchess nose and bow-shaped lips. Circled the big hoop earrings dangling from her tiny ears that, in her opinion, stuck out too far from her head. Sprinkled the freckles on her cheeks she often hid with foundation.

Jefferson may have no longer loved Gemma, and at times wished to never see her again, but not all of those old feelings had faded. He still cared for her. Which was why he'd refused Camile's offer.

"Probably mount them on spikes…"

Hearing this, the pen slipped from Jefferson's grip, tearing a hole in Gemma's portrait. "Huh?"

"Our friends. I think that's what I should do. Don't you?"

"What are you talking about?"

"See, I knew it, you weren't fucking listening! I could've said anything, and you'd just nod your head." Gemma dropped her fork on her plate of curried goat. Wiped her mouth with her napkin and tossed the lipstick-stained linen on the table.

"You were talking about how unfair it was that Camile included everyone in the article."

Gemma grabbed her club soda, sipped gingerly, and winced at the flavor. "That was like five minutes ago. No, what I was saying, if you'd been listening, is that after giving it some thought, I'm considering proposing to Camile that she replace Nevaeh in the show."

Jefferson crumpled her portrait. "You can't do that."

"I don't see why not. I don't see how her photography fits with the overall aesthetic. How can I put this kindly? Her work is a bit…low brow."

Jefferson pressed on his eyes with the meaty part of his palms to stem the dull throb. "Low brow?"

"I'm sure she's fine for somewhere less refined, a little rawer, but we're looking to target a more sophisticated audience—"

"This isn't your goddamn show, Gemma."

Gemma gasped as if she'd found a piece of hair in her food. Other diners turned their heads at the sudden outburst, surprised at the volume and sharpness of Jefferson's tone. An apology may have been in order, but he was too infuriated to speak calmly. Hand shaking, he took another sip of his cocktail and waited for his breathing to ease, ignoring all the eyes on them.

"There's no reason to shout at me," Gemma said, remaining calm as her cheeks flushed with anger. "What is it with you and that skeeta hawk anyway?"

"I told you to quit calling her that," Jefferson seethed under his breath.

"Fine." Gemma raised her hands in submission. "But lately you've been taking her side over mine."

Fuck. Did she already know? Was it best just to admit everything here? No, he needed to play it cool. "I'm not taking her side," Jefferson lied, chuckling as if the suggestion was preposterous. "But I don't think it's good to burn another artist. Do you?"

"And what was with you freaking out over that painting? Was it something you didn't want me to see?"

"It's unfinished."

"Mmm-hmm."

Jefferson took another sip of his drink to ease his nerves. What he really needed was a cigarette. "Why are we fighting about this anyway? It's stupid. Let's concentrate on what's best for us. Not worry about what anyone else is doing."

Gemma sipped her club soda, considered what he said, then smiled. "You're right. I don't know what I was thinking. I'm anxious, I guess. I really want this show to go off without a hitch. Finally prove to my parents that I'm not wasting my time—"

"—hanging out with a swamp rat from Mississippi."

"What does that mean?"

He waved off the comment. "Never mind."

Closing her eyes, Gemma sighed. "We've talked about this before. My parents don't exactly approve of me…managing your career. But this show could change all that. They can finally see that I can make a success of this. *We* can make a success of it. Do you understand why I'm worried?"

Jefferson took Gemma's hand and gently stroked her knuckles. "Don't worry, it's going to be awesome."

"You sure about that?"

"You've put too much time, effort, and money in it for it not to be a success. I mean, by next week, it's going to be publicized in the *Pelican Bomb*. Not to mention all the other stuff you've been doing."

Gemma squeezed his hand, a slight pressure. "Thanks, babe. I feel better hearing you say that. And you're going to do great. People are going to *love* your work. They're going to be talking about it all over town. I just know it."

"How about we box the rest of the food and go home to relax in front of the TV?"

"Sounds like a plan."

Jefferson pulled his credit card from his wallet.

Gemma beamed at him. "Thank you, babe. I love you."

"Love you too."

They leaned in and kissed over the table.

After he'd waived down the server and handed him the card, Jefferson excused himself to the toilet. He rushed through the slender aisle, dodging tuxedoed servers carrying heaping trays, jogged past the kitchen, and down a darkened corridor. He burst through the door and into a stall. There he genuflected in front of the toilet and dry heaved. He dabbed spittle from his mouth and slid onto the seat, laying his head against the cool stall. Maybe he'd stay there forever.

Once he'd collected himself, Jefferson texted Nevaeh, asking to meet the following day. Gemma had a nail appointment, and he could stop by after he finished a job not far from her apartment.

Nevaeh texted that she was available.

After splashing water on his face at the sink, Jefferson took a mint from the tray, unwrapped it and popped it in his mouth while giving himself a final glance in the mirror before leaving the bathroom. Camile was right. The best thing to do was keep things chill for a while. At least until he decided how to tell Gemma he was breaking things off with her.

He knew if he didn't speak to her soon, one of two things would happen. Either Gemma would find out about his cheating on her own, or Nevaeh would get tired of the bullshit and end things between them. Neither of which he wanted. If at all possible, he didn't want to see anyone get hurt, including Gemma. But it might be too late for that. If anyone got hurt, there was no one to blame but himself.

6. GEMMA

In the morning, Gemma waited until she heard the shower running before slipping from bed and digging Jefferson's phone from the pocket of his denims. While Jefferson sang over the barrage of falling water, Gemma typed in his code and searched through his texts. It didn't take long for her to find what she was looking for. The name was right at the top. The son-of-a-bitch had messaged the little skeeta hawk last night while they were at dinner. He must've done it when he went to the toilet. No wonder he was in there so long.

They planned to meet at Nevaeh's apartment this afternoon. Jefferson knew where she lived, which meant he'd been there before. How long had they been sneaking around behind her back? And how had she not noticed?

Because she'd denied it. She didn't think Jefferson had the gall to leave her, especially for some back-a-town street trash. But she couldn't deny it anymore. He thought she hadn't caught a glimpse of the woman's leg in the painting. The skin too dark to be Gemma's. The way he looked at Nevaeh when she was around. Gemma would have to be blind not to see it. And the way he'd defended Nevaeh lately. Gemma had no doubt Nevaeh was the muse Jefferson had spoken of.

How could he do this to her? What had she done to deserve this?

Gemma squeezed the phone so tight the plastic cover squeaked. She clicked out of Jefferson's text messages and returned the device to his pocket. Bit back tears, refusing to cry, then wiped her watery eyes with her sleeve, muttering *no, no, no*. She paced a streak across the polished wood floor, thinking of what to do.

Listening to Jefferson singing cheerily in the shower, Gemma pictured Jefferson's hand on Nevaeh's back as they walked through the door at Bar Marilou. Did he take Nevaeh to the same spots he took her when they first started dating? Picnics under the oak trees in City Park? Dinner at the Mosquito Supper Club? Share a croissant at Levee's Baking Company? Did he tell her about his poor childhood in Mississippi? About living on fried fish and rice and beans for months while his daddy struggled to find work? About being beat up by older kids for being too tall and too big too soon? Had he shared secrets with Nevaeh not even Gemma knew about?

What had Jefferson told Nevaeh about her?

Gemma stopped her pacing. *Get a hold of yourself, dammit.* She slapped her cheeks, the sting snapping her awake. Then an idea struck her as hard as her open hand. Using her own phone, she googled the name Nevaeh Parker. Within seconds, that skeeta hawk's address appeared on Gemma's screen.

Though she was pissed at having to miss her nail appointment, it provided the perfect cover. She'd have to be careful not to be spotted, so that nixed taking her car. She booked an Uber instead.

Gemma hurriedly dressed in the most casual clothes she owned—a knit pullover and cropped pleat pants she rescued from the bottom of her dresser—and wrote Jefferson a note that she'd received a text from the salon that they had an earlier opening. She threw on her mom's big round sun hat, chunky cat eyeglasses, and a pair of boots. In the hall mirror, she almost didn't recognize herself. She looked like a miserable Chalmation from the Parish. Give her a soccer mom haircut and a heavy smoker's rasp and she'd fit right in.

Quietly, she turned the knob, opened the door, and exited the house. It took all her energy not to slam it.

From the Le Richelieu Hotel Cafe, Gemma lounged at a table by the window, sipping an espresso and crumbling a scone as she spied on Nevaeh's crappy apartment house. Salmon colored paint peeled like a sunburn. A layer of grime smeared the arched windows. Drying laundry hung from a wrought iron gallery.

How many times had he slipped into bed *with her* after leaving Nevaeh's place? That skeeta hawk's chemical dark room odors clinging to his clothes. Nevaeh's juices slicking his cock as they fucked. She held her napkin to her mouth and took a couple deep breaths to keep from getting sick.

An hour later, Jefferson's white work van pulled up to the curb right in front of the hotel café. Gemma pulled down the brim of her sun hat. He hopped from the driver's side, dressed in a paint-stained t-shirt and jeans, opened the sliding side door, and removed something wrapped in parchment paper, that from the shape Gemma could tell was a painting. With the painting clutched beneath his arm, he crossed the street and entered the front door with a key. A key!

Once again, Gemma pictured them together, their naked bodies sweaty with lust, Nevaeh breathing hard in Jefferson's ear, legs wrapped around his torso.

When was the last time Jefferson had made love to *her*? Touched her in a way that made her feel wanted? Feel desirable?

The espresso tasted bitter in Gemma's mouth. She had to force herself to swallow it down.

The pair stepped onto Nevaeh's gallery to smoke. Such a disgusting habit. They leaned into each other. Nevaeh appeared distraught over something. Jefferson rubbed her back, consoling her. When was the last time he'd consoled her over anything? Even last night, after they'd gone home from the restaurant, he'd hardly said a word while she confided in him about her parents' constant griping about her lack of a "real job".

With her phone, Gemma snapped a few photos before being interrupted by the server, who saw one of the pictures before she had a chance to swipe to a different tab. He glanced at Jefferson and Nevaeh then back at Gemma, brow arched disapprovingly. From her purse, Gemma pulled a twenty and slid it over. The server raised an eyebrow at the bill, and for a moment Gemma thought he wasn't going to take it, but then he slipped it into his pocket, before asking if she needed anything else. Gemma shook her head.

By the time the server scampered away, Jefferson and Nevaeh had disappeared back inside. Gemma wished she could take back her generous tip. The server's interruption might have caused her to miss something important.

Moments later, they exited the creole townhouse, Nevaeh in a penguin suit. They kissed. Gemma forced herself to watch despite her mind pleading with her to look away. As much as she wanted to deny it, the evidence had been right in front of her all along. The son-of-a-bitch was cheating on her with that fucking skeeta hawk. He might as well have stolen all her money or told everyone that she was a fake. That would've hurt less.

They said goodbye before Nevaeh hurried down Chartres and Jefferson raced off in his van. Gemma waited until she was certain they were gone, paid her tab, and moseyed across the street. She rang the bell of the lower apartment. The empowering jingle of the Tamron Hall show played from behind the door, indicating someone was home. When no one answered after a few seconds, Gemma banged on the glass. Footsteps marched forward and someone flipped the locks. The door scraped opened a crack revealing the round, saggy face of an unhappy black woman in a brightly colored checkered dress.

"What you want?" the woman asked in a thick creole accent.

Gemma put on her kindest smile. "Bonjour, madam. I'm friends with the girl who lives upstairs. You may know her. Nevaeh Parker?" At the mention of Nevaeh's name, the neighbor's lip curled in disgust. Gemma was glad she wasn't the only one who abhorred the little skeeta hawk. "She asked me to come by her house for something, but she was in such a hurry, she forgot to give me the key, the silly girl. I was wondering if you mind letting me onto her gallery?"

The Creole woman cleared her throat and spat onto the brick banquette, barely missing Gemma's shoe. Gemma kept smiling, trying to remain as pleasant as possible under the neighbor's scrutiny. "Your friend is very noisy. Keeps my children up late at night."

"I apologize. I'll let her know to be quieter."

"She always playing her music loud."

"That's awful. Very inconsiderate."

"That boy always coming over. He loud too. Laughing and carrying on."

"Sinful."

"—This is a Christian household. I keep my children safe from the devil's temptation."

"Power be in the Lord." Gemma made the sign of the cross. She liked this woman already. On another day, she would've happily bought her chicory coffee and beignets to listen to her complain about Nevaeh.

Gemma held her hand over her heart. "I promise to the

Lord Jesus, I will have a serious sit down with my friend, on your behalf, and lecture her about the wrongs she has committed against you and God, if you will please let me up to her gallery."

"Bay peché," the woman muttered before slamming the door in Gemma's face. Behind it, she shouted incomprehensibly at whoever was in the house.

Gemma exhaled a heavy sigh. Now what? She was about to walk away when the door opened, and the woman invited her in.

Stepping past the threshold, Gemma followed the woman through a front room ornamented in religious relics. Above a sofa hung two crosses with the words *Love* and *Faith*. On top of the old box television, a framed prayer asked the Lord to "Bless this House." In the far corner, before the kitchen, a wood altar draped in a white cloth displayed three wax candles in a gold candelabra, a leatherbound Bible, a beaded rosary, and an ornate cup ringed with the maroon color of red wine.

They strolled through the kitchen where a brood of children quietly ate from bowls of red beans and rice. They stopped to watch Gemma, curious yet afraid, as if she were the devil mama had warned about. Gemma smiled and waved at them. Most of them ducked their heads and continued eating—as they'd probably been told—except one small boy, not much older than the age of two or three, who briefly smiled back before catching his momma's disapproving eye. He was going to cause trouble, that one.

Out the rear door, they stepped onto a tiny stone courtyard surrounded by a low brick wall. Water trickled down the fountain of an angel and a bench was shaded by ferns on either side. Laundry blew in the slight breeze from a clothesline strung from the garage to the bottom of the gallery. The woman pointed to a staircase headed to the second floor. Gemma turned to thank her, but the woman had already headed back inside.

Gemma climbed the staircase, walked around to Nevaeh's apartment, slid open the shutter, and let herself inside. Compared to the downstairs neighbor's place, Nevaeh's apartment could've been Gomorrah. The musty odor of body scent lingered beneath the sweet fragrance of incense. The spinning overhead fan meagerly fought to cool the stagnant heat. On the street below, the drunken merriments of the Quarter continued unabated. Instead of religious decorations, Nevaeh hung photography and art prints, some of them a bit on the racier side, though nothing Gemma considered pornographic. The blankets on the unmade bed were wrinkled and pulled out from beneath the mattress. Gemma could almost trace the outline of Nevaeh's and Jefferson's bodies. It made her sick in the pit of her stomach. She slid open drawers in the dresser. Recognized some of Jefferson's clothes; the vintage threads he was fond of wearing. Beyond the bedroom, the front room was home to several framed pictures surrounding a coffee table with a few pieces of unopened mail and a cabinet full of photography equipment. Threadbare rugs led through a small, tiled kitchen, an ashtray and a half-empty bottle of bourbon sitting on the round, glass dining table.

But what really caught Gemma's attention was a canvas leaning against the exposed brick wall. She knew from the moment she saw it that Jefferson had painted it. It had all his signature techniques: the thick layers of colors and bizarre assemblage and dreamy depictions of reality. Even now, as angry as she was with him, his extraordinary vision stole her breath, much in the same way it had when she first admired his work at the New Faces of New Orleans Exhibit. Yet, there was something unique about this piece. It had a much darker theme than his normally playful and cartoonish renderings of life. This painting had pain and sorrow and fear beneath the surface. Along with adoration and love. It was by far his greatest achievement.

And at the heart of the painting: Nevaeh.

Kneeling before the canvas, Gemma traced the outline of Nevaeh's slender naked body. The brown skin, smooth and richer than her own. Ran her fingers over the thick scars on Nevaeh's arms. The restless and agonized soul. Jefferson had transformed Nevaeh's suffering into beauty. Turned that ugly skeeta hawk into an angel. And in return, Nevaeh gave birth to a true artist.

There was no doubt in Gemma's mind this was the painting hiding beneath the parchment paper.

Gemma rushed over to the end table, snagged the disposable lighter, and returned to the canvas. She flicked the wheel, sparking a hot blue flame, which she held to the corner of the painting, watching as a small dark spot bloomed on the woven cotton fabric. As she watched the burn mark slowly expand, the heat from the lighter's flame blistered her thumb. But it wasn't the pain that stopped her from torching the entire painting to ash. She couldn't in her right mind destroy a masterpiece.

Gemma grabbed the painting and carried it from Nevaeh's apartment. The downstairs neighbor was folding her laundry from off the clothesline. Gemma raised the painting, "Got what I came for," she said and thanked the creole woman for her help.

"Bay peché" the woman shouted from behind as, canvas in hand, Gemma let herself out of the courtyard.

Down the road from the Carondelet Street Gallery, Gemma paid the cab to wait, not wanting to drag Jefferson's painting inside. "I won't take long," she told the cabbie.

"Give ya ten minutes," he yelled out the window as she winded through the groups of diners in line for Cafe Bearcat.

An older gentleman carrying a wrapped painting was leaving as Gemma shoved in past him, almost toppling him sideways. She burst into the gallery, nearly causing Marcel to drop the projector he was setting up on a stand in the uptown showroom. Customers paused to shoot her a contemptuous glance before returning to browsing. Breathing heavily, Marcel clutched the expensive piece of film equipment protectively to his chest. "What's wrong with you? Coming in here like Hurricane Gemma," he said, quiet enough the customers wouldn't overhear.

"Where's Camile?"

Marcel pointed at the ceiling above them. Gemma sauntered past the clusters of customers to the back stairs in the rear showroom, ignoring Marcel's calls for an apology.

At her desk, Camile ran financial calculations in a spreadsheet on her laptop, cursing everyone from the landlord to the artists whose commissions she still owed. Gemma smirked at a vision of Camile's head sinking beneath the mud of the bayou. "Looks like you might need another donation," Gemma said, leaning on the banister behind Camile.

Camile slammed shut her laptop and wheeled around on Gemma. "You think you can just pass by my office now?"

Other than a few filing cabinets, the office resembled exactly what it was: a dusty attic strung with spider webs. A single bulb from the ceiling illuminated the rugs Camile had thrown on the floor and the ratty sofa where she probably took power naps. "Is that what you call this roost?"

"What the fuck you want, Gemma? Can't you see I'm busy?" Camile pointed at Gemma's attire. "And why are you dressed like a Chalmation?"

Waving away the insult, Gemma plopped down on the corner of Camile's desk, much to her annoyance. "I want to ask you to replace Nevaeh in the show."

"Why would I do that?" Camile leaned back in her chair.

Gemma pictured Jefferson and Nevaeh kissing in front

of her apartment building but shook the image away. "Her photography doesn't really fit with the overall aesthetic."

"For a pathological liar, you'd think you'd have more skill in lying."

Gemma flicked away the remark. "What do my reasons matter? I have the money to sweep your problems underneath the rug."

"Your mamma'n'em has the money."

"It's my inheritance."

"And they'll just give it to you?"

Gemma tapped her fingernails against the top of Camile's laptop. "If I invested it, let's say, in something like the Carondelet."

"Not a chance." Camile shoved Gemma's hand from her laptop, flipped it open, and continued her calculations.

"You're not even going to consider my proposal?" Gemma said, outraged. "I don't see how you're going to last—"

"Let this settle into your swollen head, Gemma. There's no chance in hell I'll ever sell you part of this gallery. I'd let it crumble on top of me in a heap of debt before that ever happens."

"And it just might. But you know I can make your headaches go away. Cutting me in and cutting Nevaeh out. I could sponsor a hell of a lot more shows—"

Camile snorted. "There's only one person I'd like to cut from this show and she's sitting on my fucking desk."

Gemma smiled, but Camile's words stung. "You sure about that?"

"Sure as I am that after this show I want nothing else to do with you ever again." Camile's eyes drifted back to her screen. "Now get the hell out of my office."

Furious, Gemma marched down the stairs and through the gallery. "Well, that sounded ugly," Marcel said with a sneer as she passed. She replied with a middle finger—startling the customers—before shoving out the door.

Gemma crossed the street blindly, nearly getting mowed down by a car—the motorist screaming at her to "watch where she's going"—before jumping into the waiting cab. As he drove her home, she kept picturing Jefferson and Nevaeh kissing while hearing Camile's refusal play over and over in her head. Digging her nails into her palms, she knew there was only one thing that might change Camile's mind: Money. Which meant Gemma had only one choice. She was going to have to speak to her mother about her inheritance.

7. JEFFERSON

The moment Jefferson and Nevaeh entered his studio they were greeted by the comforting sweet, earthy smells of linseed oil and turpentine. Just inside the door, against the wall adorned with a mural of a hurricane raining beads over the Quarter, leaned freshly stretched canvases, the only thing not splashed with color. Next to the fresh canvas lay a precarious pile of discarded, abandoned paintings. Adjacent to the rejects, a couple new paintings—a horse-drawn carriage flying over St. Louis Cathedral, jesters juggling skulls and bones, gators dancing along the Old Basin Canal—dried beneath the windows, hidden in the shadows to keep them from fading in the sunlight. In the center, an easel displayed a painting of the End of the World during the end of the world. The last painting for the show. Perhaps, the last ever of this style.

Head cocked to the side, Nevaeh studied the new pieces. "These are really good, Jefferson. *Really good.*"

Glancing between them, he wasn't so sure. "You think so?"

"You don't?"

Jefferson shrugged. They didn't feel like pieces he'd created, so much as rendered on autopilot. "Gemma thinks they'll sell. Maybe even make me a household name," he said.

Nevaeh turned toward him. "But what do *you* think?"

"I want to paint something…inspiring. Something with emotion. Not shit tourists will buy."

"I might have something to inspire you." Nevaeh pulled her digital camera from its bag. "I took some new photos the other day at the Tree of Life."

For a brief second, it appeared a shadow brushed past her as a shiver quaked through her body.

Jefferson clasped her arm. "You okay?"

Sunlight gleamed through the window and drove the shadow to the corner of the room. Nevaeh's body relaxed. "Yeah, fine. It's nothing. Just spaced for a second." She handed him the camera. "Tell me what you think."

Jefferson quietly studied each image before moving on to the next. Nevaeh had captured the real face of a psychiatric hospital, each snapshot a graceful glimpse of life behind locked doors: residents played cards around a lunch table; a young woman smoked on a bench in a cloistered garden, a guard hovering menacingly over her shoulder; nurses handed out paper cups of colored pills like candy to a line of comatose patients imprisoned within the sterile walls. The photos were clear and defined. A doorway into Nevaeh's world.

One specific photo chilled Jefferson despite the humidity: a swarm of flies crawling along a metal door. An insectile buzz filled his ears. The rank odor of shit lingered beneath the smell of disinfectant. Blinking fluorescent lighting flashed in his eyes as darkness closed in from all sides. Cold fingers pushed through his skin and seeped into his body as if he'd plunged into icy waters.

Jefferson shook off the dreadful feeling and the room returned to normal. "Is this what disturbed you about your visit?" he asked.

Nevaeh nodded, refusing to look at the photo.

"What is it?"

"The room of a patient. A woman named Angelique."

"What happened to her?"

"I'm not sure." Once again, Nevaeh shivered. "And I don't think I want to know."

Jefferson didn't blame her. If he'd gone through what she'd gone through he'd want to bury those nightmares in the dark recesses of his own brain, far from where memory couldn't reach it. Nevaeh was courageous for bumping heads with her past.

Jefferson took her arm. Ran his fingers along her scars. "I'm sorry you had to go through all of that."

Nevaeh smiled. "I wouldn't be who I am if I hadn't."

"Seems like a rough place."

"Could be, that's for sure. But sometimes, I was more scared of what was out here than in there."

"Why's that?"

"In there, I met some really nice people who picked me up when I was down. Can't always say the same for out here.

For a long time, I didn't know who my friends were. I still don't, really."

Hearing her say this twisted a knot in Jefferson's heart. "I'm your friend."

Nevaeh studied him for a moment, as if looking for a sign that he was lying. "I hope so," she said, squeezing his hand.

Showing him these photos, Nevaeh had offered another small peek into herself—cracked open the door to her closet of skeletons a few more inches. "The photos are fucking amazing."

"I'm glad you think that," she said, sparking with renewed energy. "Because I thought we might collaborate on a little project. Something that may inspire us both."

"Lay it on me."

"I want to transform this harrowing time in my life into something healing. Perhaps, show others that you can rise from the ashes even after everything's been burned down."

"Where do I come in?"

"The other night at Bar Marilou, Marcel was talking about reinventing his art. I want to do the same. Which was why I was thinking about mixing media. My photography with your painting."

"You're talking about these photos?" Jefferson said, holding up the camera.

"What do you think?"

Jefferson scanned through the photos again. Already ideas for images and colors and brushwork patterns were taking shape in his mind. This could work. This could really work.

It might've been the best idea he'd heard in a long time. "Sign me up."

His excitement must've been contagious because Nevaeh's cheeks blushed a dark pink as a smile crossed her lips. "You serious?"

"Dead serious. When do we get started?"

"I'll upload the photos now."

As Nevaeh took hold of the camera, Jefferson pulled her close by the hem of her shirt and kissed her on the lips. "I'm super excited about this," he said.

Nevaeh looked up into his eyes. "Me too," she said, before returning his kiss.

For the next hour or so, they shared ideas back-and-forth about their new collaboration. Jefferson hadn't seen Nevaeh this happy since before the whole ordeal five days ago at the Carondelet Street Gallery. After Camile shoved Nevaeh to the rear showroom, her mood toward Jefferson was as unpredictable as the weather during Hurricane Season, calm and warm one minute, rainy and stormy the next. Of course, maybe it wasn't as unpredictable as he was making it seem. It was only when the subject of Gemma came up that an underbelly of tension bubbled beneath the surface, sometimes spilling over into an argument. But today, they fed off each other's ideas, sometimes sharing the same thought or finishing the other's sentence as they studied each photo and discussed color palettes, compositions, and materials. It was like they were speaking telepathically.

He'd never experienced this kind of connection with Gemma. It was always her way or no way.

Jefferson still hadn't told Nevaeh about his conversation with Gemma at the restaurant. He'd planned to when he picked her up after work this afternoon, but something was off about her when he arrived. She replied in short, one-word quips and seemed preoccupied with her camera equipment, checking the memory card and cleaning the lenses. When he tried to get her to open up, she changed the subject to something else. He thought it was about them. Now he suspected it had something to do with that woman, Angelique. Nevaeh had turned away from that photo as if it was too frightening to look at. Not that he blamed her. There was something strange about that image, like it carried within it an evil omen.

So, though the conversation weighed on his mind, he'd procrastinated instead of bringing it up. But he couldn't let it lie forever. Nevaeh deserved to know.

Jefferson walked over to the desk and began scraping his palette clean. "I have to tell you something."

All joy vanished from Nevaeh's face. "Let me guess, it's about Gemma Landry."

"She wants you replaced in the show."

"What?" Nevaeh slumped against the desk.

"Don't worry, I convinced her not to."

"Jefferson, you couldn't convince that woman not to jump off a bridge if she'd made up her mind."

"She's not going to do anything."

"Don't be stupid, Jefferson!" Nevaeh growled in anger as blood flooded her face. "Gemma is not going to quit until she gets what she wants. We both know that."

Jefferson scraped off a giant blob of paint from the palette like he was scraping off a scab. Dammit! They were having such a nice day until he opened his stupid mouth. "I'll fix things, I promise," he said.

"How?" Nevaeh asked. "Marcel told me what she did. Got him blacklisted from every gallery in town for breaking up with her."

Jefferson snorted. "Marcel Romero got blacklisted because he bad-mouthed half of the galleries in this town."

"That's not how Camile said it went down. She said Gemma made all that shit up."

"You trust Camile Davies? All that woman cares about is being Queen of the Art Scene. Everyone in the art community is traitorous. They'll do anything to get ahead."

"Is that why you're still with Gemma?"

Jefferson scraped harder at the palette. "Don't make this about us. I'm on your side."

"Then why haven't you broken up with her?"

"I just haven't figured out how."

"Bullshit! You're afraid."

"I'm not afraid."

"Then break up with her!"

"For the love of God, can we please stop talking 'bout Gemma fucking Landry?" Jefferson tossed his tools on the desk. Ran his fingers through his hair. How had things gone so upside down so quickly?

"Do you think she knows about us?" Nevaeh asked.

Jefferson shook his head. "I don't know. Maybe. Probably."

"You worried?"

"I'll let her down gently. She'll understand. Things haven't been good between us for some time anyway. Never know. Maybe she feels the same."

Nevaeh put her camera back in the bag. "I'm sorry, Jefferson. I want us to be together, but I'm done sneaking around like this. It ain't fair to Gemma. And it ain't fair to me. So I need you to decide. Otherwise, I will."

How long had that thought been brewing? But Nevaeh wasn't wrong. If he wanted to be with her, he needed to be *with her.*

"I'll talk to her tonight. I promise."

Nevaeh scoffed. "I don't trust you."

There was only way she ever would.

He had to tell Gemma they were over.

8. GEMMA

Gemma fishtailed off Robert E. Lee Boulevard into a strip mall parking lot. She screeched to a halt in front of a newly constructed white stucco office building and jumped out, slamming the door behind her. She ran up the stairs to the second floor and barreled into the headquarters of the Women's Republican Club of New Orleans.

Beneath shiny gold lit pendants, Gemma marched along a diamond-shaped tile floor, past closed office doors, American flags draped along the jamb, and a procession of portraits of every President of the club from 1910 to the present. At the end of the line, Gemma's mother, Ms. Mallory Landry, peered from the custom wood frame, plucked brows raised in permanent judgment, mouth clamped in a line of indignation. Her piercing eyes gazed into her daughter's soul, humiliated that her own flesh and blood was such a souring disappointment. Gemma would've enjoyed spray painting devil horns and a forked goatee on the portrait. Anything to soil her mother's glowing reputation among the elite of Louisiana.

But today, Gemma had to play nice.

At the end of the hall, a group of fancifully dressed charmers chatted in a sewing circle next to a sign announcing the afternoon's speaking engagement: representatives from the Alexis Joy Foundation, a non-profit raising awareness for postpartum depression. Gemma politely asked the ladies where she might find Ms. Mallory Landry. They pointed inside the conference hall, an imposing room with rows of cushioned banquet chairs on checkered pattern carpet, leading to a projection screen with the party's logo: a red, white, and blue elephant inside a circle of stars.

Mallory Landry stood at the front, chatting with a group of young mother types and their significant others, people who—compared to her—looked as if life had knocked them around enough times to leave them defeated. Gemma tapped a foot while she waited for Mother to finish hobnobbing. She knew better than to interrupt. Mallory Landry may have fooled some with her southern charms, but Gemma knew beneath the superficial façade lurked the heart of a tyrant.

Soon as her mother shook hands and shared a final strained laugh, Gemma stepped in to speak about an advance on her inheritance with which to buy the Carondelet Street Gallery. Though Daddy earned the money, Mother was in charge of the accounts. Nobody spent a dime without her say-so. Which was why she was annoyed whenever Gemma came around asking for more. Couldn't she make do on her generous allowance?

Upon seeing her, Mallory asked, "Gemma, sweetheart, what are you doing here?"

"I need to talk—"

"I don't have the time to talk right now, Gemma darling," Mother said as Gemma followed her toward a trio of powerful looking men in expensive tailored suits.

"But I came all the way over here—"

"And I'm so glad you did. It's really about time you got involved with the Club—"

"I'm not here for the Club."

"Have you rented the upper apartment out yet? Let me introduce you to Diana. You know she has several lucrative buildings—"

"I'm here to ask about my inheritance." This stalled Mother in her tracks. "I want to invest in a gallery—"

Mallory pinched the bridge of her nose. "How many times have I told you, galleries are a bad investment?"

"But Mommy, it's *my* money."

"No, Darling, not until your Daddy and I have kicked the bucket. And I have bad news for you. We plan on making your life hell for many years to come."

Why did her mother constantly demean Gemma for wasting time on—what she considered were—immaterial pursuits? If something didn't make money then it wasn't worth the energy. Wasn't that why her parents agreed to give Gemma the property on Prytania—in the hope she'd make it profitable by renting the top floor?

But Gemma had no interest in being someone's landlord. "Can't we just talk about this?" she asked.

"Nothing to talk about, Gemma dear…"

"Mommy, can't you please listen—"

"No time right now. If you want, you can have a seat and we'll talk about this after the presentation. Brian—" Mother shook hands with a balding fellow with a terrible comb over and left Gemma standing there, shaken.

Gemma admired her mother's tenacity, she was a real go-getter much like herself, but that didn't mean Gemma hated her any less. She wasn't leaving until she got that money. She didn't care how long she had to wait.

For a half-hour, Gemma slumped on a banquet chair, minute by minute the plush fabric becoming more and more unforgiving. She listened to a couple old hens squawk about the afternoon's guest speakers. While the representatives, mostly young mothers or spouses of those who'd suffered from postpartum, stood behind a podium in front of a projector screen, talking about symptoms and treatments and support systems, the two hens muttered snide remarks about how they endured hours of labor with no epidural, then raised the little snapping turtles all on their own, husband too busy raking in the dough to bother, until the kids were old enough to boot them from the nest. And now they only came by for a visit when they needed a handout, the ingrates. But these women weren't crying tears to anyone who'd listen about not being tough enough to take care of the sniveling brats. No, only this new generation, so fragile, so pathetic, fussing about their kids talking back and running amok and throwing tantrums when all they need is a good whoopin'…

Gemma and Jefferson had spoken about kids once. He'd mentioned it after returning from a cousin's wedding in Mississippi—the newlyweds marrying because she'd gotten knocked up. Gemma had admitted right away that she had no interest in having children. Claimed she didn't have maternal instincts. Which was true. It wasn't like her own mother was any good at it. Besides, she couldn't see herself giving up her time to wait on a child hand and foot. Waking up in the middle of the night to rock it back to sleep. Nursing when it got hungry. Changing soiled diapers. Watching it grow up into something that would only resent her. In a way, she felt sorry for these women. Maybe they'd figured it out too late that they were unfit for motherhood.

Jefferson wanted kids, eventually. Take them to the museum or on carriage rides. Teach them how to paint, among other things. He'd make a good father too. Gemma knew he'd be devoted to raising a child. Protecting it from harm and giving it all the love it needed. Was that one of the reasons he decided to be with Nevaeh? Couldn't he understand Gemma was offering him so much more than offspring? She was giving him something no one else could: recognition.

And he was throwing it away. For what? A waitress who snaps pictures of poor people. Well, Gemma wasn't about to let him ruin his career over that skeeta hawk.

A burly fella with beard stubble dressed in a flannel shirt

two sizes too big and blue jeans shuffled to the podium. As he began to speak in his loud gruff voice the mic shrieked with feedback. Mother adjusted the sound and once they killed the noise he began again. The man introduced himself as Lyle Allen Truehart.

Lyle talked about his beautiful wife Angelique and how she made him laugh when he first met her at The Camellia Grill. She'd refused his advances at first, but eventually he convinced her into letting him take her on a date. "I was the luckiest man alive," he said. Over the next year they fell in love and she moved in with him. A month later they got pregnant with their son Kellan, a fussy but happy child, and married not long after…

A photo of a pretty woman with bright blue eyes and tiny elfin ears appeared on the screen. Though she probably wasn't too much older than Gemma when the photo was taken, the years had carved wrinkles beside her eyes and grayed the hair along her temples. Brownish patches spotted her cheeks and nose.

Gemma's attention wandered. She scanned the room, seeking her mother and found her by the podium, texting on her phone, about as interested as the rest of the crowd, waiting for refreshments to be served.

"A few years ago, my wife Angelique smothered our son Kellan in his crib with a pillow. I tried to stop her but I was too late."

Gemma's ears perked. Now here was something interesting.

"People often ask me if I saw signs. Of course, I did. My wife who'd once been funny and caring suddenly became quiet and distant. It was like she wasn't there at all. Sometimes I'd come home from work, and she'd be sitting in the kitchen mumbling to herself. I'd ask her what was wrong, but she wouldn't be able to tell me. I tried to get her help. We discussed getting her into therapy and on medications, but she wouldn't hear it—"

"Liar! You know damn well what was wrong!" a woman shouted from the back.

The entire room fell silent, except for Lyle Allen's heavy breathing into the microphone. The audience turned to see a scrawny, rawboned woman barreling up the aisle, fists clenched, and spraying spit. "It was you who done it to her, you son-of-a-bitch. You poisoned my beautiful sister."

This was getting better by the minute.

"I don't know what you're talking about, Sofie," Lyle argued, hands held palms out as if to prove they were clean.

The three men Mallory Landry had talked to earlier blocked the stage. Mother tried to calm the woman—Sofie was it?— but she wasn't listening. "Oh, you like to claim you're the victim. That's why you're doing these speaking events. Wash the guilt from your heart. But God knows what you did, and I do too, Lyle Allen. We both know what you've done. You put that swamp witch's voodoo on my dear sister Angelique because she was planning to leave your sorry ass."

Lyle laughed off Sofie's ridiculous accusations. "Come on, Sofie, I'm a God-fearing man. Everyone knows there's no such thing as witches and magic. Even your sister said so." The crowd agreed, but the tinge of desperation in Lyle's voice said there was some truth behind Sofie's allegations.

"No, that was you putting thoughts in her head. Just as you always done."

"Ma'am, this is not the time or place…" Mallory Landry placed a hand on Sofie's shoulder, but Sofie shrugged her off.

Sofie pointed a truncheon finger at Lyle Allen. "Look at him sweating up there. He knows the truth. He went out to the bayou. Found the witch, he did, and poisoned my sister."

Gemma leaned in to study Lyle Allen, hopelessly wiping the sweat from his brow, mouth flapping like a catfish stranded on the shore of Lake Pontchartrain. It wasn't a cat that had snagged his tongue. It was guilt. No one else seemed to notice; they were too busy watching Sofie being escorted toward the exit by the three well-dressed men, but Lyle Allen was scared of something. And if Gemma were to guess, she'd say he was afraid of getting caught. Hadn't she just seen that same frightened look in Jefferson's eyes at dinner the other night?

As the three men pushed Sofie toward the exit, she shouted over the cacophony of the crowd, tears now spilling freely down her cheeks. "She's still rotting in that Tree of Life prison you locked her in. Speaking those same words you stuck in her head. That's all she says! Those same words. I beg them to let me take her home, but they won't release her. She's sick, they say. But you and I both know it's that spell you put her under, you bastard!"

The men dragged Sofie from the hall, but her accusations echoed down the corridor. Gemma quickly gathered her things.

The men had already taken Sofie to the lot. From behind, Mother called after Gemma, wondering where she was going, but Gemma couldn't talk right then. If what the woman had said was true, then Gemma may have found a solution to her problems.

Once outside, Gemma ran down the stairs, past the three men huddled together at the bottom landing and chased Sofie through the lot. She caught up to the woman as she unlocked her car.

"Was what you said in there true?" Gemma asked.

Sofie leaned against her car door with her arms crossed over her chest. "I wouldn't have said it if it weren't. I may be a lot of things, but as God is my witness, I ain't no liar."

"You said that man cursed your sister with a witch's spell?"

"Lyle ain't no man. He's a lying son-of-a-bitch, that's what he is."

"What makes you say that?"

"My sister Angelique was going to leave him and move in with me. Had her bags packed and everything. Then the day I was to take her and her son away she straight up refused to go. It was like she didn't know what I was talking about. Like we'd never discussed her leaving him. But I know it was Lyle who put those words in her mouth. It was like he was directing her what to say."

"Maybe she had a change of heart."

Sofie snickered. "You don't know Angelique. Once she made up her mind about something there weren't no changing it. She'd gotten tired of Lyle always bossing her around and treating her like a slave. No, she was ready to walk out." Tears welled in Sofie's eyes. Gemma handed her a tissue from her purse. Sofie thanked her kindly, dabbing her cheeks. "He gave her the witch's poison. Put her under some kind of spell, I tell ya."

"What makes you say that?"

Gemma realized her error the moment the indignant fires sparked back to life in Sofie's eyes. "Ain't you been listening? No, you ain't. You're just like everyone else. Think I'm crazy. Well, I'm not crazy!"

"I never said you were crazy," Gemma said, softening her tone.

"Lyle enslaved her with the witch's poison. If he said lie down in the middle of the street then my sister would've walked out there, traffic or not, and stayed there until he told her to get up."

Gemma was intrigued by this notion. If there was really a witch selling this kind of power then…but still, she had a hard time swallowing Sofie's story. It sounded like something from a fairytale. For all she knew, Sofie's sister Angelique was as loony as Lyle claimed. A nutjob who fell off the railing and smothered her own child.

"Why would Lyle want her to murder their son?" Gemma asked, seeing a hole in the plot.

Sofie shook her head. "That was an accident, I think."

"An accident?"

"Lyle couldn't stand it when Kellan cried. He always complained that the boy's fussing gave him a headache. Begged Angelique to keep him quiet. Well, like I said, she'd do whatever Lyle wanted, except this time it must've snapped something in her brain. And they locked her away because that godforsaken witch destroyed my sister's soul and let the devil in."

"Have you ever seen this witch?"

"Yeah, I went to see her. Voodoo Queen at the Temple of Bondye took me out there. I ain't never seen anything like her and I hope to never again."

"What happened?" Gemma said, itching with anticipation.

Sofie narrowed her brow. "Why you interested in all this stuff anyway?"

Gemma pictured Jefferson and Nevaeh together. "I suspect the same thing may have happened to my friend. He does whatever his girlfriend tells him to do. Believe me when I say she's nothing but trouble."

"How do you know it isn't young love?"

"Same way you know Angelique wanted to leave Lyle."

Sofie leaned forward so she was looking Gemma directly in the eyes. "You better hope it's puppy love, darling. Because let me tell ya, you don't want to mess with Mirlande St. Pierre. That witch is pure evil. Ever since I read that bitch the riot act, weird shit's been happening to me. I almost died from a gas leak in my kitchen, almost got in an accident on Interstate 10, and had to have surgery to remove a clot. I ain't never had no health problems before."

"Could be coincidence."

"Nah. That evil witch is fucking with me. Trying to scare me into keeping my mouth shut. But she'll have to kill me before I do that. Which she might damn well do someday. So believe me when I tell you. Do not mess with Mirlande St. Pierre."

With that said, Sofie hopped in her car and turned the ignition, exhaust coughing from the muffler as the motor revved. She squealed out of the parking lot, leaving a cloud of black smoke in her wake.

Gemma went to her car and plugged into her GPS the address for the Temple of Bondye.

9. NEVAEH

Nevaeh left Jefferson at the studio around 6 pm and caught the number 8 bus to the Carondelet Street Gallery. Camile had called, asking her to come by to talk about, perhaps, hiring Nevaeh as her new assistant. At first, Nevaeh thought that this was just Camile's attempt to assuage her guilt for delineating her photography to the back room. But Camile promised that wasn't it at all—or at least not her entire reason. She thought Nevaeh had a good eye that, with the right mentoring, might be an asset to the Carondelet. She'd also taken a glance at Nevaeh's social media pages and saw she had thousands of followers. "Which means you know how to market yourself," Camile said. "I know the last few years have been rough, but things are looking up for the Carondelet, especially if everything goes right for these next few exhibits. I'm getting lots of interest from some big collectors. Working together would be advantageous to us both."

Nevaeh had to admit this was exciting news. She'd never dreamed of working at the Carondelet. Never thought it remotely possible. It would be a huge step in her career.

She considered telling Jefferson but decided to keep it to herself…for now. Until he could figure out his own shit, best she worry about her own future.

Besides, Nevaeh had another reason to speak to Camile. She was pretty sure Gemma knew about her and Jefferson. What other reason could Gemma have for wanting her gone?

As the bus cruised along St. Claude, Nevaeh sat by the window gazing at the rainbow of colorful shotgun houses and picturesque street murals of the Bywater rolling by. The neighborhood had definitely influenced Jefferson's art. Nevaeh saw it in his striking palette of colors and the brushstrokes he used, the bohemian culture and Caribbean vernacular playing major roles in his paintings.

Nevaeh ran into Jefferson a few months after she'd moved into her place in the Vieux Carré. It had been a humid Sunday, the sidewalk around Jackson Square steaming, a haze wavering above the pavement like a mirage. Along the gate surrounding the park, artists strapped their paintings to the black bars and pitched sales to the tourists passing by. Nevaeh was headed to work when she saw Jefferson standing like a giant among them, hocking his artwork to the mob of sweaty tourists ambling in front of St. Louis Cathedral, speaking in his fast Mississippi accent, the words so closely strung together you didn't know where one ended and the other began. Nevaeh was happy he hadn't given up on his dream.

Still, Nevaeh was stunned to run into him there. Though she didn't believe in things like fate, it certainly felt like something had brought them to the same place. She must've stood staring for a good five minutes just to make sure she wasn't imagining it. He hadn't changed at all since she'd last seen him. Same vintage threads he bought from places like Funky Monkey and Swamp Rags. Same curly black hair. Same peach fuzz mustache she always tried to convince him to shave. She was nervous Jefferson wouldn't remember who she was. He may not have changed much, but she sure had. Sometimes she'd catch her reflection and not even recognize herself. Having almost died had hardened her like clay heated in a kiln.

As she approached, Nevaeh called out his name. Squinting into the sun, Jefferson's confused expression quickly melted into surprise. He ran up to her with lanky strides and lifted her in his beefy arms, catching her off guard. "Where the hell have you been?" he asked, spinning her around until she had to beg him to put her down before she got dizzy. After they caught up for a few minutes, they exchanged numbers and made a promise to meet for coffee. Nevaeh floated the rest of the way to work, unable to stop smiling. She was even more ecstatic when he called her the next day.

They started hanging out once in a while, going for Irish Coffees at Envies or dipping in for a drink at the Rusty Nail. He told her about his job painting murals. He didn't exactly love it, but it paid the bills and allowed him to use a brush. Besides, it afforded him a van in which to transport his artwork to shows. Other than that, he'd managed to squeeze his work into a few galleries around town, hoping to make a name for himself. She told him about her photography. After seeing some of her photos, he encouraged her to get her stuff out there. Even wrote down some names and numbers for her to call.

"Do you really think I'm any good?" she asked while sipping an old fashioned.

"Good," he said. "You might be the next Diane Arbus."

Flattered, Nevaeh couldn't stop her cheeks from blushing. It was because of Jefferson's enthusiasm that she went home that night and created a portfolio. He was the only person to celebrate with her the first time her photos were displayed in a small café in Tremé.

Though they didn't get to see each other often, when they did, they always had fun. They'd wander the New Orleans Museum of Art and argue over which art movement was the best: he liked Expressionism, she preferred Abstract Expressionism. Lunch in the sculpture garden. Take the streetcar back to the Quarter, talking about everything and anything. They fell right into their old patterns from their Academy of Fine Art days. It was like all that time apart had never happened.

Eventually, he got around to asking where she'd disappeared to. Unashamed, she rolled back her sleeve and exposed the puffy scars traveling along the veins of her arm. Unlike most people she knew, he looked at them without judgment. The rest of that afternoon, they talked about her stay at Tree of Life. While she walked him through the halls of that horrifying place, he listened intently, not with disgust or pity, but empathy. And instead of offering advice or feeling sorry for her, he bought them King Cake and they walked down to the pier to eat it, where she smashed frosting into his face and he chased her down the Moon Walk, always running out of breath long before she did.

The only thing she found strange was Jefferson never stayed long, always checking his phone any time it dinged. Then he'd make some lame excuse why he had to go. Nevaeh let it slide for a while, but finally she called him out on it. He admitted he was seeing someone. That was the first time Nevaeh heard the name Gemma Landry.

Nevaeh pretended to be happy for him, but deep inside she was crushed. She should've stopped seeing him then, but she'd never connected with anyone quite the same way she had with Jefferson. When they were around each other, he never spoke of Gemma. Not until Nevaeh started asking about her. He spoke highly of her. Talked about how she gave him confidence. Introduced him to people she knew in the business. Bragged to anybody who would listen about his talent. Yet he didn't seem happy. Always sighing when her name blinked on caller ID.

Then there was the night of the Nouveau Collective Exhibition. The night Gemma got in a fight with Barbara Stone and stormed out on Jefferson for taking Barbara's side. Jefferson called Nevaeh soon after and she invited him to her apartment. He came by with the painting of the old man in City Park wrapped in a soggy box. Hung it on her wall after she complemented its beauty. She figured he'd vent about what happened, but instead they sat at the dining table, reminiscing about the good times they had picnicking beneath the Singing Oak and walking along the Bayou St. John. Rain drummed on the roof and Jefferson dripped a puddle onto her wood floors, shifting uncomfortably in his drenched clothes. From her dresser, she grabbed the biggest shirt she could find, still much too small. When he pulled off his damp threads and bared his torso, without hesitation she reached out to glide her fingers down his abs, surprised by both her longing and the boldness of her gesture. Next thing she knew they were tumbling onto her bed, kissing and clawing at clothing. At each other. Like a levee had finally given way to a torrent that rushed all around them, making it impossible to distinguish one body from the other. For a bear of a man, Jefferson touched her gently in ways she'd ached to be touched. Gave her skin the same attention to detail that he did his art. Like she *was* his art. Afterwards, Jefferson still wrapped around her, Nevaeh fell asleep, feeling safe for maybe the first time in her life. She enjoyed the most peaceful dream, a dream where they stood kissing on Langles Bridge.

Jefferson's ringing phone woke them early in the morning. As if scolded by the sunlight, he hopped out of the bed, scooped up his phone, cursing—Shit! Shit! Shit! Suddenly nauseous, Nevaeh wrapped the blankets tightly around herself, the slight bleeding and pain from having sex for the first time nothing compared to the ache in her heart. At first, she pretended like she was still asleep while eavesdropping on the conversation before opening her eyes wide enough to see Jefferson scrambling to put on his clothes, phone tucked between his ear and shoulder. Gemma's voice crackled through the speaker, admonishing Jefferson, wondering where he was and why he hadn't come home. He lied, of course, saying he'd fallen asleep at the studio after he'd dropped off his paintings and supplies.

But Gemma had driven by the studio. Of course she had. His van was still there, parked in the lot. Jefferson halted, buckling his pants, fear frozen on his face, and looked right at Nevaeh as if he expected her to help him. But what could she do? Gemma would hear her if she spoke, so she remained silent. Just as fast as he'd stalled, Jefferson stammered out another lie. "I got called in early for a job. I'm painting a mural in Treme," he said, a neighborhood he knew she wouldn't dare wander. This calmed her enough for him to promise to be home soon and end the call.

"I should probably go," Jefferson said, though he didn't make a move to put on his shirt or shoes.

Nevaeh could only bring herself to nod. This was not how she'd wanted their night to end. She slid out of bed, blankets still wrapped tightly around her and started for the bathroom. Jefferson took a step towards her, hand outstretched, and asked if she was okay. Nevaeh didn't doubt that his concern was genuine. He understood what she'd offered him and what it meant. But once again, all she could do was nod. Because, at that moment, despite his promise to call her, she was uncertain whether she wanted to see him again.

She could've walked away then. She almost did. For days, she ignored his calls. Ignored his attempts to see her. Ignored his texts and his apologies. Then the calls fell silent from his end. She tried to move on, tell herself it was for the best. Still, she yearned for the smell of paint solvent on his clothes. Yearned to hear his raspy laugh. Yearned to feel his strong hands brushing across her body. So, when he walked into her work place two weeks later and asked if she'd like to grab a drink after her shift, she happily agreed.

This was why Nevaeh had offered to collaborate with Jefferson on her project. Did he recognize this as her opening the door to her heart; a step toward sharing her darkest secrets? Was it a mistake? Had she opened up too soon? Or not soon enough?

Jefferson promised to finally break things off with Gemma and Nevaeh hoped he meant it. Maybe Gemma finding out about them wasn't the worst thing that could've happened. It may have pushed Jefferson to make his decision. But Nevaeh highly doubted Gemma was going to let him go so easily. Things could never be that simple.

***

Soon as Nevaeh stepped across the threshold at the Carondelet, Camile swept in from the backroom, carrying a glass of wine. "I'm so glad you dropped by," she said, waving for her to follow to the bar. "Now I don't need an answer tonight, but I thought we might go over what some of your duties…"

"Camile." The Queen of the Art Scene clomped to a halt. "I need to speak to you about something first."

Air hissed out of Camile's nostrils. She walked back toward the bar and poured them both a glass of Pinot Grigio. Nevaeh accepted. "You heard about Gemma's little visit."

"What did you two talk about?"

"She asked me to replace you."

"And?"

Camile put her hand on her heart in mock surprise. "I said no, of course."

Nevaeh wasn't buying the savior routine. "You moved me into the backroom."

"I made a bad decision and I seriously regret it. But I had to give Gemma something. Whether I like it or not, I owe her a lot of money. And if that psycho has her way, she'll buy the gallery out from under me. Well, I'm not about to allow that to happen. I've worked too damn hard for too damn long to let her take what's mine."

Whether Nevaeh liked it or not, she needed Camile more than Camile needed her. If Gemma was in charge, she'd do whatever she could to prevent Nevaeh from showing in this city ever again. No, she had to ally with Camile. It was her only choice. "What are we going to do about it?" she asked.

"I'm making some moves. Reaching out to some old friends. Collectors who have money and are willing to spend. Just gotta hope they like what I have to show them."

"Or?"

"We all might be up the Mississippi."

Guilt seeped into Nevaeh's bones. Hearing Camile tell it like that, it seemed she and Jefferson weren't the only ones on Gemma's hit list. "I think she knows about me and Jefferson."

"Well, duh." Camile rolled her eyes. "It's not like you've done a great job of hiding it."

Face flushed, Nevaeh looked at her shoes and took a sip of her wine. Was there anyone who didn't know about her and Jefferson?

Marcel appeared on the staircase from the upstairs office. "What are you two ladies gabbing about?" he asked, walking down to join them.

"Your favorite topic," Camile said, putting an arm around Marcel's shoulder as he came to stand next to her.

Marcel gestured with his chin toward Nevaeh. "I take it you told her about Gemma's visit?"

"Seems our friend knows about Nevaeh and Jefferson's dalliance."

Marcel scoffed. "Better be careful girl. Gemma's crazy. She'll fuck you up if she even *thinks* you're moving on her man."

"What? She'll try to ruin my career…"

"Oh, she'll do more than that. Trust me."

"I think we could all use a little more wine."

Upstairs, Nevaeh took a seat on the opposite side of the desk from Marcel. Camile grabbed a bottle of pinot from the minifridge, unscrewed the top, and took an unladylike slug before sitting on Marcel's lap and passing the bottle. They each took turns sipping the tart beverage.

"How long have you known Gemma?" Nevaeh asked Camile.

"I met her about five years ago. Ran into her occasionally at an art show here and there and eventually we struck up a conversation. It was obvious she had a firm understanding of technique and style and color theory. Thought she was just another scenester, but eventually we started hanging out. Go to dinner or go shopping. Just gab like two girlfriends about artists we thought were hot or things going on around New Orleans we were interested in. Shit like that. The weird thing is I really liked Gemma back then. She was outgoing and smart and had this very dark but funny sense of humor. She was a bit judgy, but then again, so am I."

"Two regular peas in a pod," Marcel chuckled as he reached for the bottle.

"Eventually, she started bugging me about giving her a job at the gallery. She didn't know shit about the business side of things, but was eager to learn. I figured I could use some help. Just someone to answer phones and greet guests and check-in deliveries. Same kind of things I was hoping you'd do if you accepted the job. I thought I might be able to guide her through the ranks the same way Margaret guided me. Boy, was I fucking wrong."

Camile took a swig, wiped her mouth with her sleeve, and shook off some random thought. A smile returned to her face to hide the pain. "After about seven months, Gemma started bugging me about letting her organize an exhibition. Of course, I turned her down. I said she needed to learn the ins and outs first, most of which I'd been doing myself. I asked her to have patience. But Gemma wasn't interested in grunt work. She wanted to be the star of her own show. But that's not how things go in this business. She seemed to take it alright at first. I had no idea she was doing things behind my back."

"Like what?" Nevaeh asked.

"One day I got a call from one of my collectors about some artist I supposedly represented. I'd never heard of the person and had no idea who he was talking about. He said my assistant had put him in touch. The reason he was calling was that he thought something was peculiar when my assistant asked if she could bring some of the work by his place. The collector said no, he'd rather drop by the gallery, which was when things turned weird. My so-called assistant started making all kinds of excuses why he couldn't see the work at the gallery. Well, come to find out Gemma had been canvassing my connections for her own purposes. I don't know how she thought she was going to get away with it. Like word wouldn't get around."

"You're kidding me!" Nevaeh said, unable to contain her astonishment.

"Nope. And when I confronted her about it, she flat out denied it. I was really hurt. Felt betrayed. So I let her go."

"Damn, the girl has some gall. But if she did all that, why did you borrow money from her?"

Camile chuckled to herself though it was obvious it wasn't over anything funny. "I was in a bit of a bind. Hell, I'm just now starting to get back on my feet. Even now, after the pandemic, a lot of main collectors have cut down drastically on the number of acquisitions they purchase, and my sponsors are less willing to take risks unless I can guarantee a return, which in this business, isn't always easy to predict, even for the Carondelet. So, a few months back, I launched a Kickstarter hoping to draw up sponsors elsewhere. Well, who should reach out to me? Ms. Gemma Landry herself. I hadn't heard from her since all that shit went down. We talked for a while. She apologized, and I believe in second chances. She offered to donate a big chunk of money. Looking back, I should've told her to go fuck herself, but I was desperate. Trust me when I say there isn't a day gone by that I haven't wanted to kick myself for opening that can of worms. Gemma has been nothing but a pain in my ass ever since."

Camile snatched the bottle from Marcel. "But that's nothing compared to what she did to poor Marcel here. I'm sorry I introduced you two. If I'd known she was crazy I would've told you to run away"

"You introduced them?" Nevaeh asked.

"She sure did." Marcel squeezed Camile around the waist. "I'd dropped by the gallery one day to show Camile some new pieces and there's Gemma seated at a desk in the front room. The three of us practically spent the entire day together, talking about art and going out to lunch. Gemma took a personal interest in my work. I had to say I was flattered.

Nothing beats a boost to the ego. Camile suggested I invite her to my next expo at Studio Be. So I did."

"Before he goes on, let's get it out that my darling Marcel here had the hots for Ms. Landry. I thought I was just doing him a favor."

"And she looked great that night. Woo-wee! Sleek red dress and heels. We were having a great time talking and hanging with the other artists. But I should've seen the flags. They were waving all over the place, red as that fuckin' dress. She didn't leave my side the entire time. Not for a moment. Even when she had to use the restroom, she asked me to go with her and wait outside. And any time I spoke with another woman she'd always inject herself into the conversation."

"But you slept with her that night anyway, you dog," Camile teased.

"You know what they say about crazy women? They're crazy in bed too."

This was more information than Nevaeh wanted to hear.

"Next thing I know that girl is calling and texting all day and night. When can I see you? Why haven't you called me back? What are you doing tonight? Sometimes she'd just show up on my doorstep. But none of that was half as bad as her trying to run my art career. She began talking to gallery owners for me. Booked me in shows I wasn't even interested in. Tried selling my art on an Instagram page she set up. She'd throw a damn fit whenever I asked her to stop. Finally, I had to tell her we were over. As you can imagine, that didn't go over well at all. She stormed out of my apartment, crying and screaming every insult you could think of. My neighbors came out to check if everything was okay. I thought it was, but that's when the real hell started."

Nevaeh shifted uncomfortably in the chair and took a swig of wine. "And you think she'll do the same to me and Jefferson?"

"Darling, we don't know what Gemma will do," Camile said. "But if she knows about you and Jefferson you best be prepared for anything."

<hr>

It was late by the time Nevaeh arrived home. Before she left the Carondelet, she agreed to start working for Camile after the exhibition. By then, hopefully this mess with Gemma would all be behind them. She looked forward to the time when the only drama in her life was presented in her artwork.

Nevaeh stumbled drunkenly from the cab and leaned against her apartment door, dropping her key multiple times while trying to insert it in the lock, laughing at her own ineptitude. How can something so commonplace be so hard?

At the sound of Nevaeh's joviality, the front shutter scraped open and out stepped Ms. Batifole. The pinkish flesh around her beady eyes wrinkled as she narrowed Nevaeh in her sights. Her saggy jowls fluttered as she grunted. Not in the mood for one of Ms. Batifole's sermons on propriety, Nevaeh pulled at her door while wrestling with the lock.

Ms. Batifole sniffed the air. "The devil's in the poison you drinking."

"Is that so?" Fuck! Why wouldn't the lock budge? Stupid clumsy fingers.

"Devil's poison make you do bad things."

Not as bad as the shit Gemma pulled. What would Ms. Batifole think of that? "Just trying to get this lock to turn," Nevaeh said, shaking the key.

"I had a husband who drank the devil's poison. Always drunk. Got in an argument with another drunk. That man struck my husband. He fell and hit his head on a table. Died a couple days later. That other man in jail now."

"I will definitely be more careful with the devil's poison." The lock twisted open. Nevaeh breathed a sigh of relief. She didn't know how much more of Ms. Batifole she could take.

But before she could say goodnight…

"Did your friend bring you the painting?"

Nevaeh stopped with her foot just over the threshold. "What painting? What friend?"

"The young lady. Red hair."

Gemma!

Without responding, Nevaeh raced upstairs, leaving the door wide open and Ms. Batifole shouting at her in Creole she didn't understand. The jolt of adrenaline quickly sobered her up. She flipped on the lights and searched her apartment. It didn't take long for Nevaeh to discover what was missing: Gemma had stolen the portrait Jefferson had painted of her.

Nevaeh pulled her phone from her pocket and dialed Jefferson, praying he'd answer.

10. GEMMA

Within fifteen minutes of leaving the Women's Republican Party's headquarters, Gemma passed along the canal of the Bayou St. John, where locals threw frisbees, picnicked, and walked their dogs on the grassy banks. Kayakers and paddle boarders raced under the bridge. Gorgeous historical mansions and raised cottages and brightly colored shotgun houses dotted the waterway. The neighborhood was a far cry from its sordid past. Move it from the lakeside to the riverside and it'd rival the Garden District. But as Gemma drove further along Orleans Avenue towards Tremé, a seedier element reared its ugly head, derelict houses fallen into disrepair, boarded up abandoned storefronts tagged in graffiti, glass and debris on the sidewalks, unkempt lots. Something ominous raised the goosebumps on Gemma's arms and pumped her heart faster as she drew closer to Broad Street. The air felt like it'd dropped a few degrees, a sudden chill sinking into her bones. A murder of crows perched in the branches of the oaks lining the roadway, cawing as if warning her to stay away. Being early evening, it was strange to find the streets empty. No cars passed in the opposite lane as if the world had disappeared.

Gemma flipped the locks. What had she been thinking coming here?

A few minutes later, she pulled in front of a squat cottage the color of a bruise, faded yellow rimmed with purple trim. A sign in the shape of an upside-down triangle swung from an ornate mount between a pair of double hung windows. Scribbled in white lettering it read: The Vodou Temple of Bondye. The shutters were swung open, but the place looked completely dark, like no light was allowed to enter. Perhaps that was why two terrifyingly demonic statues guarded the doorstep: one a homeless man smoking a pipe with a pack of grisly mutts at his feet, the second a skeleton in a top hat and tailcoat. They both reminded her of the dregs that begged for pocket change on Bourbon.

Gemma remembered something her mother once proclaimed about messing with things like voodoo dolls and gris-gris during the Krewe of Boo. "Mess with spirits and they mess with you." Well, sometimes you had to walk through mud even when it rose to your knees. This was something else Mommy-Dearest said. And this was one of those times. Stepping out of the car, Gemma thought, *Spirits be damned*.

The store gave Gemma the heebie-jeebies as soon as she stepped inside. As she squeezed between the tightly packed tables cluttered with African masks and spooky porcelain statues, it felt like layers of dust coated her skin. Filthy shelves hung loosely from the walls, packed with trinkets that looked parooted from a witch's junk drawer. Gemma picked up a hand-carved wood doll from a table. Spanish moss sprouted into a fright wig on its head. A black satin cloth draped its stick body. The thing appeared to glare at her from behind empty sockets.

Gemma grabbed a nail from a tray and imagined those who'd betrayed her. She imagined Camile sipping a cocktail at Bar Marilou and jamming the nail into the doll's heart. *Thunk!* Camile clutches her breast, sucking for air, and collapses on the counter, her drink spilling on the floor. Imagined Marcel setting up the projector in the gallery. *Thunk!* He folds into two and vomits his guts out his mouth. Imagined that skeeta-hawk Nevaeh kissing Jefferson on her balcony. *Thunk!* Nevaeh screams in terror as she falls to the street. Jefferson screams down to her. A footstep draws his attention to the open shutters where Gemma stands, clutching the doll with one hand, the nail with the other. Jefferson crawls over to her and begs for mercy. Locking eyes with him, Gemma hits the nail. *Thunk!*

"Oh fie, no play with that." A chubby black man in a checkered waistcoat and a bowler hat came running from behind a beaded curtain. He snatched the doll from Gemma's hands and placed it back on the table. "It's no toy," the shopkeeper admonished her like a small child caught messing with grownup things.

"I was only looking," Gemma replied, not seeing what the big deal was.

"This pwen is a talisman against sickness and death."

"I thought it *caused* sickness and death."

The shopkeeper scoffed, offended. "You watch too many Hollywood movies, cher. Vodou no harm people. This pwen of the Lwa, Baron Samedi."

"Lwa?"

"Spirit. Sort of like an…" he snapped his fingers "…angel. They guide and offer advice through dreams and prayer."

Bored of the lecture, Gemma crossed over to the opposite side of the store, where a variety of herbs, oils, and powders were stacked on shelves. Devil Root. Skullcap. Dragon's Blood. With names like that, she wondered whether the poison she was searching for could be found here. "I heard there's a witch who sells a potion that puts its victim under your control."

"We don't sell nothing like that here. We're a respectable business. Where'd you hear such foolishness?"

"Is it true?"

"Rolando, who's the couillon asking about coup de poudre?" Atop a spiral staircase, a bearded woman in a peacock sequined dress scrutinized them.

The shopkeeper shrugged. "Beats me, Isabel. I walked out from the storeroom and caught her playing with a pwen."

"You know about the poison?" Gemma spoke to Isabel, but eyed Rolando.

For a big woman, the Cajun lady descended the stairs in her heels as gracefully as a jazz dancer performing the cakewalk. "Chance has it we know 'bout lots of things, souer. The Rougarou that prowl the bayou. The feu follet. The ghost in the cimetìere. But what tickles my feetsies is what's a beauté like you want with a dark spell, hmmm?"

"That's my business."

The bearded lady glanced toward her partner. "I bet she jalousie over a beau. Is that right, beauté?" she tittered.

Rolando spat his words with contempt. "I don't care what she wants it for. Mal and trickery are not to be trifled with."

Gemma was tired of being pulled from pillar to post. It was stretching her patience thin. "Do you know where I can find Mirlande St. Pierre?"

Mention of the witch's name wiped the smirk from the bearded lady's face. Rolando lowered his head and hid beneath his bowler. Isabel crossed her arms across her busty bosom. "What you know about la sorciére?"

"I hear she has this poison. What you called coup de poudre. Perhaps you can help me contact her?"

"Cher, you don't wanna have nothing to do with her. She's trouble with a big ole' T," Rolando warned her.

Isabel nodded in agreement. "Rolando's right. You mess with the diable, the diable likely to burn you."

Gemma was once again reminded about what her mother told her.

"Now if you want a card or a palm reading or some gris-gris for good luck then we can help. Otherwise, c'est tout."

"I'll pay," Gemma said, a bit too fast. She could've kicked herself for appearing so desperate.

Isabel stopped in her tracks. "How much?"

Rolando shook his head and said something disapproving Gemma didn't understand.

"Whatever the witch charges for her poison, I'll pay you half that amount."

Isabel snickered. "Beauté your age ain't got that kinda payola."

"Wanna bet?" Gemma challenged. Suddenly the bearded lady was as quiet as Ash Wednesday. "Just put me in contact with Mirlande St. Pierre."

Rolando begged his partner not to do it, but Isabel ignored his pleas. "Alright cher, let me grab my things."

By the time they exited civilization and entered the Bayou Sauvage, the sun had lowered behind the trees. As they moved toward the pale nite-lite in the sky, deeper into the noisy swampland, with its chittering bugs and croaking reptiles, Gemma stirred restlessly in the backseat. Night swallowed the last flickers of day. Tiny lights burned above the dark swamp water. Her chauffeurs bickered relentlessly. As much as she hated listening to the two shopkeepers airing their grievances with the vinegar of a soured marriage, it was a nice distraction from the claw-like branches of the skeletal trees reaching out from the darkness.

In the passenger's seat, Rolando groaned about the dangers of dealing with la sorciére. Not that he'd ever met the witch, only knew her through reputation, but that was enough to keep him away. Clutching a crucifix around his neck, he said, "The cockroach should never be silly enough to approach the henhouse."

It wasn't like Gemma didn't know the dangers of getting involved with a witch. The reward better be worth the risk.

Steering the wheel, Isabel Lovelie puffed on a fat cigar. The foul-smelling smoke billowed into the backseat, where Gemma shooed it from her face and out the window. The bearded lady sniped at her partner to stop his grumbling. "You're not even making any damn sense with those old proverbs."

Leaning against the window, Rolando glared at his wife as if she'd insulted his entire family. "What are we doing delivering this nice young lady to evil's doorstep?"

"I'm twenty-six, I'll have you know," Gemma said, poking her head between their seats. "I'm mature enough to make my own decisions. Thank you!"

"Good enough for me." Isabel flicked ash onto the floorboard.

Rolando huffed. "What if she gets hurt? Or worse? That will be on our heads—"

"I take full responsibility for whatever happens." Gemma raised her hand as if taking a pledge.

"—And for what? Money?"

"A good roll of money." Isabel patted her cleavage where she'd stuck the bundle. "Mamma has to eat and look pretty too." The bearded lady slapped her partner's thigh and snorted.

"You're unbelievable," Rolando sighed.

"Honey, you don't know the half of it."

For the rest of the ride, everything remained quiet except the cries of the bayou. The silence was a welcome relief but left her susceptible to the whispers of apprehension about heading into unknown territory. A territory with its own brand of folklore and spook stories. Though she'd never admit it, Gemma was terrified. Strange things lurked this far from the city.

Moments later, they pulled into a clearing and the headlight beams captured a ghoul with flesh the color of clay. Isabel hit the brakes. The tires locked and slid across the moist ground. All three passengers screamed. Gemma thought for sure they were going to run him over, but the Caddy rattled to a stop, the bumper kissing the ghoul's knobby knees. The passengers breathed a collective sigh of relief. The ghoul never blinked his pale eyes. A striped shirt hung off his bony shoulders, unbuttoned in the front, displaying his caved in chest and ribcage, which didn't appear to move. Was he even breathing? In a claw–like hand he held an oar.

If Gemma wasn't really having second thoughts before, she was definitely having them now. What was this ghoul doing out here in the middle of the bayou? "Who is he?" she asked.

Isabel relit the stub of her cigar. "That, cher, is the boatman. He'll take you to see Mirlande St. Pierre."

"Are you kidding me? I have to get into a boat with that… thing?"

Roland looked at Gemma over his seat. "You can always forget about this foolishness."

No, she couldn't. It was the only way to get everything she wanted. The Carondelet. The admiration of the art community. Her parent's respect.

Jefferson.

As much as he'd hurt her, she still loved him.

She opened the door and stepped out into the night.

Without any acknowledgement, the boatman trudged across the muddy bank toward a dock where a pirogue wavered on the water. Gemma took a deep breath, waved "see you later" to the odd shopkeepers, and followed the ghoul.

What in God's name had she gotten herself into?

This wasn't one of those crackpot voodoo shops in the French Quarter where they hawked tarot card readings and gris-gris at $200 a pop. No, this place was nothing more than a rusted tin shack, blotched with mold, dropped on a square patch of centipede grass in the middle of the bayou. A pale light behind the mesh windows flickered with every crackle of a bug zapper. A gator skull opened its mammoth jaws above the front door, not so much a welcome as a warning. In the woods beyond, stringy gray hair of Spanish moss dangled from the trees, crawling with chiggers. Somewhere in the darkness, a barred owl screeched like a woman giving birth to death.

The Creole boatman steered the pirogue alongside a rickety dock, tied it to a post, climbed onto land, and offered Gemma his filthy clawed hand. He glowered at her, not so much as though he was seeing her, but instead looking at what breathed beneath her skin.

"No, thank you," Gemma said.

Louis Vuitton purse slung over her shoulder, Gemma planted one foot on the dock, but as she lifted the other, the pirogue tilted, and she lost her balance, flapping her arms as if she were treading water. The boatman hugged her narrow waist and heaved her ashore. Her skin trembled beneath his icy touch. It was as if every last drop of blood had been drained from his body.

"I'm fine." She smoothed the wrinkles of her cotton midi dress.

She'd be lucky if the mosquitoes didn't eat her alive. The humidity had already frizzed her hair and dried her skin like a fried onion. She glanced around at the moss hanging from the deathly gray trees and the sludge floating on top of the water and wondered what the hell a prim belle like herself was doing out in this steaming hell.

They sloshed through the mire up to the hut, mud splashing Gemma's $600 ankle high boots. The humidity breathed hot on her neck, and pearls of sweat slithered down her spine. With a handkerchief from her pocket, she dabbed her damp forehead. A pair of stripped lawnmowers, along with other bits of random rusted machinery, cluttered the patio that groaned beneath her footsteps. She had to be careful not to step on the nails poking out of the wood. She didn't come all this way to contract tetanus.

The screen door creaked open and out of the brightly lit interior floated a black woman with a svelte body swathed in a checkered madras dress. The witch was nothing like what Gemma expected. But then again, she didn't know what to expect.

For one thing, Mirlande was young and beautiful, not a wrinkled old crone. Bushy hair bloomed around her full, round face. Her lashes fluttered like moth wings and a Nubian nose perched above bee stung lips. Colorful beads wrapped around her long neck and the hem of her dress fluttered around her ankles.

Mirlande eyed Gemma as if she already knew everything about her. "You gonna come by my house, child, or congregate with the 'squitos?" The witch didn't wait for a reply and glided back inside. The boatman nodded at Gemma as if to say, "move along."

Despite its striking sparseness, the room felt claustrophobic, shadows reaching from the corners, forcing Gemma to tread a narrow path. A boombox on a milk crate played Caribbean rhythms across from a sofa patched together with various materials. Inside a wire cage, a parrot plucked its feathers, its bald spots matching the sofa. "Noctua want a crawdaddy," the bird squawked as Gemma passed, its beak broken into a jagged nub at the curve.

Gemma moved to the opposite wall, freaked out by the bird's cloudy eyes, and banged into a shelf. A jar dropped and crashed to the floor. A grayish tongue flopped around in a puddle of formaldehyde.

"What the—?"

"Leave it." Mirlande waved Gemma forward.

Mirlande took a seat at a round table covered in a scarlet cloth embroidered with stars and spirals and faceless stick figures. Next to the table, a tiny hodgepodge kitchen where a pot of fishy roux cooked on the stove. She beckoned Gemma to join her. Gemma sat down.

Mirlande snapped her fingers and held out her hand, palm up. "Me coin."

Gemma pulled the five grand from her purse, but as Mirlande grabbed for it, she yanked the bills out of reach. "How do I know this isn't a fucking scam?"

Hand still held out, fingers stroking the air, Mirlande replied, "The question you should ask yourself, darling, is do you want it to work? A man who dies and resurrects is never the same."

"How so?"

"Once a man been looking at the other side…well, dares a reason the catlicks call it hell."

Gemma wasn't falling for the witch's scare tactics. "Will he be mine?" she asked.

"That he will."

"Then I don't need him to be the same."

Throwing back her head, Mirlande cackled. "What this man do to you? Pass a good time wit' ouch-ya?"

"You could say that."

"Leave-a wild horse to pasture, it bound to run."

"Not if you tie them to a hitching post."

"Why don't ya forget him and get yourself another fella? You're young. You got money. Save yourself a load of trouble."

"Because I want him and no little skeeta hawk is going to take him from me." Gemma tossed the cash in front of the witch. "Now, how about you give me what I came for?"

Mirlande snatched the bundle up like a hungry gator and counted the hundred-dollar bills. Once satisfied, she rose from her chair, strode into the kitchen, opened a cupboard, and retrieved two glass vials: one yellow powder, one green powder.

The witch held up the yellow powder. "Mix dis in with his café or soft drink. But I warn ya, once he ingests, dare ain't no going back."

"Yeah, yeah."

The witch pounded her fist on the table, making the candle jump. Gemma pushed back her chair, preparing to book it. The witch came around the table to hover over Gemma. "Listen to me, chile, cause I ain't fooling. After his heart and breathing slows, ya'll need to bury 'im."

Gemma snatched for the vials, but it was the witch's turn to pull an offering out of reach. "Bury him? Where am I supposed to do that? The backyard?"

"No my concern. But ya'll need to do so to bring 'bout the end. Wait a full night and dig 'im up. Then give him the second dose. You can't forget to give him the second dose, you hear me?"

"What will happen?"

A smile cracked the witch's lips. "Nothing you want to know." Mirlande placed the vials in front of Gemma. "After that he's all yours."

"You make it sound easy."

"Nothing in life easy, chile."

With a snort, Gemma gathered her stuff. She'd had

enough of the witch's ominous riddles. She scooped up the potions and made her way toward the door.

"Chile," the witch said as Gemma stepped outside. "Remember what I say, a man die and resurrect, he not come back the same."

Gemma turned around and shook the vials at the witch. "This better fucking work. Because if this is some parlor trick, well, let's just say, I know where you live."

Mirlande nonchalantly picked up a paring knife resting on the edge of a shelf, lifted the dehydrated tongue from the floor, sliced a piece, and dangled it above the parrot's cage. The bird squawked, "Noctua want a crawdaddy." The witch dropped the morsel into the parrot's mouth. He slurped it down his throat like a worm.

"You be safe on your return now," Mirlande said to Gemma, slicing another morsel to feed her bird. "That hungry swamp swallowed many a forgotten soul." As if to punctuate the statement, the bird chirped and slurped once more.

Gemma opened her mouth to respond but saw a glint in the witch's eye that dared her not to push it any further. She had what she wanted. Leave it at that.

Once outside, she crossed the mire to the dock where the boat rocked. Before she boarded, Gemma opened her fist and contemplated the vials in her palm. All she knew was that they better work.

As the boatman pulled the pirogue from the dock, a billowing fog, the color and thickness of soot, rose off the murky swamp water and drifted toward the witch's hut, the wispy tendrils erasing it from existence. Eventually, the corona of the lamp hanging outside faded into nothingness—like it'd never been there at all.

11. JEFFERSON

A text dinged. Jefferson wiped his hands on a paint splattered towel and pulled his phone from his pocket. It was a message from Gemma: *Where are you?*

That was when Jefferson noticed the time: 10 pm. How had it gotten so late?

Ever since Nevaeh left, he'd slipped into the zone, the photos transforming into images in front of his eyes, flowing from mind through the pencil and onto the paper. He'd finished three sketches in a matter of hours. Incomplete sketches. Smaller versions of what he had in mind. But he'd never finished anything this fast. Normally it'd take him days of trial and error before an idea clicked, and that was if he didn't destroy it, but these had taken on a power of their own, as if he were merely a vessel from which they were born. For the last several hours, he'd hardly been aware of what he was doing, much less, what was going on outside his studio door. Headphones over his ears, jamming a mix of his favorite music, he'd entered a kind of trance. It was magical.

Jefferson thought about ignoring Gemma's text—he

hated being interrupted when he was in a groove—but he'd promised Nevaeh he'd break things off with her. There was no point in dragging this out any longer. Gemma deserved to know that he was not in love with her. That he appreciated all she did for him, and he still wanted to be friends, and hoped he could be there for her if she wanted him to be, but he could no longer pretend that everything was fine when they both damn well knew it wasn't. And it was all his fault. Of course, she'd be hurt. Probably curse him every which way until Sunday. Might even try to get him thrown out of the show—the same way she'd tried with Nevaeh. He'd take his lickings until she calmed down long enough to speak reasonably. Then they'd have a talk. He prayed everything would go smoothly—as smooth as could be expected.

There were a couple other text alerts. He'd have to look at them later. Probably just Gemma wondering where he was. No need to rush off just yet. Why spoil the mood when he could enjoy the evening a little longer?

Before jumping in his van, Jefferson gazed at the stars in the sky. There were two, side by side, right above him. He took this as a sign.

***

Lights were on in the lower apartment of 2919 Prytania. For a moment, Jefferson thought he saw Gemma's silhouette standing behind the white curtain. Had she been watching for him all this time?

The glow of the streetlamps washed him in a golden haze.

The front gate creaked as Jefferson let himself inside. He gently rested it against the latch to keep it from banging shut. Quietly, he climbed the brick stoop to the porch. The old wood groaned beneath his feet as he leaned against a pillar to pull his keys from his pocket. He slipped the key into the lock but didn't turn the handle. Peering through the long, rectangular window into a hallway of framed photos that led to the kitchen in the rear, Jefferson saw no movement.

This was his last chance to run. He could head back to the studio. Spend the night there and face Gemma in the morning. *Stop being a chickenshit.*

What was the worst she could do? Give him an earful? Throw him out? Hit him or burst into tears or accuse him of cheating? None of which changed his plans. No, this ended tonight.

Jefferson turned the handle and strolled inside. He slipped his shoes off in the foyer. There was a layer of mud caked on Gemma's boots. Normally she despised getting dirty. He'd seen her change an entire outfit over the slightest stain.

"Jefferson!"

In the front room, Gemma turned off the flatscreen and placed the remote next to a half-drunk mug of tea that was busy sweating onto a damp coaster on the coffee table. She rose from the emerald velvet sofa and sauntered in her bare feet across the distressed rug. Her nails weren't painted. Didn't she go to the salon a day ago? And what was with the mud on her boots? What the hell had she gotten into these last couple days?

Jefferson was about to ask her when Gemma threw her arms around his neck and kissed him, warm and gently, on the mouth. "I missed you," she said, snuggling against him.

Hesitantly, he placed his hands on her waist, not knowing what else to do.

"I feel like there's been a wall separating us lately. Me on one side, you on the other. I'm not blaming you. It's my fault too." She massaged his shoulders.

"It's the show. We've both been stressed."

Gemma placed her palms on his cheeks and stared directly into his eyes. "I thought the same thing. Is that why you were at the studio so late?" Jefferson nodded. "Oh, you poor baby." She rubbed his arms down to his wrists and hands. "You work so hard. Have I pushed you too hard? I have, haven't I?"

"No, you haven't. I want the show to be a success. For both of us."

"And it will be. I'm sure of that."

When she dove in for another kiss, Jefferson turned his head. "I'm covered in paint."

Gemma peeled a strip of dry paint from his brow, crumbled it between her fingers. "Why don't you go get cleaned up? Get in something comfy. Have you eaten supper? I bet you're starving. Go wash up and I'll make some food."

Once in the bathroom, Jefferson stripped, and sat on the edge of the tub while he ran a bath. What the hell was going on with Gemma? Whatever she'd been up to today, it was like the old her had slipped out from the crusty shell of her deranged doppelganger. But it was far too late for things to go back to the way they were. Jefferson had made up his mind. He was leaving.

Jefferson dug in his pocket for his phone. Checked his text to see if he could find a clue to Gemma's weird behavior. The messages were from Nevaeh. He clicked on the first one sent a few hours ago. Read the message.

Suddenly, everything made sense.

After Jefferson put on fresh jeans and a buttoned shirt, he returned to the front room where Gemma waited on the sofa. On the coffee table sat a steaming plate of rice and beans. Next to it, a cold Coke. Gemma patted the cushion next to her. "Come talk to me while you eat," she said. Reluctantly, Jefferson did as she requested.

Jefferson took a forkful of rice and beans and chewed to give him time to think of what to say. Relaxed against the sofa's arm, Gemma watched him with a menacing smile. "How is it?" she asked.

The rice and beans had a kick. Burned going down. "Spicy, but good. Thank you," he said, then took a gulp of Coke.

Gemma slid next to him, brushing her knee against his thigh as she crossed her leg beneath her. Jefferson scooted over an inch. "Listen Gemma, I have to talk to you about something..."

"Let me guess..."

He choked and rubbed his throat. Took another sip of

Coke. "Wow! This food really has some heat." He placed the fork on the plate. Waved his hands in front of his face as he began to sweat. "What did you put in it?"

Gemma measured him like she was readying to mount his head above the mantle. "You're fucking that little skeeta hawk."

"How did you?…How did you?…" The spice tingled on his tongue. He tipped the bottle and drank a large gulp of Coke this time.

Gemma showed Jefferson the photos she took with her phone. Jefferson letting himself into Nevaeh's apartment in the Quarter. The two of them sharing a smoke on the gallery. Holding hands in front of her building door on Chartres. There was only one way in which Gemma could've taken these shots without them noticing. She was watching them from the hotel across the street. Which meant she knew he was heading to Nevaeh's that morning.

"You looked through my phone?"

Gemma shoved an accusatory finger in his face. "Don't you dare make me the villain here, Jefferson."

Hacking, Jefferson took another swig of soda. "What is wrong with you?" he asked, rubbing his throat, which now felt like he'd swallowed a fiery coal. He pushed the plate away.

"Wrong with *me*? I'm not the one cheating, let me remind you." A tear rolled down Gemma's cheek, yet her expression remained solid as stone.

Jefferson shrugged, shook his head, fell against the cushions. "I planned to tell you…"

"When? After the show?"

Even after all Gemma had done, there was a part of him that felt guilty. She didn't deserve this. Jefferson took another sip to quench his burning throat. "I didn't mean to hurt you. It all just sort of happened," he bumbled.

"Happened?" Gemma scoffed. "Like you accidentally slipped your dick inside her."

"No, no, we were just hanging out and…"

"And what? You decided to fuck that skeeze."

"Nevaeh's not a skeeze."

Gemma leapt from the sofa and paced in front of the coffee table. "She's fucking *my* boyfriend! That makes her a skeeze."

Jefferson coughed again. The burning in his throat was worsening, like he'd inhaled a lit cigarette. "The night of Barbara….gag…Stone's…gag…"

"You ditched me to fuck her!" The anger raged in Gemma's brassy tone.

"I didn't ditch…"

The fire in Jefferson's throat spread into his chest. He started to wheeze. "*Gag*…you were…*gag*…and she was…" He took a deep breath then guzzled the Coke in hopes of cooling it down. "I'm sorry…Gemma?"

"Damn straight you're sorry! After all I did for you! Introduced you to the people I know. Got you exhibits with galleries that would've laughed in your face! Made you something. Someone. Without me you'd still be selling vignettes for pocket change down in Jackson Square! And this is how you repay me?"

Cold sweat poured down Jefferson's body. He wrapped his arms around himself but could not get warm. His heart seemed to slow, its languorous thud thundering in his head. The room spun as the walls closed in. Shadows swirled around Gemma as she faded in and out of focus.

"I'm not feeling well," he said. "What did you say you put in the rice and beans?"

Gemma spun on her heels then looked him in the eye. "Tell me something, Jefferson, is it hard to breathe? Is your heartbeat slowing? Is that little voice in your head freaking out? Saying help me…help me…help me."

"What, what, what…did…you do?"

Gemma slipped into the opposite chair.

Jefferson began to panic. There was something seriously wrong. He needed to see a doctor. In between coughs, he begged Gemma to call an ambulance, but her blurry image just sat there, watching, doing nothing. Why wouldn't she help him?

Jefferson coughed again. Blood splattered on his hand and shirt. He tried to get to his feet, but he was too dizzy, and his legs noodled under him. He crashed across the coffee table, knocking it over with the plate of rice and beans and the dregs of the Coke, which spilled an unfamiliar foam, thicker than the fizz of carbonation.

"Gemma…call…ambulance," Jefferson wheezed, soles kicking the hardwood. "Please…"

Gemma grabbed him by the arm, and with all her strength dragged him onto his back. He flopped over like an unspooling ball of yarn. Gemma straddled his hips. Jefferson clasped at her collar, but she grabbed his wrists and pinned them to the floor as he writhed beneath her. As strong as he was, he couldn't buck her off. To him, she weighed as heavy as his van. It didn't take long before he lost whatever fight remained. His breath came faint and shallow.

"Sssh, it's okay, sweetheart. Don't struggle." Gemma rested her head on his heart. Boom! Boom! Boom! "I'm going to make everything right as rain. I promise. After tonight, no one will get between us again."

Those last words echoed in Jefferson's mind as the light faded.

PART TWO

12. JEFFERSON

It wasn't the darkness that frightened Jefferson. Nor the squelching heat roasting him like a crawfish in a broiler or the hard stone floor breaking his spine. Nor the rats burrowing into his clothes or the stench of rot. It wasn't the bones and ash of the dead piled at his feet, and it wasn't the ghosts of that ash and bone clawing at the brick walls, hopelessly wailing for someone to let them out.

No, it was the emptiness.

This drifting in an endless void of nothingness, where time nor space existed, where reality was a thing of the past, where all that remained were dreams, flashing from one to the next, but not long enough to hold beyond a fleeting glance. This void devoured the soul and left the body hollow like a shed cicada shell. Jefferson was void of emotion. Void of feeling a goddamn thing. Reduced to nothing more than a plant breathing air.

Jefferson couldn't twitch a finger or wiggle a toe or grunt a syllable. He could still blink, which he had to do often to keep the dirt and gravel from his eyes. Even in the silence, there was no heartbeat pounding in his ears, only the bubbling of damp air drowning his lungs.

A spider crawled across his face, legs scratching his cheek. It probed his lips before climbing into his mouth and dancing on his tongue. Jefferson didn't have the strength to spit or bite or cough. Imagining a cluster of baby spiders inhabiting his body, he prayed it wouldn't lay eggs. Stringing webs along his skeleton, nestling in the folds of his organs. But eventually the spider got bored and crawled out.

Echoes of Nevaeh as he'd last seen her flashed before Jefferson's eyes in a fragmented collage. He pieced them together into a memory and strained to frame them in his mind. The two of them at the bus stop at the corner of Poland Ave. and St. Claude, fellow passengers waiting at the station, playing on their phones or staring into traffic. One man quarreled with an invisible friend—maybe a ghost. Everyone else ignored his wild ramblings. Nevaeh's head rested on Jefferson's shoulder, hands slid in the pockets of her houndstooth jacket, bouncing one of her fishnet stockinged legs and clicking her tongue ring against her teeth to the beat in her head.

Damn, she was cool.

There, Jefferson sat biting on a loose hangnail. Why didn't he say something? Why did he have to be so timid? This beautiful girl who held his heart. Who set his soul afire. Who made him smile and laugh with her wit. She was right there. And he said nothing.

The purple RTA bus rolled down the road. *Say something!*

Jefferson opened his lips and coughed black bile. It splattered the corners of his mouth and ran down his cheeks into the dirt. His eyes rolled in his head as he twitched and convulsed. He tried to move his arms or flip on his side, but his body resisted, straining against the blight festering inside his entrails.

The sound of a metal grate scraping along the stone floor snapped Jefferson from his waking nightmare. Blinding white light pushed the shadows to the corners of the tomb. Two bulky hands gripped Jefferson beneath the armpits, lifted him slightly, and dragged him out of the crypt. The groundskeeper, a grimy Cajun with thinning hair and a slack jaw, heaved Jefferson onto his feet against the mausoleum, the names of the Landry family's deceased etched into the chambers of the adjacent wall.

"Take it easy, bon ami," the wiry groundskeeper said, propping Jefferson upright to keep him from slumping on the ground.

It was still night. The light came from a nearby streetlamp. Above him stars blinked, but he could no longer find the two he'd seen earlier. How long had he been inside? A few hours? A few days?

Across from them, dressed in a black suit tailored for a funeral, Gemma texted a message on her phone. Jefferson pictured wrapping his hands around her scrawny throat, but he was unable to lift his hands under his own volition. He couldn't even wipe the dirty drool spooling from his lips onto his chin.

Gemma grabbed a handkerchief from her pocket and walked over to wipe his mouth. "Jesus, you smell terrible. Nothing a bath and a clean set of clothes won't fix. And don't worry. You'll regain your strength soon." She pulled a vial of green powder from her purse. "I know behind that blank expression you're probably thinking horrible thoughts about me, but I promise you, I did this for your own good. Soon you'll learn to love me again." She placed her hand on his cheek. "Not that you have a choice."

"Hold him up," Gemma ordered the groundskeeper as he struggled beneath Jefferson's bulky frame. She unscrewed the lid to the vial. As she lifted the powder to Jefferson's lips the groundskeeper lost his grip. Jefferson slipped from his hands and fell into Gemma, knocking the vial onto the ground, where it smashed into pieces. The breeze scattered the green powder in the dirt.

"You fucking idiot," she cursed the groundkeeper as he regained his grip. "If this shit doesn't work, I swear—"

Gemma told Jefferson to grab the groundskeeper by the throat. Before he could stop himself, Jefferson wrapped his fingers around the scrawny man's neck and picked him off his feet. The groundskeeper kicked his feet in the air and clawed at Jefferson's arm. Jefferson wanted to let go—he was afraid he was going to snap the man's neck—but his hand was no longer under his control. What the hell was going on?

"Holy shit!" Gemma snickered with glee. "That witch wasn't playing."

She got in the groundskeeper's face. Spittle flew from his

teeth as he pleaded for her to call Jefferson off. "Count your lucky stars I don't bury you too." She pulled a wad of cash from her purse, counted out the bills, and stuffed them in the groundskeeper's pocket. "And if a word of this gets out to anybody my beau will be paying you a visit." Gemma tapped Jefferson on his shoulder. "You can let him go now."

Jefferson wanted to but his hand just kept squeezing. The man struck his soles against the tomb. His face was turning blue. Jefferson looked at Gemma. She didn't seem to know what to do either.

"Jefferson. Let him go."

Of its own accord, Jefferson's hand released the poor man. He slid to the ground, sucking for air. Jefferson glowered at his hand as if it were something wicked. Something inhuman.

Gemma appeared just as surprised as he felt. What had she done to him? Snapping out of whatever toxic thought poisoned her mind, Gemma regained her composure, and slid her arm around Jefferson's. "Let's get you home, love," she said. The entire walk back, Jefferson couldn't stop staring at his hand.

⁂

At Gemma's apartment, Jefferson soaked in the tub, a days' worth of grime floating in the murky water, his face reflected beneath, void of emotion. The hot water did nothing to revive the stiffness in his muscles or remove the stench from the tomb that clung to him like enamel. Neither could it wash away the memory of what happened, the pain he suffered at the hands of death, the fire burning in his lungs as it strangled his throat, the beats of life stalling as a fist squeezed his heart, the blood congealing in his veins, bowels releasing fluids through his orifices, the rodents and bugs feasting on his flesh, the ghosts screaming at him to free them from the limbo of endless nothingness, where the only thing that remained were echoes of what was. The same echoes that had flashed before Jefferson's eyes before the groundskeeper pulled him from the tomb.

How could he ever forget something like that? There was a reason most people didn't come back once they'd stepped through to the other side. But here he was. Trapped somewhere between life and death. A revenant.

One of the last things Nevaeh said before they last parted company rang like a church bell in his head. *Gemma deserves to know.* His coming clean had nothing to do with Gemma's feelings. It was a test to see if Nevaeh could trust him. Their relationship may have been born of dishonesty, but Nevaeh would be damned to continue uncertain of his loyalty to her. Which was why she'd grown frustrated when he'd continued to put off the confrontation with Gemma. Why did it take him dying to realize this?

Jefferson thought about the moment he knew he was in love with Nevaeh. He'd climbed out of her bed early one morning and strolled into the kitchen to make them chicory coffee in her French press while she was still asleep. He added a teaspoon of sugar and a splash of milk as she liked it. Carried the two mugs back into her bedroom, where Nevaeh was just waking up. When she saw what he brought her, her eyes lit up. It was drizzling outside, but the rain had cooled the humidity—unusual for New Orleans. They sat on the gallery and drank their coffee in perfect silence as they watched the city rise with the sun.

He'd never really had a moment like that with Gemma. From the time she woke up until the time she fell asleep, she was always on the go, rushing around like she might miss out on something. Whenever he'd tried to share a quiet moment with her, she'd grow bored and complain. It was exhausting always trying to keep up, like being tethered to a wild horse fleeing its own shadow.

And now she'd lassoed him to her. How long until his body dropped?

From the look of his reflection in the bathwater, not long.

Gemma stepped into the bathroom wearing a nightie. Sitting down beside the bathtub, she dipped the loofah in the water, and began tenderly scrubbing the filth from Jefferson's skin. "Tell me about the first time you saw me." Gemma asked.

"It was at an installation at the Maria Cousteau Gallery."

"That's not what I meant silly. I want to know what you *thought* of me."

"I thought you were bossy. You yelled at me for hanging a picture crooked…" Jefferson said, unable to stop his admission, but not regretting it either, chuckling on the inside.

Gemma stopped washing him. "Why haven't you ever told me that before?"

"I didn't want to hurt your feelings."

"Shit, I forgot you only do what I say now. Which includes answering questions honestly. I guess I need to be more careful from now on." She returned to her gentle scrubbing. I was thinking more about when you approached me outside the exhibit. Tell me about that."

"You were reading Maroger's, *The Secret Formulas and Techniques of the Masters* on a bench outside the gallery. I asked what you thought of it."

Like everything in Gemma's life, the book was only for appearances. Jefferson should've known then she was a phony. But he'd been flattered on how much she'd tried to impress him with her knowledge about painting techniques, when it was obvious she'd only skimmed it.

"Then what happened?"

"I tried to sell you a painting."

"City Park in the Evening."

Jefferson thought about that painting hanging in Nevaeh's apartment. The vibrant depiction of Langles Bridge arched above the glistening waters of the canal that when he looked long enough appeared to undulate as the oaks swayed and the stars twinkled. A trick of directional brushwork and impasto textures and contrasting warm and cool colors. The old man waved at him from his seat on the bench. Even appeared to wink. To grin in a sinister way. Something else moved across the water and trees and stone behind him. Something that hadn't been there before. Shadows peeled from the canvas and climbed over the frame, beckoning him.

"And I said?" Gemma asked.

In a hauntingly similar imitation of Gemma's voice, Jefferson replied, "Why should I pay for what I can already see?"

"And you said?"

"You've never seen it like this."

The face of a dark-skinned woman emerged, smiling, from the bathwater. Stars aglow in her eyes, she cackled as her long arms tangled around Jefferson's torso so he couldn't move. Shadows crawled across the tiles, beckoning him to come with them. Back where he belonged. Jefferson shut his eyes and waited for them to quiet. The witch's cackle faded.

Gemma laughed at the memory. "Later, you asked me for my number. I went home and waited, hoping you'd call. A couple days later you did and you took me to lunch at Birdy's, even though you barely had enough money to pay. After a long discussion about your desire to make a living off your art, and after you showed me some of your work on your Instagram page, I saw you had potential: as an artist and a boyfriend. You just needed the right woman to come along and give you confidence. Which *I* did. That's why I can't let you go, Jefferson." Gemma brushed his sweaty hair from his face and pecked his lips.

I'm not your creation, Jefferson shouted in his head.

"Whatever happened to that painting?"

As much as Jefferson tried to stop his traitorous tongue from confessing, it spat the truth about giving it to Nevaeh.

"I already knew," Gemma said, fiercely scouring Jefferson's

back. "I just wanted to hear you admit it." He would've cried out in pain, but he was unable to make nothing more than a grunt. "Tomorrow you'll end things with Nevaeh," she said, dropping the loofa in the tub and pulling the stopper. The dirt and ash swirled down the drain.

Inside his head, Jefferson shouted, "Fuck you! I won't do it."

But he knew he would.

He had no choice.

13. NEVAEH

Inside Lafayette Square, Nevaeh sat at the feet of Henry Clay, the shadow of his hand holding her. She toked on a cigarette to calm her nerves and searched for Jefferson among the pedestrians strolling along St. Charles and Camp. Government workers filed out of the gray stone towers of the Edward Hebert Building and a convention crowd spilled from between the pillars of Gallier Hall. The park was practically empty. A homeless woman scrounged the garbage cans, skateboarders practiced ollies, and a dog sniffed about the bushes while its owner bopped along to his earbuds. A flock of pigeons pecked at a dropped Muffuletta in the grass, good eating for scavengers.

There was no breeze. Nothing to stifle the damp humidity. Though it was only March, the unbearable heat had dipped in for an early appearance. Sleeves rolled to the elbows and pants to the knees, Nevaeh sweated in her tuxedo uniform, having come here straight from Two Sisters. She checked the time on her phone again. She hadn't heard from Jefferson since she left him at his studio two days ago. Then in the middle of the weekend brunch rush, he'd texted her to meet him at the park at 4. They needed to talk, he said. About what he didn't say. Which worried Nevaeh. Now it was nearly 4:45. Where the fuck was he?

Nevaeh took another drag and blew smoke signals toward the sky. What had happened since they parted? Had Jefferson broken things off with Gemma? Maybe they had a huge blow up. If so, it might explain why he was late. Or had he chickened out? Let Gemma talk him into staying? Nevaeh saw how Jefferson bent to her will. Didn't have the balls to tell her how he truly felt. Well, if that was the case, then Nevaeh was through with them and their drama. Maybe they deserved each other after all.

In some sick, twisted way, Nevaeh understood Jefferson's fears about leaving Gemma. Since the time she was old enough to talk, Nevaeh's folks had reminded her that God was watching and every sinful act she committed earned her a ticket closer to Hell. Her entire childhood they'd forced her to ask God's forgiveness at her bedside, at the dinner table, at the church. She wasn't allowed to watch TV or listen to music her folks deemed unsavory—which was almost everything. Every evening, once her homework was finished, she had to recite passages aloud from the Bible, her folks withholding dinner if she didn't remember them perfectly. The chore of pleasing them grew increasingly harder as she aged. How many nights had she gone to bed hungry?

Eventually, Nevaeh stopped trying to please them and the real fight began. Once her dad ripped a hole in her earlobe when he saw she'd pierced it with an ice cube and a hoop she'd borrowed from a classmate. She'd recently started hanging with Jefferson and wanted to look pretty for him. Another time she came home to the minister seated at their kitchen table; her momma having asked him to come over to shame Nevaeh for hiding contraceptives in her dresser. After he'd lectured her on the dangers of premarital sex, and gone about his day, her momma told her she'd never allow a whore to sleep in their home and threatened to throw her out on the streets.

Nevaeh prayed her folks never caught her with Jefferson. Still, she'd continued spending time with him, hoping their friendship might turn into something more. At the time, he was her only escape from the hell her folks created. Unfortunately, he wasn't enough.

Seeing no other way out, Nevaeh tried to take her own life with a razor and a warm bath. She might have succeeded if her folks hadn't come home early and noticed the pool of crimson flowing from the bathroom and called 911. Her dad had broken down the door and lifted her from the tub to the sofa. Her momma slowed the bleeding with gauze and applied pressure until the paramedics arrived. At the hospital, they stitched Nevaeh's wounds, earning her hypertrophic scars as a memento. Her folks never forgave her for what she'd done. Suicide was a sin in God's book. From that moment forth, she was tarnished in their eyes. An irredeemable sinner.

After her release from Tree of Life, Nevaeh found the job at Two Sisters, working double shifts to avoid her folk's relentless judgments and criticisms. They tried to pull her back into the church, begged her to ask God for forgiveness, but she refused. He died that day in the bathroom along with the person she once was. Her folks tried interventions and, when that didn't work, they threatened to throw her out. The only reason they didn't was because they believed they could save her—and still do. Eventually she saved enough money to afford her apartment. In the last fourteen months, she could count the number of times on one hand she'd spoken to her parents, each of those times ending in a vicious argument.

Now that she was free, Nevaeh refused to ever allow anyone control over her again. But she had sympathy for anyone struggling to take that initial step, including Jefferson.

Soon as she saw Jefferson's mushroom cloud of curly hair bouncing above the shrubs surrounding the statue of Benjamin Franklin, the anger Nevaeh harbored for him drained, and she jogged up the cement walkway to greet him at the entrance. But she came to a halt the moment she saw Gemma clamped to his arm, pulling him along like a service dog leading the blind. She whispered in his ear then nuzzled against his shoulder. The wicked smile cutting across Gemma's face irked Nevaeh. She steeled herself for a confrontation.

Jefferson looked like he hadn't slept in days, his eyes two dark orbs staring at her from the sunken hollows of his sockets, his skin paler than a mime's makeup, his mouth swinging open. He shuffled with the slumped gait of a beaten man. Nevaeh had flashes of Angelique Truehart in a white gown, meandering in that same walk past her room at Tree of Life.

Nevaeh shook off the image. Whatever was going on here, Nevaeh didn't like it.

"What's she doing here?" Nevaeh asked Jefferson, voice shaky with concern.

But it was Gemma who answered. "What am I doing here? I'm his girlfriend. I should be asking you the same question."

"He texted me." Nevaeh showed Gemma the message. Neither her nor Jefferson looked surprised.

"Seems you've been sending texts for some time." From her pocket, Gemma pulled Jefferson's phone and read aloud from their correspondences.

Once again, Nevaeh ignored Gemma and spoke to Jefferson. "What is this about?"

"Jefferson, what is it you wanted to tell your little friend Nevaeh?"

Without blinking, Jefferson leered at Nevaeh, but he didn't seem to be all there. As if there was nothing behind those eyes. "I don't want to see you anymore," he said, like he'd rehearsed the line.

There was something unusual about his tone. The words spoken without inflection. Still, those words crushed Nevaeh with the weight of a grand piano falling from a fourth story window. How could he change his mind overnight? After he agreed to their collaboration? It didn't make sense.

"What do you mean you don't want to see me anymore?"

"Can't you see? He still has feelings for me." Gemma squeezed Jefferson's bicep, but he just stood there, mouth agape.

"I'm asking Jefferson."

"Tell her you still have feelings for me."

"I still have feelings for her."

Nevaeh couldn't believe what she was hearing. "Where is this coming from, Jefferson? What about the other day? What about our project? You told me you were leaving her. Now it's me you want to leave? I don't get it. Why?" she said, unable to hold back the tears.

Gemma pouted. "Did you really think he'd choose you over me? You were a revenge fuck, honey. A piece of ass to get back at me. But thankfully," Gemma wrapped her arms around his bicep tighter, "Jefferson has come to his senses."

"Why don't you let him answer?"

"Tell her how you made a mistake, Jefferson."

Jefferson leaned in close. He smelled…off. A fruit gone sour. "I made a mistake."

"You love your Gemma."

"I love my Gemma."

"She gives me everything I need."

"She gives me everything I need."

"Stop speaking for him," Nevaeh shouted in Gemma's face.

Gemma just smirked. "I have no idea what you're talking about. You heard it right from his mouth."

Jefferson's face was frozen into a mask of apathy, eyes staring far off into nothing. Just like Angelique Truehart. "What the fuck did she do to you?"

"I didn't do anything to him," Gemma said, acting offended by the accusation.

"Bullshit!"

"Are you sure you're not saying that because your feelings are hurt?"

"Let's go and talk somewhere private," Nevaeh said to Jefferson. Her eyes darted back to Gemma. "Somewhere without your ventriloquist."

But Gemma remained posted at Jefferson's side like she was afraid of what he'd say if they were separated. "Can't you see he wants nothing to do with you? Now why don't you mosey along. We have an opening night to prepare for. Which, if I were you," Gemma picked at a crusty ketchup stain on Nevaeh's shirt and flicked it away, "I wouldn't bother coming."

Gemma tried to push past, but Nevaeh blocked their path. "Jefferson, talk to me." Nevaeh grabbed him by the sleeve. "There's something weird going on. You don't look right. You don't sound right. You're not acting like *you*."

Jefferson's appearance suddenly changed. His eyes glared at each other from either side of his nose, the bridge a barrier between the warring parties, and one side of his mouth fell open in surprise while the other bared teeth in anger. The left hand clamped the right wrist and forced it to remain at his hip. Was he having a stroke?

"Jefferson, are you okay? You're scaring me!"

"Stay away from him!" Gemma shoved Nevaeh.

Nevaeh swung at Gemma. Gemma cowered and shouted at Jefferson to stop her. Jefferson caught Nevaeh's wrist inches before it cracked Gemma in the nose. He twisted Nevaeh's arm hard enough she thought he might snap it. She dropped to her knees.

Gemma squatted next to Nevaeh. "If you know what's good for you, you'll forget about him," she lectured her in a tone that sounded much like her parents when they were giving a sermon about hellfire and damnation. "Jefferson's mine now, and nothing's going to change that. So don't even try fucking with me or you'll end up just like him." She glanced into Jefferson's pale eyes. "You can let her go now, Jefferson."

Jefferson released his grip. Nevaeh fell onto the grass. She called after him as they strode away, but it was like Jefferson didn't hear her. Nevaeh watched as they turned down St. Charles. Soon as they were gone, an image flashed in Nevaeh's mind. Angelique's face twisted into a permanent mask of terror.

14. GEMMA

The following evening, several portraits of Gemma littered the cement floor of Jefferson's art studio. None of them moved her. Not in the way Nevaeh's had. They were bland portraits that didn't dig beneath the surface. As if she were nothing more than a pretty face.

Why couldn't Jefferson see there was so much more to her? A whirlpool of emotions swirled inside, threatening to pull her under where she couldn't breathe, which was why she sometimes had to break the dam, drown every goddamn thing beneath a raging sea. But what did he give her? A fucking still life. In his addled brain, she was no better than a bowl of plastic fruit.

Gemma ripped the sketch paper in half and tossed the pieces in the pile. "Garbage," she sneered at Jefferson.

He didn't flinch in the slightest. Didn't move a muscle. Didn't appear hurt in the least. Just sat on his little stool, a brush and palette in his paint-stained hands, staring at her blank-faced, like one of those wood manikins with movable limbs that artists used to strike poses. This infuriated Gemma even more. Under her control, Jefferson was a canvas waiting for her to supply the paint.

Where was the boy who once had the idea to paint random things in her apartment? A riverfront of steamboats flowing across her bathtub. A lamp dancing the Lindy Hop in her living room. A streetcar cruising along the floor to the garden outside. Now he couldn't paint a simple portrait. Everything rendered without feeling or style. An exact copy.

Where was the boy who surprised her with a late-night Gondola ride through the lagoon and signed them up for a scavenger hunt through the city and took her to film screenings at the Ace Hotel? Where was the boy who introduced her to Muffulettas, food her family would've considered beneath them? Part of Jefferson's attraction was he showed her a whole new way of living. He revealed to Gemma parts of herself she'd never known. But now Jefferson was as spontaneous as a game of Simon Says. A mirror reflecting everything Gemma hated about herself.

What was going on in Jefferson's mind? Was he fantasizing about killing her? Could she blame him? Or was he wishing for death to finally come? Claim him from this world in which he no longer belonged.

Gemma snatched the palette from Jefferson's hands and cracked him across the mouth, splitting his lip. In that moment, Gemma saw a hint of animosity stirring behind Jefferson's eyes. It was the most alive she'd seen him since that night he'd admitted to cheating with Nevaeh.

"There you are, sweetheart," she said.

She waited for Jefferson to grab her by the throat as he did in her dreams. Wished for it, really. At least then she'd know somewhere within that husk his spirit existed. But as soon as the drama ended, he returned to being a lifeless doll. Gemma dropped the palette at Jefferson's feet and turned away, unwilling to let him see her upset.

Was this what the swamp witch's cryptic message meant? Once a man resurrects, they never the same. Had she been wrong to give Jefferson the potion? Things definitely weren't turning out as she hoped.

She opened a window to aerate the studio and, with a flowered kerchief, she shooed the cloud of flies that had begun to swarm. She lit a stick of lavender incense to fumigate the room of Jefferson's sickly-sweet odor. Looking back, she'd probably overreacted. Nobody deserved this. But he'd broken her heart, and in that moment, she had broken the dam again, gone a little…*cuckoo*.

The portrait of Nevaeh leaned against the opposite wall alongside several unfinished projects. She studied the scars on Nevaeh's wrists. The angels casting her from Heaven and the devils welcoming her to Hell. Gemma never put much faith in religion. In her opinion, Heaven and Hell were already here and she had one foot in each door.

She was jealous Jefferson had been able to capture Nevaeh's authentic beauty. Something in the portrait revealed something missing in Gemma. She was intent on discovering what it was.

"Tell me, what is it about Nevaeh that you're able to bring

her to life on canvas in ways you can't with me?" Gemma picked up a handful of the scattered sketches and tossed them at Jefferson. They fluttered around him momentarily before falling to the ground.

Jefferson took a long look at the painting. A spark ignited in his eyes. If she hadn't felt the need to know, Gemma would've regretted asking. "She knows who she is," he said.

"Are you saying I don't know who I am?" Gemma spat her animosity at Jefferson.

"Is that what you want me to say?"

"I know who I am, dammit!"

"You know who you are."

"You think it's easy being me, don't you? Rich girl from the Lower G has everything given to her on a golden platter. A nice house. New clothes. Tuition paid. No financial burdens. But nobody understands what consequences come with being the daughter of real estate moguls. What's expected of me."

Gemma snagged a tube of paint from the desk. "I lied to you before. I was never accepted into Parsons. When my parents found out I was interested in painting they bribed the chancellor to let me in. They told me I was going to be the best. A huge success. They bragged to all my friends and their parents about this big opportunity I didn't earn."

She squirted black paint onto her index finger and traced dark circles around Nevaeh's eyes. "But from the first day, when I saw the other students' portfolios, I knew I was phony. I ran to the dorm where I was staying and called my parents, begging them to come get me." She squirted red paint on her palm and slapped handprints over Nevaeh's naked body. "But they forced me to stick it out. Said I wasn't allowed to embarrass the Landry name. Even though in the end, I still disappointed them. Not that I could ever impress them with art. They got exactly what they wanted. For me to see what a waste of time it was."

"When I came home, I found I was no longer inspired to make art. I'd sit down to paint, and nothing would come out. Just a blank canvas. I hardly left my room. Slept for days. Which was why I started looking for someone to give me the thrill I once felt when I painted. So I did what my parents wanted for me. I studied business at Tulane. I wasn't happy, but I learned some things while I was there. My parent's plan was that I'd join them in the real estate market. But I had other plans. I threw myself into the art scene, which was when I met Camile. I knew from the moment I started working for her that one day the Carondelet would be mine. Which was why she fired me. She was afraid of me stealing her spotlight."

"Then I met you, Jefferson. And you made me feel alive again…You are also the key to me finally getting what I deserve."

Pulling open a desk drawer, Gemma rummaged until she found a utility knife. She slid open the blade and pointed it at Nevaeh's ruined portrait. "…and she took you away from me." She stabbed the knife into Nevaeh's chest. "Now tell me what it is about Nevaeh that makes her *so fucking* special!"

"What would you like me to say?"

Gemma grabbed Jefferson by the shirt collar and tried shaking him awake. "The truth."

"Nevaeh knows who she…."

Rage boiling over, Gemma shoved Jefferson off-balance, causing him and the stool to topple over. She kicked him in the ribs. Kicked him in the arms. Kicked him in the nose. Blood squirted from his nostrils. She continued to kick him, hoping maybe he'd do something to protect himself, but he just lay there like a broken doll. Finally, sweaty and exhausted, Gemma collapsed in the far corner, the stone wall the only thing holding her up.

Once again, she studied Nevaeh's portrait, the scars on her arms. There was a perfection to the painting's imperfection. The array of bright colors in the background popped compared to the stark darker hues of Nevaeh's image. As if she were merely a shadow invading a square of light. Yet it was she who drew the eye. She who demanded attention. Everything around her manifested from her presence.

"It's her pain. That's what it is," Gemma said, not expecting Jefferson to answer. "You believe you can save her. Where you think there's no saving me. I'm too far gone. Tumbled off the deep end." She laughed to herself. "You may have something there, darling. I'm the wound that never scabs. But you can't save anyone. You're too chickenshit to do what needs to be done. And as much as I hate that skeeta hawk, I'll give her this: she isn't afraid to look death in the eye. So I don't know if it's her that needs saving." She knelt down beside her bleeding beau. "Do you think she loves you enough to save you?"

From his pocket, Gemma shook a cigarette from

Jefferson's half empty pack and slipped it between his split and bloody lips. "Take a drag," she ordered him as she lit the tobacco with his lighter. He inhaled, the cherry glowing bright orange. She held out her arm. "Burn me."

Jefferson pushed the red-hot cherry into Gemma's bicep. The stench of fatty pork hit her as the hot ember sunk into her flesh. Stinging pain radiated down to her wrist and up to her shoulder. Gemma's eyes watered as she gritted her teeth, but she refused to let a tear drop. Let Jefferson see how far she'd tumbled. How far she still had to go before she hit bottom. The torment soon dissolved into a comforting tingle. "Enough," she said, and he drew the cigarette away. The cigarette branded her with a bright red circle tinged with a crisp black outline.

Gemma begged Jefferson to kiss the wound. He pressed his bloody lips to the lesion. The pleasure intensified, briefly, before it was gone, fading to a dull throb.

Yes, it was true that Jefferson never had any chance of saving her. She was far too gone by the time they met. Instead, she'd drag him down into the depths with her. No one ever said love existed for only the happy and content. There was love in madness as well. Can anyone love as deeply as those who suffer together?

"I now know what will bring us together."

Snapping her fingers, Gemma ordered Jefferson to his feet. His bulky body rose from the floor like Frankenstein's monster, rigid and clumsy, but even in his deteriorating condition, he was strong enough to cause harm.

"Hit me!"

Jefferson wrenched his arm back, wheeled around, and cracked Gemma in the mouth. A stinging pain spilled across her jaw as her head whiplashed. Her knees buckled beneath her and she crashed to the floor. Blood dripped on the floor in front of her. She touched her bottom lip. Her finger came away with a streak of red.

Gemma laughed tears of joy as she stumbled to her feet. "Do it again!"

15. JEFFERSON

"Let's take a look at you." Gemma came around from behind, ushering Jefferson gently by the arm toward the mirror.

Though Jefferson knew it was his reflection, the stranger gazing back at him from the mirror wasn't someone he recognized. Inside hollowed sockets, his eyes were lifeless, a dark void from which no light escaped. The stranger had his mouth. A mouth that no longer smiled. A mouth that spoke words that were not his to speak. A dummy waiting for the next performance. Waiting for Gemma to reach inside and pull his levers.

Gemma had fitted him in a navy-blue suit of fine merino wool, stiff in the arms, legs, and crotch—or maybe that was just him. Had rigor mortis finally started to settle into his muscles and joints? They creaked and popped whenever he bent down or rose from a lying position. Already his pores were emitting a faint odor—like he slept in a basement. To hide the stink, Gemma doused him with an opulent floral-scented cologne. It didn't help much. Now he smelled like a dug-up graveyard. She cinched a matching tie tightly to his throat; a noose with which she'd drag him through the streets.

When she finished, Gemma backed to the opposite corner of the room and studied him from several angles like she would a piece of art. "That'll have to do, I guess," she said. "Wish there was something we could do about those sunken sockets, but at least you don't look dead." Her skepticism didn't soothe Jefferson's anxiety.

Gemma masked the crack along her bottom lip with red lipstick. Foundation covered a purple half-moon encircling her left eye. Still, she had to wear tinted glasses to hide the broken blood vessels spotting the white of her sclera.

"We need to make an impression tonight. I'm going to make Camile one last offer. If she refuses, well, things might get ugly." Gemma kissed him on the lips. "Let me freshen up and we'll get going."

Jefferson hoped Nevaeh would be there. Only she had the slightest idea of things being out of the ordinary. He'd seen the concern in her face at the park. He needed to somehow tell her Gemma had poisoned him and brought him back from the dead.

Would she believe him? It sounded insane, even to himself, but it was the truth. Maybe, she could take him to Tulane Medical Center. Maybe, the doctors there could do something for him. Was there a cure for the undead?

He prayed she hadn't given up on him.

If she had, then perhaps he could try to speak with Camile

or Marcel. They too had warned Jefferson about Gemma, said she was dangerous, but he'd blown off their warnings, blaming their accusations on jealousy. Now he wished he'd listened.

If he was going to have a chance to get a message to anyone he'd have to wait until Gemma left him alone—if she left him alone. And even then, would he be able to speak without her permission? Either way, he had to try. It was his only chance.

They rode the number 12 Canal streetcar upriver along St. Charles. Fellow passengers kept their distance. Gemma glared at them, inviting them to say something. Nobody dared.

They hopped off at Howard and walked the few blocks up Carondelet. Wrapped in a gold and turquoise lace dress, red hair twisted in an updo, Gemma led Jefferson along by the hand, squeezing his fingers hard enough to cut the blood supply—if any blood still pumped to his digits. Her impatience resounded in the clackity trot of her high heels along the stone sidewalk.

Lights blazed from the island windows, a beacon guiding Jefferson home. The white stone and blue trim and tall squarish structure even put him in mind of a lighthouse, like those he saw as a child along the Gulf. Balloons floated on either side of the entrance, welcoming guests. The swinging horns of Dixieland jazz and a cacophony of voices mingling in conversation greeted them at the door. Already a small crowd had gathered in the front rooms, clutching plastic go cups of wine, a select group of Camile's close associates—journalists, interior designers, business owners, and collectors—specifically invited to this private showing.

Hand on his back, Gemma ushered Jefferson into the gallery. They weaved through the small mob admiring Jefferson's paintings clustered on the walls. A few of the guests greeted them with smiles and flattered them with compliments. Under any other circumstances, Jefferson would've been ecstatic over the praise his work was receiving—it appeared many were impressed—but at the moment, he was too busy searching for Nevaeh among the strange faces.

Perhaps, she was in another room—or maybe she hadn't arrived yet. There was a chance she might not come at all. Jefferson prayed she would. She had to know in her heart it wasn't him who'd harmed her.

"Everyone, please meet one of tonight's magnificent artists, Jefferson Fontenot," Camile announced to the crowd as she strolled in from the backroom in a sleek charcoal suit.

Next to him, Gemma stiffened, a grimace decorating her snide expression. It must've irked her that Camile had introduced him and not her. Jefferson had to give it to Camile, she really knew how to wrinkle Gemma's appearance. But Camile ought to be careful or she'd end up like him.

Ignoring Gemma completely, Camile opened her arms to embrace Jefferson but paused a foot in front of him. "Boyo, you look…sleep deprived." She pinched her nose. "And what is that cologne you're wearing? Stinks like the incense the Catholics dose their churches in during vespers."

Jefferson opened his mouth to speak, emitting a groan and a string of drool.

Gemma answered for him. "Jefferson's recovering from a nasty flu that left him bedridden for several days. Isn't that right, honey?"

It wasn't no goddamn flu. The wicked witch of the arts district had transformed him into her slave. "Flu. Bedridden," Jefferson told Camile.

Camile patted his shoulder. "Well, I'm glad you're up and walking. Because there are a whole bunch of people who want to meet you."

Jefferson wrestled with his own mouth to speak the truth he was desperate to spill. If he could just tell Camile that Gemma put him under a spell. He squeezed air from his lungs. Constricted his throat. Pressed his tongue against his teeth. What sounded like a gag gargled in his throat.

"Don't get too close to anybody, darling." Camile curled her lips in disgust. "No reason to share your contagion."

"He's fine," Gemma lied.

"If you have a minute, I'd like to speak to you in my office about our deal," Camile addressed Gemma.

A genuine smile crossed Gemma's face. "How about right now? Jefferson follow—"

Camile grabbed Gemma's arm. Gemma shook her loose. "Let's leave your boyo to mingle while us two girls chit-chat." Camile called over a few of her friends, bohemian New

Orleanians in flashy clothing that made even Gemma look cheap.

Looking panicked, Gemma tried to mumble something to Jefferson, but Camile steered her with an arm around her shoulder toward the backroom, leaving him alone to field questions from the circle of curious patrons.

At first, Jefferson remained mute, apart from the occasional groan. The krewe of wealthy art aficionados glanced at each other in confusion. An elderly woman in a floppy wide brim hat and paisley print dress raised her voice. "What inspires you to paint, Mr. Fontenot?" she said, waiting patiently for his answer.

Nothing now, only death. Festering inside like rot at the core of a tree. Why couldn't they see the corpse standing before them? Jefferson strained to alarm anyone to his torment, his cries for help withering on his tongue.

A shadow crossed Jefferson's path. Not a shadow on the wall or the floor. Nor a dark reflection tethered to a person. A shadow severed from its owner. It crossed the room and disappeared down the narrow hall then appeared again on the other side. Beckoned Jefferson to come with a wave of its hooked finger. But Jefferson was uncertain whether he could move of his own volition.

Grunting, Jefferson peeled his foot from the floor and slid it a step forward. Just the slightest movement sapped his strength. But he had a feeling the shadows wanted to show him something urgent. He took another step. Then another. And another. Pushed through the circle of patrons, leaving them baffled by his sudden exit in the middle of the conversation. "Well, that was rude," he heard the old woman say as he shuffled toward the doorway to the connecting front room.

With each rigid step, Jefferson thought he might collapse into dust. It was like walking upstream with boulders tied to his ankles. Shadows passed through the wall like clouds of black smoke, faces twisted in agony. These spectral visitors reached out of the mist to take Jefferson from the world he no longer belonged in. They reached inside him only to find the body untenanted. A house abandoned. A fate far worse than they had ever known.

As Jefferson approached the connecting front room, a speaker played Caribbean rhythms behind a bluesy zydeco accordion. It increased in tempo as Jefferson dragged his stiff body into the well-lit room. The drums beat in his ears like his heart had once done. He stood in the middle of the crowd admiring the art. A computer connected to a projector on a stand mapped a 3D impressionistic painting of life on the bayou onto the rear wall. It was composed in a gumbo palette of murky greens and earthy browns and twilight purple. Shrimp boats floated on the brackish water. Gators sunbathed on rocks. Cypress trees rose like giants and spread their thick limbs toward the sky, the awl-shaped leaves trembling in the wind. Laundry hung outside huts on stilts where dark-skinned aborigines danced in the yard and pelican girls carried caskets of clothes as they disembarked from pirogues onto the shore.

The paintings pulsated with a life of their own. The

moist humidity dampened Jefferson's skin and the damp moss squished beneath his feet and frogs croaked and swans trumpeted. Warmth spread into his limbs as if the cold hands of death had released him from its clutches.

"Jefferson!" A hand clapped him on the shoulder from behind. "Wha'chu think, my friend. Beautiful, isn't it? Yes, sir, the future of art right here," Marcel said, sleek in a white suit and fedora.

The piece was truly beautiful. Any other time, Jefferson would've complimented Marcel's artistry. But right now, he needed to convince Marcel to call an ambulance.

Jefferson pushed his tongue against the roof of his mouth and constricted his throat. "Gem...Gem...Gem..."

Marcel glanced around the gallery. "That bitch with you tonight? I don't know what you doin' still hanging 'round with her. She bad juju, my friend." Lowering his voice, Marcel said, "A little birdie tells me you seeing Nevaeh Parker on the sly. Best be careful. Gemma finds out and you won't show nowhere in this town. Take it from somebody who knows."

Teeth gritted together; Jefferson sounded out the next syllables. "Kill...kill...kill..."

"Kill your career. Yeah, she surely will."

Oh, how Jefferson knew.

The thing about artists, they love to talk about themselves. If Marcel would just shut up and listen for ten seconds, he might hear what he was saying, "I...dead...I...dead..."

"Gemma already knows about...?" Marcel whistled. "Ah

boy, yea, you dead. Well, it was nice knowing you. I guess I'll see you around Jackson Square. Hell, I'll even give you my space on the gate. It was kinda yours anyway."

Handheld drums started playing a syncopated rhythm over the speakers. A chorus of voices chanted, *Eh! Eh! Bomba, hen, hen. Canga bafio té…* Lights flickered. The shadows flew around the room and into Marcel's digital painting, infecting the program like a virus. Spanish moss strangled the Cypress Tree, wilting the leaves and rotting the bark. The water churned into a green sludge that swallowed the shrimp boats, their hulls capsizing in the muck. The wooden stilts of the huts splintered as heavy winds sheared the roofs clean off like a can opener. Gators calcified and shed their skin into papery flecks while the pelican girls' flesh wrinkled and melted from their bones. All around them was death, but yet Marcel kept right on talking like nothing was out of the ordinary.

Jefferson trembled as he lifted his hand. Reached out toward the wall, bony fingers twitching. Blood dripped from his nose and splashed on his shirt. His eyes rolled back in his head. His teeth chattered as he tried to speak. Tried to warn them.

Marcel took a step backward. "Jefferson. You alright, man?"

Patrons gaped, terrified, wondering what was going on.

"Jefferson!" Even in a fit of panic, Nevaeh's voice made Jefferson tear in relief.

Next thing he knew she was standing before him, more beautiful than ever in a tight-fitting skirt with her hair braided and cheeks rogued. She'd outlined her heart shaped lips with a deep burgundy. He ached to kiss her, but his body wouldn't allow it.

"What's wrong with him?" Nevaeh asked Marcel.

Marcel backed away with the rest of the crowd watching in horror. "I don't know. He just started tripping."

Nevaeh placed her hands on his shoulders and spoke calmly. "Jefferson, listen to me, tell me what's wrong…"

On the wall behind Nevaeh, a rusted tin shack on an island in the swamp appeared out of a dense fog. The shadowy figure of a woman, outlined by an aureole of shimmering pale light, sauntered onto the cluttered porch. The figure inside the painting turned her head in his direction, her face momentarily brightened by the pale light. A beautiful black Creole woman with untamed hair. Who was she? What did she want from him?

The swamp woman's arm transformed into shadow as she reached through the screen and into the room.

"Jefferson, talk to me," Nevaeh begged.

The swamp woman pried open his chest and slipped her hands into his ribcage.

Nevaeh turned toward Marcel and the crowd of horrified onlookers. "Call 911…Now!"

The swamp woman clutched Jefferson's heart and squeezed. Sharp pain radiated outward, down his arms and legs, up into his head where it pulsed with blazing light. Jefferson convulsed as if he'd touched a live wire. His eyes twitched back and forth like balls on Newton's cradle.

Nevaeh wrapped her arms around Jefferson and pleaded for him to hold on while Marcel spoke to the emergency hotline. "Stay with me, Jefferson! It's going to be okay! Help will be here soon," she said.

Unable to take the pain any longer, Jefferson screamed as the swamp woman tore out his beating heart.

16. GEMMA

Upstairs in the gallery office, Camile pulled a bottle of champagne, wrapped with a red bow, from the minifridge. Obviously, something she'd purchased for a special occasion. But what were they celebrating exactly? Had Camile finally surrendered to the reality that the gallery wouldn't survive without Gemma's partnership? If so, it was about time.

For a brief moment, Gemma saw the brass key dangling from Camile's neck before it disappeared beneath her silk blouse. She touched her own chest, pretending to feel the key's cool kiss on her skin. She imagined how much better it'd look around her neck.

"You always wear sunglasses inside?" Camile asked, loosening the thin, wire cage around the cork.

Gemma pushed the glasses up the bridge of her nose. "There's a certain gleam in here that hurts my eyes."

Camile snickered, catching on to the vaguely cloaked insult.

From downstairs rumbled the white noise of conversation.

It had better be worth it for Camile to drag Gemma away. There were dozens of collectors' asses to kiss.

Holding the bottle between her legs, Camile twisted the cork. "I hope you don't mind me asking, but I'm a bit concerned. Did you and boyo have an accident or something? You're both looking a little rough."

"We're fine."

"You don't seem fine to me. I noticed you have some—" Camile drew a circle around her own face—"bruising."

Gemma thought about Jefferson downstairs, alone. The image didn't sit well in her mind. Without her, who knew what he'd do? It'd only take him spouting one wrong thing to spoil her plans. She needed to get back to him in a hurry before he did anything stupid. But she couldn't leave quite yet. Finally, Camile had come to her senses and decided to cut her in on ownership of the gallery. How long had Camile thought she could keep going when the money was all gone? Camile had her time at the top. Now it was Gemma's turn. It wouldn't take long for her to shove Camile out the door on her face.

But until then, she had to play it cool.

"Everything is fine. Just a little…mishap. That's all."

Camile popped the cork. The wooden plug shot from the neck like a cannonball and hit the ceiling with a thump. Foam ran over the lip, spilling a puddle on the floor. Camile laughed with glee as if it were the funniest damn thing. Gemma was not so amused. She didn't like having her time wasted.

"You want to tell me what the hell we're doing up here?" Gemma asked, slightly irritated by the charade.

From the cupboard, Camile poured the champagne into two glasses and handed Gemma one. "I know you're not much of a drinker—something I'll never quite understand and that's okay—but I thought tonight you might bend the rules. Since a toast is definitely in order."

The bubbles fizzed like Gemma's impatience. "Toast to what?"

"It seems Jefferson's art has made quite a splash with some of my more prominent collectors."

"I don't see why it shouldn't. I told you from the beginning he had talent, didn't I?"

"I never said you didn't have an eye for what sells."

"Oooo…it must hurt for you to say that." Gemma sipped the champagne. Normally she despised the sweet fruity flavor, but tonight it tasted cool and refreshing.

"Yes, well, they like it so much I sold the entire collection."

Bubbly sprayed from Gemma's mouth and nose. "You're fucking kidding me!" she said, coughing.

Camile tossed Gemma a package of napkins from the counter. "Some have even asked to commission him. Of course, you can imagine once word gets out that his collection is sold that offers will start flooding in from everywhere."

Wiping her mouth, Gemma couldn't believe the good news. They did it. They really fucking did it.

Then she pictured Jefferson as she'd left him downstairs. Or that drooling, mumbling thing that was once Jefferson. Could it even paint? Not from what she'd seen so far. Fuck! What the hell was she going to do? But she needn't panic yet. Jefferson had to do what she said, right? She'd make him paint until he found inspiration.

Hand shaking, Gemma took a sip to calm her nerves. "What kind of money are we talking about?"

From the inside pocket of her jacket, Camile pulled an envelope and slapped it on the desk. It had Gemma's name scribbled on the front. "This here is your portion. The money I owed you along with Jefferson's half of the split."

"Wait, you just said there were commissions—"

"I know what I just said."

"Am I missing something here?"

"I don't know? Are you?"

Then it hit Gemma like a hangover. "You're cutting me out."

Camile smirked as she sipped her champagne.

"You can't do that. We have an—"

"Agreement?" Camile tapped her nails against her glass, causing the bubbles to rise. "Have you read it?"

When Gemma didn't answer, Camille strolled around her desk, opened the top drawer, pulled out the contract, and flipped a page.

"How about I remind you of a few things?" Camile cleared her throat. "Part one, Section C. states: Artist, meaning Jefferson, will consign possession of all artwork to gallery as the sole distributor. Gallery shall have the right to sell artwork in *any manner* as *solely* determined by the gallery."

"What are you getting at?"

"Let me explain in simple terms for you, Gemma. All

commissions for Jefferson's work arranged by this gallery must go through me. That's what sole distributor means. But here's the real kicker. And I think you're going to love this. Part 2, Section D., states that regardless of termination of contract by either party, it's the gallery's right that all commissions made during the contract shall survive the termination of this Agreement. Now I happen to have in a very safe place, along with the original copy of our contract, signed agreements from all my valued collectors stating they will exclusively buy Jefferson's art through me and only me."

It was Gemma's turn to feel the sting. "This isn't fair. I found Jefferson when he was nothing. I made him what he was. He's mine, goddammit. Mine!"

"He's a grown boy, Gemma. A very big grown boy. He's allowed to make his own decisions."

Gemma whipped the flute at the wall, shattering the glass and spraying the sparkling champagne into a mosaic. Camile laughed. Remarked how the mess looked like a Pollock. Gemma tore off her sunglasses and glared at Camile with her bloodied eyes. "Jefferson will never paint for you."

"He will if he wants to make it in this town."

"What if he refuses?"

"Then he's finished too." Camile sipped from her glass. "Because here-in lies your problem, Gemma. You may have a good eye for art and mommy and daddy's money to throw around, but you're missing a vital piece of what it takes to make it in this business. Do you know what that is? Friends. You don't have any friends, Gemma. So who the hell is going to buy Jefferson's art from *you*?"

Rage shook through Gemma's body from head to foot. Camile was right. As much as Gemma ached to rip Camile's guts from her stomach and strangle her with them, the fucking bitch was right. She was screwed. And there was nothing she could do about it.

Camile stuck the envelope in Gemma's handbag. "I tried to be your friend, Gemma. Welcomed you in my house when you had nothing, offered to show you the rooms, but you had to go parooting through my shit. Decided you had to have the house and everything in it. Well, I have the key to the house—" Camile dangled the key in front of her—"and I'll be damned before you ever set another foot inside these doors." Finished with her drink, Camile placed the empty glass on the desk in front of Gemma. "Excuse me, I have friends to entertain."

With a smile of satisfaction, Camile headed downstairs. Gemma rushed to the edge of the top landing and shouted down at Camile's retreating backside. "Where were your friends when you were out of money, Camile? Nowhere, that's where. You'll come begging again. When you're hard up you'll come crying, and I won't be there. Ha! No, I will *let* them take your house from you! Then we'll see who has the key!"

The champagne soured in Gemma's stomach. She fell to her knees next to Camile's desk, grabbed the wastebasket, and wretched, the heaves shuddering through her. Gemma plucked another napkin from the package and wiped the spittle from her chin. Camile had set a trap, and she stupidly fell for it. Stupid! Stupid! Stupid!

Gemma slapped her cheek hard enough to snap her head to the side. Enough, she told herself. Then she picked herself up, put her glasses on, grabbed a mint from her purse and popped it in her mouth. Straightening her shoulders, she ambled down the stairwell to join the party.

There was no one in the backroom other than the Tulane Art student volunteering to serve wine. The pimply-faced pigtailed weasel offered Gemma a glass. She snagged it from the girl's hands and downed it in one long gulp, spilling some on her dress, then took another. The wine went immediately to her head. Numbed the pain of watching her dreams crushed beneath Camile's chunky heels.

Everyone was crowded in the front rooms, the people in the rear hopping to take a look at whatever was going on. From the baffled expressions on their faces, Gemma wondered what abstract piece of garbage Marcel had put together for the exhibit. The moron had a talent for overestimating his audience. Gemma stumbled along the short hallway, sipping from her drink, and was about to inquire from the nearest person what was going on when…

"Aaaahhh!"

Dropping her cup, Gemma pushed through the crowd, shouting at everyone to get the fuck out of her way.

In the center of the room, Jefferson convulsed as if he were having a seizure, body trembling, eyes bulging wide, wailing in agony as if he were being electrocuted. Nevaeh grasped his shoulders, feebly trying to calm him down long enough to tell her what was wrong. Marcel spoke to someone on the phone about paramedics while Camile tempered the crowd, promising her guests everything was under control.

"Get away from him!"

Gemma pried Nevaeh from Jefferson and tossed her into Camile, sending them tumbling to the floor. Clamping her hands to the side of Jefferson's head, Gemma forced him to look at her. She'd never seen fear like she saw in Jefferson's eyes. The pupils were two dark infinite wells. "Listen to me, Jefferson…" but before she could say another word, he knocked her to the ground with the swipe of his arm.

Jefferson clawed at his collar, popping buttons, and heaved as if he were being strangled. Veins strained at his temples and neck like cords pulled taut. Bloody foam leaked from his mouth. Some onlookers glanced away, terrified.

"Help is on the way," Marcel announced, hanging up the phone.

"What did you do to him?" Gemma accused Nevaeh with a rigid finger as she and Camile got back to their feet.

"What did *I* do to him?" Nevaeh rushed at Gemma, but Camile held her back. "It's you who did something to him, you evil witch! You turned him into this…"

Marcel motioned toward the wall. "We were watching the video and he just…he just…"

Gemma glanced over her shoulder. Projectors flashed digital paintings of the bayou. Something he'd seen in it must have snapped his brain. She snatched the projector from the stand. Before Marcel could stop her, Gemma smashed the machine to pieces on the floor. The images on the wall blinked into static then vanished from existence.

"What the fuck…?" Marcel fell to his knees and cradled the broken pieces to his chest.

The crowd stood around in shock, not knowing what to do.

Jefferson's screams squealed to silence. His body shivered like there were things crawling beneath his skin. His legs wobbled, but before he collapsed Gemma and Nevaeh caught him beneath the arms.

Once they had him securely on his feet, Gemma pulled Jefferson away. "You stay away from him!" She dragged him toward the hallway. "All of you stay away from him!"

Nevaeh stepped forward, but Camile blocked her path. "I think it's best you both leave," Camile said to Gemma. "Now."

"You can't let him go with her," Nevaeh said, struggling against Camile and Marcel. "Can't you see there's something wrong with him?"

Feeling all eyes on them, Gemma ushered Jefferson to the entrance, the crowd clearing a path, while Nevaeh argued with Camile. Gemma pushed through the door and guided Jefferson outside. In the distance, the roar of sirens approached. They needed to get out of there in a hurry. Last thing Gemma wanted was the police involved. Thankfully, right at that moment, a cab turned onto Carondelet from St. Joseph. Gemma hailed it.

Just as the cab pulled up to the sidewalk, Nevaeh burst from the gallery and chased them across Carondelet, calling for Jefferson to wait. Gemma snatched open the car door, pushed Jefferson inside, then crawled in after. She gave the cabbie Jefferson's studio address and ordered him to drive as Nevaeh grabbed the door handle. Gemma slammed the lock. She cautioned Nevaeh to step away.

"Jefferson, listen to me, don't go with her, she has you under some spell…"

"Can't you see there's a crazy lady out here? Go! Go!" Gemma said to the cabbie as he honked for Nevaeh to move.

When Nevaeh banged on the window the cabbie threw the car into drive and peeled out. Nevaeh pursued but lost her grip and stumbled in the street. Gemma watched out the rear window as Marcel and a few others came to Nevaeh's aid. Gemma sighed with relief and slumped in her seat.

The cab turned down Poydras toward the Bywater. Beside her, Jefferson shuddered, mumbling incoherently. Gemma grasped his hand and put it in her lap and laid her head on his shoulder. She promised Jefferson she was going to make everything right.

One way or another.

17. NEVAEH

Later at home that night, Nevaeh washed pebbles from her hands and knees with a warm rag then lathered the wounds with antibacterial ointment before wrapping them in gauze. The wounds throbbed and made it difficult to hold things or kneel. She'd definitely ache for the next several days. It was going to make lifting and serving trays of entrees difficult.

How could she have let Gemma take Jefferson away? Not that she could've done much about it. Would Jefferson have come with her even if she'd begged him? Nevaeh doubted it. Gemma had him under her control—even more so than before. This control seemed supernatural, like something out of a twisted fairytale.

Nevaeh hobbled through the front room to her bed, where she collapsed on the soft mattress. The rain tap-danced on her shutters as cars splashed by. Occasionally, revelers caroused past her building from the bars. Nevaeh tried to fall asleep, but she knew it wouldn't come easily. Every time she closed her eyes, she saw Jefferson standing above her, clutching her wrist, looking down at her with a stony expression.

She'd never feared Jefferson before. Even as big he was, she never thought him capable of harming her. Thought of him more as a cuddly bear than a grizzly. But he'd have snapped her wrist if Gemma had ordered him to do so. Nevaeh tried to put the thought behind her, but she couldn't. Bruises still marked her wrist where Jefferson's fingers had squeezed.

Then there was tonight at the gallery. The cold vacantness in his eyes. The putrid stench. The stiffness in his limbs. And those screams. He was like a child suffering night terrors. What had triggered them?

Marcel said it was something in his video, but Nevaeh hadn't seen anything in the digital paintings that would scare anyone. Only 3-D historical depictions of bayou life. Yet, something in the exhibit terrified Jefferson. Was it from something in his past? Or had Gemma shown him something horrifying out in the bayou?

For the last few hours, every time Nevaeh shut her eyes, the face of Angelique Truehart rose from the depths of the dark, whispering her haunted incantation. *Please, quiet child, please…*

It was during Nevaeh's first month at the Tree of Life when they admitted Angelique into the recovery center. From the beginning, she felt something was severely off about the poor woman. Angelique shuffled along the tiled floors in her slippers as the orderlies escorted her to a room across the hall and placed her in a chair in front of the clouded window. And there she stayed. A strange, rotten stench permeated the room. The nurses sanitized it with bleach and air freshener, which deadened the odor but never eliminated it. Didn't stop the flies from breeding in there either. They crawled along the windowsill and light fixtures and beneath the blankets. They crawled on Angelique's legs and hands and face. She never bothered to shoo them away. Just sat there, perfectly still. Nevaeh would've thought the poor woman dead if it wasn't for the barely perceptible rising and falling of her chest beneath the hospital gown. The orderlies complained so much the facilities finally hired an exterminator. But it seemed the bugs were attracted to Angelique. They came back no matter how often the room was fumigated. Sucking on the black blood that appeared to flow through her veins.

Any time Nevaeh walked by, she'd find Angelique staring out the gloomy window at the parking lot. Nevaeh figured she was dreaming of the outside. Dreaming of freedom and the things that came with it. But now, looking back, Nevaeh wondered if she had any thoughts at all. Nevaeh couldn't remember Angelique moving in the slightest unless the staff demanded her to. Then she'd do whatever they asked as if under hypnosis.

The same as Jefferson.

During her stay, Nevaeh avoided Angelique whenever possible. After she transferred to the lower floors, she erased the woman from her memory. Now, here Angelique was again, haunting Nevaeh from beyond the brown brick walls and barred windows of the Tree of Life Recovery Center. If Nevaeh could convince Angelique to speak with her, then maybe she could provide answers to whatever spell Jefferson was under.

Early afternoon the following day, Nevaeh once again was sitting in the lobby of Tree of Life, waiting for Ms. Hebert. She'd called her former activities director that morning and asked if she could make another visit. For the photo project. Ms. Hebert was hesitant at first—"today's not a good day"—but after Nevaeh haggled, saying it was for an upcoming show, she finally agreed. "Just make it brief."

While she waited, Nevaeh looked at the photos Jefferson had texted her of the new sketches. He'd taken the bleak surroundings of the hospital and transformed the photos into something magical, blending textures into extraordinary scenes of beauty. In the first drawing, Valentin and London shuffled cards around a table, laughing, their comfort with each other a stark contrast to the gloomy surroundings of the cafeteria and the somber expressions of the staff and other patients. In the next, a small group of patients lined up for their daily meds outside the nurse's station, their stoic faces and stiff postures imbued with undertones of anger and sadness. The last showed Emery whistling at a sparrow perched on the branch of a bald cypress, attempting to reach beyond the walls of her isolation. This image brought Nevaeh to tears. Emery had always talked Nevaeh down off the ledge whenever melancholy's cloud hovered over her head. Now Nevaeh was going to ask her for another favor. A huge one.

"Did you do those?" Nevaeh had been so engrossed in her own musings she hadn't heard Ms. Hebert approach. She wasn't smiling like on the last visit. A look of concern marred her face.

"Jefferson did them," Nevaeh responded.

"Is that your beau?"

Nevaeh nodded.

Ms. Hebert touched Nevaeh's wrist, studied the bruises, and bandages wrapped around her hand. "What happened here?" she asked.

Nevaeh couldn't meet Ms. Hebert's gaze. "Bicycle accident."

"You're not lying to me, are you?"

This time Nevaeh forced herself to meet Ms. Hebert's eyes. "No." Shame warmed Nevaeh's cheeks. She hoped her friend wouldn't notice. This friend who'd bent over backwards for her when everyone else had written her off. But Jefferson's life was on the line.

For a moment, Nevaeh thought Ms. Hebert might refuse her admission into the facilities—or at least give her a lecture—but she just squeezed Nevaeh's shoulder and mumbled okay, okay. Though it did nothing to unwind the tightness in her belly. Nevaeh hugged Ms. Hebert and thanked her kindly—for more than she knew. She glanced over her friend's shoulder and saw the receptionists were busy speaking on the phone and typing on the computer. Leaving one hand on Ms. Hebert's back, Nevaeh reached down with her other hand and unclipped the keycard from her belt loop, slipping it quickly in her pocket as they released. She felt terrible doing this to Ms. Hebert, but what choice did she have?

Ten minutes later, Nevaeh was seated across from Emery in the visitor's center, showing her Jefferson's sketches while others around them played games or watched TV. Under the dreary halogen lights, Emery looked even worse than when Nevaeh had last visited. Purple saddle bags drooped beneath her eyes, flecks of dry skin peeled from her cracked lips, and she wore her greasy, tangled hair in a ponytail. But she smiled at the drawings. Nevaeh was glad to offer her friend even a brief moment of happiness.

"You really like this fella, huh?" Emery asked.

Nevaeh showed Emery a selfie of her and Jefferson sharing a sno-ball outside Pandora's. Seeing the photo, a King Cake crème mustache smeared over the tops of their lips, she remembered that day. They'd wandered around NOMA before eating a picnic in City Park then gone to Pandora's for dessert. That was the afternoon Jefferson admitted that when he first moved to New Orleans he'd spend hours riding the streetcars around the city, visiting different neighborhoods, sometimes getting lost for hours. It was his first real taste of the world expanding around him, life opening up and being much bigger than the small Mississippi town in which he grew up. Nevaeh remembered how much she hungered for that freedom—and Jefferson had shared it with her, asking nothing more than for her to be open to whatever he decided to show her. Had he not spilled his coffee on her bag would she have even noticed him, or found the courage to get to know him? Had he not brought her a café au lait the next day, would she have ever found the courage to escape her parents' grasp? No one mattered as much as Jefferson did. The freedom he brought her. The joy.

Would things ever be like that again? A heavy dose of doubt brought tears to Nevaeh's eyes. But she couldn't give up on Jefferson yet. If there was one thing she could say about him, he was a stubborn son-of-a-bitch. She prayed that stubbornness would keep him alive.

Emery touched her hand. "Where you at, darling?" she asked. It seemed unfair that Emery was consoling her rather than the other way around.

Wiping her eyes, Nevaeh dropped her voice so the guards wouldn't hear and told Emery everything she knew about what happened to Jefferson, which all in all, wasn't much. Then she went on to explain how she thought Jefferson's illness related to Angelique Truehart, which was why she needed to talk to the woman. It was a hunch, but it was all she had. The story sounded delusional, but Nevaeh continued anyway. She thought for sure the doctors or guards would overhear and lock her up again.

Emery listened, as she always did, without judgment. When Nevaeh finished, Emery bit on a thinly chewed nail. "You really think that's what's going on?"

Great! Even her own friend doubted her sanity. "I know how it sounds…"

Emery held up a hand for her to stop. "It's New Orleans, sweetheart. Everybody knows this place is crawling with voodoo and ghosts and whatnot. Besides, what you're saying would explain a lot about Ms. Creepy Creeps. But can you get her to talk—other than repeating that same damn phrase? She's been in that room a long time now and, far as I know, she ain't spoken to anybody. Not even the sister who comes by every now and then."

"I have to try."

"You have a plan on how you're going to sneak up to the fifth floor and into her room?"

"I thought you might be able to help." Nevaeh looked down at her nervous tapping feet, afraid her friend might be offended. "I wouldn't ask if I had other options."

"How do you plan on getting inside Angelique's room?"

Lowering her voice to barely above a whisper, Nevaeh said, "I swiped Ms. Hebert's keycard."

Emery chuckled. "You little pickpocket."

"I need to hurry before she realizes it's missing."

Clicking her tongue against her mouth, Emery surveyed the room. Counted the guards. Took in the number of patients. Nevaeh could see the beginnings of a plan taking shape. The guilt ate at her. She almost told Emery to forget it. But her friend would never let her talk her out of it now.

Emery leaned over the table. "Go to the bathroom. When you hear…well, you'll know."

On the verge of crying again, Emery shook her head for Nevaeh to quit that shit. If they were going through with this, she needed to be strong. Pushing down her emotions, Nevaeh mouthed the words *thank you.*

Emery winked. "Go."

Nevaeh raised her hand for an orderly, the same no neck

bullethead from before, and asked her to escort her to the bathroom. The orderly led her down the hall to the nearest one, which by bad design, was a short jaunt to the elevators. Locking herself inside, Nevaeh tore the visitor's sticker from her shirt and tossed it in the trash. Hand clutching the handle, she pressed her ear against the door and waited for what felt like forever, praying Emery hadn't chickened out, or worse, turned her in.

"Give me the remote. It's my turn. I'll smack you," Emery shouted.

Orderlies ordered her to settle down.

"Make me, you motherfuckers."

There was a loud commotion. Things being thrown. Patients having fits while the staff attempted to calm them down. Nevaeh had to give Emery this. She sure knew how to stir up trouble.

Nevaeh counted down from 3...2...1. She strolled out of the bathroom to the elevator, hit the button, took one glance, where she saw the orderlies pinning Emery to a table while a nurse prepared a sedative, mouthed an apology, before the doors swooshed open, and she was taking a ride to the fifth floor.

As Nevaeh strolled along the halls, she met the staff's gazes long enough they might confuse her for a patient, but not too long where they'd recognize her and question what she was doing wandering the facilities unattended. She knew she wouldn't have much time, and if the administration caught her, they'd call security to throw her out. Not only would she not get to speak with Angelique—if that was even possible—

she'd ruin her friendship with Ms. Hebert and maybe even get her fired.

Two nurses pushed a cart full of medications from a room. They glanced over at Nevaeh. Appeared to recognize her. She gazed down at her shoes until their footsteps faded behind her. She had a flashback of the pills in the tiny paper cups and the odd tasting water to wash it down. The heaviness of sinking into the cushion of her chair as the medication dragged her beneath the waves of sedation. It'd leave her feeling empty and hollow, like they'd scooped the soul from her body. Was Jefferson experiencing a similar feeling?

A stink, like raw sewage, clogged her nostrils. Nevaeh had to pull her shirt over her nose to block the gagging stench. A fly landed on Nevaeh's hand, crawled over her two middle knuckles, then launched into the air again, and soared down the hall. Nevaeh recognized where she was immediately. She was in her wing. Swallowing her fear, she walked forward, ignoring the shadows creeping in around her and the garbled noise of televisions.

The fly landed on the handle of door number 29S.

Angelique's room.

From behind it emanated a loud buzzing like a busted circuit. Nevaeh swallowed to wet her dry throat. Wiped her sweaty palms on her jeans before pulling the keycard from her pocket. This was a different fear than she'd endured on first arriving at this place. This was a fear of the unknown.

Taking a deep breath to slow her rapid heartbeat, she glanced around to make sure no one was watching, then slipped the keycard through the lock. For a brief moment, she panicked that it didn't work. That they'd found her out. Then the light switched from red to green. Exhaling, she opened the door and slipped inside.

The rotted meat stench churned Nevaeh's stomach and she swallowed down the vomit pushing up her esophagus. Shades were drawn over the windows and the lights shut off, only enough sun squeezed through to cast the room in a faint glow. Tiny things flew around her head. Nevaeh swatted at the flies landing on her. Black specks dotted the fixtures and shelves. Soiled blankets were curled at the end of the bed. On the wrinkled sheets, white maggots slithered in a puddle of goo. How long had it been since the staff stepped into this room? Could Nevaeh really blame them for ignoring it?

Seated in a wheelchair near the window, the gaunt figure of Angelique Truehart slumped like a tattered doll. Patches of scraggly coarse hair fell over a bare scalp that was much more bone than flesh. The head leaned sideways on her emaciated neck. Talon-like fingers curled around the plastic armrests. Beneath her breath, Angelique groaned over and over again, *please quiet, child, please.*

Nevaeh whispered Angelique's name as she approached from behind. The frail figure raised her head slightly. Nevaeh stepped around into Angelique's view. Soon as their eyes locked, Nevaeh tripped backwards, clamping her hand over her mouth to keep from screaming.

18. JEFFERSON

After the debacle at the gallery, Gemma had the taxi drive them back to the studio where she'd tried to evoke Jefferson into talking about what he saw. Not that he could explain it to her. Not in any way that made sense. The words from his mouth just further added to the confusion. Darkness, he said. Death, he said. A woman in the bayou, he said.

This last snippet caught Gemma's attention. She dug her nails into her palms and muttered, *fucking witch*. Jefferson had no idea what she was talking about. But he didn't like the sound of it. Is that where she'd bought the poison? Had she cursed him?

Gemma swore she was going to burn the witch's hut to the ground. Kill that stupid groundskeeper for spilling the powder too. She was sure it was their fault everything had gone wrong.

That was just like Gemma. Blaming everyone else for her mistakes.

She walked over to his desk where his drawing pad was open. She flipped through the pages. Inquired about the sketches he'd done for Nevaeh of the patients at Tree of Life Recovery Center. Jefferson wanted to lie, but his traitorous tongue spilled every word. Then Gemma forced him to tell everything about his and Nevaeh's plans. There were no more secrets. Everything was now out in the open.

As she listened, Jefferson saw Gemma begin to shatter. Cracks formed as she did her best to disguise the humiliation. Bending a brush between her hands, the wood cracking in the center, Gemma snapped it in half. She gawked at the two broken pieces before letting them drop to the floor. With a deep breath, she wiped her hands and walked over with his pad. Jefferson was certain she was going to destroy the new sketches.

Gemma grabbed a fresh canvas and stuck it on the easel. She handed him his palette and laid out a water jar of brushes and some tubes of paint on a worn wood table that she scooted next to him. "I don't care if it takes you all night. You will create me a masterpiece. Like you have for that nasty skeeta hawk. And it better be finished by the time I return tomorrow. Until then…" She twirled the studio keys. "…I don't want to see you."

The hardened expression Gemma had molded for the entire evening melted away into sobs. She grazed her fingernails along Jefferson's cheek. "They want to take you away from me. Nevaeh. Camile. Even Marcel. But I'm not going to let them. We started this together. We're going to end this together. They're all going to see exactly what we're made of."

Gemma kissed him full on the mouth. Then she stormed out the door and locked him inside. A few minutes later, he saw the headlights of a car and heard the door slam.

T he hours ticked by. Other than the sounds of the occasional artist leaving for the night, the place was deathly silent. The pale light of the moon wrestled with the shadows. The shadows watched him from the corners of the room, waiting for…what? Jefferson didn't know. Didn't want to know.

A blank canvas sat untouched in front of him. Jefferson mixed some paint, dipped his brush into it, but for some reason, he couldn't bring a painting to life as he'd done so many times before. It was as if inspiration had been stripped from him, wrapped in heavy chains, and thrown into the bayou.

Sometime in the night, a hazy mist gathered and billowed through the open windows. It filled the studio and slowly solidified into a dark figure. Jefferson thought he must be hallucinating. What other explanation was there? But after all he'd seen already would it surprise him that something from beyond the grave had come for his soul? Come to drag him into the darkness where he belonged?

A skeleton man in a top hat and tails stepped into the moonlight. He bit a cigar between rotten yellow teeth. Dark ruby eyes peered at Jefferson from within deep sockets. Jefferson had seen images of him around New Orleans. He was the famous voodoo spirit of the dead, Baron Samedi.

"You not looking so good, gason," the spirit said.

"Am I dead?" Jefferson asked, somehow able to speak. Was it all in his head?

Baron Samedi laughed, blowing smoke from his cigar. "As we say, Byen mal pa lanmó. Not well is not death."

Great! Just his luck.

Baron Samedi placed his cigar on the edge of the table, grabbed Jefferson by the chin, then plunged his gloved hand into Jefferson's chest. The punch rattled Jefferson. Heat flooded across Jefferson's torso and through his limbs as the spirit caressed his heart. For the first time since Gemma had pulled him from the tomb, Jefferson's heart thumped with a steady rhythm like a fist knocking on a door of an abandoned house. He took a deep breath, his lungs filling with stale air that tasted refreshing.

The shadows crept in around Baron Samedi, but he hissed for them to halt. "He's not ready."

"Ready for what?" Jefferson heard himself ask. It was strange speaking with his own tongue, not miming the words Gemma put in his mouth.

"Syèl la." Fires ignited in Baron Samedi's pupils. "Beyond."

"What waits for me there?"

"Everything."

"I'm ready to go."

Baron Samedi glanced over at the shadows. Jefferson couldn't be sure, but he swore they laughed.

"Bél antéman pa vle di paradi." Baron Samedi snatched Jefferson's wrist. Showed him the black blood flowing through his veins like ink. "A nice funeral does not mean you go to paradise, zanmi. This world isn't finished with you yet. Far from it."

"But what is here for me?"

"Nothing." The spirit dropped Jefferson's arm. "But agony."

Baron Samedi squirted a tube of black paint into the water jar of brushes and mixed it into a thick, muddy sludge. He splashed the sludge on the canvas. The sludge swirled into a maelstrom, a vortex of endless black. The paint peeled from the canvas and stretched out towards Jefferson like a monstrous snake. Wrapping around his neck, it began to swallow him, beginning with his head and working its way down his body. Trapped inside, arms pressed to his sides, Jefferson struggled to break free but he couldn't move. He begged Baron Samedi to stop whatever it was from happening, but the skeletal man grabbed his cigar and vanished into a cloud of smoke.

Jefferson tried to scream, but the enormous snake that had been swallowing him was now small, slithering down his throat, cutting off his breath. Darkness painted over the moonlight.

⚊⚊⚊

Flies swarmed Jefferson's head. They crawled on his skin. Sipped the tears from his eyes. Stung his cracked lips and burrowed into his pores. Laid eggs in the cuts on his forehead and hand. Buzzed in his ears. A loud, consistent drone that stirred horrendous visions of death.

The shirt that had been loose on him last night was now pushing against the buttons from the bloating of his belly, discolored with stains caused by the fluids leaking from his flesh. Blood pooled into purple bruises like tiny ponds across his body. A stench like rotten meat churned his stomach. Maggots broke from their eggs, squirming inside of his organs. Perhaps they'd feast on him until all that remained were bones.

The sun shone through the studio windows and traced squares of light on the floor. A woodpecker chipped away at a telephone pole outside, and a couple of dogs barked back and forth in heated confrontation. Occasionally a car rolled by on the narrow road of Japonica Street.

The front door to the building swung open and Gemma's voice carried down the hall. She was having a squabble with someone, and from the sound of it, things were not going well. What had she been doing while he remained imprisoned in this hell?

Jefferson wished he had some way to speak with Nevaeh. Wished he could call her on the phone to hear her voice. To know that she was okay. To tell her he missed and loved her. But Gemma would never let that happen. Not as long as she had control over him.

The locks clicked and Gemma pushed open the door, phone clutched between her shoulder and ear. She wore the same gold and turquoise lace dress from last night, ruffled as if slept in. Makeup smudged and peeling, exposing the bruising beneath.

"What do you mean you no longer think his art is right for your gallery? A few weeks ago you were practically begging to show his work. Things have changed? What the fuck has changed? You're booked solid. For the rest of the year. Well, you're going to regret not getting a piece of him right now. Because by next year, let me tell you, Jefferson's name is going to be everywhere. Yeah, you can bet on it."

Gemma hung up. Blew a stray strand from her face. Her expression curled into one of disgust. "Jesus, it stinks in here. And what's with all the flies?" With a frantic wave of her arm, she shooed the swarm away and walked over to open the windows even wider. Hearing voices from the outside, Jefferson tried screaming for help, but he gagged on his own cries.

Gemma turned toward the easel. "What have you been up to all night? Hopefully something productive." Her expression shifted from disgust to anger. "What the hell is this?" She picked up the canvas and shoved the big black splotch of dried paint in Jefferson's face. "You call this a masterpiece?" When he didn't respond, she snarled, "Tell me what this is."

"Nothing," Jefferson muttered.

A jittery laugh spluttered from Gemma's throat. "I can see it's nothing." She tossed the canvas to the side. It crashed to the floor. "You paint beautiful things for Nevaeh, but you give me *shit*."

Jefferson thought Gemma was going to have another one of her fits, but she walked over to the windows and put her hands on her hips. Her shoulders slumped and, for a moment, he thought she was crying.

"All day I've been calling everyone who owes me a favor, trying to get you in another gallery. Is Nevaeh doing that for you? Camile? No, they're not. But how do you expect me to help you when you give me *nothing*! That bitch Camile has flapped her lips all over town already. Now everyone wants to cut us out."

Gemma snapped her fingers. "Get up and pack your things. I'm taking you home. Maybe you can find some inspiration there. God knows this stink hole isn't doing you any good. Then I'm going to talk to our good friends at the Carondelet. Let them know exactly how it's going to be."

As she stepped out of the light, the shadows creeped in around Gemma like they had with Baron Samedi. They seeped into her flesh and peered through her eyes. From behind her mask of disdain they smiled.

19. GEMMA

ain pelted the windshield as the wipers swiped frantically to clear the streams floating along the glass. Wind shook the tendrilled branches of the oaks along the sidewalk, as if the trees had come alive. Fingers gripped knuckle white on the steering wheel, Gemma pressed the gas pedal, speeding in her BMW along the flooded streets, tires spraying the grassy strips of neutral ground dividing St Charles. Headlights pierced the murky fog.

On the seat next to her lay the envelope with the check inside. What the hell was she doing giving it back? Had she finally lost it? She could just walk away from all of this. Take the money and start afresh. Camile had said that Gemma had a good eye for what would sell. Why not make her own connections? Show them all she didn't need them. Any of them. Including Jefferson.

But then she imagined Jefferson as she'd left him at home: flies buzzing around his stinky carcass, nasty goo leaking from his pores, the soulless husk miming back to her what she told him to say. If Jefferson was in there somewhere, he was trapped inside his own private hell. Buried beneath all that rot.

What was it the witch had said? *Once a man has seen the other side he's never the same.* The scene Jefferson caused at the gallery and his talk of shadows and spirits certainly indicated that. For all she knew, he was lost to her. Another reason for her to take the check and walk away.

But if she did that, Camile and Marcel would win. They'd already proven themselves capable of destroying her reputation. Walk away now and they'd have her banished from the art community. Gemma was sure of that. And where would that leave her? Nowhere.

No, she couldn't let that happen. She'd never be able to live with herself knowing those two had gotten the best of her…again.

Marcel always moaned about how she'd ruined his career. But it wasn't like he didn't deserve it.

For months, Gemma was Marcel's lover, confidant, and business partner. They'd met through Camile, when Gemma was still working at the gallery, and hit it off immediately. She should've known he was a charlatan from the way he bragged, the pompous ass, but she was taken by his swagger and talent. Unlike Jefferson, Marcel walked down the path to success without any hesitation about where it led. His only problem was he wasn't exactly beloved by the art community. Too cocksure. Too mouthy. Too arrogant about his own skills. So Gemma had helped smooth some things over. Nothing a little charm and charitable donations couldn't solve. It all seemed to go rather well, for a while. She booked him some shows around town, and he provided her with the attention she desired.

Then one day he decided he didn't need her anymore. Invited her to meet him for coffee. He was already seated at a sidewalk table when she arrived. He tried to hide his nervousness behind his usual cool stance, but she knew something was off when he kept swirling the foam in his cappuccino. The son of a bitch said he felt she was suffocating him. Stifling his imagination. Holding him back. Blamed her for his inadequacies as an artist, lover, and friend. Embarrassing now, but she'd actually begged him to reconsider. He must've enjoyed that. He loved having his ego stroked even more than his cock.

He pretended to bring her down gently. "I'm sorry, this isn't working for me," he said. Gemma stalked off that day, broken-hearted, but determined not to let his rejection crush her.

This wasn't Marcel's take on things, of course. Told some of their friends she stalked him, not only through social media, but waited outside his job and apartment when he wasn't home. All an exaggeration. She'd messaged his family and friends about the money Marcel owed her from his sales from the exhibits she'd gotten him into. But being a forgiving soul, Gemma tried to give Marcel a chance to apologize and take her back. Since he refused to answer his phone, she dropped by to have a conversation. She had no idea he'd turn it into a big deal.

The last time Gemma had passed by Marcel's he'd called the police on her. There was nothing the pigs could do about it since she'd arranged for the post office to deliver some of her mail to Marcel's apartment, making it officially her residence too. Marcel blew his top and talked the landlord into writing her an eviction notice.

A week later, Gemma broke into his studio, took photos of paintings he'd committed to certain galleries, and uploaded them for sale on his Instagram. The galleries were furious and threatened to bar Marcel permanently. To make matters worse, Gemma used Marcel's profile to leave nasty comments on the galleries' social media pages. The idiot had shared his password with her. She lambasted the galleries' events and criticized the artwork with emojis and GIFS, causing quite a stir. By the time Marcel figured out what was going on he was two feet in the mud and sinking. He tried to speak with the gallery owners and convince them it was none of his doing, but they'd had enough. He'd dug his own hole over the years, knowingly criticizing others' work to people he thought were his friends. Gemma just tossed the dirt on top.

But the whole thing circled back to Camile.

She was jealous that Marcel lavished attention on Gemma. It was so obvious in the way she stalked them whenever they hung out at the Carondelet. How she'd suddenly find things for Gemma to do so she could pull Marcel aside and whisper in his ear. She'd treated Marcel like a servant before he started dating Gemma, having him run errands and unpack artwork and assist with installs, which he gladly did for a chance to display his art in the backroom. Gemma tried to prove to Marcel he was better than that. And what was the thanks she got for it? He stabbed her in the back as soon as Camile gave the order.

But Marcel wasn't the only reason Camile was jealous of Gemma. She knew Gemma was more of a visionary than she'd ever be. Camile may have had the connections, but Gemma knew what sold. All those pieces she'd gotten into the right collectors' hands for a hefty price. So what if she made a few bargains? Took a bit for herself off the top? Used the connections for her own purposes? What was it Camile always said about being a successful gallerist? *You must have initiative.*

Now Marcel wanted to ruin her career and Camile wanted to get rid of her for good. Well, Gemma Landry wasn't going quietly.

⎯⎯⎯⎯⎯⎯⎯⎯

Gemma screeched to a halt in a space opposite the gallery. She slipped the check in her pocket, flipped her raincoat hood over her head, and skipped in her ankle boots across the street. She pulled on the door of 841. It was locked. She peered through the window but didn't see anyone. Yet there was a light on upstairs. Determined to have this out now, she rang the buzzer and banged on the glass.

A barista smoking outside of Bearcat glanced in Gemma's direction. "What are you looking at?" Gemma snarled back.

A curtain slid open and Marcel's sleep crusted face pressed against the glass. His jaw dropped when he saw it was her.

Marcel peeled open the door and stuck his head out. "What are you doing here?" he said, more of an accusation than a question.

"Aren't you going to let me in?" Gemma motioned at the stormy weather.

"Naw! Ain't you done enough damage already?"

Gemma scoffed as if he'd offended her. "That's not fair. It wasn't my installation that sent Jefferson into seizures."

Marcel's hardened expression softened. "How is he?"

Once again, Gemma pictured Jefferson as she left him at the apartment, seated in front of an easel, painting nothing but black shadows and skeleton-faced men. But she couldn't tell Marcel any of this. He already thought they'd lost their minds.

"Resting," Gemma said.

"Well, I hope he's okay. Give him my best."

Marcel went to close the door, but Gemma jammed it with her foot. "He'll be fine," she said. "Is Camile here? We need to talk."

Nudging her foot with his own, Marcel replied, "She don't want to talk to you. Not after you ruined her soiree the other night."

"I've come to iron things out between us," Gemma spoke in her sweetest tone.

"No wrinkles to iron."

"Not true. There are plenty of wrinkles and I'm here to apologize for the terrible things I've done."

"Well, Camile ain't here."

Gemma was quickly losing her patience. She didn't enjoy being given the runaround, especially while being rained on. "Where is she?"

"Probably cleaning your mess."

Tired of Marcel's jibes, Gemma shoved the door as hard as she could, catching him off guard, and knocking his scrawny ass off balance. "Goddamn, what's with you?"

Marching in, Gemma shook off her raincoat and hung it on a hook. "You wouldn't invite me in and it's raining. Awfully rude, Marcel." Then she noticed some of Jefferson's paintings were missing. "Where are they?"

"That's none of your…"

"Tell me!" Gemma lost her cool. Marcel took a few steps back. She straightened her blouse and smiled. "Please?"

Marcel swiveled his head as if making sure Camile was nowhere around and dropped his voice to a near whisper. "After what happened the other night, many of the collectors withdrew their purchases."

"How many?"

"All of them."

This was bad news.

"Camile's taking some of Jefferson's paintings around to other collectors in hopes of reclaiming some of her losses. But she wasn't too optimistic. You know how word gets around. And with the opening less than a week away…"

Gemma pulled the envelope from her pocket. "Then maybe she'll want to talk about this."

"She ain't gonna want to talk to you."

"Then maybe you can talk some sense into her."

"Why would I do that?"

Gemma strolled into the other room. Marcel had fixed his projector. She had to admit he was good with his hands. Not that he was a magnificent lover. Too selfish, too greedy. How often did he finish before she got started? Unlike Jefferson who was patient and attentive. Marcel lacked Jefferson's talent in many things, including his art, but he was determined and unapologetic in what he wanted. Which was why he was a useful ally. The trick was to convince him to join her side.

"You know, I didn't come here just to iron out things between me and Camile. There are things between us too."

"You talking about how you tried to derail my career? No forgiving for that, lovely. Don't matter none anyway. My feet are back on the ground and in the gallery. It's you the one standing outside looking in."

"Don't be mean, Marcel. I never tried to…"

"Bullshit!" He pointed an accusatory index finger. "Because of you no one would hang my paintings. I had to sell them in Jackson Square."

Gemma would've enjoyed twisting Marcel's stubby appendage until it popped, but she played nice. "So, I did some terrible things. I'm truly sorry. But you did some terrible things too. Doesn't mean we can't be friends."

"Why would I want to be friends with you?"

"We both know Camile is struggling. How much longer do you think she can keep this place running, huh? And what are you going to do when she closes?" She waltzed over to where Marcel leaned in the doorway. "Maybe we can come to some arrangement." Marcel tried to step away, but she blocked him in. "We could give it another go?"

"What the fuck is she doing here?" Over Marcel's shoulder, Camile leaned one of Jefferson's paintings against the wall. Blood flooded into her cheeks as she seethed between gritted teeth.

Marcel moved to Camile's side. "She's come to talk."

Camile clomped forward in her heels. "We have nothing to talk about."

"Came to apologize." Gemma waved around the check. "Brought this back. From what I hear, you can use it."

Marcel glanced down at his shoes as Camile shot him a knowing glare then focused her rage on Gemma. "Came to save your ass, that's what you're doing. But me and you, we're done. So you take that check, darling, and stroll on out of my gallery. Because I don't ever want to see you again."

"There must be something we can work out."

"Little too late, I'm afraid…"

"That's not true. I'm willing to make another sizable donation."

"With ya mamma n'em's money," Marcel remarked.

Gemma squeezed her hands into fists. "Does it matter where the money comes from? I can get it. Now what do you say you put the coffee on and the three of us talk about an arrangement?"

Camile glided over until she hovered a step from Gemma, casting her in shadow. "How's that working out for poor

Jefferson?" Gemma swallowed. "And don't be telling me he sick with no grippe. Both of you are on something and I want nothing to do with it."

"I don't know what you're talking about."

"Yes, you do. Now get the fuck out of my gallery. We're done here."

As Camile turned her back, Gemma grabbed her roughly by the arm. The flick of a blade clicked next to Gemma's ear. Marcel slid his arm around her chest and pressed the sharp edge of the knife to her throat.

Camile yanked free of Gemma's grasp. "Throw this trash out the door."

"I spoke to the landlord not long ago," Gemma blurted. With a squeak, Camile stopped in her tracks. "He was interested in cutting a deal with me."

Glancing over her shoulder, Camile accused Gemma of lying.

"Am I?" For once, she wasn't, and Camile knew it. "I can make a call to my mother right now."

Smirking, Camile clipped over to the window and closed the curtain again, darkness swallowing the light in the room. What the fuck was she doing? Gemma struggled against Marcel, but his grip was too tight, the blade pressing harder against her neck. "Don't make me slip now," he said. "Hate to nick an artery."

"Did I ever tell you how I got my start as a gallerist?" Camile asked her, but continued on before Gemma could respond. "It was right here as an art handler for the previous owner, Margaret Carroll. Talk about a tough old bird. She'd lay into me if I didn't handle the art properly. Once she slapped my knuckles with a piece of wood from an expensive frame I accidentally cracked. You can bet I never did that again. Another time she overheard me talking badly about a sculptor's work she was representing. She made me personally apologize. It was maybe the most humiliating moment in my life. You must respect the art and the artist, Margaret would say. Otherwise, what are you doing this for?"

Camile snatched the envelope from Gemma's hand. Ran her finger along the crease.

"I spent eleven years busting my ass for her. For a long time, I did every shit job in the business. Everything from washing windows to sweeping floors to answering phones to running out and finding Margaret a nice cup of hot tea. If I complained, well, there was the door. And a few times I almost walked."

"But as hard as she was, Margaret was also very generous. She paid me a decent wage and was always willing to front me a little extra cash when I needed it. She taught me the ropes. How to maintain an inventory and ship expensive pieces of art and organize exhibits. But most importantly, she taught me how to garner my own stable of artists and collectors. By throwing the best opening night and remaining loyal to those who are loyal to you."

Camile tore the check in half. Then again into fourths. She stuck the pieces into Gemma's pocket.

"I remained loyal to Margaret Carroll. For my loyalty,

when she retired, she gave me the key to this gallery. Now it's my turn to take on a protégé. Someone I can show the ropes. A while ago, I'd hoped that person might be you. But you wanted too much too quickly. So, I've chosen Nevaeh. I think she'll make a fine addition to the Carondelet, don't you?"

Gemma struggled against Marcel's tight grip. "She won't be here for long. Not once I buy this place and throw her ass out the door. Along with yours."

From beneath her shirt, Camile pulled the brass key and dangled it in front of Gemma's eyes. "You go ahead and make your threats, darling. Because I can make them too. You try to buy me out and I will bury you. There's a lotta swamp in the bayou, dearie."

Marcel nicked Gemma. Ah! She flinched. *She fucking flinched!* She did her best to play it cool, resume her deadpan expression, but from Camile's satisfied grin, she knew she saw. Blood dripped down Gemma's neck.

"What did I tell you, Marcel? Apply enough pressure, even the hardest sculpture cracks."

"Sure do."

Camile traced a sharply filed fingernail across Gemma's brow and down her cheek. If she didn't have a knife to her throat, Gemma would've smacked her hand away, but she didn't trust Marcel. He may have thought he was street, but Gemma knew the motherfucker's roots were firmly planted in the rich, man-made soil of Lake Vista.

"You can fill those cracks, of course," Camile continued

her analogy. "Repair the piece with putty or epoxy. Might even look brand new. But everybody knows it's broken. The cracks remain."

"You going to cut my throat, Camile? Go on then! Do it," Gemma snapped.

Camile shook her head. "Nah, cher. Death's too good for you. No, I have something that cuts far worse. You're finished in this town. Both you and that boyo. You can damn sure bet on that."

"Fuck you, Camile! You'll see I ain't done."

"Marcel, do me a favor. Take out the trash. It's starting to reek."

Marcel dragged Gemma to the front, opened the door, and shoved her out into the rain. She slipped and fell on the sidewalk, bruising her hip. "Best you get by your house. Stick a Band-Aid on that boo-boo," Marcel said, tossing her coat at her.

Screaming, Gemma leapt to her feet, only to receive the door in her face. She pulled on the knob, but it was locked. Banged on the window until her knuckles hurt and shouted at Camile and Marcel until her voice went hoarse. It was only once she'd tired that she noticed the small group of customers waiting to be seated in the café staring at her.

20. NEVAEH

Hand clamped over mouth, Nevaeh hyperventilated, frozen by Angelique's ghastly silent scream. The poor woman's jaw was locked open, her swollen purple tongue flopping inside her black hole of a mouth. Her skull leaned against the ball joint of her left shoulder; the spinal discs of her neck too weak to hold it straight. Filmy, opaque eyes pointed at Nevaeh blindly inside cavernous sockets. Sinewy strips of flesh and muscle dangled off bones like moss on a cypress tree. The hospital gown draped over her slumped cadaverous frame, sucked in against the contours of her ribcage, the hem ending an inch above her knobby ankle bones, the right shifted to an awkward angle where she must've once broken it, wooly grayed socks disguising her clawed feet. Flies clambered over her remains and burrowed inside her exposed crevices. Nevaeh would've thought Angelique dead if she weren't mumbling, *Please, be quiet, child, please.*

The Tree of Life Recovery Center. More like the Museum of Death. How had the hospital allowed Angelique to remain this way? They had left her to wither to dust.

Nevaeh's heart broke for the poor woman. Left alone to rot in hell. Who could do this to another human being?

Someone like Gemma. That was who. If Nevaeh didn't find a cure—if there was one for this curse—then Jefferson would suffer the same horrific fate. She had to hope Angelique was able to speak something other than that repeated phrase.

Nevaeh grabbed a chair from the corner and placed it in front of Angelique. She didn't appear to notice. Did she even know Nevaeh was there? Was she aware of her surroundings? In a way, it was better for her if she wasn't.

Letting go of her fear, Nevaeh reached out for Angelique's cold emaciated hands, pulling them gently into her lap. "Angelique, can you hear me?"

Angelique's jaw moved slightly. Air hissed from her lipless mouth. It sounded like she wheezed the word, *Yeeeeaah,* but Nevaeh wasn't sure. Then she mumbled, *Please, be quiet, child, please.*

"What happened to you?"

Tears dribbled from Angelique's opaque eyes and slid down her ossified cheeks. *Please, be quiet, child, please.*

"Please, help me understand. My boyfriend. He too is poisoned. I have to save him. I can save you both. But I need to understand what happened."

Nevaeh was crying now too. This was hopeless. Why did she come here? What answers did she expect from a dying woman? For all she knew, Angelique Truehart's mind was as rotted as the rest of her. Reliving the same memory over and over again. A rerun of her past.

Angelique started to groan like she was in pain.

Nevaeh glanced toward the closed door. Shadows flickered across the square patch of light. Footsteps clapped along the tiled hallway. Two staff members stopped outside the room and chattered unintelligibly. Placing a hand on her shoulder, Nevaeh begged Angelique to calm down. To relax. Nevaeh expected the nurses or orderlies to barge in any second. What would they do if they caught her? Lock her back in the facility? It wasn't like they followed everything by the book around here.

Nevaeh stayed quiet, listening to Angelique's agonizing moans. The two staff members outside the door finished their conversation and parted ways in different directions. Nevaeh exhaled a long sigh of relief. She hadn't realized she'd been holding her breath.

Once again, she pleaded. "Please, Angelique, tell me who did this to you?"

Angelique clutched Nevaeh's hands and squeezed tight, cutting off the circulation to Nevaeh's fingers, the tips blanching white. Head thrown back, eyes rolled toward the ceiling, Angelique's body trembled, the wheels of her chair squeaking back and forth on the tile. Her tongue fluttered against her blackened gums. *Please, be quiet, child, please,* Angelique unleashed the phrase in a high-pitch scream.

Flies fluttered in a frenzy around her skull. They flew into the window, their smashed bodies pinged like raindrops in a storm, smearing their insides on the glass. Feet pounded down the hallway outside. Shadows devoured the patch of light.

The door was shoved open, bouncing against the wall. In the doorway stood a skinny middle-aged black woman dressed as if she'd just come from church. She was flanked by two orderlies. "Who are you?" she asked Nevaeh with alarm in her voice. "And what are you doing with my sister?"

"Please, let me explain…"

But before Nevaeh could speak another word, the orderlies in white scrubs plunged through the swarms of flies, grabbed her by her arms and tried to pull her from Angelique. The sick woman held on with a vice-like grip. Her jaw clacked open and shut, open and shut, as she muttered over the roar of an alarm, *please, be quiet, child, please.*

The orderlies lifted Nevaeh off her feet. She leaned her ear in close to listen to what Angelique was trying to tell her. The skinny woman demanded the orderlies drag Nevaeh from her sister's room.

"Who did this to you?" Nevaeh pleaded as the orderlies pulled her from Angelique's grasp. "Please, Angelique, I need to know!"

Nevaeh slipped from the orderlies' clutches. Grasped onto the bed rails. One of them hugged her around the waist while the other tried to pry her fingers. "I know you know something. So please, help me!"

Angelique shuddered in her chair. Nevaeh lost her grip. The orderlies dragged her, shoes scraping black marks on the tile. In a last-ditch effort, Nevaeh stomped on the toe of the orderly hugging her waist, slipped from his hold, and raced over to Angelique. "Tell me, goddamn it, who did this to you?"

Angelique lifted her head off her shoulder and leered at Nevaeh. Color flooded into Angelique's eyes as they snapped into focus. In a clear voice, she wailed, "Mirlande St. Pierreeee!" before collapsing into the wheelchair and resuming her raspy breathing of *Please, be quiet, child, please.*

There it was. The name Nevaeh had been searching for.

As the orderlies dragged her from the room, past the woman who stood staring at Angelique in awe, Nevaeh thanked Angelique. She wished there was more she could do for her, but Nevaeh knew it was already too late.

Hopefully it wasn't for Jefferson.

The orderlies marched Nevaeh down the hallway to the elevators, followed by the skinny woman. Patients stuck their heads out of their rooms to watch the excitement. Nevaeh threatened to report the facilities to the state. "You're keeping a dying woman prisoner," she shouted as they turned onto the administration wing, the video cameras catching the entire episode on film. Charging ahead, the orderlies ordered the receptionist to call the police. They had an intruder in the building. The receptionist picked up the phone and started dialing.

When they reached the first floor, Ms. Hebert came running from her office. Upon seeing Nevaeh restrained, she demanded the orderlies unleash her. The orderlies were unfazed by Ms. Hebert's interference, explaining that they'd found Nevaeh harassing the patient in room 29S. Seeing her keycard in the orderly's hand, Ms. Hebert's expression morphed from confusion to concern to anger. She knew that Nevaeh had snagged it from her belt loop.

"What were you doing in Ms. Truehart's room?" Ms. Hebert tersely asked.

Ashamed, Nevaeh hung her head. "I needed to speak with her."

"About?"

"The spell she's under."

The staff smirked at each other, but Ms. Hebert's expression never changed. Even hearing herself say it, Nevaeh realized how unbelievable it sounded. But she couldn't lie to Ms. Hebert. Not after all she'd done for her. Besides, what else could she say? She'd broken her friend's trust. Things between them would never be the same.

"You know about Coup de Poudre?" Everyone turned to see the woman standing directly behind them.

On Ms. Hebert's insistence, the orderlies released Nevaeh into her custody. She instructed them to resume their duties. Nevaeh still couldn't look at her. She'd crumble if she saw Ms. Hebert's disappointment.

Then Ms. Hebert glanced over at the woman. "Nevaeh, this is Ms. Sofie Truehart. Angelique's sister."

Sofie approached them, clutching her handbag. "How do you know about that poison?" she asked Nevaeh.

"Someone used it on my boyfriend," Nevaeh replied, voice shaken.

Ms. Hebert looked between Nevaeh and Sofie, baffled. "What are you two talking about?"

Sofie Truehart stepped forward. "If you could excuse us, Ms. Hebert," she said. "But me and this young lady have something we need to discuss in private. About *my sister.*"

Ms. Hebert left them alone in the lobby. Nevaeh and Sofie fidgeted next to each other on the bench, looking out at the garden, the cypress tree, the same spot Nevaeh had sat with Emery only a few weeks ago when everything was still normal. Now here she was with Angelique's sister watching the rain splash. A complete stranger, but the only person who had any clue what she was going through.

Sofie ran her thumbs along the handle of her handbag. Though she maintained a calm presence, Nevaeh could tell there were a million things running through her mind. They were both struggling to broach the problem before them. It wasn't every day you had to deal with black magic spells.

Finally, Sofie cleared her throat. "My sister spoke to you. I don't know how that's possible. She hasn't spoken anything but that horrible phrase for years."

Nevaeh hadn't given it much thought. "I'm not sure."

"When she spoke to you, I saw a spark of life…" Sofie's voice caught on the last word. She removed a tissue from her bag and pressed it to her eyes. "It was brief, but it was there."

"Who is Mirlande St. Pierre?" The name had rung in Nevaeh's head ever since Angelique screamed it.

"She's a witch who lives out in the Bayou Sauvage," Sofie spat the words out in disdain.

"Why did she do this to your sister?"

"That witch just supplied the potion. It was my brother-in-law, Lyle Allen who done this to Angelique. She and my nephew were going to leave and he decided he couldn't have that. So he found a way to…"

"Control her." Nevaeh thought about her shouting at Angelique to tell her who'd done this to her. "Perhaps that's why your sister talked to me. I demanded an answer."

"I don't understand what you're saying."

"This potion. I think it turns people into some sort of… slave. They can only do what you command. Otherwise, they're…"

"Empty." Sofie squeezed the tissue in her fist. "That's how Lyle convinced my sister to stay."

"What will you do now?"

"There are definitely more answers that are long overdue. I'm sure the police might be interested in them too. Whether they'll believe Angelique, I don't know. But to give my sister some justice, it's worth a shot."

"Why didn't you go to the police about Mirlande St. Pierre?"

"NOPD don't care about what goes on in the bayou. Especially when it has something to do with voodoo."

Even more so than before, Nevaeh felt like she was on her own. If the police wouldn't help, who would? "The poison you mentioned. Coup de Poudre. Is there a cure?"

"If there is, only one person knows, and you can bet she ain't givin' it freely."

"Do you know how I can contact her?"

"You sure you wanna do that? Mirlande St. Pierre ain't someone you wanna be messing with. Trust me, I know…"

"I have to help my boyfriend."

With a deep sigh, Sofie fell silent. From the way she bowed her head, Nevaeh could tell there was something Sofie wanted to share but didn't know if she should. But then, lifting her face, something like awareness bloomed across Sofie's features "You said someone did this to him. Was it a haughty red head?"

"You met Gemma."

"Shit! Honey, I might be partially to blame for what happened." Sofie twisted the handle of her purse. "I knew I shouldn't have said nothing to her, but I was just so mad at the time…"

Touching her arm, Nevaeh assured Sofie it wasn't her fault. There was only one person to blame. And that was Gemma Landry.

Digging in her wallet, Sofie found a card and passed it to Nevaeh. On the card, "Vodou Temple of Bondye" was printed in an old charlotte font, topped by a symbol of a heart and a pyramid. "Isabel Lovelie will take you to Mirande St. Pierre. She's the only one that witch trusts."

"Thank you."

"I just pray I didn't dig your grave too."

As Nevaeh stood to leave, Sofie took her hand. "Please, be careful girl. The witch has caused enough harm. I'd hate for something terrible to happen to you."

Nevaeh promised she would.

21. GEMMA

The following morning, Gemma headed over to Drago's Seafood to have lunch with her mother. She'd called her mother the night before on the pretense of spending some mother-daughter time together. Surprisingly, Mother agreed. Even sounded excited by the proposition. "I feel we have some things we need to discuss," Mallory said. Of course, Mother picked the restaurant, which was fine, considering she was paying. What she didn't know was that Gemma had a discussion topic of her own: getting the money to buy the Carondelet.

On the drive lakeside along I-10, Gemma practiced the speech she was going to give her mother, beseeching her to fork over the money from her inheritance. "Art is a long-term investment, but unlike many of your investments, it doesn't depend on the stock market…"

Gemma had created an entire presentation on her laptop. She'd crunched numbers, taking in the aesthetic value and potential inflation hedge and profit to loss margins based on the location. Designed a spreadsheet of different ways to create revenue including offering home installations, providing decorating consultations to businesses and offices—many of them her mother's friends—and increasing sales commissions. Added in the value of the space itself, a historic building in an up-and-coming neighborhood, knowing full well the old dodger who owned it would sell for the right amount. It was a no-lose situation.

After the disappointing meeting with those two criminals, Camile and Marcel, Gemma had gone home and bandaged the wound on her neck. She was nearly in tears over the way they'd manhandled her. Well, they'd get their comeuppance soon enough. No one treated Gemma Landry like a piece of trash.

She'd tossed the torn check then looked in on Jefferson. The sight of him startled her. Stuck in their darkened bedroom, flies crawling over him, he painted those horrid paintings she couldn't look at without the graze of ghostly fingers sliding down her spine. Sometimes Gemma swore she saw shadows swirling around Jefferson; heard whispers coming from behind the closed door. Whispers from voices that were not Jefferson. To block the sounds, she left the TV on all day. With each passing day, it felt more and more like her home was a haunted house. And not the kind tour guides took gullible tourists to in the Quarter. The real deal.

The paintings too seemed to come alive on the canvas, as if by painting them, Jefferson had brought his torment to life. The last time she checked in on him, bringing him a Po-Boy from Adam's Street Grocery, the skeleton man he was painting glanced over at her, startling her so badly, she dropped the sandwich on the floor and ran out of the room. As she left the house, grabbing her coat and keys, a guttural chuckle followed her out the door.

Gemma no longer knew if she could count on Jefferson. He'd already stained his reputation with his sideshow performance at the viewing. And only the criminally insane would buy the horrors he was creating. Who else would want those nightmares on their walls?

Which was why she needed the money to kick Camile out of business. If things didn't work out with Jefferson—and that seemed a likely possibility—at least she'd have the gallery to fall back on. She could always find other artists. But there was only one Carondelet.

Above the doorway of the cement block building, a mammoth lobster smiled down upon the parking lot, the Drago logo written in bold black lettering above its massive pinchers. Gemma hoped Mother was in the same cheerful mood, and that somehow the seafood restaurant's mascot heeded a good omen. Laptop tucked beneath her arm, she entered the swinging glass doors.

Ignoring the cheerful welcome from the host at the front door, Gemma darted into the dining room, but screeched to a halt on the tile floor when she saw her mother seated at a big round table in the center of the brightly lit room, surrounded by members of the Women's Republican Club of New Orleans, a brood of stern-faced women who were looking for any reason to complain to the server about the plates of charbroiled oysters and Fleur de Lis Shrimp. Flashing her pearly smile, Mother spoke exuberantly about the history of the club and its part in electing reliable officials who exemplified their conservative values. "People who put God and family first," Mallory Landry proclaimed, though Gemma knew those were the last things her mother ever put first. Obviously, since she'd tricked Gemma into attending this meeting on the pretense of a mother-daughter luncheon. The women around the table clapped, more impressed by the speech than by the portions of aioli tuna. If only they knew the truth about Mallory Landry.

Gemma crossed the tightly packed dining area, heels clacking across the tile floor. Soon as she passed the open kitchen, the flames from the grills as hot as her desire to have this conversation over with, her mother caught sight of her, and stopped speaking as her jaw dropped mid-sentence.

"Hello, Mother. I didn't know we'd have company."

Mother rose from her chair on jittery legs, dropped her fork into the leaves of her house salad, and stumbled around the table. The rest of the club members followed her gaze. They too paled as if they'd suddenly been struck with a bad case of food poisoning.

Gemma smiled, a slight jolt of pain from her split lip. "Good morning, ladies," she said. "How's the grub? Good I hear. Now, where's my seat?"

The members pushed their plates away. One of the ladies

even tried to conspicuously spit a gator nugget into her napkin.

Mallory hugged Gemma, almost maternally. Stepping away quickly, a smile plastered on her face, she spoke in an artificially cheery voice to the table. "Well, look who finally made it. This is my daughter…Gemma. "

"I didn't know we'd have an audience. I need to speak with you privately."

"Gemma, darling, let's not be rude to our guests. Can't it wait until later?"

"It's important."

Mother turned toward her underlings and gave them her winningest apology. "Excuse me, ladies, I need to speak with my daughter momentarily. As I was saying, family first. But we'll be right back. You enjoy the food and company."

As Gemma was ushered toward the restrooms, the members began murmuring behind their backs.

Mother pushed through the door and checked the stalls to make sure no one was inside. God forbid anyone hear her being uncivilized. Might ruin her preciously sculpted reputation.

Finally, her mother concentrated her attention on Gemma. "What's wrong with you? Being so unladylike."

"I'm sorry, but it's really important I speak to you."

"That's not what I'm talking about."

What was she talking about? "What *are* you talking about?"

"Have you seen yourself lately?"

Gemma glanced at her reflection. "Okay, so I didn't have time to do my hair, and threw it into a bun. So what?"

Mother pulled off Gemma's sunglasses, spun her by the shoulders, and forced her to look at herself in the mirror. A yellowing bruise colored her eye and a cut split her lip and a spot of blood had dried into a rust-colored splotch on the bandage on her neck. "Who did this to you?" Mother asked with genuine compassion in her voice.

It surprised Gemma.

"Doesn't matter."

"Is it that boy you're seeing? Because if it is…"

"No, Mother. Can I please speak with you? It's about the gallery I mentioned before." Gemma opened her laptop. "Now I've been crunching some numbers and…"

"Sweetheart." Mother pushed a loose strand of hair from Gemma's face. "Are you taking drugs?"

"What?" Had she really asked her that? "No! Why would you think that?"

Mallory stalled, choosing her words carefully. "You seem, well, unstable lately. Listen, there's no shame in admitting you have a drug problem. Your Uncle Tim did, and we got him help. We could do the same for you…"

"Mommy!" Gemma stomped her heel. "I'm not on drugs! I really think buying this gallery is a great investment. Now if you can take a look at this chart." She opened the Excel spreadsheet. "You'll see that the average profit margin…" But her mother was no longer listening. She'd drifted into her own thoughts, rubbing a thumb back and forth on her shoulder, a tic she had whenever she needed to make a hard decision.

"Are you listening to me?"

"I'm worried about you."

"I'm fine."

"You're not fine. You show up here looking like a cat after an alley fight. You're dating some loser artist who for all I know is beating you…"

"He's not beating me."

"Going on about that gallery that I've told you a thousand times isn't worth burning money…"

"How do you know?"

"Because none of them ever last." Mallory raised her voice loud enough Gemma was certain she could be heard outside.

Gemma slammed her laptop closed. "You and Daddy never care about my interests," she said, raising her voice to match her mother's.

"We're worried you're throwing your life away."

"They're the ones who did this to me." Gemma tore the bandage off the cut on her neck.

Mother grimaced at the sight of the wound. "Who did this to you, sweetheart?" She sounded on the verge of breaking into tears.

The door opened and a businesswoman walked in. She smiled at them before locking herself in the stall. Gemma lowered her voice, but there was still bite to her words. "Camile and her boy, Marcel. They held a knife to my throat."

"Why would they do that to you?"

"They know I'm taking their gallery. I've already spoken to the landlord. I just need some of my inheritance…"

"No!"

The word hit with finality. "What do you mean…*no?*"

The toilet flushed. The woman came out of the stall and washed her hands. Did her best to pretend she hadn't overheard the two of them arguing. Gemma glared at her mother, hardly able to hold back her rage. Mallory met Gemma's stony gaze with one of her own. She waited until the woman left and made sure no one else was about to enter.

Mother reached for Gemma's hand, but she pulled it away. "I don't think you should be mixing with this crowd."

"I'm not a teenager anymore. I can take care of myself."

"No dear, you can't. Your dad and I thought if we loaned you the property on Prytania you'd finally start learning some responsibility. Instead, you leave the upstairs unrented and gallivant around the city with a bunch of hoodlums. Living out a wild fantasy about being an artist. Coming to me with a black eye and a busted lip and a cut on your neck to beg money for some failing gallery. Can you understand why Daddy and I are worried?"

"You have no need to worry. I'm fine."

Mother put her hand on Gemma's shoulder. "Why don't you come home for a while? We can talk then."

For a moment, Gemma considered it. She could put all of this behind her. Move on and do something else. But that would be giving up. That would be letting Camile and Marcel win.

Once again, Gemma cracked open the laptop. "If you'll take a look at the numbers…"

Her mother gently shut the lid. "Honey, sweetie, what in heaven's name do you know about running an art gallery?"

Wow, she might as well have slapped her. It would've hurt less. "I know a lot about running a gallery…"

"No, you don't. Otherwise, you'd give up on this ridiculous dream and begin living in reality. Which is why I think it's best if you came home. You could start helping out with my charities…"

"You'd like that, wouldn't you? Having me under your thumb again. Well, you can forget it! You don't want to give me my inheritance. Fine! You want to kick me out of that house, so you and daddy can sell it. Fine too! You don't want to help me with the gallery. Fuck it! I don't need you! I'll take care of it myself."

"Gemma!" Mallory called out to her as Gemma burst through the bathroom door, nearly knocking down one of the ladies from the meeting, who chirped at her in surprise. Mallory chased after Gemma, calling for her to come back. "Let's talk this out. I just want what's best for you."

How the hell did her mother know what was best for her?

As she strode across the lot to her car, cursing her mother every foul name in the dictionary, tremors of anger juddered through Gemma's entire body. Now she knew. *Everyone* was against her. Even her own family. Well, she'd show every last goddamn one of them. At any cost.

22. JEFFERSON

Maybe he'd watched a video online, or heard it off some weird podcast, but the ghostly shadows and nightly visits from the cigar smoking ghoul reminded Jefferson of stories from random people about their near-death experiences. A man who'd died in a tragic car crash in Kentucky watched as paramedics hurried to resuscitate his body, his head split open from where it smashed through the windshield. He said he'd never believed in spirits until he was hovering above the scene of the accident for a brief few seconds before the medics revived him. At that moment, it was like something had grabbed him by the legs and pulled him inside of his body. And for a second, he saw himself in two places, lying on the ground and floating in the air.

Another woman who almost died in childbirth listened to her baby's cries while invisible hands sunk her into a watery abyss that filled her lungs and stole her breath before she was allowed to surface for air. A professor of theology described being torn apart by gray human-like creatures with gnashing teeth and claws during a surgery to repair a ruptured intestine.

There were, of course, those who spoke of seeing tunnels of light or were sung to by a choir of angels or were led down a path by their deceased loved ones.

A few weeks ago, Jefferson would've thought it was all B.S. But looking at the paintings scattered around the room—an endless black circle, shadows peeling from the walls into the light shining from the bedroom window, a skeleton man smoking a cigar in a hazy mist—he couldn't say for sure whether it was true or not. Was this all a hallucination or was it proof of some sort of Purgatory? Jefferson didn't know anymore. What would people think if he could tell them his story? Would they call him a liar? A fraud? Could he blame them? There was a part of him that truly believed he'd lost his mind. It was the most rational explanation.

On the easel in front of Jefferson, a painting of a woman lit in a shadowy doorway of a tin roofed hut in the bayou beckoned him with a wave of her longish fingers. A gator head with glowing eyes menaced from the wall above her head. Flaming orbs drifted in the air, reflecting in the green swamp water lapping at the sagging wood porch. Fog rolled in through the branches of the mossy cypress. The harrowing cries of loons screeched inside Jefferson's head. A pirogue floated near the dock, where a dark figure stood hidden within the gloom. All this a scene which had come to him in a dream.

Jefferson didn't remember painting the piece. Of course, he didn't remember painting any of them. While he drifted between reality and whatever hellish landscape resurrected before his eyes, his hands performed the work Gemma instructed them to do. But these weren't the paintings she wanted. She wanted pieces like he'd created for Nevaeh. Not these atrocities. These paintings terrified Gemma. He'd seen the fear when she peeked in on his progress yesterday. Before she hurried from the house and drove away.

Perhaps, Gemma could no longer stand the sight of him. In the mirror, his reflection revealed the horror Jefferson had become. This pitiful creature of seeping oozy flesh.

Jefferson didn't want to die. He'd done so little in his 25 years. He'd never been anywhere outside the Gulf. Never seen the Statue of Liberty or the Louvre. Never hiked in the Grand Canyon or sailed in a boat across the ocean. Never ridden a motorcycle or jumped from a plane. He'd never let his folks know how much they meant to him. How he appreciated how hard they worked to pay his college tuition. How he was glad they accepted him for who he was. Were always proud of him. He wished he could speak to them now, but Gemma would never allow it. Instead, she put the words in his mouth. Told him what to say to his parents. Created a false belief that everything was fantastic. His art was taking off so much that he had so much to do. Was just tired from all the success, that was all. And what reason would his folks have to suspect any different? This was their son they were talking to. Not an imposter.

She forced him to quit his job. The boss really laid into him about not showing up for a few days only to walk away without notice. He might not have loved the work, but they'd treated him well. It infuriated him to be a bystander while Gemma dismantled his entire life in a matter of weeks.

But his biggest regret was never having the guts to tell Nevaeh he was in love with her. How many opportunities had he allowed to pass without saying those words?

On a chilly, overcast afternoon, Nevaeh had called Jefferson asking for a favor. She wouldn't specify what she needed, but from the tremor in her voice he knew it was important. At the time, they'd just started hanging out again, and he found himself thinking about her more and more, longing for the next time they could see each other between long stretches of separation, so when she'd begged him to accompany her to Westwego he hopped in his van after work and raced to her place, telling Gemma that he was finishing a job and would be late getting home.

"Where are we going?" Jefferson asked her.

Without looking in his direction, she responded, "To the place I grew up."

The entire thirty-minute drive from the Vieux Carré to Westwego, Nevaeh hardly spoke, nodding her head and making little grunting noises of agreement while Jefferson babbled about random nonsense to fill the dead air. He tried to pry from her the secret of their destination, but Nevaeh's lips were sealed as tightly as a vault. Though he had no idea what they were doing, Jefferson decided if she wanted him to come along that was enough justification for him to be there. They spent the last portion of the ride passing by the border of transmission towers dividing the communities that encompassed the Jefferson Parish—a name they'd laughed about on the way home.

After pulling off the Westbank Expressway, they ended up driving down a narrow road through a crowded residential area of modular homes. On the corner of Avenue A and 6th Street, Nevaeh directed him to pull into an empty lot on the side of a church. A marble plaque read, The Light of the Sacrificial Lamb. The building looked more like a government office than a place of worship. The center rose to a triangle, adorned by a cross, the only symbol identifying the property for what it was.

Turning off the ignition, Jefferson asked, "You're not trying to convert me, are you?"

Nevaeh didn't even crack a smile at his sad attempt at a joke. "I just have a question for God," she said, opening her door and jumping out. She didn't wait for Jefferson, strolling around to the front and slipping inside before he had a chance to respond.

The chapel was nothing more than a high school-size auditorium of cushioned seats encircling a waist-high stage. A statue of Christ's crucifixion hung on the wall behind a podium and a makeshift altar. The faint echo of a choir sung a psalm of praise. He thought Nevaeh must've heard it too. They both looked around for where the sound was coming from, but the chapel was empty. Somewhere in the vicinity, a vacuum whirred, a janitor completing his duties.

Nevaeh took a seat. Not knowing what else to do, Jefferson sat next to her. They stayed like that for some time, her communing silently with the holy relic, he shifting uncomfortably, unsure if he should fold his hands or close his eyes and say the one short prayer he sort-of remembered. But Nevaeh wasn't doing any of that. She met the Lord's sorrowful gaze with this look on her face like she wanted to fight him—and maybe she did. From the few things she'd said about her upbringing, it didn't sound like she had the happiest of childhoods. And if this was the place she grew up, then he expected she had every reason to be angry.

"Did God talk to you yet?" Jefferson asked after enough time had gone by. Churches had always given him the creeps. He hated being there any longer than he had to.

Nevaeh shook her head. "I wasn't expecting him to."

"Then why did we come all the way out here?"

"I don't want to be afraid anymore."

"Do you really think a man named Jesus died for our sins?" Jefferson asked out of the blue. He didn't know what had prompted him to ask such a serious question. Being someone who wasn't raised religious, it wasn't something he'd given much thought about. But sitting there, he suddenly feared for his soul.

Nevaeh must've known from his tone that he was being sincere because she didn't hesitate to answer. "I don't know. I just know when I look back, I don't think any of it matters."

"Are you saying there's no such thing as Heaven or Hell?"

Pulling back her sleeve, Nevaeh traced the scars on her

arms. "When I was lying in the bathtub, bleeding to death, you know what I felt? Only cold and dark."

"Were you afraid?" Jefferson had asked her.

"How can you be afraid when the pain's finally over?"

Jefferson touched Nevaeh's arm. It felt warm and pulsated with life. Then she leaned in, kissed him long and softly on the lips. Her initiative took him by surprise—he had hoped but not expected for them ever to get together—but he soon melted into her tenderness. For a moment, Jefferson forgot where they were.

N evaeh's words rang true in Jefferson's head as his brush finished the painting. There was nothing but cold and darkness in this place between life and death. How he wished for this nightmare to end. The torment he suffered was slow and excruciating.

But the real nightmare was being under Gemma's control. Painting his own insanity.

If she allowed him to speak, he would've begged Gemma to bury him in the bayou, like she threatened to do. Let the gators gnash him to shreds. Devour every last bit until nothing remained. But would that finally put an end to him? Or would he keep existing? A ghost haunted by a death it would never receive. A fate worse than dying.

After she returned home from her visit to the Carondelet, Gemma spent the entire night talking and crying and laughing to herself. Slapping her own face. Calling herself awful names.

Planning her revenge against Camile and Marcel. Then she settled down. Convinced herself she could persuade her mother to give her the money to buy the gallery out from under Camile. She'd spent the morning practicing her speech in the hallway mirror. It was disturbing the lengths she was willing to go to get what she wanted. Jefferson wondered if she was always this demented or had she slipped over the edge.

Satisfied she'd come to a decision, she'd washed, put on some makeup, and dressed in a fresh outfit. Jefferson hadn't seen Gemma this happy since his first few days of imprisonment. Back when she still derived pleasure from him. Before the sight of him disgusted her.

The doorbell rang. After a long stretch of silence, it rang again and again and again. Then whoever stood outside knocked. Knocked harder. Banged until he thought they'd break the door down. Jefferson tried to yell he was trapped inside, but his cries went unheard by anyone but himself. His lips and tongue no longer had the power of words.

A muffled voice called Gemma's name. A woman's voice. One he recognized. Then she said his name.

23. NEVAEH

It came as no surprise that Gemma lived in an antebellum house that looked like it'd been craned straight from the plantation and cemented in the Garden District. A black wrought iron fence with spiked tips warned trespassers to keep away. A finely kept lawn and sculptured garden sprouted from the blood of the help's callused hands. Standing tall atop carved quoins, the Italianate's façade arched head glared down at those passing on the sidewalk from beneath the ornate hood moldings. A veranda rested on the shoulders of decorative columns and the walls blushed a rosy pink, but behind the laced curtains the rooms kept secrets of a dark nature. Maybe it was the storm stirring her imagination, but it looked as if shadows danced around inside.

"You sure you want to do this?" Camile asked Nevaeh over the headrest of the passenger's seat.

"I'm telling you, old girl gone crazy." Marcel tapped his fingers on the steering wheel. "Nothing telling what she'll do."

"Maybe you shouldn't have stuck a knife to her throat," Nevaeh said from the backseat.

Both Camile and Marcel fell quiet. They may have been wrong to threaten Gemma, but they weren't wrong about this. Nevaeh wasn't sure she wanted to face Gemma either, but she didn't have a choice. Not after what she'd seen.

After Nevaeh had left Tree of Life the previous day, she'd gone over to Jefferson's studio, hoping to find him there. Thankfully he'd given her a spare key. The moment she opened the door she knew something was wrong. Flies swarmed around the studio like they had in Angelique's room. A horrid stench of rotting meat made her stomach curl. Nevaeh had to cover her nose to stop from vomiting while she opened the windows. On an easel was a canvas smothered in a circle of black paint. It appeared to swirl like a whirlpool, threatening to pull her in. Shadows in the corners seeped across the walls and devoured the light coming in from the windows. A cold darkness crawled along her skin and beneath her clothes. The air got thick, and she struggled to breathe. Nevaeh knew she had to get out of there, but it was like something had a hold of her. She pressed the teeth of the key hard enough against her palm for the pain to snap her from the trance. Then she ran from the studio, not looking back. Only once she reached the corner of Japonica and St. Claude was she able to catch her breath.

This morning, after a fitful night's sleep, Nevaeh had gone straight to the Carondelet and spoken with Camile and Marcel. She told them what she found at the studio, unable to stop the shaking in her voice. They brought her a cup of hot tea, sat her on the office couch, and let her explain all she knew about Jefferson's condition. She could tell they were struggling to believe her—could she blame them?—but they understood that Jefferson was in danger. Gemma had become unhinged. Which was why they were reluctant to tell Nevaeh where she lived. But in the end, she convinced them to take her.

Nevaeh opened the car door and stepped into the street. "I'll be right back."

"She gives you any problems, holler. We got your back," Camile said, leaning over Marcel.

Marcel dug his hand into his coat pocket. "You sure you don't want my knife? She may not look it, but Gemma's a feisty cat."

"I'm not going to stab her."

"Suit yourself."

Moving from behind the live oak, Nevaeh pulled her hood over her head, as much to keep the rain off her face as to hide her identity. She looked for oncoming traffic. There wasn't anyone out and about on the brick sidewalks, but a few cars hugged the curb. A couple blocks away, beneath the dreary turbid skies, the moss-stained brick walls of Lafayette Cemetery coiled an entire city block. The tops of the stone tombs peered above the ledge like pale spectral faces. The memory of Jefferson's studio sent a shiver along her spine.

Nevaeh trembled: grinded her teeth. She wondered if Gemma's family owned a mausoleum. Was that where she buried Jefferson? Allowed death to fester in his heart? Fed his soul to the rats and maggots? Was there a part of Jefferson that remained behind the cemetery walls?

Nevaeh slipped through the gate, calmly covered the short distance of the walkway, hopped up the concrete steps onto the porch, and rang the bell. She tapped her foot impatiently while listening to the raindrops tapping on the eaves. A car whooshed by, spraying a wave onto the sidewalk. Nevaeh rang the bell again. She squinted through the glass, but there was no movement. Nothing she could see anyway.

She peered into the big bay window. Through the lace curtains, the front room appeared staged, a showroom. An accent mirror above the fireplace reflected her own shadowy figure. Two brass candelabras pillared each side of the mantle. One of Jefferson's paintings hung on the blue wall. She recognized his techniques, the grattage in the paint to create the movement of the Mississippi River, the linear perspective of a steamboat giving the illusion of depth, as if it stretched far into the distance, the dreamy quality of the crescent-shape of the west riverside mirroring the crescent moon in the sky. Would he ever be able to create anything as beautiful again? Or had Gemma stolen his artistic spirit too?

Nevaeh pressed the bell. Let it ring long and loud. It echoed throughout the emptiness of the house. Maybe no one was home. It was possible. But she couldn't allow herself to give in yet. Nevaeh knocked and shouted for Gemma to open the door. Still, nobody answered. She paced the porch. The tombs in Lafayette Cemetery and the shadows flittering behind the locked door haunted her mind. What if she was too late?

She banged her fists against the door until her knuckles

ached. Shouted for Gemma to let her in. She didn't care if the neighbors heard. Let them call the police. She'd demand they bust in. At least then Jefferson would get the help he needed.

"Jefferson!"

What sounded like a low moan emanated from inside the house. It could've been the old house, groaning in the rain. She called his name again. Another moan. This time it was obviously human. From its muted tone she guessed it was coming from deeper within.

Nevaeh grabbed the baroque handle and gave it a turn, but it wouldn't budge. Thought about putting her shoulder into it, but that wouldn't do anything but hurt her arm. The door was too strong. There had to be another way in.

After ensuring no one was watching, Nevaeh dropped from the porch and crept along the side of the house, using the fence as cover. The rain had lightened, a soft patter against her hood. The muddy grass squished underfoot. She had to step carefully not to slip. When she reached the second set of windows, she stood on the spigot, grabbed the sill, and lifted herself to peek in. What she saw nearly caused her to lose her balance.

Behind the thin white curtains, Nevaeh saw Jefferson standing in front of an easel, dressed in the blue suit from the viewing, now paint splattered. Bruises the same hue marred his skin. Flies swarmed the room, vibrating with their insidious buzzing. They crawled over his face and down into his collar. Paintbrush in hand, he worked on a canvas. Nevaeh was afraid to see what he was painting.

Seeing Jefferson like this brought tears to Nevaeh's eyes. A breath escaped in hitching sobs. A white-hot fire spread from her heart outward. Getting a hold of herself, Nevaeh wiped the tears from her cheeks. Crying wasn't going to do Jefferson any good. She tapped on the window and called his name. His cloudy eyes drifted in her direction, the irises flushing with recognition to their normal deep hue.

Pushing on the lift, the window rattled open an inch, but not wide enough for Nevaeh to squeeze through.

"Jefferson, I need you to open the window."

He just kept painting as if he hadn't heard her.

Frustrated, Nevaeh pushed on the window, but it refused to budge even a little. Her feet slipped from the spigot. The copper thread scraped the flesh on her ankle raw. Blood seeped to the surface. Cursing, she scrambled back onto the slick spigot, tears of frustration welling her eyes. Then she remembered how she'd gotten Angelique to speak.

"Jefferson, open the window," Nevaeh demanded.

Jefferson came over to the window and shoved it upward so hard he damn near splintered the rail. Nevaeh had considered asking him to help her in, but after seeing what he did to the window, she decided she enjoyed having her arms in their sockets. She clutched onto the sill, and hauled herself through the curtains over to the other side.

As soon as she got on her feet, Nevaeh threw her arms around Jefferson's neck and hugged him tightly. She pressed her hand on his cool cheek. Wondered what he was thinking behind those blank eyes. "Do you know who I am?" she asked in a stern voice.

Jefferson's lips parted slightly. He exhaled the word, "yes."

"Who am I?"

Somewhere deep within, a part of him emerged from his cocoon. A light thumping of the pulse in his neck beat beneath her fingertips. "Nevaeh," he uttered, tearfully.

Once again, Nevaeh hugged him, her tears soaking into the wool of his jacket.

Along the wall were several paintings, each more disturbing than the next. Swirls of black. Agonized faces emerging from the maelstrom. On the easel was a portrait of a man in a top hat and coat, his skeletal face ending in a maleficent grin.

"Where did you see this?" she asked him, pointing at the painting

"In my dreams."

Nevaeh took Jefferson's paint-crusted hands. "What did Gemma do to you?"

Jefferson's entire body stiffened. His teeth clamped together, jaw muscles strained as if he was battling with his body to speak.

"What did she do, Jefferson?" she begged him. "You have to tell me."

"Poisoned…me."

"With what?"

"Don't…know."

What was it Angelique had called it? "Coup de Poudre?"

"Don't…know," his voice trembled.

"Relax, Jefferson."

His body sagged limp and he collapsed on top of her. Nevaeh pressed his cold hand to her lips. Kissed his knuckles.

A pang of guilt spread through Nevaeh, sickening her head and heart with its vile toxins. Her mind took her back to their last night together, waiting at the bus stop at St. Claude. She was unable to look at Jefferson in fear she'd say something she'd regret. His words slid off her like the raindrops on her raincoat were now. The voice in her head had shouted at her to run away and not look back. Leave Jefferson standing there with his false promises. And she almost had.

This might be the last chance she had to confess everything she'd wanted to tell him for so long. Finally get it all off her chest. She just hoped a part of him was alive enough to remember.

"A few weeks ago, I thought about breaking up with you. I thought you were too chickenshit to split with Gemma. Looking back at it now, maybe you had a good reason to be frightened, but I didn't know that then. The way I saw it, as long as she kept booking you shows, making things happen for you, you'd never leave. I know how much your art means to you. And what did I have to offer? Nothing that compared to what Gemma was offering. Which was what really cut me deep. Deeper than the cuts on my wrists. Because I'd never been as vulnerable with anyone as I had with you."

Nevaeh felt a light pressure on her hand. Jefferson had squeezed it. There was some life in him after all. The slight sentiment encouraged Nevaeh to continue.

"Do you remember the first time you saw my photography in class? You were captivated by my picture "The Fire Rose.""

You asked me who'd broken my heart. I had to correct you as usual, of course. Explain that in Greek Mythology, fire symbolizes the Goddess of Chaos. On the other hand, a rose represents love and devotion, but is also symbolic of a carrier of secrets. Just like me. You said that, in some way or another, the photo characterized us all, which was maybe what you found so striking about the image."

"I knew you were flirting with me, and though I never would've admitted it then, I was flattered. You were the first boy to take an interest in me. But I was scared to let you get close. Scared what would happen if my folks found out I was hanging with a boy. Which was why I initially rejected your invite to coffee. But to your credit, you persisted, and eventually convinced me to agree. I'm glad now that I did. You bought coffees and we took a walk along the river and you told me damn near your entire history. It'd be months before I'd tell you mine. But you were patient. I've always admired that about you."

A single tear slid along Jefferson's cheek. Nevaeh wiped it away then let her hand rest there, hoping to spread the heat from her skin into his cold body.

"I was so frightened the first time I was naked in front of you. You tried to undress me, but I stopped you. You apologized, of course, but it wasn't your fault. You were doing everything right. I decided to trust you like I'd never trusted anyone before. I showed you my scars. And you traced them with your fingers. Then you kissed them. For the first time ever, I felt beautiful."

Nevaeh kissed the bruises on his face. Once again, she felt the pressure of Jefferson squeezing her hand. It may have been all he could do, but Nevaeh was happy to know he was listening. The gesture made her smile.

Nevaeh's smile turned to tears, her voice cracking with guilt. "The reason I tried to commit suicide was my parents saw us walking from school together. They'd come to pick me up for a church fundraiser I'd forgotten about. When I got home, they were waiting for me in the living room. They made me kneel on the floor and beg God for forgiveness for my sinful deeds. My daddy beat my ass with a switch until I couldn't sit down. They made me promise that I'd drop out of the school and never see you again. I was too young and scared to tell them no. That's why I did what they asked. But as the weeks went by, I felt lonely and trapped in a world I couldn't escape. Then one night, I'd had enough. I didn't see any way I could ever be happy, so I locked myself in the bathroom, and…"

"Even after I got released from the hospital, I never thought I'd see you again. I always hoped I would. But I didn't even know if you were still in town. Which was why I was ecstatic the day I saw you in Jackson Square. You're the only real true friend I've ever had. The only person I've ever loved."

Nevaeh cleared her throat. "I pushed you into ending things with Gemma. I was tired of sneaking around. Tired of you going home to her, where you'd slip beneath the covers of the bed you shared, just after you slipped out of mine. Tired of wondering whether or not I could trust you. Tired of being frightened you were using me. Frightened that in the end you'd hurt me. But I should've known something was wrong. Known you were scared. I should've asked you to stay with me. I'm so sorry."

Jefferson's lips moved and words mumbled from his mouth. Nevaeh asked him to repeat what he said and leaned her ear close. "I…am….sorry….toooo."

Nevaeh laughed, partially from joy, partially from sadness. She wished she had the power to take away his agony. But only one person had that power. Nevaeh looked at the painting of the witch standing in the doorway of her hut in the bayou.

Taking Jefferson by the hands, Nevaeh used all her strength to tug him toward the window. "Get up. You're coming with me. I don't care what we have to do, we're going to find this witch and get you a cure. Then we're leaving this place behind. The two of us."

From the front of the house, keys rattled in the lock. The door creaked open. Gemma's voice echoed down the hallway. "Jefferson, sweetheart, guess who's home? And she's had a hell of a morning."

Shit!

Jefferson glanced toward the open window. Nevaeh didn't want to leave him. She was afraid of what that crazy bitch might do. "Jefferson, we have to go," Nevaeh pulled on his arm, but he wouldn't budge.

Gemma dropped something heavy on the floor, all the while whistling an annoying jolly tune. What in the world did she have to be so happy about? But the real question was: Did Nevaeh want to know?

"Hey," a voice called from outside the window. Nevaeh peered at Marcel standing at the side of the house, waving at her to move. "Come on, girl."

Nevaeh tried to pull Jefferson, but his body was stiff and heavy as a statue.

Gemma's footsteps approached from down the hall.

"Please, Jefferson, come with me. I love you."

Nevaeh kissed him on the lips. But he couldn't leave. Fear had him paralyzed. Not fear for himself. Fear for her.

Jefferson was right. She wasn't any good to him without an antidote. And definitely not if she was dead. She promised Jefferson she'd be back for him. After she found Mirlande St. Pierre.

She climbed out the window just as Gemma reached the closed bedroom door, singing Jefferson's name.

24. GEMMA

Gemma waited for Jefferson's response, but there was only silence beneath the buzz of insect activity. Flies crawled on the windowsills and the mantel and swarmed the lamps. The stench of shit and decay mingled beneath the lemony fragrance of air freshener.

Breathing through her mouth, Gemma put down the bag of supplies and canvas she'd bought at Mo's Art Supply. Shooed the bugs away then slipped off her damp coat, her arms getting stuck in the sleeves, before she finally managed to pull it off over her head, whipping it onto the floor as if it had been the one who'd attacked her. She kicked the coat in the air and snagged it by the collar, wrapping it into a tight ball and squeezing the damp nylon until it crinkled. Then shoved her face in it, muffling the scream burning her lungs.

What was she going to do now?

Without the money from her inheritance, Gemma could forget about purchasing the Carondelet. How could her mother be so goddamn selfish? She was her daughter, for God's sake. Wasn't that worth something? But she shouldn't have been surprised. Mommy had never had her best interests in mind. Only her own.

What do you know about running a gallery? Those words burrowed beneath Gemma's skin like chiggers.

In the hall mirror, Gemma caught her reflection. What a goddamn mess. Strands of hair untangled from her bun into knotted strips. Purple rivers of eyeshadow spilled down her cheeks from the yellowish half-moon shining beneath her left eye. Dried blood crusted from her swollen bottom lip. Blood stained her collar and had dried on her neck where the blade nicked the flesh. The cut was only as long as a bobby pin but deep enough to sting.

Gemma made a promise to rip Marcel's goddamn esophagus from his throat and wear it as a necklace. As for Camile, she was going to beat the queen of the art scene's pretty face into a Kaminsky smear.

Muscles relaxing, Gemma rolled the knots in her shoulders loose and cracked her spine. She unfurled her coat, smoothed the wrinkles, and hung it up in the closet. Pulled off her boots and placed them next to her assortment of shoes on the floor.

Carrying her things, Gemma strolled down the hall, her off key whistling echoing back to her. She placed her bags of goods outside the door of the bedroom. She wanted the gifts to be a surprise.

Gemma opened the door. Jefferson stood in front of his easel where she'd left him since the previous night. Flies swarmed his body. With his skin colored a shade of twilight, he reminded Gemma of Francis Bacon's *Portrait of Pope Innocent X*.

"My God, love, you look truly terrible. We're going to have to clean you up before the big opening. Can't have everyone thinking you arose from the dead."

Jefferson didn't reply. That was what she liked best about him. He always listened.

"I missed you," she said, brushing sweat from his slick forehead.

"I always knew one day that son-of-a-bitch Marcel would try to ruin me. I did blacklist his name in this town, after all." Gemma smirked at the thought. "Not that he didn't deserve it. Those nasty things he'd said about the community. And they were nasty, believe me. The problem with Marcel is he never respected anyone. Loved himself, but anyone else…So what if I was the one who posted that stuff on social media. He'd said it, I just made it public."

Gemma ambled over to the dresser. She opened her makeup kit and camouflaged her bruises with concealer, dabbed her lip with antiseptic cream then covered the injury with lipstick. Already she was starting to feel better.

"But Camile. I never thought she'd stab me in the back. After all I did for her, saving her gallery from going under during the pandemic. She couldn't sell a goddamn Picasso even if it was authentic. That's why the collectors pulled out on us. Not because of a little pre-opening drama. Hell, if that were true no painter would succeed. No, they pulled out because they know Camile's all talk."

Gemma looked at the paintings Jefferson had completed. She picked up the one with the silhouette of the witch glowing inside her hut. Even within shadow, Gemma could picture Mirlande St. Pierre's wild hair and savage beauty and penetrating eyes. Picture her feeding that disgusting bird pieces of dehydrated tongue; it gobbling the dry hunks with relish. Heard the screech of the owl from the branches of the cypress. Smelled the rot and decay. "That hungry swamp swallowed many a lost soul," the witch said.

Hands shaking, Gemma placed the painting on the floor, facing away from her. She did the same with the others. She could no longer look at them. No longer had the courage to face what was eating away at Jefferson.

Still, there might be a way of spinning this tragedy into profit. For isn't madness the sister of genius? Agnes Martin suffered schizophrenia. Munch was terrified of death. Van Gough cut off his fucking ear. But Jefferson. He'd seen beyond death. What was more marketable than that?

Gemma smiled wide, lipstick staining her teeth. It looked like she'd bitten into a chunk of flesh.

Over her shoulder, Jefferson continued his silent vigil. For a moment, Gemma thought his eyes darted toward the window, but when she followed his gaze, she didn't see anything unusual. Just the curtains blowing slightly in the breeze. When she looked at him again, Jefferson was staring straight forward. Had it all been in her imagination? Was her mind beginning to slip too? It wouldn't surprise her after the stressful week she'd had.

Gemma placed Jefferson's fingers on the cut on her neck. Pressed down hard until it stung. Until blood leaked from the wound like a cracked faucet. She grimaced, holding back tears. "Feel what those bastards did to me, baby? Probably would've slit my throat if I hadn't begged for my life. Filled my pockets with stones and threw me in the bayou for alligator meat." She entreated Jefferson to kiss the wound and make it better. He pressed his lips to the tiny gash. She closed her eyes with pleasure. "They would've killed me if I hadn't run. I'm sure of it."

An image of Camile Davies hovering above her, eclipsing her in shadow, slicing her sharply filed fingernail down her cheek, ate away at Gemma like maggots. Camile enjoyed every moment of watching her squirm, eyeing Gemma with that wicked smirk, reeling in pleasure at having the upper hand.

With a sob, Gemma rested her head on his chest, and listened to the faint beat of his heart. She burst into laughter that flowed into tears, dampening Jefferson's shirt. "They're going to ruin me," she said. "Which is why I need your help to put things right. You're the only person I trust."

Gemma removed Jefferson's jacket and threw it on the floor. Grasped the placket of his shirt and ripped the buttons and slid it off his shoulders. "Then afterwards we can go to Vienna or Florence or Paris. Just as we've always talked about. Get away from this horrible place and its horrible people. Just the two of us." She ran her fingers across his yellowed skin, tracing the bruises that seeped through like red wine soaked in a paper towel. "If you can hold it together long enough."

Gemma gazed into Jefferson's pale eyes. Placed her hands on his cold cheeks. "Tell me you'd never hurt me."

"I'd never hurt you."

His proclamation of love brought a smile to Gemma's face. She loved the way Jefferson looked at her. The same way she imagined he looked at something he was dying to capture on canvas. "You're the only person who loves me. The only person who cares. Which is why I brought you something special." She grazed his cheek with her thumb. "Stay right there. I won't be but a second." Gemma sauntered toward the door, only to pause and turn back, grinning. "Not like you have a choice."

Gemma grabbed the bag and canvas from the hall and brought them back to the bedroom. She pulled from it a package of natural hair fiber brushes, Jefferson's favorite. She placed one of them in his hand. "Go ahead," she said. "Hold it." Resting the handle against his middle finger, Jefferson curled his index finger a few inches above the tip.

"Feels good, doesn't it?" Gemma said.

"Feels good," Jefferson replied.

Gemma removed a tube of oil paint. Twisted off the lid and squeezed a dollop of paint onto the palette. She balanced the oval shaped board on Jefferson's other hand.

"Go on, dip your brush into it," Gemma said.

Jefferson smeared the blob.

"I now know why you couldn't paint my portrait. I'd locked your soul inside a cage. Like a domesticated bird that's lost its passion for song. I'm sorry I had to do that to you. But it was for your own good, you understand? No one can become a great artist until they've felt true suffering."

Gemma put a fresh canvas on the easel. "And now that you've felt it, you're ready to create your masterpiece. But first I must unlock the cage door. To do that, I will need complete confidence that you're on my side. That we're in this together. Which is why I'm going to lengthen the thread. Allow you a little freedom. But only when you're painting for me. Would you like that? Tell me you would like that."

"I would like that." He may have not been smiling, but Gemma heard the joy in Jefferson's voice. His joy made her happy. "How about we start now? You can paint me." She posed for him on the bed. "Turn me into a goddess."

Jefferson dipped the brush into the paint. His shaky hand reached toward the canvas. Bristles inches from drawing a line, a branch snapped outside, somewhere near the house. The brush slipped from Jefferson's hand and rolled across the hardwood. His eyes darted toward the window.

Gemma followed his anxious gaze. What the fuck was he so interested in? She stepped toward the window and yanked the curtains aside. Stuck her head out and surveyed the length of the narrow strip of grass between the houses. A trail of footprints stepped up right below where Gemma leaned, looking down. A clump of mud smeared the spigot. More mud tattooed the wall. Wood splintered along the window casing. Someone would have to shove this window pretty hard to cause that kind of damage. The window always stuck. You had to really put your back into it...

"Why is this window up?" Gemma said, focusing her ire at Jefferson.

He clamped his mouth tight to silence his canary tongue from confessing.

Gemma glanced at the window again. How had she missed that someone had broken into her home? *Her home.* Because she'd been too damned wrapped up in her own self-pity. That was why. But she was pretty sure it wasn't money or jewelry they were after. No, they'd come to steal her most prized possession. Take the one thing she'd never allow anyone to take from her.

Gemma ordered Jefferson to kneel. He fell to his knees like a penitent, knocking over the easel and canvas in front of him. Standing before him, Gemma snatched a handful of hair and wrenched his head back so she could stare into the whites of his eyes.

"Tell me who was in *my* house."

Jefferson's lips remained clamped. His tongue jabbed dents in his cheeks as his jaw caromed back-and-forth. It was like watching a rat scratching out of a bag. She had to give Jefferson this: even after being killed and brought back from the dead, the son-of-a-bitch still had fight.

"Tell me who it was, dammit."

Still, Jefferson wouldn't give her a name. The name she knew he was unwilling to speak. The name of the person he'd do anything for. The person he fought for. The person he stayed alive for. The name that did not belong to *her.*

Gemma whispered right into his ear. "Goddamn you, Jefferson. If you don't say her name, I swear, I'll enslave her too. I'll make her do things to herself. Things you couldn't possibly imagine. Things that'll turn your stomach inside out. And I'll make you watch the whole thing. You two can rot alongside each other."

Jefferson opened his mouth. Finally, he was going to say the name. The name Gemma was dying to hear. He stuck out his tongue. Gemma tingled with excitement. Then he bit down hard, teeth sawing through muscle and papillae and taste buds, severing the fleshy appendage. Blood sprayed the wall. His tongue flopped on the floor as a trickle of bloody spit spooled from his lips.

With a shriek, Gemma stumbled back against the door. What had Jefferson done?

Jefferson raised the paintbrush to his mouth, soaked the bristles in blood, and with a shaky hand began painting on the canvas, what looked like, the beginnings of her portrait.

Despite being nauseated by the sight of him, Gemma admired Jefferson's grit. His fortitude. He really loved that skeeta hawk. No man would ever have the devotion to do something like that for her. She both envied and hated Nevaeh for it.

From the bathroom across the hall, Gemma grabbed a washcloth and soaked it in cold water. Wrung it out until hardly a drop remained. "That damn witch, she'd seen all of this coming. I should've listened when she warned me. But it doesn't matter anymore. Soon as this is all over it's the swamp for you."

Gemma strolled from the bathroom and tossed the wet towel into his lap. "You spend the next remaining hours thinking about what you've done. Because tonight we're going out on the town. Going to have ourselves a fais do-do."

25. NEVAEH

Marcel and Camile dropped Nevaeh off in front of the Vodou Temple of Bondye. The isolated, weatherboard creole cottage darkened the cracked street corner with its gloomy twilight façade. Strange sigils marked the shutters of the double set hung windows. The first was a cross sitting atop a crown. The second sigil was a heart with two mirroring sides, each with tiny flames and stars at their center. These sides were cut in half by a staff in the shape of an upside-down arrow; a snake coiled around each shaft.

"I don't know about this," Camile said, shaking her head. "My momma always said nothing good comes from messing with black magic."

Nevaeh thumbed the card in her hand. "They're the only ones who can take me to the witch."

Marcel whistled through his grill. "I ain't never had any problems with voodooists, but a swamp witch. Listen Nevaeh, I know we're not good friends, but…"

"You're not going to be able to talk me out of it, so please don't try."

Camile and Marcel shot a worried glance at each other. Camile reached between the seats and placed her hand on Nevaeh's knee. "We don't want to see you hurt."

"I appreciate the concern. I really do. But this witch is the only chance I have of saving Jefferson."

"Then let us go with you," Marcel said.

But Nevaeh couldn't let that happen. "You both have done enough already. Besides, this witch would never agree to see the three of us. From what Sofie said, I'll be lucky if she speaks to *me*. I have to do this on my own."

Taking a deep breath, Camile relented. "Promise you'll be careful and come back to us alive."

"The opening wouldn't be the same without you," Marcel added.

Nevaeh rested her hands on their shoulders. "I'll see you in a couple days, okay?"

Nevaeh stepped out of the car and waved as her friends drove away along White Street. Though the rain had stopped, the mugginess in the air draped around Nevaeh like a wet blanket in a downpour. But there was something other than the humidity causing her to perspire. Guilt. Her parents would've berated her for opening the door and inviting the devil in. That's what you get for stepping into voodoo territory, they'd say. Unfortunately, God didn't have the power to save Jefferson. Only the swamp witch, Mirlande St. Pierre.

A tiny bell rang, announcing Nevaeh's entry. The place breathed incense and dressed the part of a cluttered occult junk shop. A narrow path weaved through tables full of trinkets, sculptures of saints, scented candles with depictions of various spirits etched into the wax, perfumes and soaps, bowls of healing gems and stones. Near the back, ceremonial masks sat atop shelves of books on Tarot, Palmistry, magical herb horticulture, and Creole history. Next to a spiral staircase, a sign with an arrow pointing up announced the services and spiritual guidance of the Priestess Isabel Lovelie.

"Bonjou, Koman lêz afaer, cheri?" a loud male voice from behind Nevaeh startled her nearly out of her shoes. Appearing seemingly out of nowhere, a dark-skinned black man in a checkered waistcoat of bright colors greeted her with a tip of his bowler hat. He looked like someone who'd own a hattery on the colonnade, not a voodoo shop.

"I'm sorry, I don't understand," Nevaeh said, waiting for her heartbeat to return to its normal rhythm.

"I asked how ye'er."

Not knowing how to answer that question, Nevaeh said, "Fine?"

He approached carefully as if she were a frightened kitten he'd found in an alley. "Mo non se Rolando." He pressed his hand over his heart. "And what's yer name, lovely?"

"Nevaeh."

"Ahhh, syél la. The heaven. Yo mamma en'em Kreyol?" Nevaeh shook her head. "Katolik?" Once again, she shook her head. "Beautiful non, eider way." Nevaeh thanked him for his kindness. "Pardon me, I should speak da common tongue, but I prefer ta speak da language of peyi mwen. It sounds nicer ta da ears than da chicken scratch of English."

Nevaeh didn't mind at all. She liked the way Rolando spoke. Despite being in a place that, honestly, gave her the creeps, his jovial accent put her at ease.

"What can I help you wit today?"

"I'm looking for a powder…"

"Oh, we have many, many powders. Powders for love. Powders for money. Powders to relax…"

"Coup de Poudre."

Rolando jolted as if he were struck by lightning. He laughed jollily to hide his discomfort. "Oh, cher, ya seen too many scary movies. We do no black magic here. Dis ounfó is a place of worship and healing. Konprann? We have many nice herbs." He grabbed a jar from the shelf full of brown flakes like peanut shells and unscrewed the lid. "Protect against negative energy." He took a whiff. "Very powerful, musky. Smell, ah?" He held the open lid under her nose.

"Coup de Poudre was given to someone I love."

"I know nothing about dat poison. Vodou is about praising Bondye and honoring the Lwa. Asking for their guidance when we need it."

"Someone told me you can get me in touch with Mirlande St. Pierre."

Taken back, Rolando's smile cemented into a tight-lipped grimace. When he spoke again, his accent had lost its joviality. "I don't know no one by that name."

"No? You don't remember taking a girl to meet her; a red head?" Nevaeh noticed a flash of recognition in the shopkeeper's eyes. "You *do know* who I'm talking about.

Well, she gave that poison to my friend, and if I don't do something he's going to die."

"No die. Not for very long time. But suffer, yes. Suffer worse than any hell imaginable."

"So, you do know something about the powder?"

"Dere are some from my country who talk about dis, yes. Dey say dere are bokors whose sorcery so powerful dey keep da dead alive. Capture the victim's ti bon ange."

"Ti bon ange?"

"Part of de soul most connected to da body."

"Do you have a powder that can reconnect that part of the soul?"

Rolando's face sunk into gloom. "I'm sorry, cher. Der's no such powder. What is done is done. Best ya can do, bury him and pray he stops breathing."

"What about the bayou witch, Mirlande St. Pierre?"

"Der nothing ya want from her. She cannot help ya. She only evil." He traced the sign of the cross.

"I must speak with her."

"Dere is nothing we can do. Now please leave."

"Mon amour, you should be ashamed, treating our customers so rudely!" A brash feminine voice shouted from above Nevaeh. Standing halfway down the spiral staircase, leaning against the railing in a purple dress with red stitching along the hem of the bodice, a robust bearded lady puffed on a fat cigar between two sausage fingers. She had the gentle features of a girl's favorite aunt. The kind of aunt Nevaeh would've trusted to solve her problems. If she'd ever had such an aunt. Nevaeh found herself walking toward her for no other reason than she needed to be near her.

"But Isabel…" Rolando slipped past Nevaeh in the narrow aisle. The woman Isabel knelt and stuck her ear between the balusters. He whispered to her. By the time he finished with his secret, Nevaeh was right behind him.

Isabel Lovelie stroked her beard as she listened. Then she puffed on her cigar and motioned for Nevaeh to step closer. "My Mon Vieux says the witch put curse on your friend."

"He's not just my friend."

"What did the couillion do to her?"

"He didn't do anything to her. She sold the powder to a girl named Gemma. A girl you took to meet this witch. Which makes you partially to blame."

Isabel pointed the smoking ash of her cigar at Nevaeh. "I'd be careful what you say if you want our help, cher." She snapped her fingers and waved her hand for Nevaeh to follow her upstairs. "Come with me."

As Nevaeh stepped forward Rolando blocked the staircase. "I'm sorry for yer friend," he said. "We never meant anyone harm. I will pray to the ésprits for his soul's peaceful rest."

Beneath the sloped roof of the attic, the priestess's sanctuary was just as cramped as the store below. Beaded sequin flags similar to the ones that hung downstairs draped the windows, letting in faint beams of light, and covered various cabinets pushed against the wall. The room glowed an amber glow like the cherry of Isabel Lovelie's cigar. An army of statues guarded the sanctuary from atop furniture, each more frightening than the next: skulls with strange markings drawn onto their bones, demonic creatures smattered in face paint, serpents with the faces of men, a devil with twelve eyes. Nevaeh got the creepy feeling they were all watching her. As if they knew what she'd come here for.

They took seats on opposite sides of an altar in the center of the room. Isabel stubbed her cigar in an ashtray, stroked her beard, and sized Nevaeh up. "Mais ya, I feel your heart beating from over here. You have deep love for this boy, ah? What's his name?"

"Jefferson."

"This why you willing to go walking into the alligator's mouth. Rolando right. Wiser you move on. Before you're bitten." The priestess leaned over the altar and gnashed her filthy stained teeth. Nevaeh didn't budge. Isabel sighed. "But you won't listen, will ya?"

"Mirlande St. Pierre. I need to speak to her."

Isabel Lovelie chuckled. "What makes you sure she'll speak to you, huh? Do you have something to offer? She don't do nothing for free."

"I know what she's done."

This time the priestess laughed so hard her belly jiggled up and down. "You think you can boo doo a powerful caplata? Hoo, Lawd!"

This time it was Nevaeh's turn to lean over the altar. She snatched the banjo lighter and flicked the flint. A hot yellow flame sparked to life. She spoke slowly and clearly so the priestess understood every word. "I will burn that witch at the stake to get Jefferson's soul back."

Isabel Lovelie grinned like a fille de joie with a dirty secret. She stuck the cigar back between her teeth and lit the cut end from the flame. Clouds of smoke puffed from her nostrils. "Tête de cabri. Okay, okay. We talk to Samedi. See if there a way to bring back your defunt beau. He says Mais ya. I'll tell you how to get to the witch's hut. He say Mais non. You do what Rolando tell you. Bury your beau and pray he stop breathing. Good?"

Nevaeh nodded.

Isabel held out her palm. "That will be fifty dollars."

"Are you kidding?"

"Cash or credit?"

What choice did Nevaeh have? "This better be worth it." She rifled through her bag for her tips.

✦

Isabel Lovelie lit a triangle of three candles on the altar. Popped the cork on a bottle of dark rum and poured it into a silver demitasse with skeletons dancing around the cup. Pulled a fresh cigar from her bodice and added it to the Lao's offerings. She then poured a cup for Nevaeh and told her to drink it.

"What's in it?" Nevaeh asked.

"You want to find your beau or no?" Isabel said, obviously not caring either way.

Seeing no choice, Nevaeh slammed the syrupy liquor. The spicy notes tingled her throat. She coughed like she'd swallowed a fly. This amused Isabel far too much. She held her belly and chuckled.

Isabel grabbed a bag of cornmeal from a cabinet and sprinkled an image on the floor, the same sigil Nevaeh had seen on the shutters outside the cottage, a cross sitting atop a crown. Nevaeh asked the priestess what it represented.

"The vévé act as a doorway for the Lwa. Allows them entrance into our world. But first they need a chwal to possess."

When she finished tracing the symbol, the priestess grabbed a big wooden rattle decorated with beads and snake bones. She danced around the vévé, feet stomping the wood floor, shaking the rattle and chanting, "Samedi nan baye-a, Samedi nan baye-a, se ou ki pote drapo."

Drums pounded a fast-paced rhythm, and an accompaniment of singers joined the priestess in the chant. Nevaeh searched for a radio but saw nothing of the kind. Shadows danced across the walls, bodies twisting around each other, around Nevaeh, their hands feeling beneath her clothes, caressing her skin. They flung her arms above her head. Spread her legs wide. Heat spread across her flesh and slipped deep inside her. She moaned in ecstasy. Her stomach swelled, pregnant with spirit. She screamed and her body shook as the thing crawled up her throat. The priestess snatched her jaw, pried her mouth open. Nevaeh exhaled smoke. A cloud poured from her lips and formed into a ghost of herself.

Nevaeh awoke seated behind the altar. Her body took a seat across from her. But it was no longer her body. A different owner possessed it. Was this how Jefferson felt?

The Lwa placed a top hat from the skull on top of *her* head. Lit the fresh cigar and puffed blue rings toward the ceiling. Drank the rum, savoring its sweet flavor with a smack of *her* lips. Isabel Lovelie stood behind the Lwa's right shoulder, eyes rolled up inside her head, showing only the whites.

"Sa a se ti fi a?" Samedi said, in a thick Haitian accent from Nevaeh's mouth before taking a puff on the cigar.

"This is the Belle," Isabel Lovelie answered.

"Very bél. Me like already." Samedi ran her hands across her body.

"Don't get used to it," Nevaeh told the Lwa. "I want it back."

"Feisty, this one."

"Tête de cabri," Isabel said, making horns with her fingers from her forehead. With her beard, she looked like a goat. "Baaaa!"

"No surprise. Aren't they all?"

"Either tell me if there's a way to get Jefferson back or get the hell out of my body and I'll speak with the witch myself."

Samedi held up Nevaeh's hands as if deflecting a blow. "O-keh! O-keh!"

"And talk to me so I can understand."

The Lwa glanced over at Isabel. She grabbed the bottle of rum and poured him another cup full. Samedi took a sip then splashed the rum on the altar. A dark puddle sunk into the flag and spread to the far edges. A hand plunged through the surface. Nevaeh jumped back in her chair. More hands pushed through the dark liquid. Then faces appeared, gasping for air, treading the thick syrup, struggling to keep their heads above.

"What is this?"

"A place for the souls who have not had a proper burial."

All of a sudden, Nevaeh found herself watching from a muddy shore, the waters lapping at her shoes. She took a step back and almost tumbled into an empty coping grave, the dirt piled into a mound on one side of the hole. Algae traced Jefferson's name etched in the marble of the headstone. There was no date of death.

Surrounding her was a cemetery. Across the potter's field, graves were marked with PVC piping and painted fence posts and moldy headstones. Others weren't marked at all. Some were lined with brick or cement or covered in dirt. Offerings such as wilted bouquets and filthy dolls and empty bottles were left for those still remembered. A massive oak tree sprouted in the center, decorated with shells and beads blowing in the wind. It started to sing the chant, "Samedi nan baye-a, Samedi nan baye-a, se ou ki pote drapo."

Samedi stood next to the mound with a shovel in his hands. His piercing eyes burned like candle flames in the black sockets of his white skull makeup. Puffing on his cigar, he walked over to the lake of dark waters and glanced over the lost souls. From the edge of the murky, black water, Nevaeh searched the drowned spirits but didn't see Jefferson among them. "He's not here."

"No, your beau's days have not expired."

"What does that mean?"

"That mean there is time for you to save him, ou konprann. But as ou konnen, a caplata has stolen Jefferson's soul and is keeping it prisoner. And only the caplata can liberate him. And she won't for free."

"You're speaking of Mirlande St. Pierre."

"I am."

"The shopkeepers say she's dangerous."

"That she is."

"What will she want from me?"

"A pretty purse. Upwards of 500. Do you have that?"

Once again, Nevaeh watched the souls drowning in the dark water, their cries of agony dying in the wind. She didn't have that kind of money. She'd have to bring what she could afford and hope it was enough. "What will happen if I can't convince her?"

"His soul will not know peace." Samedi waved for her to follow. "It is time for us to go."

Nevaeh thought about Angelique Truehart. What had she ever done to deserve such torture? She would be certain to ask Mirlande St. Pierre when she met her. "Are they in pain?" she asked, taking one last look at the spirits in the black water.

"Birth, life, death. They are all painful."

"Does it have to be?"

"That you will have to ask Bondye, kay. Only he knows."

Taking her by the arm, Samedi led her through the gates of the cemetery. They followed the cracked asphalt path to a crowded section, the graves dug right next to each other.

Nevaeh asked where they were going. He led her to another empty grave. This one had no tombstone. No marker. Just a big, bottomless hole.

"What are we doing here?" Nevaeh asked Samedi.

The Lwa took one last puff on his cigar then flicked it into the grave. The yellow fire of the cherry twirled into the darkness and disappeared. His grip tightened on her arm. Nevaeh tried to pull away, but he was too strong. He stared at her with his skeleton mask, those menacing eyes reflecting her confusion and fear.

"Let me go," Nevaeh shouted at him.

"Bon chans, jén dem," Samedi said, then shoved Nevaeh into the grave. She tumbled into the endless abyss, screaming.

26. NEVAEH

umbles of thunder boomed in every direction. A crackling fire engulfed her in its heat without singeing a hair. Beams of light illuminated a yellow line bisecting a narrow path winding beneath a tunnel of branches. The bumpy, swaying motion aroused Nevaeh from sleep to the smoky fog of exhaust fumes and the soft purr of a motor. Still in a stupor, the world around her appeared as disconnected flashes; photographs edited without composition or purpose.

Her hands rested, prayer style, on her lap. Feet tangled on the floor. Beneath her rippled a leather seat. A strap cut across her chest, fastened into a heavy fat buckle. She was in the back of a big car.

Two dark figures sat in front of her, their heads silhouettes. One drove; the other watched out the window at the gloomy landscape, nothing but trees and swamp and telephone poles connected by wire. The driver's eyes snatched glances in the rearview mirror, peering at Nevaeh with empathy. She caught snippets of their whispered conversation, but not enough to piece together what they were saying.

The voices sounded familiar, a man and a woman, having an argument. Was it her parents? Were they taking her to the Tree of Life? Pa didn't want to institutionalize her, he thought it looked bad among the church members, but Ma insisted. Didn't Christ preach about taking care of others? And she was their daughter. As much as they would've preferred to deny it, much as she'd embarrassed them with her dramatics, she almost died. What if they hadn't come home and seen the river of blood flowing beneath the bathroom door?

But the bandages were gone. Only a crosshatch of knobby scars slashed her arms. That had all taken place long ago. She hadn't spoken with her parents in some time. But if it wasn't her parents then who was she with? And where the fuck were they taking her?

"Where are we going?" Nevaeh asked the heads in the front. She recognized her own voice, but it sounded outside her like a radio broadcast turned to a low volume and hissing with static.

A black man in a bowler hat scooted around in his seat. "Zami, you wake?" he asked.

A crashing migraine split Nevaeh's skull. She rubbed her temples as the memories flooded her mind. The man was the owner of the voodoo shop. What was his name? Rolando. Which meant the person behind the wheel, studying her in the rearview mirror, was his wife, the bearded manbo, Isabel Lovelie.

"Aye-ya-yi. Couillon not look so good. Too much of da gris-gris," Isabel said, without a hint of concern.

Nevaeh slumped against the headrest, ghostly arms pulling her between two worlds, half-inside her body, half-outside.

Rolando spoke bitterly to his wife. "Told ye, no good idea. The girl is not well. We should not take her to sósyé a."

Isabel stared straight ahead at the narrow road cutting through the marshy bayou.

"Samedi say take belle to sorciére, I take belle to sorciére."

"What if Samedi wrong?"

"Samedi never wrong," Isabel snapped at her husband.

Rolando slumped against his door. It was obvious who wore the britches in this relationship. Watching him cower, Nevaeh felt sorry for the kindly Creole man. His manbo wife didn't need voodoo to control him. She was witchy enough.

But their fighting was worsening Nevaeh's thundering migraine. She couldn't take any more.

Nevaeh unlatched her seatbelt, pulled up the lock, and pushed open the door. Isabel slammed on the brakes. The tires screeched against the asphalt. All three passengers rocketed forward, Rolando slamming his pudgy belly into the dash, Isabel gripping the wheel so hard her knuckles blanched, Nevaeh clung to her seatbelt to keep from flying into the darkness.

Once the car ground to a halt, Isabel swiveled her portly figure to face Nevaeh. "Mon Dieu! Are you crazy? Get yourself dead before meeting."

"Meeting with who?"

"La Sorciére."

More memories came charging back to Nevaeh, shadows dancing in circles, the lake of lost souls, the cemetery and

Samedi pushing her into the grave, the woman standing in front of the tin hut, Jefferson and his terrifying paintings, the pain in her head like a crack against a windshield. For a moment, Nevaeh thought she was going to vomit but fought down the nausea. She shut the door and leaned against the seat and waited for her thoughts to clear. The voodoo shopkeepers watched her with concern.

Once the migraine subsided enough for her to think coherently, Nevaeh leaned forward between the seats. "Take me to Mirlande St. Pierre."

A few more miles in, the threesome turned into a small clearing cut into the brush on the side of the road. The headlights illuminated a rickety, floating dock cobbled together with 2x4s. A short pier bridged over the swamp of brackish water churning and bubbling like a pot of boiling soup. Across the marsh, the giant cypress stretched their branches towards the moon, as if it were a crystal ball in which they read a future, a future too dark to predict.

Beneath the gabled roof of missing boards, a shadowy figure lounged at a round patio table. Soon as the headlights illuminated him in their glow, he stood but neither waved nor spoke a greeting, just leaned against a wooden pillar, scrawny arms crossed over his caved chest. A threadbare rope cinched tight at the waist kept his baggy pants from falling down. The soles of his shoes were wrapped with duct tape. Waxy skin stretched over his bones. The pale white orbs of his unblinking eyes sunk deep into the sockets. He stared straight at them as they pulled to a stop in the grassy clearing. It was the same look Jefferson had given Nevaeh in the park.

"We will wait here for your return, cherie," Isabel said, no longer watching her in the rearview mirror.

"Who is that man?"

"He'll take you to la sorciére."

The humidity breathed its moist, oven hot air into Nevaeh's face as she stepped from the car. Within seconds, sweat dripped from her forehead as her clothes stuck to her clammy flesh. The musky moss mixed with undertones of sweetly fragranced flowers wreaked havoc on her sinuses. She fired a round of sneezes, the pressure drilling into her head. How she wished to be back in the city, away from the sounds of nature—the haunting wail of the loon, the guttural snore of the crawfish frog, the hiss of gators—spawning ghostly spiders that crawled up her spine. But there was no point in hesitating any longer. The clock was ticking, and the further the arms spun, the less chance she had of saving Jefferson.

Before she took a step forward, Rolando rolled down the window of the Caddie. "Us Louisiana Creole have a saying, 'Chien jappô li pas morde.' The barking dog does not bite. Remember that when you speak to sósyé a."

Isabel leaned over Rolando and dropped a doubloon in Nevaeh's palm. "For the boatman," she said.

The boards creaked beneath her feet as Nevaeh crossed the pier. When she reached the stranger, he took the coin then nodded his head for her to follow. At the end of the dock, a four-rung ladder led to a pirogue floating in the dark waters. The same dark waters Samedi had taken her to where the spirits drowned. What else lurked beneath this muddy swamp, waiting to drag her under?

As they made their way along the winding outlet, the triangular point of the pirogue sliced through the brackish water. An antique brass marine oil lamp dangling from a hook shone a circular spotlight to guide their travel and spook away predators. Nevaeh kept her limbs tucked within the boat. The skeeters were already having a feast. She didn't need anything larger taking a bite.

Off in the distance, little glowing orbs blinked behind the sawgrass and spider lilies. At first, Nevaeh thought it was the eyes of alligators, but the closer they floated, the spears appeared to hover, flickering like candle flames. Their fiery presence gave Nevaeh the chills. Feu follet. Swamp fairies. Nevaeh had heard stories about them before, but she thought that was all they were—stories. Supposedly, they are spirits of the dead who have returned to bid farewell to the earth. But Louisiana was full of superstitions. Normally, Nevaeh would've brushed off such nonsense, but after what she'd recently seen, and in the presence of her current company, she no longer knew what was real and what was folklore.

"So you work for the witch?" Nevaeh asked the boatman, no longer able to stand his eerie silence. He didn't respond. Just kept pushing the boat along with his oar. "Not much of a talker." Then Nevaeh remembered Angelique and Jefferson. "Or has the witch ordered you not to speak?" Nevaeh shifted to look at him. Though she could barely make out his face in the dark she could tell his deadpan expression had not changed. "Tell me about Mirlande St. Pierre."

"Whachu wanna know?" the boatman answered in a surprisingly deep voice.

"Where did she come from?"

"Mais I don't know! Der are dose say she born in da swamp."

"How did you meet Mirlande St. Pierre?"

"I fish'en crawdaddies. Don't know where she seen me, but lik'a my boat, yeah. Follow me to da Blind Tiger. Me, I'm drinking when she saddles over. Striking woman and me a couyon. C'est bon."

"She poisoned you?"

The boatman's grip tightened on the oar. "Drop me in gras doux."

"What about your family? Haven't they come looking for you?"

"Mais I don't know! Maybe dey lookin' and find, no. Gone long time."

"Why has no one done anything for you?"

"People talk to me, no. Mirlande, by her house dey go. Get gris-gris."

Hearing him say these words, the hatred Nevaeh harnessed for the witch burned even hotter. What kind of sick evil allowed her to do such cruel things? Swallowing her fear, Nevaeh would soon find out.

They glided around a lunette of cypress and a tin shack on

a grassy islet came into view. The same one from Jefferson's painting. Rust streaked the pitched roof, and moss grew on the walls. A bunch of junk cluttered the porch. Nevaeh would've thought the place abandoned if not for a pale light streaming through the cloudy windows. Above the doorway, a gator skull opened its jaws as if to say hello—or was it guarding the entrance from something unworldly? Either way, Nevaeh didn't like the look of the place. She told herself to be brave; the words like a prayer against the evil that awaited her.

The boatman pulled the pirogue alongside the dock, hopped on to it, and offered Nevaeh a hand. Nevaeh took it and climbed onto shore. They marched toward the shack to the chirping of crickets. The silhouette of the woman from Jefferson's painting brushed past the foggy glass.

As they reached the deck, the boatman stopped. Nevaeh looked at him curiously. "Why are you stopping?"

"Me move further, no."

"Tell me, has she demanded this?"

"No step 'cross doorstep."

Now that she was here, Nevaeh did not like the idea of going in alone. She could feel the witch watching her. After saying a quick prayer, something Nevaeh hadn't done in a long time, she walked onto the porch. Maybe she didn't believe in God anymore, but if He existed, she could use all the help she could get.

The moment Nevaeh raised her hand to knock, the screen door swung open and she was greeted by Mirlande St. Pierre. The witch eyed her up and down and tsked. She didn't seem to be impressed. Was Nevaeh not the adversary she expected? Well, she'd have to prove the witch wrong.

Nevaeh stood as straight as her spine would allow. Mirlande St. Pierre cackled so loudly her howls scattered birds from the trees. What had Rolando said? "The barking dog does not bite." What would he say about a laughing witch?

Mirlande glanced over Nevaeh's shoulder at the boatman and her eyes briefly widened. "Get back to the pier," she shouted at him. The boatman did as he was told.

With a wave of her bejeweled fingers, Mirlande invited Nevaeh inside. Bronze lanterns swung from chains hooked into the tin ceiling. Standing fans hummed as their blades twirled, stirring the muggy air. Nevaeh followed the witch down a narrow path through her front room. Next to the far end of a checkered sofa, a parrot perched on a swing inside a wire cage. It shook its remaining feathers around bald patches of puckered skin. Its skinny black tongue licked out of its broken nub of a beak. It watched them with reptilian eyes but said nothing. Nevaeh would've liked to put it out of its misery.

"What happened to the bird?" Nevaeh asked.

"Noctua want a crawdaddy," the parrot squawked.

Mirlande swatted the cage, knocking the poor things off its swing. "He talk too much."

Opposite of the cage, a bookshelf stored jars of various organs floating in—what Nevaeh assumed was— formaldehyde. From the kitchen wafted the burnt okra fragrance of gumbo. On top of the stove, a roux-stained pot burbled over an open flame.

"Stew?"

"Something like that."

Mirlande pulled out a chair and demanded Nevaeh sit. It didn't take a genius to decipher what the strange symbols on the table cover illustrated. Nevaeh repeated the mantra of "Don't be afraid" in her head.

"What canna do for ya?" Mirlande asked, remaining on her feet.

"I want to know if there's a cure to reverse the effects of Coup de Poudre."

From a cupboard above the stove, Mirlande retrieved a vial. She placed it on the table between them then took a seat. Inside the glass capsule, tiny silver crystals floated in a clear liquid. "Give 'em dis and dey regain der senses and remember who dey are." Nevaeh reached for the vial, but the witch snapped it up in her right hand. "Cost ya. Five hundred bones." The witch opened her right hand, palm up.

"I don't have that much."

Mirlande closed the fingers of her left hand into a fist. The gems of her rings dazzled brightly beneath the unnatural light from the lamps. "Den what ya here for?"

Nevaeh pulled out the cash she had and placed it between them. "You poisoned my boyfriend, Jefferson Fontenot."

The witch shook her head. "Never met 'em."

"You sold the powder to a girl named Gemma Landry."

"Never met her neither. Sure ya got da right address, chile? Lotsa sòsyé in dis swamp."

Hands flat on the table, Nevaeh leaned forward so the

witch heard her loud and clear. "Oh, I have the right address. Let me jar your memory. Vindictive little redhead, probably walked in here like her heels are a few inches taller."

"Ya talking 'bout half me customers. Who ya think comes asking favors? Surely, no catfish from Desire or insects from St. Roch. All Algereens and Chalmations and Pecans from da Garden District. Uh-uh. Me keep a clean house. No sticker thorns in here, mind ya."

"She was probably talking about the skeeta hawk who stole her beau—"

The witch held out her empty hands. "Once again, dat everybody who come asking favors."

"—paid you good money to make him her prisoner."

Mirlande stood up as she were about to excuse herself from the table. Nevaeh could feel her chance slipping away. She thought of the last time she saw Jefferson. How close he looked to death. It was as if he was…

"The boy you poisoned, *my* Jefferson, is dying. Rotting to pieces while he's still alive. Is that what you do to people? Slowly kill them from the inside?"

Mirlande's scornful expression cracked. "I kill no one. Dat girl must've fucked up the formula."

Nevaeh leaned back in the chair. "So you do remember her?"

"She hadda coin, I sell her da powder. Dat was dat. I had nothing ta do what happened which ya fella. The girl too goat headed to know what good for her."

It enraged Nevaeh how easily this witch disregarded

another's life, someone she didn't even know, to fatten her wallet. She deserved to be burned at the stake. And Nevaeh would gladly strike the match. But not before she got what she came here for. "*That* is not fucking that."

Mirlande shrugged away the accusation without any regard. "Dis no my problem. I tell da girl what she needed ta do. Sound da me she no listen."

"Same thing you did to Angelique Truehart. Sold her husband Lyle your formula. Her sister Sofie said she came to see you. My guess is you chased her away with your lies."

The most wicked smile Nevaeh had ever seen curled on the witch's lips. This woman was remorseless. She derived pleasure from her handiwork. Didn't care how her victims suffered. Rolando and Isabel were right. Mirlande was pure evil. "Now, I know dis charmer."

"Tell me something, do you think the police will agree this isn't your problem? Because you can bet your ass they're on their way. Going to storm this shithole and put you out of business."

Once again, Mirlande laughed. She didn't seem at all scared by the threat. "Yes, I hear about what Ms. Sofie done. You see I have little birdies all over da city. Well, I pay a visit to Ms. Sofie. She won't be talking to nobody. That fur sure."

There went Nevaeh's only play. She was out of cards. And Mirlande knew it.

The chair legs scraped against the wood as Mirlande pushed from the table, encompassing Nevaeh in her shadow. "Eider pay me the full coin or get da hell outta ma home," the witch tossed her money at her.

Nevaeh swallowed the words she wanted to say. They wouldn't get her anywhere but dead. And her being dead wouldn't do Jefferson any good. Not that she was any good to him anyway. Without the antidote she might as well have dug a grave and buried herself next to him.

Refusing to allow the witch the satisfaction of seeing her cry, Nevaeh grabbed her money and dashed across the shack, the parrot squawking "Bonjou" as she passed his cage. When she stepped outside the door, Nevaeh saw the boatman waiting for her at the end of the dock. He stared at the shack like someone with rage in his heart. Like he wanted to pull it down beneath the black waters of the bayou.

That was why he wasn't allowed near the house.

Nevaeh marched back to where the witch still stood on the opposite side of the table. Mirlande tried to intimidate her with a sinister glare, but Nevaeh was no longer afraid.

"What do you say we invite your boatman inside for some stew?"

"Be my guest. He's no threat."

But Nevaeh knew this was a lie. There was a subtle quiver in Mirlande's tone.

"What's his name? I'll call him now."

"He ain't got no name."

"I think he does, but you're too afraid to tell me."

"I ain't afraid of you," Mirlande seethed.

Nevaeh thought about how she'd gotten the boatman to speak about the witch. "The commands. They're the key to unlocking the soul."

Mirlande burst out laughing. "Stupid chile. Dat's all a trick." The moment the words slipped from her mouth, the witch clammed up.

It was Nevaeh's turn to smile. "Their will isn't gone, is it?"

Milande opened her mouth to respond, but the lies didn't come as easily now that Nevaeh had seen through the ruse. The witch stepped toward the kitchen, but Nevaeh cut off her path to the drawers and cabinets.

"You don't have complete power over him, do you? That poison you fed them. It made him sick, weak, vulnerable to suggestion and manipulation. Just like the drugs the psychiatrists gave us at the recovery center. They distort your perceptions and actions. Take away your identity. But if he wanted to, the boatman could burn this place to the ground. Couldn't he?"

A mumbled curse escaped the witch's lips. Nevaeh had her trapped in a corner. She watched as Mirlande St. Pierre chewed on the possibilities of what the boatman might do if freed from the shackles of her influence. The clacking of her nails against the counter insinuated none of the scenarios she imagined played in her favor.

"Whachu want from me, chile?"

"What I came here for." Nevaeh held out her hand. "The remedy."

The witch snagged the vial from the table. "How 'bout we make a deal? Ya pay me the money you brought—"

"I ain't paying you shit."

"Yer beau won't live without it."

Nevaeh glanced outside the doorway at the boatman. "And you won't live if you don't give it to me."

Without looking over her shoulder, Mirlande knew what Nevaeh was referring to. She dropped the vial onto Nevaeh's palm. Acted as if this made them even-steven. It was just another of Mirlande's clever ruses. But this time Nevaeh saw through it. Leveraging with her thumb, she popped the cap off the vial and dumped the contents into the sink, staring at Mirlande the whole time as the corners of the witch's mouth raised. Nevaeh was ashamed she'd almost fallen for the salt and water mix. But she'd been desperate for a solution. Praying there was still a chance she could save Jefferson.

"There isn't one, is there?"

Mirlande stepped forward, prompting Nevaeh to raise her fists. The witch scowled in anger at her before reaching for the cabinet above her head. This time she retrieved a different vial. A vial of green powder.

"It may be too late to save yer beau. Dat girl, I tell her to give 'im dis after she dig 'im up. Dis potion stop da poison. Stop da body from rotting."

Nevaeh didn't want to believe what the witch was saying, but she knew in her heart it wasn't a lie. She snagged the potion from Mirlande's fingers.

Staring at the dark green powder behind the glass, Nevaeh asked, "What will happen to Jefferson if the potion doesn't work?"

For the first time since Nevaeh entered this ramshackle hut, Mirlande avoided her eyes. "Like yer friend Angelique, he'll die a slow, painful death."

Nevaeh's tears boiled. The witch deserved to suffer for her part in Jefferson's suffering. Angelique's too.

Without another word, Nevaeh slipped the potion into her pocket and strolled through the front room. Mirlande St. Pierre chased after and clasped Nevaeh's arm. "Please don't let him in. I beg you."

Nevaeh shoved the witch. Mirlande St. Pierre stumbled into the birdcage. It tumbled from its pedestal and crashed onto the floor, breaking the latch, and freeing the parrot from its jail. Noctua flew at the witch, tangled in her hair, and clawed her face with sharp talons. Screaming, Mirlande St. Pierre stumbled and fell onto the sofa, batting at the bird.

The boatman was waiting for Nevaeh on the dock as she crossed over the boggy grounds. He stared at the hut, where the witch's screams carried off into the night, echoed by the calls of the bayou. From his deadpan expression, it was impossible to tell what he was thinking. He seemed not to care either way.

Nevaeh placed a hand on his shoulder and whispered into his ear what she knew to be true.

PART THREE

27. JEFFERSON

He stared at his hands, oval-shaped palms spattered with blood. Not his blood. Most of it anyway. Fingers, long and conical, the middle and ring of his right hand broken and crooked, knuckles swollen into hard stones; the pink shells of his nails cracked and grimy, ringed with black. These hands that once painted portraits of the city and people he loved had colored the walls of the Carondelet Street Gallery in gruesome carnage.

It was these hands that had twisted Nevaeh's wrist. These hands that brought her to her knees in Lafayette Square. These hands that harmed her even when she begged him to have mercy. He'd shouted at his hands to stop what they were doing. To leave her alone. They wouldn't listen. Not to him anyway. They were no longer his to control. Now they'd gone and done the unthinkable.

He wondered if Nevaeh had discovered a cure to raise him from the dead. Break the spell Gemma had cast him under. But did it even matter anymore? No potion could save his soul. Remove the guilt slowly devouring him from the inside out like the maggots feasting on his organs.

Nothing could erase the memory of Marcel's agonizing screams. The branch-like snaps of his breaking bones. The splintering of wood as his head crashed through the bar cabinets. The hollow thunk of his skull splitting open. The moans as he slowly lost consciousness. The tearing sound of his stomach ripping open and intestines spilling to the floor.

Slumped against the busted cupboards, doors hanging off hinges, Marcel cradled the guts that had spooled from his torn belly. The right side of his skull oozed brain like yolk from a cracked egg.

Jefferson had never much liked Marcel, but he didn't deserve this.

The first time they met at Jackson Square, before Jefferson started dating Gemma, Marcel accused Jefferson of stealing his spot on the gate near the corner of Decatur and St. Ann. Claimed the former owner, a friend and mentor who'd passed away earlier in the year, had bequeathed him the prime real estate. Unconvinced by Marcel's sob story, Jefferson continued to set up his display, stating plainly that he hadn't seen any title or deed affirming Marcel's ownership of this section of gate, and as far as he was concerned, it was up for grabs. Jefferson had arrived there first and unless Marcel could produce any documentation proving proprietorship then he suggested Marcel move along. Well, Marcel didn't take too kindly to Jefferson's attitude. He shoved Jefferson, which was laughable, as Jefferson didn't budge. Jefferson shoved Marcel backwards, knocking him on his ass, then grabbed him by the collar and shook his fist in his face, threatening to clean

Marcel's clock if he didn't walk away. Figuring the fight was over, Jefferson went back to assembling his display. Marcel pulled a switchblade from his pocket, cut the zip ties strapped around the gate, and began throwing Jefferson's paintings into the street. Jefferson moved to stop him, but Marcel pointed the blade at him and warned him to step away—the same knife he lodged in Jefferson's shoulder tonight—and insulted his work as amateurish. What did Jefferson do in retaliation? Grabbed his things and moved on further down the gate.

From that point on, Jefferson had always been wary of Marcel. Kept his distance in case the son-of-a-bitch got the idea to stick him when no one was looking.

That was until he started dating Gemma and they ran into Marcel at an exhibit by a local conceptual artist at the N Contemporary. Jefferson no longer recalled the artist's name, but he did remember the show; it disturbed and unsettled him for months. Nightmares about swinging balls shackled to the ceiling by chains and outlines of murder victims constructed from metal spikes and installations that resembled medieval torture devices. The sort of thing Gemma was into—and he now knew why. Marcel didn't like the work either, but not for the same reasons; he didn't like anyone's art but his own. But as soon as he laid eyes on the two of them studying a cage-like contraption fixed over a mannequin's head he rushed over and played nice.

Marcel asked to speak to Gemma privately, not caring whether Jefferson approved or not. They moved to the other side of the room, behind an iron cradle rocking in a blue light, and started arguing in whispered tones. Jefferson tried to get close enough to eavesdrop, but Marcel caught him snooping.

Before he stormed off, Marcel advised Jefferson not to trust Gemma. It wouldn't be the last time. But Jefferson thought Marcel was jealous that he'd swooped in and stolen his girl. Payback for the day at Jackson Square.

From upstairs came a loud thump and gargled groans. Jefferson climbed the stairs. Glass crunched beneath his feet where Nevaeh's photos had shattered. Bloody prints smeared the white walls. Several fist-size dents pockmarked the drywall.

In the office, Camile crawled across the floor toward her desk, broken fingernails scratching against the wood, right leg kicking forward, dragging the left, bone sticking out of her ankle, foot pointed upward toward the ceiling where Jefferson had twisted it. Her lipless mouth spewed blood down her chin, from where he'd cut off her lips with scissors and pried her teeth from her gums with pliers. Meeting Jefferson's gaze, Camile's eyes pleaded for mercy. She tried to speak but her mouth could no longer form words.

Camile had taken a risk on Jefferson, and now he'd broken her. Broken her with the same hands that painted the work that hung on her gallery walls. The work that would be shown at the exhibition tomorrow night.

Gemma hovered above Camile, grinning gleefully down upon her. When she saw Jefferson standing at the landing, her brows pinched in frustration. "I thought I told you to wait downstairs until I finished."

Jefferson's body ached to obey, his foot sliding backwards, but he clung to the post, willing it to remain. Maybe he couldn't save Camile, but he wasn't going to let her die alone.

Camile reached out toward him.

Gemma grabbed the chain, from which dangled the brass key, twisted it tight around Camile's neck, pushed the weight of her knee into her spine, and wrenched far enough backwards she lifted Camile's abdomen off the floor. The links cut a ribbon into Camile's throat, rivulets of blood staining the collar of her shirt. Camile stomped her good foot and clawed at the floor as she tried sucking in for air. Her skin turned palish-blue as her eyes rolled into the back of her head.

Unable to watch anymore, Jefferson stopped fighting his body and allowed it to head back downstairs, where he waited by Marcel's corpse. Eventually the struggling stopped, and a bang shook dust from the ceiling.

Moments later, Gemma joined him, wearing the bloody key. She finally had what she wanted. And he'd played the part of her executioner. Was there nothing he could've done to stop it? Nothing he could've done to quiet her voice in his head? The voice that shouted, "Kill them! Kill them!"

Gemma wrapped her fingers around the handle and pulled at the knife sunk to the hilt in Jefferson's shoulder. As the blade slid through the wall of bone and muscle, a geyser of black blood gushed from the wound and spread into a sticky puddle on his shirt. Gemma wiped the switchblade clean with a rag from the bar, closed it, and slid it in her pocket. She dropped the rag in the garbage. She unbuttoned

Jefferson's shirt, peeled it from his battered torso. The knife wound looked bad, small but deep, even compared to the dark purple bruises and seeping sores.

Digging through a closet, Gemma found a cloth she soaked with water in the bathroom. She washed the wound, smearing blood across his chest, then wrapped the damp cloth tightly, cinching it with a knot. Jefferson begged Gemma to let him die, but without a tongue, his lips rendered only incessant babble. It didn't matter anyway. Until she was done enacting revenge, he was her butcher.

"You'll need to clean this mess," Gemma said, wiping a smear of blood from her cheek.

"Clean this mess," Jefferson said, wishing he could tell his psycho ex to go to hell.

From the closet, she gathered a couple of old, plastic drop cloths and dragged them into the back room. Together they spread one across the bare floor. Even if blood seeped through it'd be difficult to spot.

Jefferson dragged Marcel's corpse to the drop cloth, rolled the body inside it, and carried him to the trunk of Gemma's car parked behind the gallery. Once he returned, he carried Camile from the upstairs office to the car, also wrapped in a drop cloth. Jefferson tried not to think about the crime he was committing, his part in all of this as Gemma's accomplice. *I have no control over my actions*, he kept telling himself. But the more he repeated it, the more it sounded like a lie. He had the resolution to bite off his tongue to keep Nevaeh's name a secret. Couldn't he have stopped himself from killing Camile and Marcel?

For the next couple of hours, Jefferson cleaned the gallery the best he could while Gemma sipped from a bottle of champagne she'd stolen from the office minifridge and supervised his cleanup job, pointing out places he missed, until she was satisfied they had covered their tracks. In the end, blood pools had been soaked up, floors and walls scrubbed, broken items and shattered glass tossed into trash bags. Anyone walking in the gallery would hopefully not notice anything was amiss.

They sped through the city along I-10 E. For probably the first time in her life, Gemma drove below the speed limit. The moon glowed like a flashlight behind the clouds, coloring the sky a blend of purples. The highway stretched in front of them like a long black snake.

Jefferson had never felt so alone.

Thirty minutes later, they crossed into the Bayou Sauvage. Woodland spread into the distance on either side, intermittently swallowed by mossy lagoons. A kettle of vultures circled above the tree line. Gators lounged on stones, swishing their powerful scaly tails and extending their vicious, sharp-toothed jaws. Despite the air-conditioning pumping through the vents, beads of sweat rolled down Jefferson's neck and spine. He'd never much liked the bayou. The only thing it was good for was the disposing of bodies. It made sense Gemma had chosen this place as Camile and Marcel's final resting place.

Night descended upon them like a long tunnel. Soon they were the only headlights on the highway; two lone travelers far out of their element. Gemma cut across the grassy verge, the tires bumping over the lumpy ground, jostling them in their seats, onto the gravel path of Fromage Road. She parked about a quarter-of-a-mile down, behind a copse of elms.

On the other side of the steel parapet, what looked like fireflies hovered above the stillness of the Irish Bayou. But at this far distance, they were far too big to be fireflies. Jefferson wondered where the lights were coming from. There were no buildings or radio towers in the vicinity. No airplanes flew overhead. Perhaps it was a reflection from the stars. What else could it be?

They stepped out of the car and while Gemma opened the trunk Jefferson stared at the twinkling lights. A low hum started buzzing in his head but grew louder and louder. Voices whispered. Strange voices he did not recognize. He could not make out exactly what they were saying, but he was quite certain they were pleading with him to "Let go."

Jefferson took a few steps toward the bayou, and would've gone further, if Gemma hadn't asked where he was going.

"Grab these bags and drag them to shore," Gemma said, obviously annoyed with him. "We need to hurry up before someone comes along and wonders what the hell we're doing out here. Going to be real hard explaining why we have a couple of bodies."

Together they carried the bodies of Camile and Marcel over the parapet and down a sandy embankment to the shoreline. They found some heavy stones to weigh the corpses down, loaded them into the drop clothes, and shoved the bodies into the water. The bodies floated momentarily. Gemma freaked, pacing back-and-forth, imploring them to sink. She was convinced they hadn't weighed them down enough.

The twinkling lights came to hover above Camile and Marcel, burning brightly and tracing their wrapped bodies in a golden aura. Jefferson watched with fascination and dread. He glanced over at Gemma, wondering if she was seeing the lights too, but she appeared completely oblivious to their existence. Once again, the voices inside his head whispered. This time he heard them clearly. "Let go."

Jefferson took a step into the water. The lights flickered and extinguished and the bodies sank. Silence filled the bayou. The voices were only in his head.

Gemma sighed with relief then noticed him staring out at the water. She clung to his bicep. "Don't cry for them, darling. They would've buried us at the bottom of the swamp if they had the chance."

Jefferson would've given anything to change places with Camile and Marcel. Given anything to put an end to all this. Given anything to be free from the shackles of Gemma Landry.

Gemma caressed his cheek. "My poor tongueless simpleton. I know who was in the house. You don't have to say her name. I see her portrait reflected in your eyes." She balanced on her toes to look directly into his eyes. "Even now when you're looking at me. She's right there. I can't describe to you how much that hurts. How much I envy her. But I know I can't hold onto that hurt forever."

Inside his head, Jefferson shouted at Gemma to leave Nevaeh alone. Threatened to rip out her poisonous heart if she so much as scratched her. A thread of dark blood poured from his mouth as he babbled nonsensically.

Disgusted, Gemma turned her back on him, daring him to strangle her from behind, but his hands remained at his sides, useless. "You did a good job today, darling. And tomorrow's opening is going to be the pinnacle of our collaboration. So tonight, I want you to have a little fun." Gemma smiled at him over her shoulder. "Go and see your sweetheart. You can give her one last special goodbye—" Gemma whispered in his ear. "Because after that you won't be seeing her again."

Jefferson's heart sank beneath the waters of the swamp, down into the depths alongside the bodies of Camile and Marcel, where no light could reach.

28. NEVAEH

By the time Rolando and Isabel dropped her off in front of her building, Nevaeh was completely wiped. She could barely keep her eyes open and had dozed in and out of consciousness on the drive into the city. The effects of whatever drug Isabel Lovelie had given her hadn't quite worn off, and once the adrenaline rush of confronting the witch subsided, it hit her like a bottle to the skull.

A migraine thumped at her temples and blinded her with shocking white pain whenever she caught a flash of light. The only way to bear it was by closing her eyes, but as soon as she did, she'd return to the cemetery, the pool of drowning souls, and Baron Samedi tossing her into a bottomless grave. As hard as she tried to shake it, Nevaeh couldn't escape the dream. The images lingered at the periphery even when she awoke looking out the window at the fading pink brick of her creole townhouse. The shutters were closed, and no light peeked through. Nevaeh prayed Ms. Batifole wouldn't stick her head out. What would she say if she spied Nevaeh with the voodoo shopkeepers? Douse her in holy water and pray that God saved her wicked soul?

Nevaeh thanked the shop owners for the ride home. She didn't know how she would've made it otherwise. She pushed the door open with her shoulder, stumbled onto the sidewalk, then righted herself and waited for the dizziness to pass. She reached into her pocket for her keys.

Rolando leaned out his window, called to her, and asked if she was going to be okay. There was a fatherly concern in his tone. Isabel stared out the windshield at where the headlights illuminated the carriageways of the adjoined townhouses, squeezing the steering wheel and revving the gas pedal like she was in a hurry to be gone. Was there something the manbo had seen in their little adventure to frighten her? A premonition of impending doom she'd rather not witness? Or did she know about Mirlande St. Pierre's death at the hands of the boatman? Angry that her occasional employer was no longer around to fill her pockets with extra coin?

Nevaeh leaned inside the Caddie. "Is there something you'd like to tell me?" she asked Isabel Lovelie.

The manbo remained facing forward. "I hope you not become a wooden cat."

"What does that even mean?"

Rolando squeezed Nevaeh's hand, a compassionate gesture. "She hopes to see you again. We both do."

The second Nevaeh removed her head from inside the window, Isabel threw the car into drive, and they squealed down Chartres, exhaust hanging in the air as the red eyes of their brake lights vanished down Ursulines.

Nevaeh wondered if she'd ever see them again, but the

hollow well in her gut left her doubtful. What had Isabel Lovelie meant by "becoming a wooden cat?"

Rummaging in her bag, Nevaeh checked to make sure the vial was still there and intact. Confirming it was, she let herself in through a rear carriageway, climbed the stairway to the gallery, swung open the shutter, and nearly collapsed into her apartment. Preferring the dark to ease the pounding in her head, she lit a candle from the mantle to guide her.

Though it'd only been hours, it felt like days since Nevaeh had been home. The familiar exposed brick walls and creaky wood floors and low ceilings swaddled her. She stared at her favorite painting, the one Jefferson had done of the old man in City Park, and yearned to see him again; to have him hold her in his arms.

She dropped her bag on the end table next to a stained mug with a teaspoon of black, cold coffee and a small plate powdered with sugar from a beignet. Too tired to consider washing dishes, she crossed to the kitchen to scrounge in the fridge for something to eat. On the stove, she reheated a bowl of étouffée. The peanut buttery fragrance of the thick brown roux tantalized her taste buds and teased her stomach. She didn't realize how famished she was until she sat at the small circular dining table and devoured the entirety of the smothered seafood dish.

Already the migraine had begun to ease.

She swallowed a couple aspirin with a slurp of water from the faucet. Considered taking a bath to wash off the mossy stink of the bayou, but when she saw her bed, the blankets crumpled at the foot, the shape of her body imprinted on the mattress, it called to her to rest awhile.

As soon as she lay down, she passed out cold.

An hour or so later, Nevaeh awakened to booming thunder. The wind banged open the shutter she forgot to latch while a torrential downpour flooded the gallery. Flashes of lightning snapped photos of a figure seated perfectly still in the armchair in the corner. The intruder was a massive giant slouched forward with long, spidery fingers clasping its bony knees. It sat in silence, watching her. How long had it been there? Was this a dream? But the prick of goosebumps on her flesh told her it wasn't.

Nevaeh leapt out of bed and grabbed a pen from the end table. It wasn't the most deadly weapon, but it'd have to do. "Who are you? What are you doing here?" she shouted, shuffling backward toward the bathroom, thinking she'd hole up in there if it came at her. The intruder responded with a wet gargling sound like it was clearing its throat. "You better get out of here before I call the police," she threatened, knowing full well her phone was still in her bag. Once again, the intruder made a gargling sound.

When she reached the corner of the room, Nevaeh flipped a lamp on. The light shone upon a mummified creature swathed in bloody rags. What parts of its flesh were exposed had bruised a dark purple. It stared at her with one good eye, the other awash with blood. It rose on unsteady legs, head nearly scraping against the ceiling, and tried to speak but the words were garbled nonsense. The chewed hunk of meat that remained of its tongue pulsed inside the cavernous hole of its mouth.

The pen slipped from Nevaeh's fingers. "Jefferson?"

He looked far worse than when she'd visited him a day ago. It was a miracle he was alive. From all appearances, he should've been dead. But Nevaeh was glad he wasn't. Maybe there was still a chance the antidote could save him. It couldn't reverse all the effects, but perhaps enough where he'd continue living and they could be together.

Nevaeh dashed across the room and held him in her arms. "Jesus, what has Gemma done to you?" she cried, allowing the tears to flow freely. Despite his horrifying appearance, she kissed him on the lips. He'd kissed her wounds when she felt vulnerable and hurt. Now it was her time to do the same for him.

There were so many things Nevaeh ached to know. Where had he been since she'd last seen him in Gemma's house? What happened in the hours since she slipped out the bedroom window? How had he managed to break Gemma's control and find his way to her place? Where was that bitch now? But all that could wait. What was important was giving him the antidote and finding out if it worked.

After telling him to sit on the bed, Nevaeh retrieved the potion and showed him the vial of green powder laid across her palm. "Gemma poisoned you. She was supposed to give this antidote to you to nullify the effects but, for whatever reason, she didn't. Which is why you're…" Nevaeh couldn't bring herself to say it. To say it would only make it true. "But there's still a chance you can be cured."

Jefferson gazed at her with his pale eyes, all hope lost. "Listen to me, I understand you've suffered a lot, and you don't see a way where your life will ever be the same, but that's not true! There's still a chance the antidote will stop the poison from doing more damage. Then we'll hop in a cab and go to Tulane Medical Center. They'll have doctors there who can fix you."

She took his clammy hands and gave them a squeeze. "You have to trust me, Jefferson. No matter what happens, I'll be by your side. I'm never going to leave you again. And I'm not going to let Gemma hurt you anymore. You're free of her. You hear me? You're free—"

From behind her, the wood floor creaked. Nevaeh glanced over her shoulder. A flash of lightning spotlighted Gemma framed within the doorway, smirking as if this were all a sick joke. Her hair looked fried as if she'd been struck by lightning. Speckles of—what appeared to be—blood—freckled her face. Bruises blackened her wide, crazed eyes and Camile's brass key hung from her neck; the chain stained a rust color. Nevaeh feared Gemma had done something horrible to her friends. Whatever sanity the girl once clung to must've slipped from her grasp, leaving her to swirl inside the hurricane of her own delirium. But before Nevaeh could ask…

"That's where you're sadly mistaken. Jefferson is only here because I allowed him to come."

As she stood, Nevaeh slipped the antidote in her pocket. "I suggest you get the fuck out of my house now or we're gonna have a problem."

Gemma crept inside the front room and pulled a knife from her pocket, pressed the silver button on the black handle, unleashing the pointy blade from its cradle. "We've had a problem since you decided to try to steal my man. But you're soon going to find out he's all mine. Isn't that right, sweetheart?" She blew Jefferson a kiss.

Nevaeh noticed Jefferson's shadow grow tall behind her. Felt the heat of his breath on the back of her neck. She took a step forward toward the mug of stale coffee on the end table. Switchblade gripped tight in her fist, Gemma parroted her movement.

"I visited your friend, Mirlande St. Pierre," Nevaeh told Gemma. The witch's name halted Gemma in her tracks, wiping the sadistic smile from her face. "She told me a few things. The whole thing about you having control over Jefferson. It's a trick."

Cracks split the foundation rubbed into Gemma's face as she cackled with laughter. She waved the knife at Nevaeh. "I see what you're doing here. You're trying to get into our heads. Pit us against one another. But it's not gonna work. You want to know why? Because he listens to whatever I say."

Nevaeh pulled the antidote from her pocket. Seeing the vial pinched between her fingers, Gemma gawked in surprise. "Where did you get that?" she said, voice breaking.

"Like I said, I paid a visit to your friend. She gave it to me. Then I freed her boatman and, let's just say, he resolved some issues between them. She won't be offering her services anymore. Now I'm going to set Jefferson free, and you're not going to bother us again."

"We'll see about that." Gemma glanced around Nevaeh. "Jefferson, kill that little skeeta hawk."

A heavy hand gripped Nevaeh by the shirt. "Jefferson, no…" and flung her backwards through the air. She flapped her arms like a bird caught in a strong headwind and hit the floor with a thud. The impact knocked the breath from her lungs and jostled the antidote from her grip, the vial skittering beneath a display cabinet.

A thump returned from downstairs, and the crabby voice of Ms. Batifole shouted, "Keep it down!"

Without a second to collect herself, Nevaeh flipped on her stomach and scrambled after the potion. Jefferson snagged her by the ankle, and pulled her backwards, her nails etching stripes into the hardwood.

Nevaeh saw the pen she'd dropped and nabbed it right before Jefferson flipped her around. Jefferson grabbed Nevaeh by the collar and lifted her on her feet. She stabbed him in the hand. Jefferson released his grip and pulled at the pen. Nevaeh scurried for the antidote, slid on her belly, and reached beneath the cabinet, fingers touching the smooth glass of the vial.

"Get her, you idiot!" Gemma shouted.

Before she could retrieve the vial, Jefferson seized Nevaeh

by the hair and yanked her to her feet, nearly pulling a fistful from the roots. Nevaeh tugged Jefferson's painting from the wall, and slammed the canvas backwards over Jefferson's head. This only stalled him momentarily, but long enough for Nevaeh to flip open the cabinet and snatch a tripod. She swung it as hard as she could, catching Jefferson square in the jaw. He tumbled over a chair, leg curling beneath him, and smacked his temple on the table leg.

"Stay down, Jefferson," Nevaeh demanded, tripod cocked, as he struggled to sit up from his twisted pretzel position.

"Goddamn you, I said get—" Gemma started to order Jefferson before Nevaeh launched the tripod like a javelin into her stomach. Gemma crouched forward, hands on her knees, and gasped for air.

Ms. Batifole continued to bang on the floor and shout for Nevaeh to be quiet.

Nevaeh sprinted forward and tackled Gemma around the waist. They tumbled backward out the window, Gemma landing on the gallery. A storm poured from the sky, soaking them wet. Nevaeh reared back to throw a punch. Gemma grabbed Nevaeh's wrist and gored her beneath the ribcage with the switchblade. Blood gushed down Nevaeh's side and soaked the waistband of her pants. White hot pain spread through her stomach. Gemma twisted the knife, the blade carving Nevaeh's insides. Nevaeh vomited down the back of Gemma's dress. Gemma didn't even seem to notice, so intent on engraving her name on Nevaeh's kidney.

From downstairs, Ms. Batifole opened her shutter and

demanded to know what was going on up there. "Better not be having no party," she said. Nevaeh tried to tell her to call the police, but Gemma twisted the knife, and Nevaeh screamed against the burning pain in her gut.

Wrestling for an advantage, the two of them rolled across the front room, locked arm in arm, and spat insults into each other's face. Jefferson remained sprawled on the ground, tangled in the chair, staring at the ceiling as if a fight wasn't going on right next to him. Gemma started to say his name again, but Nevaeh clamped her hand over Gemma's mouth. Gemma drove the blade deeper in her gut until Nevaeh swore it'd lodged in a rib. The pain was so excruciating she thought she might black out.

Gemma leered over Nevaeh and stroked her cheek, speaking to her in the tone of a compassionate nurse comforting a dying patient. "There were so many days I wondered what attracted Jefferson to you. Certainly, you're beautiful. Anyone can see that. But as much as Jefferson admires beauty, something alluring existed beneath the surface of your flesh, something that moved him. Honestly, for so long I couldn't figure it out, but after staring at his portrait of you it finally dawned on me what it was. You're damaged goods. Which is why I know, deep inside his heart, he could never truly love you. He deserves a woman like me, strong and confident and…artful." Gemma squeezed Nevaeh's cheeks and stuck her blurred face directly in front of Nevaeh's dazed eye. "You can look at your death as me doing him a favor. I'm lancing the boil before it fills him with pus."

Though she'd only caught snippets of Gemma's rambling monologue, Nevaeh had heard enough to suffuse her with an adrenaline rush of rage. "Then you squeeze it until the pimple goes—" Nevaeh shoved Gemma off her. Gemma fell backwards, smacking her head on the floor.

Ms. Batifole screamed she was calling the cops; the best news Nevaeh had heard all night.

Catching a second wind, Nevaeh scrambled to her feet and delivered a sharp kick to Gemma's abdomen as she tried to get up. Gemma grunted and slumped on all fours. Nevaeh crawled across the parlor, the slightest movement igniting flames in her abdomen as she pulled the switchblade out and dropped it on the floor. When she reached the cabinet, Nevaeh slowly lowered herself on her uninjured side and reached for the antidote. The minute the vial was in her fingers a sense of relief numbed the pain.

Jefferson hadn't moved a muscle since she'd ordered him to remain still. Through brainwashing and torture, Gemma had imprisoned his soul, broke his freewill until he was a slave chained to her bidding. But Nevaeh had found the key. Now it was time to free him from this jail. Give him back the life that was unfairly taken from him. And together they'd walk away from this hell.

Nevaeh untangled his legs from the chair and removed the painting from around his neck. Unable to hold back her sobs any longer, Nevaeh lifted Jefferson's head and begged him to hold her. She nearly fainted when she felt him wrap her in his warm embrace. She could've stayed there forever.

Soon everything would be back to the way it once was. Back to the way it should be.

"Jefferson, darling, time to give your sweetheart her special goodbye," Gemma said as she rose to her feet.

Nevaeh gasped as Jefferson squeezed her around the waist and picked her up as he rose to his feet. She pushed at his face and punched his shoulders as he carried her through the parlor, past the table where they once shared meals, past the bed where they once slept and made love, past Gemma who watched gleefully, and out onto the gallery where they'd had their last argument before this whole thing began. Jefferson dipped Nevaeh over the parapet, twenty feet above the empty street below.

Nevaeh showed him the antidote, the green powder inside the vial. "You don't have to do this, Jefferson," she said. "You don't have to listen to her! She has no power over you! You've had control of your own will all this time!"

"Don't listen to her, Jefferson! You're mine and you know it!"

A spark of awareness flickered in Jefferson's eyes. "Search in your heart! You know she's lying," Nevaeh said.

"Let her go, Jefferson," Gemma screamed.

Jefferson's grip loosened and Nevaeh could feel herself slipping. She clung on to his shirt. The buttons started to pop as she shouted at him over the storm and Gemma's demands. "Your soul still lives inside you, Jefferson! Locked in a cage she created! But here is the key." She shook the vial of green powder. "I can set you free!"

A single tear dropped from Jefferson's pale eye and streaked down his tattered cheek. His mouth formed her name. There he was. There was her Jefferson. Alive!

From over his shoulder, Nevaeh watched as Gemma charged Jefferson from behind, wielding the tripod. "Watch out!" Nevaeh screamed.

Gemma clobbered Jefferson in the back. He lost his grip. Nevaeh plummeted. The fall wasn't in slow motion like the movies. No dramatic muted screams or cries of anguish. It happened far too fast for any of that. One moment Nevaeh was dangling over the gallery, the next she was sprawled in the street; the blood washing away in the rain as it poured out of her.

She clutched the antidote in her hand. Refused to let go. Maybe she'd die today, but that didn't mean Jefferson had to. She could rest now knowing she'd saved him. Just like he'd saved her by coming into her life at a time when she was listless and adrift.

The shocked face of Jefferson hung over the parapet two stories above her. His hands still reached out toward her, fingers clutching at the empty air. She wanted to tell him everything was going to be okay. Wanted to tell him there was no pain. Wanted to tell him none of this was his fault and that she loved him. She'd always loved him.

As the light began to fade, she wanted to tell him to come with her.

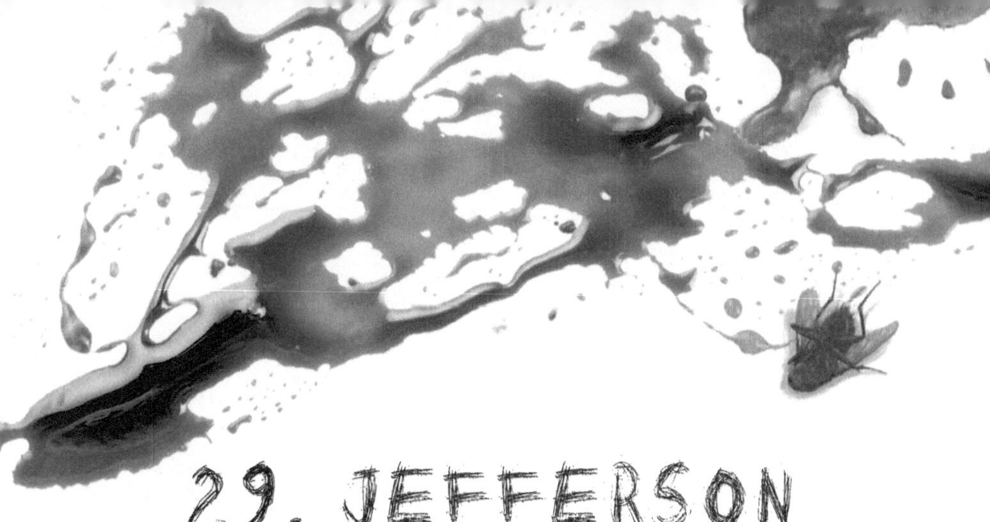

29. JEFFERSON

On a gorgeous morning in May, Jefferson took Nevaeh to the End of the World. They walked the ten-minute trek down Poland Street to the far east end of the Bywater, cutting across a set of railroad tracks, before walking along the barbed wire chain-link fence surrounding the towering abandoned Naval Defense Complex on the bank of the Mississippi. Signs warned of potential hazards and fines for trespassing on a restricted area.

Jefferson lifted a broken slice of fence, allowing Nevaeh to crawl through the hole, before following behind her. They raced across the deserted lot, weeds growing up through the cracked cement tickling their ankles, and chased each other through the winding parking garage, across the dark tunnel of the sky walk, laughter echoing inside the steel chamber. Nevaeh shouted at him to hurry when Jefferson lagged behind. The higher they ascended the faster Jefferson's heart raced. With no one else around, it was like they were the only humans alive. They screamed as loud as they could into the emptiness, only their voices answering back.

Once they reached the roof, they looked out at the long deck of a naval carrier floating on the river and the pointy skyscrapers of Algiers in the distance. A flock of seagulls soared together, a blanket of white feathers, seeming to transform into a cloud in the shape of an angel. They could hear the birds' cries of goodbye in the peaceful stillness.

They left the complex and strolled along a grassy levee looping around the industrial section of the canal. On top of bollards at the water's edge, cormorants stretched their kinked necks and made guttural noises that sounded like hiccups. A dachshund sprinted up to Nevaeh and jumped on her thighs. She petted the pup's head and let it lick her face sopping wet. When Jefferson tried to pet the pup, he growled and flashed canines. Jefferson pretended to be jealous, and Nevaeh playfully joked not to mess with her man while cuddling the pup to her chest. They chatted with the owners, a couple of young bohemians out for a stroll.

They browsed the free store, a concrete and tin shack where merchandise was traded like in the old days. Nevaeh donated a sterling silver necklace of St. Christopher. She said he'd saved her from death and now that she was safe it was time for him to protect someone else. Feeling he needed to give away a piece of himself too, Jefferson opened his backpack and pulled out his sketchbook. Nevaeh raised a brow and eyed him precariously. Jefferson told her about how he practically grew up in the Gulf South Art Gallery in Mississippi, where the local artists inspired him to pursue his own creativity. Now it was time he returned the favor.

Out past another weedy parking lot they stumbled upon a labyrinth. At the entrance, a chalkboard sign read: *Take a beautiful journey to your own center and return to the world changed.* What do you hope you'll find there? Jefferson asked Nevaeh. She stared off at the sun peeking behind the clouds above the cantilever arches of the Greater New Orleans Bridge. Peace, she said.

How about you? she asked him.

He'd already found it.

Taking Nevaeh by the hand, Jefferson led her around the spiraling kaleidoscopic maze, following the rainbow of colored stones guiding their path to the center where they faced the words OPEN YOUR EYES spray painted two stories tall along the bottom of the complex's base. Nevaeh whispered in his ear for him to close his eyes. Jefferson eagerly obliged. Thank you for this wonderful afternoon, she said. It was there, between beauty and ruin, they shared a kiss.

✦

The memory played through Jefferson's mind as he stared at Nevaeh lying shattered in the middle of Chartres Street. Eyes wide open, Nevaeh gaped at Jefferson with a look of horrified astonishment, as if she couldn't believe he'd let her go. All those memories of the good times they had together, moments he'd never relive again, taken from him, along with his will to live, in seconds.

He could see Nevaeh clutched the vial of green powder in her right hand. The antidote she'd received from the swamp witch. She held onto it despite everything.

What was the last thing Nevaeh had said before she fell? *You don't have to listen to her. She has no power over you. You've had control of your own will all this time.*

If that was true, then Nevaeh's death was his fault. And deep down inside, he knew it was true. She'd still be alive if he hadn't come here. He should've drowned himself in the bayou alongside Marcel and Camile's corpses.

He could've stopped any of this from happening whenever he wanted. He could've broken up with Gemma like Nevaeh had asked him a hundred times. He could've deleted Gemma's number and blocked her on his social media accounts. He could've dropped out of the exhibition. He could've forgotten about this whole stupid scene. So what if he'd been back to selling art in Jackson Square? Right now, he could've been with Nevaeh, instead of staring down at her lifeless body.

But he was too afraid.

Not because he was afraid of what Gemma might do. Because he was too afraid to disappoint. Not just Gemma, but Nevaeh too. Afraid he would never be strong enough for her. Afraid he didn't deserve her. Afraid she'd see him for what he was. For what Gemma always knew he was.

The tripod clanged on the gallery floor. Gemma came up beside him, admiring her handywork. She clamped her hand on the back of Jefferson's neck, digging her broken nails into the skin, and shoved him forward, causing him to lean far over the parapet, his feet balancing on his toes. Jefferson didn't fight it. If Gemma wanted to push him off the gallery to end things, then so be it. He'd gladly die in the street next to Nevaeh.

Gemma pointed a steady finger at Nevaeh's corpse. "Now that's art, darling."

Jefferson's stomach twisted with sickness. How had he ever fallen in love with such a ruthless creature? Defended her against everyone's accusations? Blown off their warnings when they cautioned him? Stayed by her side after Nevaeh offered him a way out, freed from the shackles of her vile nature?

Upon seeing Nevaeh's body, the downstairs neighbor released a piercing shriek that stirred awake the entire block. Lights snapped on behind the curtains of the hotel's rooms. A few guests stuck their heads out of windows to see about the commotion. The neighbor shouted for someone to call an ambulance as she went to attend to Nevaeh's body. A young bellhop in a gray-and-purple uniform pushed through the exit and vomited onto the brick drive at the sight of Nevaeh's body. Another employee began dialing on his phone. The neighbor glanced up at the gallery and locked eyes with Jefferson. Her jaw dropped wide open as she gawked in terror. Others joined her, pointing their fingers, and shouting about the man on the second floor.

Gemma slipped into the darkness of the apartment and hissed at Jefferson to get his ass in gear. She picked up the knife from the floor, pushed in the bloody blade, and stuffed it into her pocket. Hearing the sirens in the distance, Jefferson remained on the gallery, unwilling to leave Nevaeh, knowing he'd never see her again. He wanted to trace every line of Nevaeh's face, a portrait for him to cherish in grief for the rest of his days. What did it matter if the police threw him in prison to rot? He deserved it, didn't he?

But if he let himself get caught then he'd never have his revenge. Where was the justice in that? Blinking tears from his eyes, Jefferson said his final goodbye to Nevaeh. Then he followed Gemma down the darkened stairwell, out the rear exit, through a narrow alleyway hidden by a brick wall to where her car was parked on Ursuline.

30. GEMMA

The ice melted between Gemma's fingers into the sink as she held the cold pack to her bruised ribs. She removed a bottle of oxycodone from her purse, crushed a couple tablets and downed them with a gulp of water. Already she was concocting a story to tell the police if they caught up with her. She'd tell them she was attacked. Make a big to-do about it. The survival story of her escape from the hands of death. Jefferson went insane, she'd say. The pressure of the show must've been too much and he cracked. Killed everyone involved.

From the look of him, it sounded reasonable. Besides, she was certain there were plenty of witnesses at the hotel who saw Jefferson at Nevaeh's place. They'd verify that he was the murderer. Gemma Landry was just another innocent victim of his crimes. Oh, she could imagine the sympathy. The media depicting her as a hero. The strong woman who fought off her would-be kidnapper. Every talk show vying for an exclusive interview. *Every day I feared I was going to die,* she'd say. *He threatened to murder me if I didn't do as he asked.* She'd dedicate the reopening of Carondelet Street Gallery to the memory of Camile Davis. *She will live on through my hard work and dedication*, she'd tell every art journal. Who knew? She might even get a book or movie deal out of this.

But first she'd have her exhibition.

The ceiling creaked above. Gemma dropped the ice pack and grabbed Marcel's knife she'd kept at her side and carefully removed the easel she'd wedged beneath the knob. She flipped the latch and took a deep breath to calm her thundering heart. The heavy door rattled as she pulled it open.

Gemma half-expected Jefferson to be waiting on the other side.

She peeked from beneath the stairwell into the showroom but there was nothing. She crept up the stairs to the office where Jefferson sat tied to the chair. His head whirled in her direction as she approached. A coldness sank deep into Gemma's bones as she shrunk from the unholy darkness swirling inside those pale eyes. What was it the swamp witch had said? *Once a man had seen the other side, he wasn't the same.* The Jefferson she once knew had died along with Nevaeh. Now what sat before her was a monster.

"You think I'm afraid of you," Gemma said, holding the knife before her as she approached, doing her best to disguise the tremor in her voice. "I'm not fucking afraid of you. I made you. An artist. A lover. A killer. And I can destroy you just like—" she snapped her fingers.

Gemma grabbed a stool from the corner and took a seat in front of Jefferson. He watched her every moment like a predator waiting for the opportunity to strike. "There it is.

I see it now. The rage burning behind that pathetic mask of sorrow. You want to hate me for what I did to your little girlfriend? Hate me all you want. But know this." She stuck the tip of the blade into Jefferson's chest where his heart beat. "I'd do it all over again."

The fucker didn't squirm. Didn't twitch a muscle or groan in anger. Just glared at her. If she thrust the knife into his heart she doubted he'd flinch. He'd probably happily accept the merciful gesture.

Gemma held up two fingers. "Now this can go down two ways. One, you play your part and give me my night. I've been waiting for this moment a long time and I'm not going to let a grieving man spoil it. Do this for me and I'll make sure your art lives forever." Once again, Gemma waited for some kind of reaction from Jefferson and, once again, didn't receive any. "Two, you do anything to wreck this show and I'll be sure to make you suffer pain like you've never felt. You'll beg me to kill you." Gemma strolled around behind Jefferson and straightened his pinkie finger. "To prove I'm serious." Gemma sawed through the metacarpal bone like carving a turkey wing. Black blood dripped from the nub. Jefferson didn't kick or writhe or squeal. Gemma might as well have been filing his nails.

He followed her with ghostly eyes as she walked back around to the other side and tossed his finger into his lap. "Now, I have a show to get ready for," she said as she stepped on the stairs. "Try not to make any noise." She glanced over her shoulder at Jefferson. "Not that you can."

By 5:30, everything appeared ready. Gemma donned a flower embroidered silk lace gown she'd specifically purchased a few weeks ago for the opening. She had to look glamorous for the festivities. With Camile erased from the picture, Gemma now slipped right into her shoes as the heir of the Queen of the Arts District.

Gemma modeled her wardrobe for Jefferson. "How do I look?" she asked, twirling in circles, her hem floating through the air. "It makes me sad to think we were supposed to celebrate this night together. But, I guess, in a way we are." She kissed Jefferson on the cheek. "Wish me luck, my love."

Gemma picked up the knife from the desk and caught her reflection in the blade. She had to grasp the handle tightly to stop her hand from trembling. Even the layers of makeup couldn't disguise the ugliness beneath. Jefferson wasn't the only monster in the room.

For a brief moment, Gemma thought of calling the whole thing off, sending the caterers home and turning off the lights and ending Jefferson's misery, once and for all. Then they could all move on. But she'd worked too damn hard for this night. She deserved her moment.

Gemma pushed her shoulders back and raised her chin high. Unfolded the prepared speech she'd snatched from Camile's printer. Cleared her throat and read the words in a slow, deep voice. "Welcome everyone to the Bons Temp Rouler Exhibition. I'm your host, Gemma Landry. I hope you're ready to let the good times roll this evening. Ha! Ha! Some of you may know the Cajun French phrase 'laissez le bon temps rouler.' It's a lexeme of the famous saying I just mentioned. Well, tonight our artists have attempted to interpret our city in their own unique visions. Now please grab a drink and enjoy the wonderful collection."

Stopping at the top of the staircase, Gemma glanced over her shoulder at Jefferson, slumped in the chair, head rolling against his chest, and blew him a kiss. "I love you, Jefferson. I'm sorry things had to end this way."

At 6:30 pm, Gemma opened the doors and welcomed with a flourish the finely dressed guests to the Bons Temps Roule Exposition. She gave the prepared speech and invited them to drop by the table to grab a glass of wine and a plate of hors d'oeuvres provided by caterers Camile had hired before proceeding to the showrooms to admire the art. She tried engaging some of the more important guests in conversation, but they only cared to know Camile's whereabouts soon as they realized she wasn't there. Surrounded by the apprehensive crowd, Gemma did her best to ease their concerns. She begged them to enjoy the evening. Shoved glasses of wine into their hands. Passed them entire trays of crawfish, deviled eggs, oysters rizzuto and gator tail bites. Encouraged them to browse all the wonderful art on display. But they didn't care about any of that. They were too concerned over their missing host.

A journalist from the *Pelican Bomb* said he'd attempted to reach Camile earlier in the day. He didn't seem to recognize Gemma from Jefferson's interview—not in her current state anyway—even after she reminded him. "It's highly unusual for Camile not to answer her phone," the journalist said. "I must've left five or six messages this morning." A few of Camile's closest confidants agreed and called her cell phone only to receive her voicemail. The interrogations started anew.

Gemma assured the guests there must be a reasonable explanation for Camile's disappearance—none of which were that their beloved Queen was sunk, along with that backstabber Marcel, at the bottom of the bayou. But hey, what does everyone think about this photo of The Singing Oak? Isn't it beautiful? It was taken by our featured photographer, Ms. Nevaeh—

Just as things were unraveling like the wisps of hair from Gemma's updo, a pretentious artsy Tulane alum, not much younger than herself, mentioned the murder on Chartres Street in the Vieux Carré the previous night. Gossip about the news circulated through the crowd. No information had been released yet other than the victim was a woman. The guests speculated whether it was possible it was Camile.

A clamor of anxious voices reached a crescendo loud enough Gemma couldn't hear herself think. She clamped her hands over her ears. How had her perfectly planned evening unfolded into bedlam? She'd done everything to make sure it went off without a hitch. Was this the price she paid for killing those three traitors? They took everything from her. The gallery. The recognition. The man she loved. Well, they weren't taking this night away from her too. She didn't care if she had to lock all the guests inside until the event was over.

"The victim was not Camile!" Gemma's scream silenced the raucous guests. They stared at her, aghast and dismayed.

Realizing she'd made a ghastly error, Gemma smiled through her embarrassment and pleaded with the crowd to please forget about the violence running rampant in the city. She snagged a wine glass from a server and, raising it high, asked the guests to join her in a toast to art. Before she finished, an investor of the gallery rudely interrupted her, demanding to know where Camile had gone. An aged sculptor Camile had championed early in her career seconded that notion, saying Camile would never leave the gallery in anyone's hands, especially Gemma's. An Instagram influencer with a Dahli mustache accused Gemma of hiding the truth.

Gemma withered beneath the guests' accusations, holding up her hands to ward off any further finger pointing. "I promise you. Camile will be here soon. I really don't know what's taking her so long…"

Unsatisfied with the non-explanations of Camile's disappearance, guests started interrogating Gemma about Marcel and Nevaeh and Jefferson. Why weren't any of them here at *their* show? How was it they were all late? Was it possible they were missing too? That couldn't be a coincidence. Something strange was going on here. And it all linked to…

The aged sculptor stepped forward, flourishing her phone, and threatened to call the police if Gemma didn't provide some answers. The guests rallied behind the gray-haired hippie and closed in. Feeling trapped, Gemma entreated the mob to take a deep breath and relax. They were here to enjoy themselves. Weren't they?

A high-pitch scream from the backroom halted the angry mob. Gemma rushed down the connecting hall to see what the hell had gone wrong now. Seven guests were huddled in opposite corners, petrified by the ghastly thing stumbling down the metal staircase. Clinging to the rail, Jefferson teetered with each wobbly step. Agonizing moans rumbled from the dark cavern of his gaping tongueless maw as his ghostly eyes searched the crowd for Gemma.

The front door of the gallery banged open, and the guests ran shouting onto Carondelet Street. The last seven remaining people in the rear room bolted when Gemma unzipped her purse, reached inside, and pulled out the knife. "What did I say about you staying put?" she asked Jefferson. "But you were never good at listening. That's why everything has gone to shit! Well, I guess it's time to put an end to this. Don't you agree, sweetheart?"

Soon as Jefferson tumbled onto the landing, Gemma charged with the knife raised over her head and thrust the tip at his neck. Jefferson caught her wrist and twisted it upward at an odd angle. The bone snapped and the knife clanged against the floor. Gemma swiped at Jefferson with the nails of her free hand, but he caught that wrist and snapped it too.

Gemma dropped to her knees. Jefferson hovered over her. Hatred seeped into his ghostly eyes. But Gemma would be damned if she let this thing frighten her.

"What're you going to do to me, Jefferson? Kill me? Is that it? Go for it, baby. Let me see if you have the guts."

Jefferson picked up the knife and lifted Gemma's chin with the tip of the blade. A smile spread across his face. Gemma begged for mercy.

He shoved the blade upward.

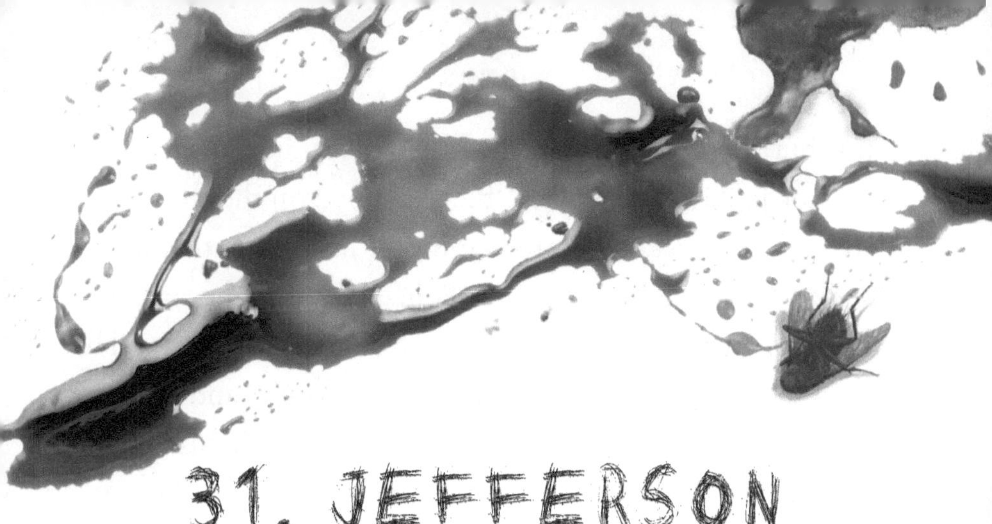

31. JEFFERSON

As sirens approached in the distance, Jefferson admired his magnum opus. It was the vilest and yet most significant piece he ever created, capturing the darkness he envisioned at the heart of the girl he once loved.

Heavy duty frame hooks strung Gemma to the backroom wall. Blood soaked the front of her dress and dripped from the brass key around her neck. Jefferson removed the blade from where he'd pushed it up through her jaw. Her head sagged, chin resting on her chest. Eyes and mouth wide, leaking blood, an expression captured seconds before a scream. In her final moments, he gave Gemma what she'd always wanted: a portrait.

Jefferson dipped his finger into a spot of blood on the floor. Scribbled his signature next to his final oeuvre. Unlike any of the other pieces he'd painted, this was the masterpiece his name would become infamous for. His art, forever tied to these monstrous murders.

The blue-and-red lights of a cruiser shaded the windows of the gallery in their recognizable hues. Car doors opened and shut. Footsteps approached the gallery in a rush. It was time for Jefferson to leave. Officers rapped on the front door Jefferson had locked before beginning his work, identifying themselves as the New Orleans Police Department, ordering him to open up. Some of the guests from the exhibit could be heard telling the police about the crazy woman and monster inside. Jefferson stumbled toward the rear exit just as the police broke through the front entrance.

Jefferson slipped through a secret passage beneath the stairs into the parking lot of the connecting building. He waited until the barricade crashed before walking out the front gate and disappearing into the traffic flowing on the sidewalks along St. Joseph. By morning, the story would occupy the news. A description of a monstrous man would headline every local Louisiana TV station and newspaper website. Tonight, he prayed no one would recognize him. But it seemed he had nothing to worry about. His revolting appearance and fetid odor provided him with anonymity. Tonight, he was just another of the unclean drifting through the streets of New Orleans.

The entire night Jefferson walked despite the stiffness in his legs and the burning from the wounds he'd suffered. Palm trees swayed in a breeze he no longer felt. How he ached for its cool caress, its airy invigorating kiss, the moisture soaking into his oozing skin. He breathed deeply but the fragrance of earth and mud—such a typical smell of New Orleans after a storm—was no longer there. Even the stench of his rotting corpse was faint, like the lingering scent of a candle long burned out.

A glimmering sheen from the previous day's rain reflected the soft glow of the streetlamps. The light scorched his eyes, his vision a tunnel without an end. Shadows closed in from every side, ghostly figures he did not recognize but who led him to a place where he could finally rest. He searched for Nevaeh among the shadows.

She was not there.

Jefferson may have been barren of feeling, but he felt that, if she were there, then it would be as if he were alive again. Where was she? Hopefully somewhere safe and far away from where he could reach her. He'd brought enough harm into her life. She deserved peace in death.

Still, a part of him yearned to hold her again. Run his fingers along the raised contours of her scars. Hear her trilling laugh. He wanted to share a slice of King Cake from Tartine's with her. Stroll the Levee Top Trail through the Black Pearl, hand in hand, from Audubon Park to Bonnet Carré Spillway, watching the diverted flood waters transfer from the Mississippi to Lake Pontchartrain. Sit beneath the Singing Oak and listen to the chimes ring their soothing melodies. Even now the memories were fading like old photographs kept in a dusty attic. How long until they vanished forever?

In a deserted block of the Warehouse District, the gloomy tall buildings and vacant lots and homeless asleep in doorways reflected the horrors of all he'd seen. A trio of shady characters dressed in shabby clothing stepped from behind the pillars of the chandlery and followed closely behind. "Wait up, man. Where you going?" a gruff voice spoke. Jefferson stopped in the middle of the sidewalk. The trio remained a couple steps back, flanking him on all sides. "We just want to talk," the gruff voice said. Jefferson turned around to face the thugs. Soon as the trio got a good look they halted. "What the shit happened to him?" the scrawniest of three muttered. "Somebody already fucked him up," a face graffitied in tattoos replied. The chunky guy with the gruff voice motioned for his boys to break. "Sorry, our mistake, thought you were someone else. Have a good night." They darted down Lafayette, shooting glances to make sure he didn't follow.

The witching hour struck as Jefferson skirted the Quarter. Here the living continued on with their existence, unaware of the unholy darkness that awaited them on the other side. A white horse-drawn carriage trotted by with a couple sunk into the cushy velvet seat, entangled in each other's arms, eyes locked on one another as they engaged in a private conversation, oblivious to the world around them.

He and Nevaeh had once taken a buggy to her place. It took some haggling on his part to convince her to go along. A promise of beignets in the morning finally sealed the deal. As much as she hated admitting it, once they were bouncing along the Rue de la Levee, she was giddy over their romantic jaunt, unable to contain her embarrassed smile as he regaled her and the driver with stories of the one time he rode a horse as a child at his aunt's ranch and was nearly thrown from the saddle.

Partygoers carried go-cups from tavern to tavern, caroling and dancing and taking selfies. Most of the shops were shut, the closed signs flipped and the lights turned out. Antique eighteenth century sconces provided the only light shining on the brick sidewalks. Near Toulouse, a woman in a sleek satin gown jogged from a center-hall cottage toward a waiting cab, barking into her phone. Everything about her mannerisms reminded Jefferson of Gemma. He knew it wasn't her, but for a brief moment, he thought maybe, somehow, her spirit had resurrected into this new being and was out for revenge. It wouldn't surprise him. If anyone could cheat death, Gemma had such powers. She'd raised him from the tomb, hadn't she?

When he reached the Bywater, Jefferson dropped by his studio. No longer in possession of a key, he shattered the window and climbed inside. There wasn't an alarm on the place, and if there were any artists working late they hadn't heard the commotion. He looked at all the paintings that would remain unfinished. The canvases the police would confiscate, searching for clues to why he'd committed these atrocious acts. Jefferson squirted a blob of paint onto a palette and wrote "I'm Sorry" on a blank canvas.

It was early morning, but still dark when Jefferson left the studio. The time when the only creatures awake were nocturnal. He walked up to the desolate warehouse area along Florida Ave. and crossed the bridge over the river. There he stood to watch his final sunrise. He waited for the rays to warm his skin. For the sweat to bead across his brow. But his body was too cold. Too lifeless. Still, it was radiant. Nothing he could ever paint would come close to it.

Jefferson followed the railroad tracks to the canal to avoid being spotted by police. He had to be careful. Whenever he saw headlights, he'd duck behind the nearest building or landform. Once, as the clouds glowed a fiery crimson, a man smoking a cigarette on his deck caught Jefferson lumbering through his backyard. Jefferson expected him to say something, but he only waved and wished him a good morning before stubbing the filter against the railing and going back inside his house. This stranger would be the last person Jefferson ever saw and he'd offered him a small kindness. It was this kindness that carried Jefferson for the rest of his journey.

The sun was high overhead by the time Jefferson stepped into the bayou. The waters steamed from the heat as a mist hovered above the waist high sawgrass. Jefferson's feet sank into the mushy ground. He lost a shoe but didn't stop. When he was far away from civilization his shadowy guides transformed into floating gold orbs. They led him into the brackish water. Basked him in a warm, glowing aura, his body sinking up to the neck as he coasted further from land.

Jefferson's heart lurched in his chest as the light traced her slender figure, the shadows painting her into existence. She reached her arms out to him. Smiled at him in welcome. Captured his reflection in her eyes. Not the monster he was now but the person he'd been only weeks ago.

Nevaeh wrapped her arms around him. He smelled her cinnamon scent. Felt her scars. A tear rolled down his cheek.

They kissed and he tasted the spice of a clove cigarette on her breath.

"I love you," he said.

Hugging him tightly, Nevaeh dragged him below the surface of the swamp into the dark. As the waters filled his lungs, she whispered in his ear, "Let go."

THE END

ACKNOWLEDGMENTS

Normally, we think of writing a novel as a solitary experience, but there are many people along the way who add their hearts and souls to this project to help bring this creation to life. Not even Dr. Frankenstein did it alone. Foremost, I want to thank R.B. Wood and Ruadán Books for taking a chance on this novel and making my nightmarish dreams come true. I will forever appreciate all you've done and continue to do for me as an author. To my editor, Anna Koon, who dedicated months of her life, pouring every ounce of her sweat and blood into this project. It wouldn't be the same without your artistic passion and insight. My mentor, Gareth Jones. You remained at my side from the time I first unearthed a rough draft until I raised this creature into a living thing. This monster is as much yours as mine. My writer's group: CJ Goldberg, Vale Vonn, and Angela Zolner, for reading early drafts and being brutally honest in their critiques. They're partially to blame for the black magic that conjured this voodoo tale. The city of New Orleans for being the inspiration for this novel. You've haunted me since I first set foot in your wickedly beautiful town. I will revisit you soon. But most of all, thank you to my lovely wife, Olivia Wong, for always supporting and encouraging me. I'm forever under your spell. I love you with all of my dark, evil heart.

J.R. BLANES lives in Chicago with his wife and neurotic dog. His short fiction has been published in several magazines and podcasts such as *Tales to Terrify, The No Sleep Podcast, Thirteen,* and *Creepy,* among others. In between bouts of writing and dog wrestling, he plays bass guitar and records music. Coffee is his nightmare fuel of choice.

Support Information for Potential POD Triggers

If you or someone you love is experiencing postpartum depression:

National Maternal Mental Health Hotline
1-833-TLC-MAMA (1-833-852-6262)

If you or someone you love is experiencing suicidal ideation or intent:

Suicide and Crisis Lifeline
Dial 988

If you or someone you love is experiencing domestic violence:

National Domestic Violence Hotline
1-800-799-7233 (SAFE)

Outside the United States:

Please check with your local government and medical agencies for assistance.

Coming soon from Ruadán Books...

Even in the shadows of skyscrapers, spring sees an awakening in the concrete jungle that we call "the city."

Spring in the City: A Collection of Dark Speculative Fiction is the next anthology in Ruadán Books' "...In the City" series that takes place in the different metropolises' around the world during the changeable, unpredictable return of life from its cold slumber.

But what awakens is not always beautiful.

Pre-Order at RuadanBooks.com

Also from Ruadán Books

Available Now

Winter in the City—Edited by R. B. Wood and Anna Koon
120 Murders: Dark Fiction Inspired by the Alternative Era—Edited by Nick Mamatas
The Black Fire Concerto—by Mike Allen

Coming Soon

Five Funerals—by Jeff Somers
Spring in the City—Edited by R. B. Wood and Anna Koon
Darling—by Mercedes M. Yardley
The Ghoulmakers Aria—by Mike Allen
Born of Malice—by Xan van Rooyen

www.RuadanBooks.com